Her Secret Crime

TANYA STONE FBI K9 MYSTERY THRILLER

TIKIRI HERATH

Rebel Diva
ACADEMY PRESS

Her Secret Crime

Tanya Stone FBI K9 Mystery Thriller Series

www.TikiriHerath.com

Copyright © Tikiri Herath 2024

Library & Archives Canada Cataloging in Publication

E-book ISBN: 978-1-990234-23-1

HER SECRET CRIME

Paperback ISBN: 978-1-990234-24-8

Hardback ISBN: 978-1-990234-25-5

Large print Paperback: 978-1-990234-46-0

Large print Hardback: 9781990234576

Audio book ISBN: 978-1-990234-26-2

Author: Tikiri Herath

Publisher Imprint: Rebel Diva Academy Press

Copy Editor: Stephanie Parent

Back Cover Headshot: Aura McKay

A Gift for You

Dear reader friend,

Thank you for picking up my book.

I write twisty thrillers that feature feisty female detectives who hunt villains and make them pay.

In my books, justice always prevails.

My stories are for smart readers who love pulse-pounding thrills and nail-biting twists. There is no explicit sex, graphic violence, or heavy cursing in my books, and no dog is ever harmed.

I'm not a marketing company or a branding firm that employs ghost writers or artificial machines. I don't hide behind a pen name or a fake avatar. I write my own books.

I'm also a reader, just like you, and I'm delighted to meet you.

Enjoy the read!

Best wishes,

Tikiri

Vancouver, Canada

PS/ There's a twisty bonus epilogue for this novel. You'll find the secret link to your story gift at the end of this book.

PPS/ All my books use American spelling because most of my readers live in North America. But I am a Canadian who went to international schools all over the world, so I write in mostly

British English. (I know. I'm a mixed up girl.)
As soon as I finish writing a book, I run a
US English spell checker, and after that, my
wonderful (American) editor double checks any
remaining errors. But words are insidious. And
sneaky. If you see a funny-looking word, please
report it. Rest assured, they will be given a sound
talk to and banished from my books.

←—•—→

Tropes you'll find in this mystery thriller series
include: female protagonist, women sleuths,
detective, police officers, police procedural, crime,
murder, kidnapping, missing, creepy cabins, serial
killers, dark secrets, small towns, plot twists,
fast-paced action, shocking endings, revenge,
vigilante justice, family lies, intrigue, suspense,
and psychological terror.

NO DOG IS EVER HARMED IN MY BOOKS. But the villains always are....

The Red Heeled Rebels Universe

The Red Heeled Rebels universe of mystery thrillers, featuring your favorite kick-ass female characters.

◂———▸

Tanya Stone FBI K9 Mystery Thrillers

Thriller series starring Red Heeled Rebel and FBI Special Agent Tanya Stone, and her loyal German Shepherd K9, Max. These are serial killer thrillers set in Black Rock, a small upscale resort town on the coast of Washington state.

Her Deadly End

Her Cold Blood

Her Last Lie

Her Secret Crime

Her Perfect Murder

Her Grisly Grave

www.TikiriHerath.com/Thrillers

←——→

Asha Kade Private Detective Murder Mysteries

Murder mystery thrillers, featuring the Red Heeled Rebels, Asha Kade and Katy McCafferty. Asha and Katy receive one million dollars for their favorite children's charity from a secret benefactor's estate every time they solve a cold case.

Merciless Legacy

Merciless Games

Merciless Crimes

Merciless Lies

Merciless Past

Merciless Deaths

www.TikiriHerath.com/Mysteries

Red Heeled Rebels International Mystery & Crime - The Origin Story

The award-winning origin story of the Red Heeled Rebels characters. Learn how a rag-tag group of trafficked orphans from different places united to fight for their freedom and their lives and became a found family.

The Girl Who Crossed the Line

The Girl Who Ran Away

The Girl Who Made Them Pay

The Girl Who Fought to Kill

The Girl Who Broke Free

The Girl Who Knew Their Names

The Girl Who Never Forgot

www.TikiriHerath.com/RedHeeledRebels

This series is now complete.

◦—————◦

Tikiri's novels and nonfiction books are available in e-book, paperback, and hardback editions, on all good bookstores around the world.

These books are also available in libraries everywhere. Just ask your friendly local librarian or your local bookstore to order a copy via Ingram Spark.

www.TikiriHerath.com

Happy reading.

Her Secret Crime

HER SECRET CRIME

AGENT TANYA STONE FBI K9 MYSTERY THRILLER

Sometimes, it's your own family who wants you dead....

It's midnight. FBI Special Agent Tanya Stone and her K9 dog, Max, arrive at a private island to investigate a suspicious death.

Tanya is undercover, on the trail of a vicious organized crime ring. What she doesn't expect to find is the matriarch of the Kensington family has just shot herself in the head.

Her blood-soaked face lies immobile on her gold-rimmed plate, red splatters on the sterling silver and pristine tablecloth.

But a deadlier danger lurks in the shadows.

A new terror rips through the mansion as a killer targets the remaining family members.

One by one.

Tanya fights off disturbing memories of her own mother's brutal death to hunt the mysterious murderer.

First, she'll have to confront the liars, swindlers, and impostors, because everyone in this twisted house is hiding a dark secret.

But one truth is chillingly clear.

The killer will protect a horrific family secret by any means necessary.

And their next targets are Tanya and Max....

A Death in the Family

"I invited you tonight to witness a death."

Honoree's voice echoed through the dining hall of Kensington Manor.

Shocked gasps swept across the long table.

"*Death?*"

"*What are you talking about?*"

"*Are you okay, Mother?*"

Honoree glared at her adult children and grandchildren.

Her captive audience didn't know she held a gun hidden in the folds of her Prada skirt. And they didn't know the night would end in blood spilled across that pristine white tablecloth.

The Kensington matriarch's eyes turned cold and flinty. She was well aware of the power she held over her clan.

"You're all liars, swindlers, and leeches."

More gasps rose from the table, but no one spoke.

The only sound in the room now was the crackle of the wood fire at the end of the hall. Honoree demanded the fire be stoked year round, even during the summer, and she always got what she wanted.

In her hand-tailored silk gown, the ten-carat diamond necklace, and her silver hair pulled into an elegant swirl, Honoree Kensington looked like she was about to visit Buckingham Palace for tea. But everybody knew her handsome, lithe look and immaculate dress were clever disguises of her true, dark personality.

Her eyes blazed in anger. "I know the real reason you came tonight."

Everyone turned away, too afraid to make eye contact.

The family had just finished a seven-course gourmet feast. They had been expecting to sing a birthday song for the grand dame, in celebration of her seventieth.

The aroma of wood fire mixed pleasantly with the remnants of the meal that had been served that evening. The atmosphere in the Kensington hall would have been congenial, if not for this unexpected turn of events.

"You're here because you want my money."

Her audience shifted in their seats. It was the uncomfortable truth no one wanted to admit.

But one brave young man sat up and cleared his throat. His mother, seated next to him, pulled at his elbow in warning.

Don't say a word.

But he had already opened his mouth.

"We came home for your birthday, Grandmother, not to get beaten up like this."

The others whirled around to him, their eyes wide, incredulous he had said out loud what they had been thinking.

Honoree's face flushed a deep red.

"You're a criminal." She glowered. "Every one of you. You're thieves. You have made my life

4

miserable, after all I've done for you. So now, it's my turn to make your life hell."

Confused murmurs rippled around the table.

"I don't understand," said a young man in a wheelchair. "Why are you doing this to us?"

"We're your family," said the man who first spoke up. "We're not strangers in your boardroom."

"We love you, Mother," said a middle-aged woman in a meek voice.

Honoree threw her head back and laughed.

"You love me? Now that's a joke!"

Her family watched her with mouths open.

"Honoree?"

The female voice had come from the other end of the table. The blonde woman in the sunflower gown had been listening silently until now, but her flushed face said she'd had enough.

"We have stuck together when things were tough. We have always protected each other. We're blood sisters. You can't treat—"

Honoree snapped her head around toward her.

"You're no sister of mine." Her lips curled into a snarl. "I know what you did. You lying, cheating whore."

Her sister froze, like she couldn't believe what she had heard. The whole family stared at her, stunned.

The sound of an ominous click made everyone jump, but relief flooded their faces when they realized who it was.

The Kensington Manor's housekeeper and her husband were standing at the threshold of the hall, holding a silver tray between them. On it was a two-tiered Belgium chocolate cake with gold leaves and rose garlands.

A celebrity baker had taken all day to create those perfect sugar roses. It was too much dessert for a party of seven and had cost an arm, but it was what Honoree had ordered.

Mariposa and Rafael stepped into the hall gingerly, like they sensed the hostility in the air. The housekeeper turned to the matriarch with a nervous bow.

"Your cake, Madame."

"Take that back to the kitchen." Honoree's voice was harder than steel. "Eat it. Give it away. Throw it in the dumpster. I no longer care. This party is over."

Rafael raised an eyebrow, but quickly rearranged his expression to an impassive butler's look.

"Yes, ma'am."

With their heads bowed, the couple stepped backward through the entrance and gently shut the doors behind them. Honoree's sister pushed her chair back and got up, like she'd had enough and was about to follow them out.

"I have made a will," announced Honoree.

Honoree's sister sat back down.

All eyes turned to her, watching, waiting. No one dared to breathe. The air in the hall turned thick with anxious anticipation.

"You think I'm just going to give it away to you all, don't you? You can't be more wrong."

A wry smile cut across Honoree's face.

"We're going to play a game." Her smile widened, like she was mocking them, gleaning pleasure from their fear. "Whoever finds my will gets everything. All you other fools get nothing."

A few faces went pale.

Honoree raised her chin.

"But the winner, if there will be one, will soon find out they won nothing at all." She smirked. "I only wish I could live to see the game play out."

A woman in a pearl choker pursed her lips and dug her manicured nails into her armrests.

"This is madness, Mother," she spat out. "Are you feeling all right? Should we call Doctor—"

Honoree slammed her fist on the table.

The crystal glass by her elbow crashed down, spraying vintage Dom Pérignon over the tablecloth.

Those who had been sitting nearest to it pulled their chairs back in alarm. The champagne spilled over the edge of the table and onto the Persian rug.

Suddenly, a babble of confused voices broke out.

"You can't do this to us!"

"Why are you playing us like this?"

"What in heaven's name—"

Honoree raised her hand to quieten them.

She scraped her chair back and unfurled herself to her full six-foot height with her heels.

Everybody shrank back in horror and a stunned silence fell in the room.

The chandelier light glinted on the black gun in Honoree's hand.

Murder or Suicide?

"She's got a gun!"

The man in the wheelchair shouted.

Everybody recognized the weapon.

It was Honoree's husband's favorite antique pistol, the one he used at the firing range on weekends. That was before he died from lung cancer three years ago, leaving his tobacco empire to his wife.

The fire crackled louder, as if to match the electrified tension in the air.

"Fools," snarled Honoree. "That's what you all are. You have been the greatest misfortune to ever grace my home."

The flames leaped up and down the chimney, like an ominous warning of what was about to occur.

Honoree raised her weapon and pointed the barrel at each member of her family, one by one. A primal fear surged through the hall like a black tsunami wave.

Panicked shrieks filled the air.

"Please don't kill us!"

"Have you gone mad?"

"Stop this! Now!"

People scrambled under the table. A few peeked over the edge as if to check if what they had seen was real.

The young man who'd dared stand up to his grandmother first screamed from under the table.

"Put that away! Right now!"

Honoree didn't glance at him.

"You will start tonight," she said, articulating each word slowly. "I wish you all a bloodied fight till the end."

With one final glare at her family, she put the gun to her forehead and pulled the trigger.

The gunshot reverberated through the dining hall.

A stunned silence fell over the room.

Honoree Kensington swayed on her feet. The pistol slipped from her hand and fell to the rug. Her body crumpled and crashed onto the table, splattering blood over the silver and crystal.

The doors banged open.

Everyone whirled around in shock as if they had expected a monster, something, anything, to explain the horrific madness that had unraveled in front of their eyes.

The housekeeper and her husband stopped in their tracks, mouths agape.

Their employer was lying face-down at the head of the table with blood spooling from an open bullet wound. Her blood was mixing with the spilled champagne, and soaking into the tablecloth.

Chaos erupted in the hall.

"Someone do something!"

"Nine-one-one! Call nine-one-one!"

"What in heaven's sake just happened?"

"Oh, my Lord. Oh, my Lord," wheezed the man in the wheelchair, a hand over his heart.

The woman in the Chanel suit clutched her pearls. "She's gone. She's really gone." She pulled on her necklace so tightly, the string broke, scattering the beads on the floor.

Through all this chaos, one person sat in their chair, their eyes on Honoree Kensington's bloodied head.

That person had never moved, even when Honoree had pulled out her gun.

And now, a small smile was creeping across their face.

No one even noticed.

Day One

FBI SPECIAL AGENT TANYA STONE

Chapter One

"Call yourself a cop? You're a stupid tax collector!"

FBI Special Agent Tanya Stone glared at the man through the bulletproof glass. He had been banging on the precinct counter for the past ten minutes.

"I'm not paying a penny, you hear me?" he yelled.

Tanya felt her blood rush to her face. She suppressed the urge to jump over and slam him on the counter.

Is this what I trained for? I fought in combat so I could deal with parking violators?

She reached to her throat and touched her Ukrainian sunflower pendant. It was a small gesture, but it calmed her whenever she felt her emotions rise.

Her K9 had the right idea.

The big brown German Shepherd was pretending to sleep by the door that separated the precinct's offices from the reception area, ignoring the human going ballistic on the other side. Max was resting his furry head on his paws, but Tanya noticed one eye remained open.

He was ready for anything, as usual.

"I was parked legally," yelled the ornery man, spittle flying from his mouth. He wagged an angry finger at Tanya. "What about the gangs, and the drugs, and the terrorists, huh? Why don't you go after real criminals instead of attacking us regular civilians?"

His face turned such a deep red, Tanya wondered if he was on the verge of a heart attack.

For what? A parking ticket?

She had far more pressing cases to deal with.

The man didn't know the woman he was shaking a fist at was an undercover federal agent, working as a contractor for the Black Rock police team.

"Mr. James?"

The deep male voice came from behind Tanya. Her heart skipped a beat, but she kept her face stoic.

Jack Bold, Black Rock's young chief of police, walked over to the front counter. He normally looked buff and sharp in his uniform, but today, his forehead was lined, his eyes were bloodshot, and his shoulders slumped.

The precinct was severely short staffed that week, which is why Tanya and Jack were left to deal with petty parking violations.

Jack stepped up and leaned across the counter.

"We don't make up these rules, Mr. James," he said in his voice reserved for unreasonable citizens. "These are municipal bylaws. Personally, I don't care if you pay, but the city will come after you. The mayor—"

"Mayor Bailey can go to hell!" The man thumped his fist on the counter. "That jackass—"

A gunshot rang through the air.

The man jumped a foot high and grabbed his chest.

Max scrambled to his feet, whirled around, and let out a volley of angry barks.

Jack yanked the door handle, his sidearm in his hand. Before Tanya could say anything, Max darted through the opening.

"Heel, Max!" hollered Tanya as she dashed toward the main entrance.

She and Jack surveyed the outside, their weapons at the ready. Except for two parked squad cars and the lone vehicle of their unhappy customer, the front of the precinct was empty.

"No! Justin!"

The terrified scream came from the back of the building.

Tanya swiveled around, her adrenaline spiking.

"It's Stacey!"

She pulled the front door open.

"No! No!" came Stacey's horrified voice again. "Someone help!"

Jack and Tanya bolted out and ran along the wall toward the back of the building, their weapons drawn, their backs taut, and their shoulders tight.

Max kept in step with Tanya, his body close to her legs, like he had been trained.

A sense of dread whipped through Tanya's stomach as she approached the end of the wall. Stacey was a paramedic. For her to get so hysterical, something terrible had to have happened.

When they reached the edge of the wall, Tanya slammed back and scanned the mostly empty city parking lot behind the precinct. It was where Stacey and Justin normally parked their ambulance during breaks.

Stacey was standing by the vehicle, staring at something inside, shaking hard.

The sound of a car engine came from a nearby street, but she was alone in the lot.

Jack swiveled his head, sweeping the parking lot for the shooter.

"See anyone?"

Tanya shook her head. "Negative."

"Let's go!"

Chapter Two

Tanya and Jack dashed toward Stacey.

Stacey whirled around and gestured wildly. "Justin's gonna die!"

Tanya yanked the driver's side door open, her heart hammering.

The younger paramedic was slumped over the steering wheel, one hand on his chest. His blood was splattered all over the ambulance's dashboard.

"Justin?" called out Tanya, her heart in her mouth. "Justin?"

His eyes were closed, but his hands were trembling.

Jack darted to the passenger door and jumped inside, making the vehicle rock.

"Still breathing," he said, leaning over to Justin. "Shot went above the heart. That should be good news."

Tanya spun around to face Stacey.

"We need a Stop-the-Blood kit."

Stacey stared at her like she didn't understand.

"Get it! *Now!*"

As if she'd got an electric shock, the senior paramedic jumped. She spun around and ran to the back of the ambulance.

"I need a pressure bandage!" yelled Jack.

Tanya holstered her weapon and started removing Justin's shirt. Using his clothing as a makeshift gauze, she pressed her hand against his wound.

Jack whirled around and grabbed the first-aid kit from Stacey.

"I'm so sorry," blubbered Stacey, wiping tears from her cheeks. "I don't know what happened. I wanted to do something... Why would anyone do this to Justin? Is he going to be okay?"

"He's alive," said Jack. "What happened?"

"I went... I went to get us drinks. He was doing paperwork. I just came out the back door with our coffees when I... I heard the shot."

"Who was it?"

"I didn't see." Stacey's voice rose like she was about to have a panic attack. "I wasn't paying attention.... I was so shocked to see him..."

"Did you see *anything*?" Jack's voice had hardened.

"All I could think of was... Justin...." Stacey's face scrunched like she was on the verge of bursting into tears. "I didn't know what was going on. I started running... I'm so sorry."

She broke down sobbing, covering her face with her hands.

"It's okay, hun," called out Tanya. "You were in shock. It can happen to anyone."

Jack ripped the first-aid kit open and plucked a gauze out of its plastic wrapping. Tanya grabbed it and placed it on Justin's chest.

She leaned close to him.

"Hey, buddy. You're doing fine. Stay with us."

Justin's eyes remained closed, but a twitch of his fingers told her he was listening.

It's a miracle he's still breathing, thought Tanya.

Jack pulled the pressure bandage out and turned to the injured man.

"Hey, buddy? This is going to hurt, but it will help, okay?"

Jack whipped his head around to look for Stacey. She was still standing by the vehicle on his side, looking helpless, like any mother would to see their only child injured badly.

"Stacey? I need you to get Dr. Chen now."

This time, Stacey didn't hesitate. She raced toward the precinct, her phone to her ear.

Jack leaped out of the vehicle.

"The stretcher! We need to get him out of here and into the clinic asap."

The ambulance bounced up and down as Jack rooted around the back for the equipment.

A low moan came from Justin.

Tanya put an arm around his shoulder as she applied pressure on his wound with her other hand. She blinked away the tears brimming in her eyes.

"Stay with me, Justin," she whispered hoarsely. "You're doing fine. Stay awake. Do you hear me?"

He moaned in reply.

Tanya held him close. All she could think was Justin was a paramedic who saved lives. He was twenty-one. Just a kid. The nicest guy. Always ready with a silly joke and a friendly smile.

Why would anyone shoot him?

Suddenly, Justin turned his head. He opened his lips and closed them.

"Don't move," said Tanya.

His head lolled to the side and fell against her shoulder. His chest was heaving harder and his breath was getting raspier.

Tanya held on to him, trying to calm her own heart down. A sob caught in her throat.

Please don't die on me.

Chapter Three

A loud bark made Tanya look up.

A whirl of brown fur was rushing across the parking lot, toward the ambulance.

Max!

She had been so engrossed with Justin, she had forgotten to check on her K9. Max had darted off to the back road where they'd heard the car engine, and was now returning to the scene.

Justin lifted his head again and moaned. Tanya turned her attention back to him.

"Stay still."

Justin blinked and swallowed hard.

He needs water.

She scanned the inside of the ambulance.

Justin's head wobbled as he struggled to keep it upright. Then, to her surprise, he reached out with a shaky hand and clutched her arm. He opened his mouth to speak.

She leaned in closer.

"What is it, Justin?"

He squeezed her arm.

"Mom, Mom... She...."

It was a croaked whisper, mingled with gurgles from the blood pooling in his mouth.

Tanya's brow furrowed.

Did he say mom?

In her undercover role, she had made it her mission to learn as much as she possibly could about the people in the town.

As far as she knew, Justin didn't have a family. Everybody thought he had been an orphan in the foster care system all his childhood. He never wanted to talk about his past, so no one pressed him.

Stacey and her husband, George, had adopted him unofficially into their family when he was only fourteen. He had even taken their last name, Richardson, and had become the son they'd never had. And soon after, he'd become the younger brother to everyone in the precinct.

But Tanya had never heard him address Stacey or George as Mom and Dad. He used their first names, like everyone else did.

She leaned closer and whispered. "Do you mean Stacey, hun?"

"No…"

"Who then, Justin?"

Before he could answer, Jack popped his head through the open door.

"Let's get him out!" he hollered, bringing the stretcher toward the driver's side.

A door banged. Tanya looked up. Two figures emerged from the back of the precinct and started running over. One was a petite woman in a lab coat.

Dr. Chen.

Tanya breathed a sigh of relief.

"The perp knew their target," said Jack as they laid Justin on the stretcher. "This wasn't an accident."

He placed Justin's hands on his thighs so they wouldn't dangle while they carried him.

"Given the angle of the shot, I'd say he was looking directly at the shooter," said Tanya.

Justin's chest heaved. He gurgled for a second before his head moved to the side. Then he fell still.

"Justin!" cried Stacey, falling to her knees by the stretcher.

Dr. Chen pushed her away.

"I need him at the surgery. Now!"

Tanya leaned over to bring the stretcher up, when Dr. Chen blocked her with her arm.

"You want to spread that all over the place? You're risking an infection."

Tanya stared at her blood-soaked hands and shirt. She had been so busy working on Justin, she hadn't realized how much of his blood had got on her.

The doctor waved her away.

"Go wash yourself. I don't have time for more patients. Not today."

She signaled to Jack and Stacey to pick up the stretcher. Carrying Justin between them, they followed the physician to the clinic located next to the police building.

Tanya stayed by the ambulance, staring at their disappearing backs. She was still reeling from what had happened, and wanted nothing more than to know if Justin would be okay.

Dr. Chen never talked to people. She barked orders and demanded everyone listen. She had transferred over from Crescent Bay to fill Black Rock's empty medical examiner position, so Tanya was just getting to know her.

Max, who had been sitting faithfully by her feet, whined. He barked once, as if to say, *how come we're not going with them?*

"The doctor's right, bud," said Tanya, wishing she could give him a treat. "I've got to clean up before I go to the clinic."

She surveyed the ambulance. The shooter had taken a clean shot through the driver's side window, but they had been several yards away, or that bullet would have gone through Justin.

Was it Stacey?

Tanya's brain buzzed.

Stacey would never do something like this. Plus, Justin had become part of her family.

Then again, most times it wasn't strangers—it was your own family that wanted you dead.

Tanya let out a heavy sigh.

After witnessing her mother get killed and her brother snatched away to a torture camp, she'd had to fight to survive. Trust was a currency she no longer had.

"Stacey looked devastated," she said out aloud, looking down at her pup. "I can't see her doing—"

She stopped as she spotted something on the ground in between Max's paws. He got up and pushed it toward her with his nose.

Tanya kneeled next to her pup.

"What's this, bud?"

She reached into her belt and plucked out a pair of gloves. Pulling one over her right hand, she picked up the crumpled note.

"Where did you find this? In the parking lot? On the road outside?"

Max licked her face in reply. Tanya shook her head, wishing, not for the first time, that her dog could talk.

Using her gloved hand, she unfolded the paper.

There was only one line printed on the note. Tanya whispered the words as she read it.

You're not welcome back. You never deserved your family.

Chapter Four

"She held a gun to her head and fired."

Jack spoke, shaking his head in disbelief.

Tanya threw her hands in the air. "Justin's fighting for his life and you're sending me on an administrative job?"

"Every time we get a nine-one-one call and a dead body, we have to investigate," said Jack.

"It was a suicide."

"It's procedure."

"You need to hire more deputies, Chief Bold." Tanya spoke in a sharper tone than she intended.

"Lopez and Fox are still stuck at the training camp. Until that darned hurricane clears and the Orlando airport reopens, we'll need to get by for another day or two."

Jack's face was haggard, making him look years older than his thirty-five.

"I know I hired you as a contractor, but you've proven yourself," he said, his voice strained. "Whatever work you did in the past has given you a set of skills more valuable than any local cop. I can't pay you more, but I'm asking for your help."

"I don't need more money," snapped Tanya. "I hate wasting time. I want to find out who shot Justin, not run off to a rich family's private island to take statements about a suicide."

"Someone's got to do the job, and you're all I've got."

"What about that weird note Max found?" said Tanya. "I don't think it's a random piece of paper that floated over. Someone dropped it in the parking lot. It could have been the shooter."

"The note is with the state forensic lab. They'll investigate and send us a report."

"*They'll* investigate?"

"You said it yourself. We need help. I wrangled two junior state troopers as well. They're supposed to arrive tomorrow. Thank goodness Chief Baptiste owes me one, or we'd be in more trouble."

Jack leaned against his desk and crossed his arms.

"There's nothing we can do for Justin right now, Stone. Dr. Chen's taking care of him. Let her do her job."

"*Taking care* are big words. The woman has no bedside manners."

"She's the best physician around here. Sheriff Adams isn't happy she left Crescent Bay, but boy, am I glad to have her," said Jack. "If anyone can save him, it's her."

He stepped up to the corkboard on his office wall and pulled out a coffee-stained, home-printed brochure. He handed it to her.

"There's a small ferry by the pier that gives folks lifts to the islands around the bay. The captain doesn't have a usual route to Kensington Island, but if you ask nicely, he should take you."

Tanya raised a brow. "How does the family get around if they don't have a regular ferry to the island?"

Jack gave her a knowing look. "You'll see when you get there."

"How long is this going to take?"

"Fifteen minutes to get to the island on a good weather day like today. An hour to take statements from the family, and another fifteen to return, tops."

"Two hours of valuable time."

Jack raised his tired eyes at her.

"Mayor Bailey is a friend of this family, and he's already raising a ruckus. If we don't take care of this now, he'll be on our case. If that happens, trust me, we won't get *any* work done."

"So, that's why you're pushing me." Tanya glared at the chief. "If I hear that man's name one more time today, I'll—"

"Don't even think of it." Jack's voice turned a notch harder. "He's the reason I can afford to hire you. I'm not an independently elected county sheriff. I work for the mayor and the council, and that means you do as well, Stone. Please remember that."

Tanya sighed and flipped the brochure open.

"The captain needs twenty-four hours' notice to take your car," said Jack. "I don't think that boat can take more than a couple of vehicles to be honest, so I'd suggest leaving your Jeep at the pier's parking lot. You can go aboard as a foot passenger."

"Won't I need my car on the island?"

"You can walk from one end of the island to the other in half an hour." He glanced at his watch. "Might want to hurry. If you leave now, you'll be back in no time to help with the investigation."

Before Tanya could respond, she felt a buzz in her cargo pants' pocket.

She had two phones.

One number was public and registered to her name. She had shared this with the local police chief, his deputies, and anyone who needed it in Black Rock. No one knew of her second mobile. It was a burner cell issued by the FBI headquarters in Seattle.

This secret phone was the one buzzing.

"All right, Kensington Island, here I come," said Tanya, before turning around to leave. "Come on, Max. We've got a job to do, bud."

She marched out of the precinct and into the parking lot with her dog at her heels. The buzz in her pocket stopped, but started again almost immediately. Whoever it was, they were insistent.

Tanya's heart beat a tick faster.

Every number that called her burner cell showed up as *restricted.* So, she never knew if it was one of her colleagues from Seattle, her immediate boss, or even the FBI director, Susan Cross, who phoned from time to time about urgent matters.

Tanya made sure she was inside her Jeep before she pulled the burner phone out.

No one in Black Rock knew she was working undercover for the feds, and she wanted to keep it that way.

She clicked the green button and took the call.

Chapter Five

"Where the hell have you been, Agent Stone?" came a crusty male voice.

Tanya closed her eyes for a second to summon enough patience for this call.

"Good Morning, Ray."

The ultimate doppelgänger for Morgan Freeman, Ray Jackson was also the opposite in personality.

He was an embittered old man who was tired of people, and didn't hesitate to show it. Having lost his family to a serial killer several years ago, he had retired to a small ranch near Black Rock, where he raised goats and read science fiction novels.

Though he had left the FBI a decade ago, the current director considered him a mentor. As Susan Cross's business confidante, Tanya suspected, he was still on the bureau's payroll, though he pretended he wasn't.

"I'm on my way to catch a ferry," said Tanya. "I don't have time to chat, Ray, unless this is urgent."

"Your boss has a job for you," said Ray, who seemed in a worse mood than usual.

Tanya's heart ticked faster. "Director Cross?"

"Yes, the big boss. She wants you to find your way into Grimwood Estate."

"Did you find something?"

"We have our suspicions but no evidence. None we can take to the courts, anyway."

"What do you need from me?"

"Your mission will be to get inside and siphon as much intelligence as you can. We need to know what they have inside those walls. Who lives there? What operations are they running, if any? Who has come in and out over the past month?"

Tanya frowned.

How am I supposed to do that?

"Get the local police chief to send you on an errand," said Ray, as if reading her mind. "Tell them you got complaints about their security guards mistreating delivery folk. Or you got privacy complaints about their surveillance equipment and you just want to ask a few questions. Use your imagination."

In the back seat, Max whined as if to say *can we go for a ride now?* Tanya merely stared ahead, her mind elsewhere.

After she had cleaned up and changed her shirt, all she had wanted was to race into the clinic to see how Justin was doing. That was before Jack had cornered her and handed her an administrative task on Kensington Island. And now Ray Jackson had a mission for her.

But this was harder to ignore.

"Ray, one of my colleagues at the precinct got shot in the chest an hour ago." Tanya spoke slowly, her mind whirling with images of the young paramedic's head lying on her shoulder, his blood on her hands. "Right now, I need to find out who attacked him."

"Heard the news." Ray sighed. "You're getting too close to them. Didn't I tell you not to get involved with the locals? These people can take care of themselves. Remember who you work for."

"This *is* my job." Tanya clenched her jaws. "I can't just go off, inquiring about noise complaints right now. If I go rogue, Jack will get suspicious. If he finds out my real identity, he'll fire me. Then, what?"

"Figure it out," snapped Ray.

"We have a brief window of time before the evidence disappears or gets wiped. I'll wrangle my way into Grimwood as soon as I'm done here. Please don't ask me to leave this case and let the shooter get away with it."

"I was a rookie undercover a long time ago, so I know what you're going through." Ray's voice had softened. "But I can't solve all your problems for you. That's why you went to Quantico and got your badge, Padawan."

"But—"

"I'm only a messenger. And I've done my job."

Before Tanya could reply, the phone clicked.

Ray Jackson had hung up.

With a resigned sigh, Tanya glanced down at the ferry brochure on her lap. As Jack had mentioned, there were no scheduled trips to Kensington Island.

She opened a browser on her phone and punched in her destination.

A black-and-white image of an expansive mansion stared back at her. She scanned the article, her eyes widening to learn this was the only photo of the manor. The public and journalists had been banned from the island for over five decades.

Tanya put her phone away and turned the Jeep's engine, her mind swirling like a gale. The strange note Max had found by the ambulance flashed to mind.

You're not welcome back. You never deserved your family.

She put the car in gear and pulled out.

"Was it meant for Justin?" she whispered to herself. "What does *family* mean?"

In the backseat, Max heard her mutter to herself, and whined in reply. Tanya usually talked back to her pup, but that note whirled in her head, challenging her.

Maybe Stacey had something to do with it. She is family, and she was the one who found him....

Tanya turned onto the main road and headed toward the pier.

Everyone considered the senior paramedic to be the nicest person in town, the good Samaritan who'd visit people in hospital, cooked meals for homebound seniors, and volunteered at every Christmas charity function during her time off.

Stacey and George had taken in a lost teenage orphan from the street.

Who does that? Good people. Stacey couldn't have had anything to do with this....

Tanya swallowed hard, recalling a lesson she'd learned during her combat days.

Never assume. That's what gets you killed.

Chapter Six

"Over my dead body," snapped the old man.

"This is police business," said Tanya.

"Do I look like I care?"

The ferry captain was sitting on an ancient oak barrel, tying a marine rope into a ball.

His white hair poked out of a peaked cap that looked as old as he was. His wrinkled face was kind, but there was a stubbornness to it that said he didn't tolerate people, especially strangers.

Tanya sighed.

Another crusty Ray Jackson type. Why do I keep attracting them?

His ferry was more of a barge than a boat. It had enough space for two vehicles but no cover for foot passengers. Tanya wished she could jump in, but the captain didn't look like he'd appreciate an unwanted passenger.

"That island is cursed," he said, not looking up from his task.

"Cursed?" said Tanya. "How?"

"Last time I stepped on that gawdforsaken island," he said, his voice dry, "the man fired at me."

"The man?"

"Mister Charles Kensington."

Holding on to the boat's railing, Tanya planted one foot quietly on the barge.

"You're not a fan of the Kensington family, I gather?"

"Can't stand them."

She sized the captain up. An old salt. Likely a loner and probably widowed a long time ago. He preferred his routines. And here she was, an out-of-towner asking him to do something he didn't want to.

"Is everyone afraid of Charles Kensington?" said Tanya, her curiosity overcoming her, despite her mind roiling with worries of Justin.

"Died three years ago or thereabouts," said the ferry driver. "Lung cancer. Served him right too. He made his money from his tobacco empire.

When you profit off other people's suffering, it's gonna come back to you one day."

He lifted his chin and narrowed his eyes.

"What is it you young people say these days? Karma is a...?"

"What about Mrs. Kensington?" said Tanya. "The one who died last night."

"That woman was a terror. The devil's daughter herself." The captain crossed himself. "Good riddance, I say. No way, am I going over to that infernal island."

Tanya kept her face straight. This was going to be harder than she'd thought.

The screech of a seagull made her look up. The sky was clear, and the ocean was calm. It would have been a pleasant morning for a boat ride, if the day's events hadn't darkened her thoughts.

Two hours. She clenched her jaws. *That's all I need to get this stupid job done.*

"Any idea why this woman would kill herself in front of her family?" said Tanya.

"Rich people do funny things for funny reasons." The captain shook his head. "Now, if you told me she massacred her entire family, I wouldn't have blinked. But shoot herself in the head? Never thought I'd live to see the day."

Max, who had been investigating every nook and cranny of the quay, trotted over. He sneezed a hello at the captain and started sniffing the barge.

The old man's eyes lit up.

"What a good-looking boy."

He reached over the railing and patted Max on the head. Max licked his hand. A slow smile cracked on the captain's face.

"What's he trained for?"

"Search and rescue," said Tanya. "Lost people and cadavers, mostly."

"I had one like him, once. A yard dog. Not trained, but a good pup."

Tanya perked up. Maybe there was a way to convince him after all.

"You had a German Shepherd?"

"Alaskan Malamute. He was bigger than my little wife, but he was such a sweet pup. Gentle like a baby."

Max wagged his tail and licked the man's hand, like he understood what he was saying.

"Oooh, look at you." The captain bent down and scratched Max's ears.

"We got him when he was a wee one. It broke my heart the day he passed." The man lifted his wrinkled eyes at Tanya. "Told my wife I'd never get another, because no one can replace Major."

"That's a good name for a—"

Before Tanya could stop him, Max jumped onto the barge, his tail swooshing back and forth. The ferry driver cackled as he hunched down to rub the dog's back.

"You're a good doggo, aren't you, my boy? I tell you, I'd trust you more than I'd ever trust a human."

Max whined in reply, his tongue lolling, happy to get this attention.

"Sir?" Tanya called out. "Would you take me and my dog to the island, please?"

She pulled out her wallet, plucked a hundred-dollar bill out, and waved it in the air. As soon as he saw the money, the old man's smile turned into a scowl.

"You think you can bribe me?" he scoffed.

"Not a bribe. An... incentive..."

Tanya quickly slipped the bill back in her pocket.

Great. Now I've offended him.

With a drawn-out groan, the captain got to his feet and turned around. He shuffled toward the open cockpit with Max trotting along with him, like he'd known the man all his life.

Tanya frowned, wondering if she should call Max, when the ferry engine spluttered to life. It revved up, creating waves in the back.

Tanya leaped onto the deck.

Without a glance back to see if she had landed inside the boat, the driver pulled away from the pier. The waves of the Pacific Ocean lapped against the barge, tilting the boat from side to side.

Tanya grabbed on to a wooden beam to balance herself.

"Where are we heading?" she called out, but the barge's engine drowned her voice.

The boat gathered speed as it headed out to the open sea. With one hand on the railing, she stumbled onto the nearest wooden bench and plopped down.

She watched the growing wake behind them, but her mind whirled with worries of Justin.

She hadn't heard any news, but Dr. Chen wasn't one to take interruptions lightly, especially when she was in the middle of surgery. Tanya knew she had to wait until someone called.

A pair of seagulls swooped over her head. She ducked and peered at the open sky. A small cloud was drifting across the sun, like a Pac-Man eating it, bite by bite.

The two hours she'd planned were stretching to infinity now.

She glanced at the bow. Max was inside the cockpit, seated on a wooden bench next to the captain. The captain's weathered hands gripped the wheel of the small boat with the expertise of someone who had been doing this job for decades.

Every few minutes, he took one hand off the wheel to pat Max on the head. Max wagged his tail in response.

At least one of us is enjoying the ride.

If there was one thing Tanya could depend on was her pup's doggy instincts. If he trusted someone, she knew she could too. But she wondered if they were heading to her destination.

Or someplace else.

Chapter Seven

Max barked up front.

Tanya turned toward the bow and squinted.

They were approaching a small island that stood alone in the wide open sea.

The barge swayed from side to side as it chugged closer to the land mass. Holding on to the nearest beam, Tanya got to her feet to get a better look.

They had left Black Rock ten minutes ago, but she could already make out the sprawling mansion on the islet.

Kensington Manor.

The house was a mirror image of what she had seen in that online article. It was like time had slowed down on the island. Or had stopped altogether.

The house stood on a large verdant estate, enveloped by an overgrown rainforest. The evergreen trees looked like sentients protecting the building from outsiders, or hiding something inside they didn't want anyone to see.

A shiver went down Tanya's back. Something about that house made her feel uneasy.

The boat was edging toward a protected cove on the east side. Its emerald green waters glistened under the sun, belying the island's family tragedy.

Tanya stepped toward the bow, holding on to the railing.

They were entering a tiny lake through an inlet that connected it to the ocean. On the far end of the cove was a waterfall that streamed from the woods above. Tall fir trees huddled around the lake, their tops swaying to the ocean breeze.

Tanya stepped up to the cockpit and smiled at her pup, who thumped his tail on the bench. The driver kept his eyes ahead, peering over the wheel, focused on his job. Either that, or he was ignoring her.

"Thank you, Captain," said Tanya.

He pointed at the lake. "See that pretty little waterfall over there?"

Tanya nodded.

"That's a good spot to sit and ponder about life." The captain shot her a side glance. "Some say there's a nice loot of treasure buried by that fall."

"Okay," said Tanya, trying to suppress an eye roll, but failing.

"You'd do well to listen to an old man who knows what he's talking about."

An old man who can spin a good yarn.

"You told me you never come here," she said.

"Only when the entire family is out of town, which doesn't happen often these days." He paused. "You have to admit this is a pretty getaway."

"You told me the island is cursed."

"It is. But only when the family's in the house."

"So, you're saying the *family* is cursed, but the island is fine?"

The captain scrunched his eyes, but kept his hands on the wheel as he navigated the boat through the inlet.

"First time I came here was ages ago. The day my wife died."

Tanya blinked. She hadn't expected that.

"I didn't know what to do with myself," said the captain. "I almost.... I sat in my boat and listened to that waterfall, and decided she'd want me to keep going."

Everybody has a story, thought Tanya, feeling humbled. *I just need to listen.*

She shifted her gaze to the waterfall at the far end and watched it roll over the edge of the precipice and splash into the lake. Even from where they were, she could see the ripples it created on the lake's surface.

It would have been an enchanting, sentimental place, if she hadn't felt a sense of foreboding come over her.

"I shouldn't be bad-mouthing these folk," said the captain, as he slowed the engine. "They've had more than their share of bad luck, themselves."

"Like what?" said Tanya, turning to him.

"The granddaughter hung herself about two years or so ago. A wee slip of a girl. Only eighteen, I think. Terrible waste of a bright life. She worked for the Black Rock Adoption Agency. Nicest of the lot, and now she's gone."

He shook his head and crossed himself.

"One of Charles' sons-in-laws died 'bout nine years back, from a car crash. He worked for the family firm and smoked like a chimney. Every time he took my ferry, he'd lit one up, even after I told him this is a no-smoking boat. Like I said, these people have no respect for the rest of us."

Tanya wrinkled her forehead.

"Why did Charles Kensington shoot at you?"

The ferry driver chuckled.

"He hated intruders. All I was doing was helping Mrs. Kensington with her bags. Her husband came out with his hunting rifle, but missed. Maybe it was a warning shot. I dropped 'em bags and ran back to my boat. Never took off as fast in my life, I tell you. I never came here after that."

"Except to ponder about life by the waterfall when no one's around."

"Aye. Don't tell anyone."

"So, this is a very private family, huh?"

The captain turned to Tanya, his wizened eyes boring into hers. "Will you take a word of advice from an old geezer?"

Tanya raised her eyebrows.

"You're an outsider," he said. "They won't want you here. Just give me the word and I'll turn around. I'll take you back to the mainland. It's safer there."

Tanya shook her head. "I work for the Black Rock police precinct. This is official business and they know I'm coming."

"You think you can flash your badge and ask smart questions? Even if you had one of 'em special FBI badges, they'll kick you out before you open your mouth."

Tanya bit her tongue.

He didn't know it, but she had one of *'em special badges*. It was tucked inside a high-security safe on Ray Jackson's ranch.

The driver turned his attention back to the front. They were heading toward a wooden wharf on the side of the lake. Docked to the pilings was a fifty-foot luxury yacht, a speedboat, a trio of bright-colored kayaks, and a cute sailboat.

That's how this family gets in and out, thought Tanya with a wry smile. *A yacht, a speedboat, and a sailboat. Do they have a helipad on this island too?*

At the very end of the dock was a steep ramp for vehicles to disembark from the ferry. It joined a narrow pathway which cut across the grounds.

This little lake must be deep, thought Tanya as they chugged past the yacht.

The boat lurched forward as it hit a rubber buoy, and Tanya grabbed a pillar to steady herself. Sensing their arrival, Max jumped down from the bench and wagged his tail, like he couldn't wait to get on land again.

"Hang on, big boy," said the ferry driver as he maneuvered the barge alongside the ramp. He picked up a rope and leaned over to wrap it around a mooring cleat on the dock.

Max leaped onto the ramp and trotted off, his nose to the ground, like he was excited to explore this unfamiliar territory.

"Appreciate the ride, Captain," said Tanya. "I'm happy to pay—"

"Go do your job," said the captain with a dismissive wave. "I'll be back in an hour to pick you up. I'm not bringing body bags, you hear me? Stay safe."

"Thank you."

Tanya jumped out of the boat to follow Max, when her phone rang. She glanced at her cell phone's screen.

Dr. Chen.

Her heart missed a beat.

Please be okay, Justin.

With her heart in her mouth, she clicked on the green button and put the cell to her ear.

"Stone?" came Dr. Chen's gruff voice from the other end.

"How is—"

"Justin just passed."

Chapter Eight

Tanya fell to her knees.

No!

She clutched her throat, feeling like she wanted to vomit.

After a dry description of what had happened, Dr. Chen had hung up, without waiting for a reply. It was how the doctor made her calls, but this time, it had felt like a stab to Tanya's gut.

Justin can't be dead.

But the physician had been clear. The bullet had severed a large artery. Justin had died while still under anesthesia on the surgery table, and there had been nothing they could have done.

A tingling sensation crept through Tanya's body, like her limbs were turning numb.

But that bullet went through muscle above his heart, didn't it....? She shook her head. *What do I know about human anatomy? I need to talk to Dr. Chen. I need to see Justin.*

Tanya turned around on her knees, toward the boat.

"Hey!" she called out, waving. "Stop! Wait up!"

But the barge was halfway down the lake, the diesel engine drowning out her voice.

She pulled out the crumpled brochure from her pocket and scanned it for a phone number. She cursed under her breath.

Of course, he has no phone.

She got to her feet, feeling dizzy.

I can't believe Justin died.

But a part of her had been expecting this news all along. Still feeling numb, she glanced around to take stock of her surroundings.

Max was running along the gravel trail toward the big house, his nose down, like he had picked up a scent. She let out a heavy sigh as she realized there was nothing she could do about Justin.

She was on the island now. All she had to do was take statements from the family and get on the ferry when it returned. Then, she could go back home to Black Rock, to Jack, to Stacey, to Dr. Chen.

And to Justin.

Max stepped off the walkway and cut through a clearing by the woods. Tanya squinted into the distance. He was in what appeared to be a small park next to the cove. He weaved in and out of the stone slabs that jutted out of the ground, like he was searching for something.

Wait. That's not a park.

"Hey, Max!" she hollered.

He stopped sniffing a tombstone and turned around.

"Get out of there!"

He ran back toward her, his tongue lolling.

"What do you think you're doing, stepping over a family cemetery?"

Tanya stopped herself as she realized her anger had little to do with Max's explorations, and everything to do with the news she'd just received.

She kneeled as he trotted up to her. She pulled him in and buried her face in his fur, trying not to cry.

"I'm sorry, bud—"

An earsplitting screech came from the woods.

Max twirled around and barked. Tanya jumped to her feet, one hand on her holster.

A petite woman burst out of the woods.

She looked to be in her mid-forties and was wearing a gray checkered cardigan and black pants. With her thick glasses and her hair tied back, Tanya would have pegged her as a stereotypical librarian or professor.

Max didn't rush up to her, but remained in his spot, barking at the intruder who was heading their way.

The woman scrambled down the wharf, panting hard, and gesturing in a frenzy.

"Stop the ferry! Tell it to wait! Stop it!"

She halted by Tanya.

"This is an emergency! I have to get to town!"

"The boat just left," said Tanya, pointing at the inlet. "It should be back in an—"

"My son!" cried the woman, her face scrunching, like she was about to burst into tears. "My boy!"

"Excuse me?"

"He's dead!"

A chill went down Tanya's spine.

The woman whirled around and scrambled down the dock, shouting at the ferry that was now inside the inlet.

Tanya stared at her, her mouth open.

Black Rock was a small town. If there had been any other unusual deaths, she would have heard about it, but so far, she only knew of one shooting in the area.

But she knew that wasn't the only way people died, and people died all the time. This could be unrelated.

Tanya scolded herself for letting her imagination run wild, but Justin's dying words refused to leave her troubled mind.

"Mom... Mom."

That's what he had gurgled through his bleeding mouth.

Tanya stared at the woman who had now jumped inside the speedboat.

Is that Justin's mother?

Chapter Nine

Tanya shook her head to clear it.

Impossible. That's too much of a coincidence—

A bark from Max made her turn.

He was halfway up the pathway to the Kensington Manor. He seemed more interested with whatever was going on in the island than with the hysterical woman on the wharf.

The woman was now rooting by the outboard motors. The engines roared to life, and soon, the speedboat careened across the lake, racing toward the inlet.

Taking a deep breath in to settle her mind, Tanya followed her dog toward the manor. If that was really Justin's mother, she'd have many more questions for this family.

Her phone buzzed in her pocket.

She pulled her public mobile out and squinted at the screen. She clicked on the text app, thinking Jack had messaged her about Justin.

Her heart jumped to her mouth.

She stared at the text, a sinking feeling coming to her stomach.

"Your brother is alive."

This was the fourth message she had received from ANON since she'd arrived in Black Rock.

ANON, whoever it was, was always brief. They never replied to her messages or took her calls.

Tanya gritted her teeth.

Who the heck is ANON?

Her finger hovered over the delete button.

She knew she could send these anonymous threats to Ray Jackson and ask him to find out who this was. Though he denied it, Ray had access to FBI equipment and tech teams, resources she didn't have as a rookie undercover agent.

Up ahead on the trail, Max turned around and barked again.

"Hang on, bud," said Tanya, her voice breaking. "Give me a sec."

She wiped her eyes, wondering why anyone would torture her like this.

Her brother was no longer alive. The same Russian militiamen who had executed her mother in cold blood had kidnapped, tortured, and killed him.

Sharing this message with the FBI would mean she would have to tell them what she had done when she was eighteen years old. The day she found out what had happened to her brother, she had hunted his killers down and made them pay.

None of them had survived.

An eye for an eye.

But that had been in another country, another era, another lifetime. It wasn't a story she could share with the federal law enforcement bureau who now employed her. No one, except for her closest friends and found family, knew what she had done to avenge her brother's death.

But someone in Black Rock was aware of her past.

Who are you, ANON? Why are you taunting me?

Her hand shook as she clicked on the text. *No, the FBI can never know about this.* She forwarded the note to the only other person who could help her, before closing the app, and thrusting the phone into her pocket.

Tanya blinked away her tears and looked up to see Max waiting for her. He wagged his tail as he saw her look.

She plodded along the trail, following in her dog's footsteps, her head spinning.

Losing Justin felt like losing her brother all over again. A young, innocent man who had meant no harm to anyone, but had been viciously attacked.

Her heart ached for Justin, and her blood boiled to think what he had gone through.

Tanya took in a deep breath. She hadn't been able to save either her brother or Justin, but she could fight for their justice.

All of a sudden, every step she took toward the house felt heavier and heavier.

The massive colonial manor that sprawled across the immense grounds seemed to be glowering at her. Large tree trunks towered over the gable roof, their scraggly branches covering the top windows, sealing some shut. It was like the forest was slowly claiming the mansion, hemming it in.

Though the sun was out, the teeming foliage made the building feel darker. It was the kind of old house that would have hidden passageways and secret doors.

A shiver went through Tanya.

Is this Justin's childhood home? Why didn't he tell us?

Maybe this suicide isn't what it seems...

Tanya and Max reached the front steps of the manor when the main doors banged open. A tall man stood by the threshold, scowling, like he hadn't expected her.

Tanya's eyes went to the hefty tool he was carrying in his right hand. It was big enough to crack a human skull.

What's he doing with an ax?

Chapter Ten

"I'm here from the Black Rock police precinct."

Tanya wished she had a proper badge to flash at him, but something flickered on the man's face.

"The family's in the living room, ma'am," he said with a slight bow, to her surprise.

He turned to Max who was standing by Tanya's feet and gave him a small bow as well, as if the dog would understand.

"And you are?" said Tanya.

"Rafael." He opened the door wider for her. "I'm the handyman. I'm also the butler, the gardener, the hunter—"

"Hunter?"

"Venison." He gestured with his chin at the forest by the house. "Every fall, I go out and catch a few deer, skin them, butcher them, and fill up the freezer. Lasts a few months."

He pointed at the front foyer with his ax.

"Would you like to come in, ma'am?"

Tanya glanced at the darkened corridor that seemed to go on forever inside this big house. The faint smell of a woodfire wafted over from somewhere within. A childhood lullaby her mother used to sing to her at bedtime sprang to mind.

"Will you walk into my parlor?" said the spider to the fly. "'Tis the prettiest little parlor that ever you did spy...."

Funny, she thought, how kids' fairy tales told the most gruesome stories.

Keeping her hand on her holster, Tanya stepped inside the foyer with Max close to her heels.

"Who are you?"

Tanya spun around. A woman was stomping toward her through a side hallway.

She was in her early or mid-sixties and was wearing a bright flowery skirt, unusual attire for a household member in mourning. Her strawberry blonde hair was pulled up into a neat bun. Her cheeks were rosy and the light makeup made her face look flawless.

Tanya's heart skipped a beat.

Even before she got close, Tanya sensed the woman's eyes piercing into her, sizing her up, judging her. But it was the golden sunflower necklace that stopped her. It glinted on the woman's neck, even under the somber light.

It looked a lot like the Ukrainian sunflower necklace she had received from her mother.

"I said, who are you?" came the woman's voice again, harsher this time.

Tanya collected her thoughts and stepped forward with her hand out.

"Tanya Stone from the Black Rock police precinct."

The woman didn't take her hand. "Why are you here?"

"I'm here on behalf of Chief Bold."

Until a few minutes ago, Tanya had been planning on taking a few statements and heading back to the mainland as quickly as possible. But now she realized there might be a connection between Justin's death and the suicide in this family, she wanted to prolong her stay as much as they would allow.

"What do you want?" said the woman again.

"The dispatch got a nine-one-one call from this residence late last night," said Tanya. "It was a hang-up. When dispatch called again, whoever was on the other line said it had been a mistake."

The woman frowned. Tanya wondered if she had known someone had called the emergency line from here.

"If it was a mistake, why come?"

Tanya stared into those icy blue eyes. While she looked a lot like her mother from afar, up close her eyes weren't as gentle as her mother's had been.

"According to our regulations," said Tanya. "we must investigate every emergency call we receive. Even the mistaken ones and the hang-ups."

Especially the hang-ups.

"I would have come last night," continued Tanya, "but we're short staffed at the moment. Given it's a suicide—"

The woman's face turned dark. "Who told you that?"

"Dr. Chen calls the police chief in case of a sudden and unnatural death."

Tanya thought she saw a jerky gesture from Rafael. The woman noticed it too. She spun around to him.

"That will be all. Tell Mariposa to prepare a light lunch today. Thank you."

Rafael lumbered through the corridor toward the back of the house. When Tanya turned back to the woman, she noticed the pink flush creeping up her neck.

"This is a gross invasion of privacy," said the woman. "I told Dr. Chen this was a private matter. She's our family physician. She has no business telling anyone about it."

Tanya spread her hands. "I'm sorry. But now we know, we can't ignore what has happened."

"And how are you going to help?"

Tanya ignored the sarcasm in her voice.

"I've a job to do, but I can make it painless. I only need statements from those who were with the deceased during her last moments."

The woman's neck flushed deeper.

"That would be everyone."

Tanya still didn't know who this woman was. She put her hand to her throat and touched her sunflower pendant. The woman squinted, then her eyes widened.

"Ukrainian?"

Tanya nodded, hoping she'd made a connection.

The woman's eyes traveled from Tanya's boots to her face, as she sized her up with fresh eyes.

Tanya cleared her throat. "Are you the head of the household?"

To her surprise, the woman offered her hand.

"Veronika. I'm the sister of the deceased." She pushed an errant hair from her face. "She was fifteen years older than me. We came to this country together, alone. That was well before she married into the Kensington family. And now... she's gone."

"My sincere condolences on your loss," said Tanya, taking her hand.

Veronika let out a heavy sigh.

"Everyone's upset. No one slept last night. It was my sister who kept us together. We were very fond of—"

An angry disembodied female voice cut through the corridor.

"I hated her! I hate you more! Get out!"

Chapter Eleven

Tanya spun around, trying to pinpoint the voice.

"You deserve nothing! Nothing, you hear me!"

She, whoever she was, sounded furious.

It wasn't what you would expect from a grieving family member. The pink flush that had crept up Veronika's neck spread to her cheeks.

"Who's that?" said Tanya.

"We're all upset, as you can understand."

Tanya frowned.

Veronika turned abruptly and stepped into a side corridor.

"I'll take you to the dining hall. That's where she, er..., is...."

Tanya followed her out of the foyer.

"I trust you didn't move the body?"

"I've been too busy trying to calm everyone down." Veronika stepped briskly ahead of her, her face stubbornly turned away from Tanya. "We were waiting for Dr. Chen to clean her up so we could bury her."

Clean her up?

There wasn't much fondness for a dead sister in those words.

Veronika walked at a rapid pace, her posture straight and her arms swinging.

With Max closely following behind, Tanya trailed after the blonde woman through the long corridor. Her profile was so familiar that flashbacks of her mother swirled through her mind.

Stop it, she scolded herself. *Focus, girl, focus.*

The Kensington Manor was as formidable inside as it was outside. Mahogany dark furniture lurked in every room, enhancing the heavy and somber atmosphere of the house.

They passed a narrow door made of stainless steel inset into the wall, with a panel of buttons on the right-hand side.

An elevator.

Tanya wondered what other modern amenities were built into this old-fashioned home.

As they approached the end of the corridor, Veronika pulled an unusually large key from her skirt pocket. She thrust it into the keyhole of an ornate wooden door.

Tanya's eyes widened.

This was no normal dining room. It was an opulent hall with wood-paneled walls, a high ceiling, and a massive chandelier, with sufficient space to entertain dozens and dozens of guests.

She stepped inside, gaping at the luxury, but stopped in mid-stride.

What had caught her attention wasn't the antique furniture or the old hunting paintings on the wall. It was the silver-haired woman lying face down, crashed on a gold-rimmed plate at the head of the long dining table.

Tanya unconsciously reached for her choker and gripped her sunflower pendant. The woman's blood-soaked head, the gaping bullet hole in the side, and the stillness of her body, all reminded her of a similar scene she had witnessed when she was eighteen years old.

Mother.

Even with her jacket on, Tanya shivered. For one brief moment, she felt like she had traveled back to a time when she had felt lost and alone.

She swallowed hard and pushed those dark memories to the back of her haunted mind.

Max raised his head and cocked it, his brown eyes on her, as if to ask, *Are you okay, Mom?*

"Hang tight, bud," she whispered.

Tanya swept the room with her eyes.

Most of the chairs around the table had been pulled back or overturned. Glass shards were scattered on the floor at one end of the table, twinkling under the chandelier's light. Round white balls that looked like pearls lay strewn on the red Persian rug.

Someone had closed the doors and windows, and switched on the air conditioner at full blast. She wondered whose smart idea that had been. Her money was on Rafael, the handyman, whom she garnered as the practical type.

She refocused her attention on the victim.

The cool temperature wasn't perfect for preserving a dead body, but it had helped. No rotting odor emanated from the corpse.

Yet.

Instead, Tanya caught the faint scent of expensive perfume in the air. But she knew that would change soon.

It had been fifteen hours since the emergency call. If the phone call coincided with the death of this woman, rigor mortis would have set in. The body would be cold to the touch. Soon, decomposition would begin, and the cells would start eating themselves from the inside out.

Tanya shivered again. This time, not because of the cool temperature.

Crash!

Max whirled around, barking. Tanya swiveled her head. It had sounded like a glass object had been flung against a wall.

"I wish you were dead!"

The disembodied woman's screech had come from the room next to the dining hall.

Tanya spun around to the connecting door which Max was sniffing with great interest. She yanked the door handle, but it was locked.

"Who's that?" she said, turning around to Veronika.

Veronika's face flushed, like the outburst embarrassed her.

"M... Monica." She gulped. "This has been hard on all of us."

"Is that one of your sisters?"

Veronika's eyes widened, as if the very thought of Monica being her sister horrified her.

"I had only one sister." She glanced at the dead body at the table and looked away. "Monica is my niece. Honoree's oldest daughter. Her mother's passing has overwhelmed her."

Monica sounds more angry than sad, thought Tanya.

"I would like to interview each of your family members."

"Is that really necessary?" said Veronika. "We need to give them time to grieve."

Tanya noticed the nervous tick on the side of Veronika's neck.

"It's procedure. I'll be brief."

That was partly a lie.

The image of Justin's bloodied shoulder had been swirling through her mind ever since she had entered this big house. Tanya had no intention of leaving the island before she figured out the question burning in her belly.

What connected a young ambulance driver to this upper-crust tobacco dynasty?

"I met someone when I arrived at the wharf." Tanya squinted, as if she was trying to recall the person. "A petite woman in her forties or so, with black glasses.... Now, what was her name again...."

"Hazel."

"Right, Hazel. What's her relation to your sister?"

"She's Honoree's younger daughter."

"Does she live here?"

"Her husband, Rupert, died in a car crash a long time ago. She's been living with us ever since, so she could be close to the family."

"Does Hazel have a son?"

"Stanley."

Tanya stared at Veronika.

Stanley? Was that Justin's birth name?

"Stanley lives upstairs." Veronika gestured vaguely at the ceiling. "He owns a few car dealerships in Seattle, Portland, and Vancouver. He sells BMWs, Audis, and that sort of thing to wealthy clients, and is always traveling."

That definitely isn't Justin.

"Does Stanley have a brother, by any chance?"

Tanya thought she saw Veronika swallow quickly, but she wasn't sure. Veronika blinked and looked away.

She's hiding something.

"Do you know a Justin?" said Tanya, eyeing her. "A Justin Richardson?"

Veronika clasped her hands over her mouth, like she hadn't expected to hear the name.

Tanya straightened up. "Tell me, was Justin a Kensington?"

Veronika stood frozen in place. Her lips were trembling, but she had gone mute.

Chapter Twelve

"Justin," said Tanya, her eyes on the other woman, "died a half an hour ago from a gunshot wound."

Veronika staggered back with a cry and grabbed a chair to steady herself.

"No!" she screamed.

Startled, Max jumped up and barked, but sat back down by Tanya's feet as he realized she wasn't a threat.

How odd, thought Tanya. *Why didn't Hazel share such a significant piece of news with the rest of her family?*

"When did Justin leave home?" she asked.

Veronika put a hand on her chest like she was having trouble breathing.

"I know he was part of this family," said Tanya. "There's no hiding it."

"He was thirteen. He left... I didn't know he...."

"Why did he leave?"

"He didn't... get along... Charles kicked him out."

"Charles Kensington?" Tanya raised her eyebrows. "His grandfather?"

Veronika lifted her face and whispered, "Does Hazel know? Does she know Justin's... that he's...?"

Tanya nodded.

Veronika put a hand over her mouth like she was stifling a cry again.

"I'm sorry for your loss," said Tanya, though a part of her wondered how much this family truly cared for Justin when he was alive.

"I lost a son... too," said Veronika in a broken voice, her eyes turned down. "Losing your child... is the worst experience a mother can have."

Tanya let her shoulders drop. The woman looked and sounded genuinely grieved.

"They told me it was a stillbirth... but I knew in my heart he was alive inside of me. He was breathing... but he stopped minutes after he was born."

She lifted her face, tears welling in her eyes, as if the memories were too hard to bear.

"Poor Hazel. She must be devastated."

Tanya frowned. "Why didn't she tell you what happened?"

Veronika shook her head.

"Losing Honoree has been such a horrible thing, but there's no feeling like that—when the baby you nurtured, protected, and had so many dreams for... dies so suddenly. It was the saddest day of my life."

Tanya watched her, wondering why she had evaded her simple question.

The ferry captain had been right. This family had more than their share of tragedies. Having all the money and power in the world hadn't shielded them from common human struggles.

Tanya sighed.

Learning about Justin's death seemed to have triggered difficult memories for Veronika. Her cool and aloof demeanor had changed completely, but now, Tanya wasn't sure she'd get anything sensible from her in this state.

She turned to Max. "Stay put, bud."

He lay down and rested his face on his paws, but his eyes followed her as she walked around the room.

Tanya pulled her phone out and stepped toward the head of the table, making sure not to tread on any evidence. She leaned over to inspect the dead woman.

The family matriarch is dead.

Honoree Kensington was bent over in the most undignified position anyone could have at the dinner table. Her face was pallid, the deathly white of one who had bled heavily.

Tanya tried not to grimace at the blood splattered all over the cutlery and white tablecloth. Not in front of a family member.

Dr. Chen's interns will have a heck of a time cleaning her up.

She spotted the antique silver pistol on the table. It was several feet away from the dead woman. On the floor, next to her upturned chair, was the lone shell that had ejected from the gun.

Tanya snapped photos quickly and discreetly.

The victim's mouth was wide open, as were her eyes. Her frozen features expressed shock, like she couldn't believe she was about to die.

Is this suicide or murder?

Tanya leaned over and scrutinized the woman's hands. What she really needed was a gunshot residue kit to confirm her suspicions.

"Why didn't Dr. Chen come?"

Tanya looked up to see Veronika hunkering by the dining hall entrance, like she couldn't wait to leave the scene.

"Shouldn't the doctor be here with you?"

"The doctor's hands are full at the moment," said Tanya.

Dealing with Justin's death, the son your family cast out.

Veronika wrung her hands. She glanced at her sister's immobile body. "We can't leave her like... like this all day. We need to bury her."

"I'm afraid an autopsy will be in order."

"No!"

Tanya stared at her, surprised at the force of her reaction.

"Don't you realize what this family has gone through?" Tears rolled down Veronika's cheek. "Can't you see we're in mourning? You'll be elongating our pain for nothing. Let this family be. I beg of you."

Tanya felt a tinge of sympathy and guilt for encroaching on their grief, but she had a job to do.

"I'm sorry for what happened. I truly am, but I'm afraid my recommendation will be for an autopsy given the inconsistencies."

"What inconsistencies?"

Tanya pointed at the pistol on the table.

"I would have expected to find that on the floor."

Veronika stopped wringing her hands. Her eyes swept toward the gun, and that pink flush crept up her neck again.

She's not telling me the whole truth.

"Who touched the gun?" said Tanya.

Silence.

"Tell me exactly what happened here last night."

Veronika leaned against the wall, trembling, like she couldn't get herself to speak.

Tanya waited for an answer. The longer she remained in this house, the stronger was her feeling that not all was what it seemed.

What are they hiding?

"Everybody was s... screaming and crying." Veronika sniffed and wiped her face. "I wasn't paying attention. I... didn't see the gun fall when... she crashed down.... It happened so fast. It was horrible."

She pressed her hand against her heart, as if trying to stop herself from hyperventilating.

"Why would she do this? I never expected Honoree to..." She looked up at Tanya, her eyes pleading. "Bad things aren't supposed to happen to good people, are they?"

Good people?

Tanya stopped herself from scoffing out loud. Everything about this family was peculiar and unlikable.

Except for Justin. He was the nicest guy....

She caught herself.

How well can you know a friend with a secret past?

Chapter Thirteen

"Can you tell me who was at the dinner table last night?" said Tanya.

"Everybody," said Veronika, "except for the help."

Tanya noticed her hands were shaking again.

"One... one minute we were sitting down to celebrate her seventieth b... birthday. She had been talking about it for weeks. The next minute, she... she... did the unthinkable."

Veronika shuddered.

"Who organized the dinner party?" said Tanya.

"Honoree, herself. She wanted to make sure everyone in the f... family would be here. Insisted on it, actually. Monica and her son, Peter, flew down from New York."

Veronika blinked and looked away.

"Craig, Monica's h... husband was held up in the city. On business."

Tanya watched her closely.

That was a lie.

"Hazel, Stanley, and the others reside here," continued Veronika, oblivious to, or ignoring Tanya's scrutiny. "This is a big house and we... have our separate lives, b... but last night, we were all here for the c... celebration dinner."

She was stammering and stuttering. Tanya knew that could be due to shock, but the way she averted her eyes made her wonder.

She's rattled. Is it her sister's suicide or is it something else?

Tanya's first impression of Veronika was a woman anxious about what others thought of her and her household. This meant she wouldn't air dirty laundry about her family.

"To tell the truth," Veronika was saying, "if they... they had known what she was going to do, no one... would have turned up."

"What happened just before she died?"

"We had finished the last course. M... Mariposa and Rafael brought in the cake, but Honoree sent them back to the kitchen. That was... when we realized s... something wasn't right."

Veronika turned to a painting on the wall, like she was trying her best to keep her eyes away from her dead sister. Or Tanya.

"Then, my sister got up and...," Veronika hugged herself, "shot herself to death."

"There was no warning? No previous indication she would do this?"

Veronika covered her face.

"It was horrible. We were terrified. Everyone's on edge now. We've never had to deal with such a thing like this before."

Tanya raised a brow.

Really?

"I was under the impression you had a similar death in your family recently."

Veronika spun around and stared at her, her eyes wide.

"A young woman," said Tanya. "Two and a half years ago, or so."

Veronika gasped and took a step back like she had slapped her.

"I only ask," said Tanya, softening her voice, "because sometimes these incidents could be connected."

"She... she...," Veronika spluttered. "Poor Lisa...."

"What happened to Lisa?"

"She started a new job at the... adoption... agency. She was having a hard time fitting in. It was her first job out of high school. We... tried to support her, but I guess... it was too much for her...."

An eighteen-year-old doesn't commit suicide because she was having a tough time on a job.

"How did she die?" said Tanya.

"She hung herself," came a male voice from the doorway.

A volley of angry barks echoed through the dining hall. Max was on his feet, facing the entrance, howling at the intruder.

Tanya whirled around to grab his collar, but missed. Before she could stop him, he darted toward the open doors. A loud mechanical whir came from the hallway outside, like an electric bicycle was speeding down the corridor.

Tanya dashed outside.

Max was bounding after what looked like the fastest electric chair in the world. Tanya blinked once to make sure she was seeing correctly.

"Max!" she roared. "Heel!"

Her pup screeched to a stop and turned back, his tongue hanging.

"Now!"

With a disappointed glance at the wheelchair, Max lumbered over to her, his head down.

"Peter!"

Tanya turned to see a frazzled Veronika behind her.

"Peter!" she called out. "It's okay."

The mechanical whir came again from somewhere. Soon, a portly young man rolled out of a side room and into the corridor in an electric wheelchair. His cheeks had turned pink and sweat was rolling down his forehead.

He pointed at Max, a livid scowl on his face.

"Keep that damned mutt away from me!"

Max glanced up at Tanya and whimpered.

"Stay, bud."

She sized up the newcomer.

Peter looked to be in his mid-twenties. Rolls of skin from his plump arms and legs folded over his chair, so that it took a second to make out the wheelchair from the front.

The elevator. They built it for him.

A closed laptop sat on his extended potbelly, and an extra-large Coke was squeezed into the cup holder on his armrest. Miraculously, neither had fallen off during that short and hasty chase.

The man was wearing the thickest glasses she had ever seen. Behind those spectacles, Tanya noted intelligent eyes, but it was the smirk on his face and the smug glint in his eyes that told her he wasn't just smart. There was something sinister about him.

She felt it in her bones.

Max feels it too.

He growled as the wheelchair whirred toward them. Max stood by Tanya's feet, hackles up, waiting for the command to jump on him.

Tanya held on to his collar, but her gut tightened.

The children's poem she'd recalled when she'd stepped into the manor popped into her head again. There was a dangerous spider web woven around this family.

She and Max had walked right into it.

Chapter Fourteen

"Lisa was my sister," snarled the man in the wheelchair.

"My condolences," said Tanya.

Peter grimaced as if those words pained him.

"I don't need your stupid fake sympathy. Nobody cared when she killed herself, and nobody cares now."

Tanya inhaled deeply to summon her patience.

They were sitting in the lavish living room of the manor, the one next to the dining hall. A quick glance around showed the telltale marks on a side wall where Monica had smashed a glass vase. The broken pieces still lay on the rug. But Monica was nowhere to be seen.

Veronika shifted uncomfortably on the couch next to the man in the wheelchair.

Tanya turned her attention to him.

Peter was wearing the biggest Rolex watch on his wrist, a gaudy hip-hop chain around his neck, and golden rings on every finger. This was someone who wanted the world to know he was rolling in dough.

"Did you see anything amiss last night," she asked, "anything that would help me understand what happened?"

Peter's lips curled into a scornful smile. "You mean an explanation for that old bat shooting herself in the head?"

Tanya didn't answer.

"I thought she was going to kill us all. Do you know she only tolerated us? We tolerated her back. Actually, she hated us and we hated her right back."

Tanya raised an eyebrow.

Keep talking.

"She was a control freak. No one in her executive suite lasted a year. She went through board members like she went through underwear. She was a bloodthirsty, power-hungry, witch. Nasty business."

He slurped his Coke.

Tanya cringed.

She hardly knew the suicide victim, and the more she learned about Honoree Kensington, the less she liked her. Still, this man's behavior felt disrespectful. Honoree had been his relative, after all.

Or had she?

"So, yeah," said Peter, that smug smirk coming on his face again. "I didn't think she'd do a hara-kiri on her birthday, right in front of us. But it was pretty cool to see."

Cool?

"If I could have gotten to my phone in time, I would have had it all on video for you. Too bad, but it was dope."

Peter turned to Veronika as if to confirm his sentiments, but the older woman's attention seemed elsewhere. She was staring at the scuff marks on the wall, but Tanya doubted she noticed the streaked mess on the wallpaper.

Tanya turned back to Peter.

"Did the deceased give any warning of her actions to come?"

"You mean what that dingbat did before she pulled the trigger?"

Tanya nodded.

"She said whoever finds her last will and testament wins it all. Everyone else gets nothing. She called us fools. Idiots. Can you imagine?"

Go on.

Peter's nostrils flared. "No one calls me an idiot!"

"What did she mean by *win it all*?" said Tanya.

He gestured around the living room with his Coke cup.

"This hellhole to start with. A white elephant. Who would want a crumbling house on a remote island in the middle of nowhere?"

Veronika smothered a cry. Peter shot her a condescending look.

"Rafael keeps saying there's buried treasure in the cove, but that's an urban legend. Only village idiots would believe something so stupid."

He slurped his drink again.

"Oh, and just before she offed herself, she said, 'I wish you all a bloodied fight till the end.'"

Tanya straightened up.

Interesting.

Peter turned to Veronika.

"I told you we should have put her in an institution. Grandmother was mental. I swear she would have bankrupt the company if she had lived."

"The tobacco company," said Tanya, sitting up. "Her shares are probably worth a lot."

Peter grimaced.

"Who needs a dying industry in their portfolio? Might as well beat a dead cow. Stock prices have been dropping like a stone for decades. After this, they'll sink to the bottom."

He turned to Veronika, put his fingers to his lips and puckered them.

"And you can kiss your valuation goodbye."

Peter threw his head back and laughed. Tanya stared at him, lessons from her behavioral psychology classes at Quantico swirling through her head.

This man's a psychopath. Or, on his way to becoming one.

Peter tapped his laptop. "I can make more cash in one day than that stupid company makes in a month."

"How do you do that?"

He pursed his lips.

"Please answer my question," said Tanya.

"You think I'm gonna share my secrets with you? It's none of your damned business, that's what."

He pushed a button on his wheelchair.

Tanya leaned forward. "I'm here with the Black Rock police precinct—"

"Screw you."

Max growled, but remained in his spot.

Peter whirred his chair around and lifted his free hand to give her the one-finger salute. Then, he sped out of the room and down the corridor.

Max looked up at Tanya and whined, as if to ask, *Can I go get him?*

"Stay, bud."

Tanya turned to Veronika.

"What's his relationship to Honoree?"

"Her grandson. He's Monica's son." She gave her an apologetic look. "He doesn't have an excuse for being rude. He was born that way."

Like mother, like son?

"Do they live on the island?" said Tanya.

"New York. Monica's husband is a hedge fund manager on Wall Street. They flew in for the birthday party." Her mouth turned down. "To them, I guess we're just village idiots."

"Why didn't you tell me what your sister said before she shot herself?"

Veronika opened her mouth and shut it a few times, like a goldfish struggling to breathe. Tanya remained quiet, waiting, watching.

Sometimes silence is the best response.

Veronika sighed.

"Honoree said a lot of things. Hurtful things. I was so shocked, I wasn't really paying attention. All I remember was her waving that gun around. I was scared for my life."

Veronika's eyes filled with tears again, but Tanya noticed the stammering and spluttering had vanished.

Had that all been an act?

"If you really have to know, Honoree was mean," she was saying. "I know it's bad to speak evil of the dead, but she treated everyone horribly. Nobody liked her."

Veronika swallowed hard. "It got worse recently."

"How?" said Tanya.

"Stanley thought it was Alzheimer's. Monica said she had dementia and we should institutionalize her. All I know was Honoree got nastier and nastier. I wouldn't have been surprised if she had turned that gun on every one of us."

Tanya frowned. "You said earlier that she kept the family together. That you were all fond of her."

"It's what you're supposed to say when someone dies." Veronika blinked rapidly. "To be honest, it feels like a dark cloud has lifted from this house. Now, at least, we can breathe."

"So, you're glad she's dead?"

Veronika turned away, but not before Tanya missed her expression.

Tanya stared at her. She hadn't expected this woman, who resembled her own dead mother, to show such hate.

"Help!"

Max scrambled to his feet and barked. Tanya jumped out of her chair and spun around.

It was a panicked female voice, with a slight accent.

"Thief! There's a thief in the house! Help!"

Chapter Fifteen

Tanya glanced around Honoree's master bedroom.

"What happened here?"

It looked like a typhoon had whipped through it.

A corner table had been overturned and the lock on a dresser had been smashed. Every drawer in this room had been pulled out, their contents flung on the carpet. The king-sized mattress had been turned upside down, and the sheets and pillows thrown on the floor.

Max was by the side desk, sniffing the papers that had been strewn over the floor, his eyes and nose intensely focused.

Tanya stepped up to the opened oak-paneled cabinet next to the armoire.

Someone was looking for something.

She leaned over to inspect the weapons. They were antique collectibles, ones you'd see in an auction with a price tag of a few thousand dollars, if she had to guess. They looked polished to a shine and well-maintained.

Three hunting rifles stood in a row. Next to them was a smaller space for handguns. A shiny silver pistol took one spot, but the second spot was empty.

Tanya's mind went to the sidearm that lay on the bloodied tablecloth in the dining hall.

The gun Honoree killed herself with. She got it from here.

"He went to the firing range every Friday," came a shaky voice from behind her.

Tanya turned to the two women huddled by the doorway. Neither Veronika nor Mariposa had dared enter Honoree's room. It was like an invisible barrier had sprung up by the threshold, which only she and Max had broken through.

"Charles," said Veronika. "This was his collection. He insisted on having this cabinet built into their bedroom."

Tanya nodded.

"I was about to clean the room...." A shaky voice came from next to Veronika. "It wasn't me."

Mariposa put her hands on her face, like she couldn't bear to witness the mess. "Rafael was in the garden. He was there all morning. We didn't come up here. I swear it."

Tanya turned to the housekeeper.

Rafael wasn't in the garden all morning.

He had opened the front door for her. With an ax in his hands.

"When was the last time anyone was in this room?" said Tanya.

"Honoree locked herself in here all day, yesterday," said Veronika. "She told us not to disturb her. She threatened to disinherit us if we did."

Tanya raised a brow.

Veronika shrugged. "She said things like that all the time."

"When did she come out of her room?"

"About five minutes after the dinner party had already started. She liked to be fashionably late."

Mariposa shook her head, her horrified eyes sweeping through the mess. "If Madame was still... alive... she would have killed me to find her room like this...."

"You didn't come up to clean the room at all?"

"She told me I didn't need to make her bed, yesterday. I was so busy getting ready for the party, I didn't have time, anyway." Mariposa spoke fast, like she wanted to let it all out. "Besides, she just fired the chef, so Rafael and I had to do all the work. Rafael was really upset when she called us in the kitchen that afternoon. It wasn't like we had time for special requests."

Tanya frowned. "Why did she call?"

"For a tumbler of whiskey." Mariposa wiped her eyes. "She said she needed something stronger than the cold glass of carbonated water, which is what she drinks. I always leave a fresh bottle in there."

Tanya turned to look at the mini fridge in the corner. It was still running, but the door was wide open.

"What time did she make that call?"

"Just before dinner, around six thirty."

"Did you come inside the room?"

"Of course not." Mariposa shook her head. "I knocked and gave Madame her drink, and ran back down to finish dinner. I was running late, and I was so worried. But I got a peek when she opened the door. Everything looked normal. I swear."

Mariposa gulped.

"I never went inside this morning, either, I promise. I knew Dr. Chen was coming for her, and I wasn't about to touch anything. The only times I come up to this floor is to clean the rooms in the morning, and for the milk run at night."

"Milk run?"

"I bring a tray of mugs for everyone before bedtime. Madame said milk helps them sleep better. She did it ever since the young ones came."

From the corner of her eyes, Tanya noticed Veronika jerk her head back ever so slightly. It was such an insignificant gesture, she would have missed it if she hadn't been focused on Mariposa, who was standing next to her.

Tanya had so many questions, but rushing this family wouldn't help.

She glanced around the room.

"Whoever did this came in between six thirty yesterday afternoon and this morning."

Mariposa wiped her eyes and nodded.

"Did you have a visitor last night?" said Tanya. "Or today?"

"Everyone was already here for the party," said Mariposa. "They arrived two days ago. Nobody came in after you today. The ferry hasn't come back yet."

Tanya nodded, her mind buzzing.

That means whoever trashed Honoree's room is still in the house.

Chapter Sixteen

G iving the wreckage a wide berth, Tanya stepped toward the large bay windows in Honoree's room.

Thick vines covered half of them. The crust built up along the panes told her these windows hadn't been opened for months, maybe years.

Why didn't Rafael remove the foliage growing around the house?

She stepped to the small window at the end, the only one that looked like it could open. She pushed it out and bent over the pane to scan the estate grounds below.

They were on the third floor of the mansion. A row of rosebushes lined the wall three stories below, and none of them looked crushed. If anyone had jumped down, it would have been a painful experience.

Tanya's eyes went toward the horizon. She had a sweeping vista of the ocean from up here.

The town of Black Rock was visible across the bay. Tanya wondered what Jack was up to. Now that Justin had died, they had a full-on murder investigation on their hands.

She retreated from the window and turned to the two women by the open doorway.

"You'd have to be a professional ninja to jump and not break a leg. Whoever did this came up the stairs and went back down it. Any idea who that would be?"

Veronika shook her head violently, like she couldn't believe what she was hearing. Mariposa stared at her, her plump cheeks red and her eyes lined with anxiety.

Tanya put her gloves on and bent down to pick up the loose papers on the floor by the desk. They were sections of an annual report of the family's tobacco company.

By law, annual reports must be sent to shareholders and made available to the public, most of the time. So, this couldn't have been what the intruder had been looking for.

Tanya looked up at Veronika. "Did your sister keep any valuables in her bedroom? Other than the antique weapons."

Veronika jerked up. "Yes, yes, of course."

Tanya detected a slight uptick in her voice.

Veronika broke through the invisible barrier by the threshold and entered the room. She scurried toward the large walk-in closet at the other end.

Tanya and Max followed her inside. Mariposa scrambled behind them, sticking close to Tanya's heels, like she didn't want to be left alone in the dead woman's bedroom.

"Jewelry worth almost a million," said Veronika. "Pieces from Tiffany's and Mikimoto's. Even a few from Chopard. They're irreplaceable."

She pointed at the large gray safe in the corner of the closet. "She kept it all in there. No one was allowed to touch it."

Tanya stepped up to the safe and got on her haunches. Using her gloved fingers, she examined the combination lock, wondering how a simple suicide case had gone sideways so fast.

Wait. It's open.

With her heart beating a tick faster, Tanya pulled at the safe's door, feeling its weight in her hands. She stared at the darkened inside and let out a low whistle.

Max trotted over and poked his nose under her arm.

"Stay back, bud," she whispered, nudging him aside. "I'll need you, but not right now."

Tanya pulled the door open all the way.

"Oh, my Lord!" came a shriek from behind her.

She turned around to see Mariposa staring at the empty safe, her hand on her mouth, her eyes bulging.

Tanya turned to Veronika. "Did you have access to this safe?"

"She... she never allowed that."

"Who has the combination number?"

Veronika placed a hand on her throat and swallowed. "I... I don't know. She didn't give it to me...that's all I know."

Mariposa needed little motivation to break into a puddle of tears.

"I swear it wasn't me!" she wailed. "It wasn't Rafael either. We're not thieves. Please don't jail us."

Tanya gestured for her to calm down.

"Hey, no one's going to do anything to anyone, okay? Right now, I'm only looking for evidence to what happened here."

Mariposa sniffed and nodded forlornly.

Tanya turned back around to snap photos of the interior of the safe when something winked at her from a corner. She reached in and plucked a small and hard object from the back. She held it in the air and gasped.

It was the largest diamond earring she had ever seen.

She turned around, holding up the piece of jewelry.

"Seems like our thief might have the other earring."

Both women stared at the diamond, but it was Veronika that caught her attention.

"How could they do this now?" cried Veronika, raising her fists in the air. "How dare they? This is scandalous!"

Tanya couldn't help but wonder why she would react more dramatically to the disappearance of this jewelry than to her sister's violent suicide.

Is she having me on?

Tanya's gut was churning, signaling red flags everywhere.

Don't believe anyone in this house. Everyone's lying.

Chapter Seventeen

*T*ime to call Jack for backup.

"We'll have to dust the room for prints," said Tanya. "Until we're done, this room is cordoned off."

Veronika's eyes widened. "But, but, you can't..."

"That's not negotiable." Tanya turned to Mariposa. "Tell me, what was it like to work for Honoree Kensington?"

Mariposa shot a scared look from under her lashes at Veronika. To Tanya's surprise, Veronika shrugged.

"Tell her."

"We... we were all scared of Madame." Mariposa's face turned a slight pink, like she didn't like speaking ill of her employer. "If she wasn't happy with something, we'd be in big trouble. She fired so many people, I've lost track. I don't know how Rafael and I have managed to stay these years. She was always threatening to deport us."

Tanya raised her brows.

"Deport you?"

"Back to Cuba. She... never let us forget she helped us with our immigration papers. If we could find another job, we would have, but we didn't have a choice. We owed her...."

Mariposa started crying softly.

"Are you going to deport us?"

Tanya softened her voice.

"We're investigating an alleged suicide and, now, what looks like major theft. All I want to find out is how this happened and why."

What she really wanted more than anything was to find out who murdered Justin. Her bones were telling her the answers lay in this massive mansion, somewhere between the matriarch's suicide and the stolen jewelry.

"We worked so hard for her," Mariposa babbled, wiping her nose with a tissue. "Madame went through chefs and cleaners like she went through clothes. A new dress every week. A new gardener or cleaner every other week. One day she fired a server because she put the fish fork in the wrong place—"

A peculiar snort stopped her.

Tanya turned her neck.

"Max?"

Max had been sniffing an antique armoire in the corner of the walk-in closet. He wiggled his head violently, like he was trying to shake something off the tip of his nose. He sneezed and glared at the armoire.

Tanya stepped over to him, her brow furrowed.

"You okay, bud?"

Max backed away, like he detested whatever was inside the wardrobe.

Tanya pointed at it. "Any idea what's in there?"

Neither woman answered, but Tanya thought she saw a flicker of worry go through Mariposa's face.

While the two women watched from the doorway, Tanya pulled the top drawer open. She reached in and felt a silky softness.

"Scarves," she muttered to herself. "And underwear."

Behind her, Max sneezed again.

Tanya sniffed the air.

A tobacco odor permeated the closet. It was so faint she hadn't paid it much attention. Besides, she was in the bedroom of a tobacco empress, after all.

She shut the top drawer and pulled open the second one.

She froze.

She pulled open the next drawer and the next.

"Wow."

"What is it?" came Veronika's shaky voice.

Tanya turned and glanced at the housekeeper.

"When you clean her room, do you come here to arrange her clothes?"

Mariposa shook her head, but her face had turned a bright red.

"Madame never allowed us to touch her things. My job was to dust the surfaces, vacuum the carpet, clean the bathroom, and get out of her hair. That's all I did. I promise you on the name of Baby...."

Tanya raised her hand to interrupt her. Mariposa was the kind of person who could wind herself up into a panic at a moment's notice.

She pulled her phone out and took pictures of the cardboard boxes that had been placed in neat rows inside the drawers. She clicked on the search engine and typed in the brand name on the labels.

Cohiba Behika.

Her eyebrows shot up.

Each box sold for $18,000. If she counted all of them, there would be more than a half a million dollars sitting right here in Honoree's chest of drawers.

Cuban cigars were illegal in the United States. Rafael and Mariposa hailed from Cuba and worked for Honoree. It was easy to make the connection, but something didn't add up.

Tanya frowned.

Why break into the safe to take the jewelry, but leave the more accessible cigars behind? A special diamond would be easy to smuggle but hard to unload, while a box of cigars would be easier to sell for a good price.

If Rafael and Mariposa had anything to do with the disappearance of the jewelry, they would have hidden the cigars first, so they wouldn't get implicated.

Tanya turned to Mariposa.

"Are you sure you don't know what's in here?"

Mariposa sniffed. "We're legal. We have our papers. We did nothing wrong. I swear on my mother's grave."

Tanya reached into a drawer, pulled out a box, and held it up.

"Have either of you seen this before?"

Mariposa clutched the doorway, and for a second, Tanya worried she was going to faint. Next to her,

Veronika stood frozen like a statue, but her hands were trembling.

Tanya watched the two women, who stared back at her wordlessly.

What are they not telling me?

Max barked in warning, breaking the ominous silence.

"Who the hell let you in?" shouted an angry male voice.

Everyone whirled around.

A twenty-something man in a beige linen suit stomped inside Honoree's closet.

Mariposa jumped with a frightened shriek to see him. Max barked his head off. Tanya grabbed his collar to hold him back.

"Stanley!" cried Veronika.

The man whipped around to her, his face red in fury. He towered over his aunt, his arms raised like he was about to hit her.

"Are you sharing family secrets with the whole damned world now? Why don't you invite the paparazzi and media next? Maybe put an advertisement in the paper, huh?"

"Stanley Kensington?" called out Tanya.

The man spun around and glared at her.

Tanya glowered right back. She knew the type. A self-entitled son of a wealthy family who thought he could order everyone around.

"Can you explain what you mean by family secrets?" said Tanya.

Stanley's eyes narrowed. "How dare you walk into our house like this?"

Veronika spluttered. "Stanley, I was only trying to...."

But the man's fury was focused on Tanya.

"This is none of your business. Who do you think you are? The FBI?"

Tanya bit back a snark.

Keep this up, and I may get the feds involved.

"I'm from the Black Rock precinct."

His eyes blazed. "Get a warrant! Get out or I'll throw you out!"

Tanya kept her voice and gaze steady.

"I have a few questions for you, Mr. Kensington."

With an angry hiss, Stanley sprang toward her, his fist raised in the air. Tanya was ready. She blocked his punch and ducked, then grabbed his shirt collar with both hands and slammed him against the closet wall.

Max jumped into the foray, pulling on his pant leg.

Stanley kicked and wiggled like mad, screaming at Tanya.

Suddenly, all three came down with a thundering crash.

Chapter Eighteen

"You're missing all the drama, Jack."

Tanya licked the cut on her lip with her tongue, then turned back to her phone.

"Stanley's hopping around like an orangutan on acid, threatening to sue me, but the rest of the family's begging me not to arrest him. They've already called their family law firm."

On the other end of the line, she heard Jack slam his fist on his desk.

Tanya had found a small bedroom on the third floor of the Kensington Manor to make the call. She glanced down at her dog sitting faithfully by her feet. Max thumped his tail and nudged her leg with his nose.

She bent down and scratched his neck.

Good boy. You did a real good job today.

"They're asking for leniency," said Tanya. "The trauma from seeing his grandmother shoot herself has supposedly impacted his mental health."

"Mental health, my foot," growled Jack. "He assaulted an officer of the law."

"Not technically," said Tanya with a wry smile. "I'm a contractor."

Stanley Kensington had actually attacked an undercover federal officer, but that wasn't a conversation she could have with the local police chief or this family right now.

"I sent you there in the capacity of a deputy from my team," said Jack. "I can't have this town think they can get away with these things."

"If it makes you feel better," said Tanya, "the man's hurting far more than me. He'll be sporting a couple of black eyes tomorrow. He won't forget this day. Max almost tore his leg out. I think we're even."

Hearing his name, Max wagged his tail.

"I'd like to see that sleazebag in one of my cells," hissed Jack.

"They're trying to protect their family's reputation." Tanya sighed. "I need these people to open up and talk to me. Hauling one of their precious sons off to jail won't help."

She paused.

"Besides, I negotiated a postmortem for letting Stanley go."

"You did what?"

"They were going to block Honoree's autopsy. I told Veronika if the family won't fight the medical examination, I won't charge their precious little boy."

"You can't make deals like that."

"Already done."

Jack fell quiet on his end. Tanya swallowed hard.

They remained silent for a few seconds. She knew he was trying to figure out how to best broach the topic, just like she was.

"Dr. Chen called...." Tanya blinked. "Have you found anything?"

"I've checked all security cameras within the vicinity of the parking lot."

Jack's voice was heavy, like he was grappling with their loss as badly as she was.

"I have cameras on the precinct, but none of them capture the city lot in the back. The mayor and council voted down my proposal for privacy reasons, a year ago. I've been pounding the pavement, but so far, no one saw or heard anything."

He sighed.

"Justin never told us he was a Kensington, did he?"

"Having met the family, I can understand why," said Tanya, feeling her swollen lips. "A lovely bunch, they are. I would have changed my name too."

"On the good news front, I got through to the state PD," said Jack. "We'll get backup soon. Their lab's looking at that note you found, and their forensics techs should come over to examine the heist. It might be a while for them to get over, though. There was a nasty multiple murder-suicide case in Seattle today."

"Oh, no."

"Secure the main bedroom and the dining hall while we wait for them to arrive."

"Already done."

"Stay on guard. Once forensics comes over, I'll need you in town asap. We need to do more interviews."

"Roger that." Tanya nodded, though he couldn't see her.

"I'll have a chat with the family and the couple who takes care of the house, while I wait. The grandsons will give me a fight, but I think the others will open up if I speak with them privately."

"Watch out for that car salesman. I've had my eye on him for a while. I've never had anything solid to pin him down, but my cop gut says Stanley is as crooked as a fish hook."

"I think he tried to push me out because he's hiding something," said Tanya. "He could have been behind the jewelry theft. And those cigars could be his. Maybe it's a sideline of his business, and his grandmother was storing them for him."

"I can understand why he reacted the way he did," came Jack's dry voice. "Cuban contraband could get you ten years in the slammer and a million dollar corporate fine. Not to speak of plummeting stock prices and a tarnished reputation."

"We need to find out if the housekeeper and handyman are part of this racket," said Tanya. "Or if the family abused their power to force them to smuggle."

"I'll put my money on the latter, but we need evidence we can take to court."

"Do we have any idea who called emergency last night?" said Tanya. "Whoever it was, wanted our help."

"I've listened to that nine-one-one recording a dozen times," said Jack, "but all I can hear is panicked screaming in the background."

Tanya frowned. "What I don't get is how they called dispatch from a landline. This is an island.

They should only have satellite or cellular. Are you sure it came from here?"

"If you have a few million to throw around like Charles Kensington had, you can get an underground cable from Black Rock to the island. That's how they have a landline."

Tanya's head cleared.

"That makes sense—"

A knock made her turn around. The door creaked open, but Max didn't bark. He merely cocked his head and stared at the newcomer.

Mariposa was peeking through the door.

"Ma'am? I think you need to see this."

"Gotta go, Jack," said Tanya, hanging up. She turned to the housekeeper.

"It's Lisa," whispered Mariposa, poking in her face some more.

Tanya frowned.

Lisa? Isn't that the granddaughter who killed herself?

"What about her?"

"Someone trashed her room. Just like they did the master bedroom."

Day Two

Chapter Nineteen

Tanya clicked her tongue.

"Come on, Max."

Max stopped sniffing the fire hydrant and got back in step with her. She and Jack were hurrying toward the Black Rock pier, with one goal in mind.

Tanya had returned to town on the ferry as soon as the forensics team and Dr. Chen had arrived on the island.

People's memories faded and important clues got buried, which meant they had a short window to gather the relevant evidence on Justin's shooting.

"Stacey had to have noticed something," she said, picking up her pace.

"She was in shock," said Jack. "She had a full-blown panic attack at the clinic after we took Justin in."

"You don't suspect her?"

Jack didn't speak for a second.

"I've known Stacey and George for years," he said finally. "Justin was like a son to them. Stacey was happy Justin decided to join the paramedic team. She was proud of him."

He paused.

"No. I can't see her having any motivation to do something like this."

"I'm glad Justin found good people to take care of him," said Tanya, "because I can tell you his birth family doesn't care."

"I've given them a moratorium. No one can leave the island until we question every one of them."

"That's not enforceable. They can challenge that."

"They already are. Their lawyers are hounding me, but I'm not taking their calls. I'll let them sweat a bit. Meanwhile, we need to figure out who targeted Justin."

"Stacey's a seasoned professional," said Tanya. "A few well-prompted questions might jog her memory."

"We both scanned the parking lot before we entered," said Jack, turning to her. "Did you see anything? Hear anything?"

"I heard a car engine. So did Max. That's why he took off like that. He was checking something out for us."

Jack glanced down at the K9 trotting in between them.

"Too bad you can't talk, big boy."

Max looked up and barked in reply, but neither Tanya nor Jack smiled.

Jack sighed. "I need a real team. Glad I have you, at least, Stone."

Tanya didn't reply.

Her FBI burner phone felt like an albatross in her pocket. It was a reminder of her actual day job. She had been ignoring Ray Jackson's request to get inside the Grimwood Estate, but all she could think of right now was Justin.

She narrowed her eyes.

When I find who killed him, they will pay.

Jack and Tanya turned from Marine Drive onto Black Rock's pier.

The spot was crowded for a Tuesday afternoon.

Located at the farthest point of the long pier was Stacey and George's Dog House Pub, which gave it the illusion of being adrift on the ocean.

Waves lapped against the quay's wooden piles. Two paddleboarders floated by the quay.

Families strolled along the wharf. Seagulls squawked above them, their laser eyes beaming down for scraps from someone's fish and French fries takeout.

It would have been a cheerful scene, if they hadn't lost Justin, only thirty hours ago. Neither Jack nor Tanya had slept, and it showed.

"This has to be the strangest case I've faced yet," said Jack as they stepped around a tourist snapping photos of a seagull eating a fry.

"A tobacco baroness's suicide in front of her family. Two bedrooms ransacked. A dragon's horde of jewelry missing. A wardrobe full of smuggled Cuban cigars. And the family's black sheep shot to death in a parking lot."

He rubbed his tired brow.

"I can't make head or tail of this."

"Mariposa told me Honoree kept Lisa's room like a shrine," said Tanya. "But someone turned it upside down last night. Whoever it was probably searched Honoree's room first, found nothing, then went to the dead granddaughter's room next."

"I'd bet all my pension the missing jewelry is a diversion," said Jack. "They were searching for something far more valuable."

"Honoree's last will and testament." Tanya nodded. "Either a few or all of them have taken the inheritance challenge she issued just before she killed herself."

They pushed their way through the crowd, the only two people on the quay in a hurry.

The pub at the end looked quiet and dark. It was closed in memoriam of Justin.

But Tanya knew Stacey and George were inside, cleaning up, fixing appliances, doing paperwork, whatever it took to get their minds off what had happened to their adopted son.

The Dog House Pub had been standing at the end of the pier for fifty years now. Stacey's grandmother had catered to passing sailors, train workers, and out-of-towners until it had burned down from a fire twenty years ago.

The family had rebuilt the oceanfront establishment plank by plank. Stacey and her husband, George, ran the show now.

It was a popular eatery. A place where folks could hang out after work, listen to the waves, and watch kayakers and paddleboarders along the shore.

Jack and Tanya were halfway down the pier, when they heard the yell.

"Whale! Look! A whale!"

Tourists stampeded down the pier, phones, and cameras out, shoving each other to get a good look.

"Take a picture!"

"Do you see it?"

"It's on the other side!"

"Where is it?"

Tanya grabbed Max by the collar as the crowd scrambled from one side of the pier to the other, like a bunch of crazed paparazzi who had spotted a celebrity star.

Jack shot a frustrated glance at a man who had almost bowled him over.

"Whales don't come this close to the shore," he muttered. "Water's too shallow and they know better than to get close to these stupid—"

That was when the Dog House Pub blew up.

The explosion rocked the pier.

Frightened screams rang through the air.

Chapter Twenty

A fireball had engulfed the Dog House Pub.

Tanya's heart pounded.

"Stacey!" she screamed.

Max bounded toward the end of the quay, barking like mad. Tanya and Jack tore after him, ignoring the frightened shrieks from the crowd behind them.

"George!" hollered Jack as they approached the burning pub. "Stacey! Where are you?"

A second explosion rocked the building. Wood debris flew in all directions.

Jack and Tanya slammed to the ground.

Max kept barking on his feet. Tanya pounced on him, pressed his body to the ground, and wrapped her arms around his face.

Her heart thudded hard, and the heat from the blaze beat on her head. Underneath her, Max wiggled, pointed his snout toward the west end of the burning building, and whined.

Tanya turned.

She noticed the silhouette simmering behind the flames by the side door.

"Over there!" she cried. "Someone's by the kitchen entrance!"

Jack leaped to his feet.

"Stacey!"

The shadow was struggling to get out.

Tanya scrambled up and yanked Max by the collar. She dragged him down the quay, ignoring his huffs as her hand dug into his neck, but she didn't let go. Severe discomfort was better than being burned alive.

"Stay here," she said in a firm voice, as she pulled him over to a pillar. "Got it, bud?"

Max plopped down on his haunches, but his entire body was trembling. He barked at her, as if he wanted to tell her something urgent.

Tanya looked up to see the fire extinguisher strapped to the pillar above him. She ripped it out of its base and raced back to the pub.

She got to the side door as Jack pulled Stacey out.

"Roll!" he shouted, as he pulled her to the floor. "Roll, Stacey!"

He slipped his jacket off and threw it over her, to kill the flame that was traveling down her pant leg. Tanya plucked the pin out of the extinguisher and aimed the nozzle at her.

"Stacey! Shut your eyes!"

She swept the foam up and down Stacey's body until the canister was empty. She threw the extinguisher away and kneeled next to Stacey.

"It's okay, hun. Stay with me, you're going to be okay. We're getting you out of here."

"George," whispered Stacey hoarsely. "Pebbles."

Stacey closed her eyes and dropped her head, like it hurt too much to speak.

Sirens wailed from somewhere on Marine Drive, mixed in with the shocked and frightened cries of the onlookers.

Tanya looked up to see a fire truck at the opposite end of the pier, its lights flashing. The fire team was hauling a heavy hose down the pier, and soon, the thundering sound of their boots beat on the wooden platform.

"George! This way! George!"

Tanya spun around to see Jack waving at a second shadow inside the pub's blazing foyer. He was trying to pull George out, but the flames were battering him back.

Tanya raced over and ripped off her jacket. Using it as a shield, she stepped toward them.

The crackling fire and the creaking wood sounded like someone had set off firecrackers all around. The heat beat on her face.

Suddenly, the hinges of the pub's front door tore away, and a flaming piece of wood dropped at her feet. Tanya jumped back to avoid it.

A panicked yell made her turn.

She whirled around, her heart pumping a thousand miles a second. The pub's heavy door had crashed down, breaking the weakened plank they'd been standing on.

Where's Jack?

"Hey!"

She saw the hand grabbing on to the edge of the pier.

Jack was holding on, but the rest of his body dangled in the air. It was a long way down, even if it was into the water.

Tanya dropped to her knees and seized his hand just as the piece of wood he'd been hanging onto crumbled into the sea.

"Hold on!"

She gripped his arm with both hands. Jack swung his free hand up and grabbed on to the mangled wharf. His face flinched as he felt the heat.

Tanya felt a small and furry body bump into her.

Max snatched Jack's shirt with his powerful jaws. Using both him and Tanya as leverage, Jack thrust his body up and fell onto the quay. He lay in his stomach, catching his breath.

"You okay?" shouted Tanya.

"George!" said Jack, coughing a raw cough. "Get him out!"

Tanya jumped to her feet and spun around. Jack stumbled behind her.

"Help!" cried George, holding his arms out. "Help me!"

Jack and Tanya jumped through the flames, propelled by pure adrenaline, and grabbed him. They hauled him out. All three crashed onto the pier while Max ran in circles around them, barking.

"Back!" an unfamiliar voice hollered. "Get back!"

Tanya whipped around to see two firefighters race over, extinguishers in their hands. The sting of the foam hit her eyes and she covered her face.

She got on all fours, panting hard.

"Oxygen!" shouted one firefighter. More footsteps pounded on the pier. A third firefighter was rushing over to George with a first aid kit.

But George had gone immobile.

Jack sat up and wiped his brow.

"Stay with us," he said, panting hard. "You can do it, George."

Tanya turned and glanced at the pub.

The inferno had taken over the entire structure. An ominous black cloud swirled above them, and the acrid smell of smoke burned into her lungs.

Stacey and George's lifelong retirement dream was now a bombed-out wreck. Tanya wondered if the pub would burn itself into the ocean.

Max was circling her, agitated, barking like he wanted to tell her something. She squinted through the blaze, her heart pounding.

Is someone else inside?

She spotted a movement.

Tanya leaped to her feet.

"Get back!" Jack pulled on her leg, but she shook him off.

Tanya approached the remnants of the pub's entrance when a ball of fur streaked through her legs.

Pebbles.

She whirled around to see if the cat was okay, when a bang came from above.

The roof was crumbling down.

"Tanya!" shouted Jack. "Get back!"

The wooden beam hit the back of her head. She slammed face first to the ground.

Then, the world went black.

Chapter Twenty-one

Tanya's eyes shifted to the window across the hospital waiting room.

She didn't recognize the reflection staring back at her. Her jacket was scorched, her face was streaked in soot, and a tornado had whirled through her hair. Jack, who was sitting next to her, clicking through his phone, hadn't fared any better.

She glanced down at Max, who was sleeping by her feet, having succumbed to exhaustion. She would have killed herself if he had got hurt.

Tanya had convinced the medical team not to hospitalize her, but they were watching. They had already given her several warnings to not leave until they gave the green light.

If she had a minor concussion as they suspected, she didn't feel it. All she knew was she had a pounding headache, and the painkillers they'd given her had been of no help.

She and Jack had been camped outside the hospital's burn unit for several hours. They had been here for so long, she no longer smelled the strong antiseptic that seeped through every hospital corridor.

People shuffled by them, giving them funny looks before turning away, as if they were embarrassed by what they saw.

We look like we fought zombies.

"Suicide?" said Jack, sitting up, his mobile to his ear. "Are you sure?"

He put his phone on speaker mode and nudged Tanya with his elbow.

"We found gunpowder residue on her right hand." Dr. Chen's voice crackled down the line. "The shot was at an angle commensurate with a self-inflicted wound. Cause of death was loss of blood from massive trauma to the brain."

The doctor's voice sounded robotic and distant. Tanya squinted at Jack's phone under the stark corridor light, trying to ignore the throbbing in her head.

"My team will run a few rapid toxicology tests to make sure there's nothing else in her. We have enough samples now, so I can release the body to the family shortly."

Jack let out a relieved sigh.

"Thank you, Doctor."

"Brace yourself for a lawsuit. They're not happy I went against their wishes on the autopsy."

With that, Dr. Chen hung up.

Jack wiped the sweat from his brow and leaned back in his chair.

"I'll cross that hell if we get to it."

Speaking of hell, thought Tanya, as the memory of Stanley Kensington flying into a rage crossed her tired mind. He had railed at Veronika about her speaking with outsiders.

She turned to Jack.

"I don't think they'll complain. They don't want any more exposure than they already have."

She paused. "That family is shrouded in secrets, secrets they don't want anyone to find out."

"I'm willing to bet it was one of them who blew up the pub." Jack rubbed his face and rolled his shoulders. "The only reason we didn't have more casualties was because of that nonexistent animal. Whoever yelled 'whale' did us all a favor."

"Stacey saw something. This was an attempt to silence her." Tanya's face turned grim. "And to think she was on my suspect list. I thought she could have shot Justin. I can't believe I—"

"That's our job, Stone. You can't beat yourself up about it. We sift through data and come to the most logical conclusion. Until then, everyone is open to questioning, even friends and colleagues."

Jack let out a weary sigh.

"I'm glad we were there when the pub exploded. I don't think the perp had bargained for two cops—"

"Chief Bold?"

A woman in blue scrubs and a mask was walking down the corridor, a stethoscope around her neck.

Jack got to his feet. "Dr. Dar."

The surgeon nodded. "Chief," she said, and turned to Tanya. "Detective."

Tanya's heart beat faster. "How are they doing?"

Dr. Dar stared at her for a few seconds, like she was an alien. She turned from Jack to Tanya and back again, her eyes scrunched in concern.

"You two look like you're in need of a medical checkup," said Dr. Dar. "Was it you who pulled them out of the fire?"

"We're fine, Doctor," said Jack, a hint of impatience in his voice. "It's Stacey and George we're worried about."

The doctor sighed.

"Stacey has first-degree burns on her arms. She's otherwise healthy and fit, so my prognosis for her recovery is good."

"What about George?" said Tanya, feeling her throat going dry.

The doctor looked down at her feet.

Jack furrowed his brow. "He's... he's not...."

"His injuries are more serious," said the doctor. "We have cleaned and dressed his wounds, but he'll need to remain under observation for now."

"Can we see him?" said Jack.

"George is off limits until I say so."

"What about Stacey? Can we see her?"

The physician turned around and gestured for them to follow her. Jack stepped forward when Tanya's phone vibrated.

"You go," she said, digging into her cargo pants pockets. "I'll join you."

With a shrug, Jack followed the doctor through the entrance to the burn unit.

Tanya sucked in her breath and plucked her mobile out with trembling fingers. The events of the day were slowly overcoming her. She didn't have the energy to deal with mean messages from that psycho ANON.

Not now.

All she wanted was to crash to the floor next to Max and fall asleep, right there in the open corridor.

She checked the screen.

Asha.

Her heart skipped a beat. It always did when any of her found family members called, as she braced herself for a life-threatening crisis.

She clicked to take the call.

Chapter Twenty-two

"Tanya!"

Two cheerful voices chimed in.

Max woke up, and barked as he heard his favorite aunts over the phone.

"Hey, Max!" cried Asha.

"How's our good boy doing?" cooed Katy.

Tanya leaned into her cell. She didn't have time for this. She needed to talk to Stacey and get back on the investigation.

"Is everything okay at home?"

"Of course," came Katy's bubbly voice. "Why wouldn't it be?"

"How are you doing, hun?" said Asha.

Tanya sighed. That wasn't a question she wanted to answer right now.

If she told them what was really going on in Black Rock, they would fly over on the first red-eye to help her with her investigation. But the last thing she needed was to have her family under her feet.

A nurse scurried by, shooting her a curious look. Tanya turned her face away.

"Seriously? Are you mad we called?" Asha sounded injured. "This is a *care* call."

"Heard you got another nasty text from that ANON guy," said Katy.

"Yesterday morning." Tanya sighed. "I already passed it to Win."

"Maybe they're not wrong," said Katy, speaking slowly.

Tanya frowned. "What are you talking about?"

"Maybe your brother escaped the Russian camp after all, and is now looking for you."

Tanya took a sharp breath in. It was a possibility she never wanted to contemplate, because if it wasn't true, her heart would break all over again.

"Did you see him?" said Asha. "His... dead body?"

Tanya choked back a sob. The images of Justin swirled with the images of her brother.

"No."

"Then, maybe—" began Katy.

"My brother would never play these sick games," snapped Tanya, speaking in a harsher tone than she intended. "He's dead, okay?"

Asha and Katy went silent.

"Whoever it is," said Tanya, "they know what happened in Ukraine and wants to get back at me. We have to track the nut job. That's all. When we do, I'll take care of him or her. Got it?"

"Win promised to dive into the texts as soon as she gets a break at work," said Asha. "She works ninety hours a week for that tech company. Poor girl."

"Poor? They pay her like a queen," said Katy. "But if anyone can get to the bottom of this, it's her."

"Tell Win thanks," said Tanya, rubbing her throbbing forehead, wishing she could end this call. She had work to do.

Katy and Asha had fallen silent again.

Tanya's spidey senses tingled.

These were her best friends. They were like younger sisters, her only family in the world.

They had been there to catch her when she'd learned her brother had been killed. The three of them had grown up together through the toughest times of their lives.

They made regular calls to her, but their strange silences told Tanya they had more up their sleeves that day.

"Why do I feel like you're about to drop a bombshell on me?" said Tanya.

"Who?" came Katy's voice. "*Us?*"

Tanya sighed. "Tell me the bad news first."

"Do we always call with bad news?" huffed Katy.

"Okay, what's the good news?"

"We're coming to visit," said Asha.

"Now isn't a good time," said Tanya.

"We have a client in Black Rock."

Tanya recognized the eager tone of her friend, one that always came with a hint of self-assured pride. That was how Asha got every time she bagged a well-paid P.I. case.

"I met him the last time I was in town," continued Asha, oblivious to the thunderstorm raging through Tanya's head. "I gave him my business card, and he called me a week ago. He said he didn't have anyone else to ask for help."

Tanya remembered the last time Asha had been in town well.

When Asha had learned Jack was understaffed and under-resourced, she had smelled an opportunity. She had placed a deck of her private investigator cards on the chief's desk, then went out to hand them to anyone on the street who would look at her.

It had been embarrassing.

"You can't come here," said Tanya, frustration swirling up her spine. "We're dealing with a nasty mess at the moment."

"Maybe we can help," said Asha.

"You don't understand. We have a case that's growing like an octopus with a hundred legs. It's dangerous."

"Sounds interesting. We can manage two cases at the same time. Not a problem."

"Isn't Jack, that cute chief, strapped for staff and cash?" said Katy. "He'll welcome our help."

"No!"

Tanya's shout made a passing patient jump. She shot him an apologetic glance and lowered her voice.

"Don't you have more important things to do in New York?" said Tanya. "If this is some dude trying to find out if his wife's cheating—"

"Do you think that's all we do?" Katy sounded indignant.

"It's an inheritance case," said Asha.

Tanya sat up. Asha's voice had come clearly down the line. She hadn't imagined those words.

"What did you say?"

"A wealthy family that owns a tobacco empire lives near Black Rock," said Asha. "Everyone's supposedly fighting over a will. One of them hired us to find it."

"We got a fifteen-thousand-dollar retainer," said Katy. "Can you believe it?"

Tanya's mind whirled.

Stanley.

She could just imagine him recruiting a private detective agency so he'd be the first to claim the family fortune for himself.

"I think I know who your client is."

"Guess!" cried Katy.

"Stanley Kensington."

Silence.

Tanya gripped the phone. "Are you still there?"

"That's not the guy who called us," said Asha.

Just like Stanley to give a pseudo name.

"What name did he give you?"

"Justin Richardson."

Day Three

Chapter Twenty-three

"Don't tell anyone."

Hazel's frightened whisper echoed inside Tanya's head.

After spending a sleepless night in hospital, the last thing Tanya wanted was to climb back into the rickety barge with a grouchy captain, heading to Kensington Island.

She shivered under her jacket in the back of the open ferry. She was glad Max, at least, had been allowed the warm spot next to a space heater by the cockpit.

Hazel's panicked call had jerked her up at five in the morning. It had taken Tanya a few seconds to orient herself.

She had been dozing on the most uncomfortable chair by Stacey's hospital bed, while Max had slept on the cold floor at her feet. Jack had kept vigil by George's ward inside the burn unit, forbidden to enter, but allowed to stay close enough to monitor him.

Two junior state officers were on their way to assist them, and another had been dispatched to the island as a night guard. Until they had backup, neither Tanya nor Jack wanted to leave the injured couple from the Dog House Pub alone.

While the fire chief was still investigating, Tanya knew in her gut, the explosion was no accident.

Whoever tried to kill Stacey and George would try again.

Tanya had taken her early morning call outside, so Stacey could rest undisturbed.

Her headache was gone but her eyes ached in the stark hospital light. She had leaned against the corridor wall, and placed the phone in her ear.

"Tanya Stone."

"Monica's gone." Hazel's voice had been laced in fear. "Please.... I don't know what to do."

"Who is this?"

"Hazel. Justin's... mother...."

Tanya had straightened up, fully awake. It was the woman she had seen race down the island's wharf and take off on the speedboat only two days ago.

"Are you on the island?"

"I'm in Black Rock."

"How do you know Monica's gone?"

"Mariposa called me. She gave me your number."

"What about the others?"

"Everyone's still sleeping. Mariposa found out, but didn't know who to call. Can... can you help us?"

Tanya had frowned.

How does anyone disappear on that small island?

Her eyes swept the solitary islet across the bay now. It looked dark and forbidding in the gray light of dawn.

Up front, the captain pushed the throttle, making the boat buck the waves. Tanya grabbed on to the railing, trying to ignore her churning stomach.

She knew he was punishing her for rousing him from bed for a trip he would rather not go on.

Tanya plopped down on the closest wooden bench and tried to focus.

Monica Kensington, married to a hedge fund manager in New York, was one of Honoree's daughters. She was Hazel's older sister.

Though Monica and Hazel were siblings, they had very different personalities. Come to think of it, they didn't look like sisters. They didn't look like their mother, Honoree, either.

Strange.

Monica had refused to speak to her the last time she was on the island, but Tanya had heard her enraged voice reverberate through the hallways of that manor.

So, now Monica's gone?

Did she leave on her own accord?

Did she have something to do with Justin's murder? Or the explosion on the Black Rock pier?

The images of Stacey and George trying to escape their burning pub mingled with that of Justin bleeding in the ambulance. Tanya placed her head in her hands.

Who is attacking this family?

A subdued sniffle pulled her out of her dark thoughts.

She glanced at her only fellow passenger.

Hazel sat huddled on a bench at the back of the ferryboat, looking like she would break into a million pieces at one wrong word. Her face was red and blotchy as though she had been crying all night. She was wearing the same clothes, crumpled now, like she had slept in them.

As Tanya watched, Hazel swallowed another sob and clutched her chest, apparently trying not to burst into a flood of tears.

Tanya leaned over. "I'm sorry for your loss."

Hazel looked up, startled, as if she hadn't realized someone had been talking to her. She pulled out a tissue from her pocket and wiped her nose.

Tanya watched her quietly.

Dr. Chen didn't welcome visitors to her surgery. She was known to chase away family members and strangers alike. Tanya wondered if the physician had made an exception for this grieving mother.

"Justin was a good guy. We all liked him," said Tanya, wondering how to placate Hazel. "I'm glad you got to see him in the end."

Hazel sniffed. "She didn't let me."

Tanya raised a brow. So, Dr. Chen hadn't been as gracious as she had thought.

"I'm going to do everything I can to find out who did this," said Tanya.

Hazel gave a timid nod.

Tanya's brain buzzed with so many questions.

Why did Charles Kensington kick his grandson out? Who in the Kensington family wanted to harm Justin and his adopted parents?

But she knew this wasn't the time to interrogate Hazel. Talking to her would require an infinite amount of patience and the softest kid gloves Tanya could find.

"What happened to your speedboat?" said Tanya.

"S... Stanley told me to leave it at the marina." Hazel sniffed and wiped her nose again. "He... he was worried I'd crash it...."

Tanya nodded. "It's probably safer to get a lift from the captain."

Hazel didn't answer. She dropped her chin and retreated into herself, like she wanted to roll herself into a ball and disappear.

Tanya recognized the personality type from her behavioral science classes at Quantico.

Hazel was meek, too scared to tell the truth, even if concealing it jeopardized her own safety. She was the sort of woman who would defend her abuser. Maybe even let someone chase her own child out of the house. This type usually misremembered, lied, and misdirected their anger at someone else.

Stockholm syndrome.

Tanya observed the woman discreetly.

Was Hazel always like this?

Or, did someone in the manor bully her into submissiveness?

Chapter Twenty-four

The captain throttled down the engine and reduced speed.

They were heading toward the cove with the waterfall on Kensington Island.

They passed the yacht, the sailing boat, and the row of kayaks, toward the end of the wharf which was connected to a loading ramp. The captain slid the barge next to the wharf, but kept his hands on the wheel and the engine still running.

Tanya got up from her wet bench with a sigh.

He hadn't bothered to tie up the boat, so they would have some stability as they got off. But Max didn't seem to mind.

With a thank you bark at the ferry captain, he leaped off the boat and onto the platform. He shook himself vigorously to rid himself of the salt water from their ride.

The captain held an arm out to protect himself from the doggy water spray, but Tanya noticed the indulgent smile on his face.

Max barked at her, as if to tell her to hurry.

Tanya turned to Hazel and extended a hand. The woman was shivering and hugging herself.

"Come," said Tanya. "You can hold on to me."

Hazel got to her feet shakily and clutched her arm. Tanya led her to the easiest spot on the barge to step out. The captain had gone back to ignoring his human passengers, focusing on something in the water now.

"I'll walk you home. We'll find Monica soon."

Hazel wrapped her arm around Tanya's and leaned against her. Tanya slowed her pace to match hers and followed Max.

Behind them, the ferry revved its engine as it reversed and headed back toward the mainland.

Max was already halfway along the path toward the house, trotting along like he was on a very important mission. Hazel hobbled beside Tanya, her hand on her arm, but her eyes on the manor in the distance.

Tanya thought she noticed an uncanny glint in the woman's eyes.

She's scared.

Or is it something else?

Max barked.

Tanya glanced up to see two people hurrying across the grounds.

Mariposa and Rafael.

"We're so glad you came," called out Mariposa, as she scurried over.

Tanya noticed Rafael limping, as he tried to keep up with his wife. She scrunched her eyes to recall if he had been limping the day before, but without sleep and with so many incidents that had happened over the past forty-eight hours, her brain felt foggy.

"We're so scared," said Mariposa, her cheeks pink from the short run. "So many bad things are happening in this house."

"Have you found Monica yet?" said Tanya.

"She's gone. Her bedroom door is open. It's like she never slept in her bed at all."

"What about the officer?" said Tanya. "The night watch we sent over?"

"He hasn't come back."

"What do you mean?"

"He went to look for her but he never returned," said Mariposa. "Rafael found his mobile dropped near the woods. That's when we called...."

That explains why the trooper hadn't returned Jack's calls for the past hour. Tanya shook her head. *Hope this won't turn into a search for two missing people.*

Rafael came over, and to Tanya's surprise, took Hazel's other arm. Hazel let go of Tanya, pushed her away, and clutched onto him as if she trusted him more than her.

"I swear, this house is cursed," Mariposa was saying.

"There has to be a good explanation for her disappearance," said Tanya. "Show me her room."

She gestured for Mariposa to follow her and stepped ahead of Rafael and Hazel.

"I don't know if I should...," said Mariposa, running to keep up with her. "I'm not sure how to say this...."

Tanya stopped and turned to her.

"What is it? You can talk to me."

Mariposa sucked in her breath, like she was debating whether to share something.

"It's Peter." She gave a side glance on either side, like she was worried about eavesdroppers, though they were in the middle of an empty lawn.

"It was past midnight." Mariposa leaned in, like she was about to divulge a national secret. "He was in his mother's room. I heard them from downstairs. They were fighting."

"What about?"

Mariposa's face reddened. "I shouldn't gossip. I...."

Tanya shot her a steely look. "This might help us find Monica."

"Monica was shouting something about... She said, *You think I have millions lying around? Somebody stole your inheritance, you idiot.*"

Mariposa swallowed hard.

"Then, I heard Peter shout back, *I hate you.*"

Tanya raised a brow.

Mariposa lowered her voice to a whisper.

"And then, I heard him say, *I'm going to kill you.*"

Chapter Twenty-five

"Where's Veronika?"

Tanya turned to the housekeeper and the handyman who were hovering by the threshold of Monica's bedroom.

"A terrible migraine," said Mariposa. "She asked for two extra-strength Tylenols last night. I took it up to her. She didn't look too good."

"What time was that?"

"Around quarter past two in the morning."

"Is everyone else accounted for?" said Tanya.

Mariposa and Rafael nodded.

"Did *anyone* see Monica this morning?"

Mariposa and Rafael shook their heads.

Tanya sighed. "I gather she doesn't go out by herself on night walks on a regular basis?"

Rafael shot her a curious look. "I heard the front door open last night."

Tanya turned to him. "When?"

"After midnight, after she and Peter fought in here."

"Did you go to check? Did you ask her where she was going?" Tanya crossed her fingers, hoping for a few more clues to the woman's disappearance.

Rafael rubbed his face. He looked at her, then his wife, like he didn't want to answer the question.

"I thought she went outside to clear her head. After the fight, you know. I didn't want to interfere...."

Mariposa turned to Tanya, her face dark. "Monica doesn't... talk to the help."

"Is that right?"

"I'm only allowed to clean her room when she's not here. She's very particular, and she can get very.... We try to not upset her."

Tanya remembered the crash of glass against the wall in the living room when she and Veronika were in the dining room next door. She could imagine why this couple would have been reticent to talk to the bad-tempered woman.

"I heard her shout at someone in the living room the last time I was here," said Tanya. "Was that Peter?"

The couple glanced at each other and shrugged.

"She's always shouting at someone," said Mariposa. "It could have been anyone."

Tanya glanced around Monica's bedroom.

Mariposa had been right about one thing. Other than a handbag at the foot of the poster bed, the room looked like no one had slept in it.

An empty suitcase lay on a luggage rack, and her clothes hung neatly in the closet. There were no electronic devices, or her phone to be seen anywhere.

Did she go out to meet someone? By the wharf? In the woods? Did someone visit the island last night?

She was about to check the night table when a bloodcurdling scream made her jump.

Mariposa shrieked in fright and clutched Rafael's arm.

Chapter Twenty-six

Max whirled around and barked.

Tanya closed her eyes as she realized what the hair-raising sound was.

An electric guitar had screeched to life. The thud of a bass drum followed, and the deep-throated scream of a popular metal song echoed through the floor.

The vibrations of the music thumped through the hallway, making Tanya feel like she had stepped into a heavy metal bar. It wasn't a pleasant sound to hear anytime of the day, let alone, early in the morning.

Mariposa covered her ears and scrunched her eyes.

"It's David."

The drumbeat was so loud, Tanya could feel it banging on her bones. She raised her voice so they could hear her over the noise.

"A fourth grandson? I thought it was only Stanley, Justin, and Peter."

Rafael shook his head. "David is Madame's son."

Tanya's brow furrowed. That didn't make sense. Honoree had turned seventy.

"How old is this kid?"

Mariposa leaned closer to her ear.

"Forty-four. Best to stay out of his way or it's never good."

His mother killed herself two days ago, and he's already partying. Tanya frowned. *Is this a celebration? Did he find the last will and testament?*

"How come no one told me about him?" she said. "I asked to speak with everyone the last time I was here."

"He never leaves his room," said Rafael. "Except for meals."

"I need to talk to him," said Tanya.

Mariposa shot her a warning look. "I don't think that's a good idea."

"Why?"

"Be careful." Rafael tapped the side of his head and made a face. "He's, er, a bit..., you know?"

The music stopped as soon as he uttered the words.

The house fell quiet once again. No one spoke for a few seconds, overwhelmed by the sudden assault on their eardrums.

"Veronika won't be too happy to be woken up like that," said Mariposa, with a tsk. "What with her headache and all."

Tanya sighed.

"David can wait. My priority is to find Monica. I need a piece of her personal clothing."

Mariposa stepped into the closet and plucked a blue silk blouse from a laundry container.

"She wore this yesterday," she said, holding it out.

Tanya took it and held it by her knee. "Max, come over here."

Max, who had been busy investigating all corners of the room, trotted over. He sniffed the blouse and wagged his tail.

"Good boy," said Tanya. "Let's get to work, bud."

She turned to the couple.

"Tell Veronika I'm going to search the island. When I get back, I'd like to talk to everyone in the house, including the party boy I missed last time."

She pushed the bedroom door open.

"Let's go find Monica."

Max trotted out of the door, his nose to the ground. Tanya followed him, Monica's soiled blouse in her hand. They were almost at the stairway, when a ferocious roar came from somewhere.

Max twirled around, barking.

A second monstrous roar followed, louder than the last one. That wasn't a canned heavy metal scream from a sound system. It had come from a live human.

Max darted back up the corridor. Tanya turned and scurried after him.

"Max, come here!"

Her dog stopped at an open doorway of the room halfway down the hallway. His hackles were up and a low growl emanated from his throat. Tanya could hear the music again, this time at a lower volume.

She stepped up and peeked inside the room. A foul odor wafted to her nose, making her gag.

For a split second, she wondered if she had entered the twilight zone.

The more she got to know this family, the more idiosyncratic they got. All the disturbing personalities she had learned about in her psychology class seem to live in Kensington Manor.

Heavy metal posters adorned one wall of this room. A large sound system was stacked next to a drum set—the source of the deafening music. A dry aquarium took up the entire length of another wall, which Tanya was sure was where the stink was coming from.

This was a teen boy's dream room.

Except the person standing in the middle of the room, and roaring like mad, was a giant in his mid-forties. He was about two hundred pounds of muscle and six foot, six inches at least. The man was built like an ox, like someone who worked out regularly.

Or had spent time in prison.

He appeared disheveled and unwashed, in a torn wife-beater shirt with army camouflage pants. But it was the thing wrapped around his neck that had Max growling and Tanya frozen in the spot.

A large albino python was curling around his torso. It meandered around him, while he stood in the middle of the room, eyes raised to the ceiling, swaying on his feet.

Tanya had defeated war mercenaries, barbaric traffickers, and drug lords, men who struck fear on entire populations, but seeing this animal made her blood go cold.

Her mind raced.

If he's screaming, he can breathe. That's good.

She stepped inside the room.

"Sir?"

He didn't look at her.

"Sir, are you okay?"

Max barked, but the man didn't move. Tanya wondered if he was in a trance of some sort.

David roared again. The enormous serpent curled around his shoulders and disappeared behind his back. It reappeared by his neck and turned toward David's chin, flicking its forked tongue.

Tanya felt like vomiting.

Suddenly, David gagged, like he was choking, He reached over to his neck and tried to pull the snake off.

"Don't move!" shouted Tanya, pulling her weapon out, and pointed it at the python's head, her heart pounding.

"I can take it out if you stay still!"

The man let out another roar and grabbed the snake where it had curled around his neck.

"Stay still!" shouted Tanya. "You're agitating it!"

To her surprise, he unfurled the animal from his neck, and buckled from the weight of the massive serpent in his arms. He heaved the snake onto his bed like he was throwing a sack of potatoes.

Tanya stared, her mouth open.

David whirled around and let out another hair-raising scream. Without a warning, he lunged at her like a wayward train engine.

She ducked, but he was fast for his size.

He slammed her against the wall, screeching in her ear.

"You murderer!"

Chapter Twenty-seven

Tanya turned as David's foul breath hit her face.

It was like someone had cracked open a case of rotten eggs.

She grabbed David by the throat.

From behind him, she spotted a whir of brown fur rush in. David's legs buckled. He bent backward, screeching in pain.

Good boy.

David's gigantic fist rose in the air.

Tanya ducked but kept her chokehold. His hand hit the wall behind her with a sickening thump.

That would have been my face.

His meaty hands clamped down on hers, tearing at her skin as he tried to free his neck. With an angry roar, he slammed her with his body. Tanya felt the breath rush out of her lungs. Using all her energy, she raised her knee and kicked him between the legs.

He crumpled to the ground, screaming.

Max sunk his teeth into the man's leg, growling like an angry wolf who had captured its prey.

"Let go, bud."

Max gave a final shake before releasing his jaws. Then, he sat down by the prostrate man, his tongue out. David writhed on the floor, clutching his private parts, whimpering.

Tanya doubled over, panting hard.

Her heart was hammering like she had run a sprint. All she could hear now was the *whoomp, whoomp* of her blood pounding in her ear canals.

"Good work, bud," she said, wiping the sweat from her upper lip.

Max thumped his tail.

Tanya had expected a long and bloody fight, given David's size and all that roaring, but it hadn't taken a lot to bring him down.

What a day.

Max whirled around and barked. A movement on the poster bed caught Tanya's eye.

The snake was slithering over the bedsheets, its forked tongue darting in and out. The white and gray scales on its back moved in undulating waves as it headed toward the aquarium.

Tanya turned toward the open doorway.

Mariposa and Rafael were staring at her, like they couldn't believe what they'd witnessed. Hovering behind them was the junior trooper who had been posted on the island as night guard.

Tanya straightened up.

"You found your way home, Trooper?"

He didn't answer, his widened eyes on the snake crawling across the bed.

"Appreciate you backing me up."

The officer tore his eyes away from the python and turned to her.

"Sorry, ma'am. You... looked like you had everything under c... control."

"Where's Monica?"

"Er..., I swept the woods. I looked everywhere. I didn't see anyone."

"You dropped your phone," said Tanya, in an exasperated voice. "The chief's been trying to reach you all morning."

The young man's face reddened. He rubbed the back of his neck.

"I, er, didn't realize...."

Tanya sighed.

She couldn't blame him. He had pimples on his face and looked barely of legal age to walk into a bar. State troopers didn't normally investigate homicide cases, and had their plates full with their own jurisdictional issues. It made sense they had sent their least experienced cadet to help them out.

She turned back to Mariposa and Rafael, and pointed at the snake who was spilling into the aquarium now.

"What the heck is that thing?"

"That's Xena."

Tanya stared at Rafael.

"Burmese albino python," said Rafael in a flat tone like he had explained this many times before.

"Xena's almost twenty foot long. Considered a delicacy in some parts of the world, but they make very good pets too. That's what David told me."

Tanya's stomach turned.

"Is that species legal here? Does he have a valid permit?"

The couple looked away, like they didn't want to answer that question.

"She was going to kill Xena!"

David had found his voice again.

Rafael stumbled into the room and kneeled next to the figure on the floor. Tanya stared at the child-man who was still clutching his private parts, his grimy face stained with tears.

"I hate her!" he screeched. "She was going to shoot Xena!"

Mariposa gave Tanya a warning look and lowered her voice.

"I told you. We leave him alone."

Rafael helped David sit up. David leaned against the handyman, whimpering and sniffing, like a helpless child.

"Was he born this way?" whispered Tanya to Mariposa.

"We were so sure Madame would send him back," whispered Mariposa.

"Send him back?"

Mariposa nodded. "I was surprised they kept him."

Chapter Twenty-eight

David flailed his arms and screeched.

Rafael whipped around to Tanya. "You're making him nervous. You need to leave."

Tanya looked for Max. He had seated himself in front of the aquarium, his eyes on the snake, like he was ready to pounce on it if it thought of slithering out again.

"Come on, bud," she called out as she stepped out of the room.

Mariposa scrambled by her, like she was in a hurry to leave. Tanya put a hand on her arm to stop her.

"What do you mean they *kept* David?" said Tanya. "He's a human being, not a pet."

Mariposa scrunched her face.

"So, nobody told you?"

Tanya narrowed her eyes.

There was more going on in this family than met the eye.

Without waiting for a reply, Mariposa scuttled down the hallway and down the stairway.

With a sigh, Tanya looked down at her pup.

"Let's go find Monica, bud. She's our priority."

"And me?"

She glanced at the junior officer, hovering in the corridor.

"Remain inside and keep an eye on the family."

"Sure thing."

"And make sure the aquarium's locked tight. We can't have that thing escape again."

"How... How am I supposed to...."

"Figure it out, Trooper."

Tanya was still reeling from her altercation with David. Just when she thought things couldn't get any more bizarre, they had.

Her phone vibrated as she headed down the stairs with Max. She pulled out her public mobile and checked the screen.

Asha.

She took the call and held the mobile to her ear, hoping they had taken her advice and found another detective gig. A tinge of guilt shot through Tanya as she recalled the fib she had told her friends to keep them away.

"Where are you?" came Asha's voice.

Tanya's heart skipped a beat as she realized why she would ask that question.

Katy's cheery voice came over the air.

"This is such a beautiful island. What a gorgeous waterfall."

Chapter Twenty-nine

Asha waved at the ferry driver, who lifted his cap to her.

"Sweet man," said Katy, blowing him a kiss. "We gave him a huge tip."

The barge bobbed in the waves as it turned around to head back to the mainland.

Tanya glared at her friends who were busy greeting Max. He had been twirling around their legs and yapping in happiness ever since he had bounded over to them on the wharf.

"A hundred-dollar bill tucked into his jacket," said Katy, "and he regaled us with sea shanties."

Tanya spluttered. "You're not licensed to operate in this state."

"We're a private firm with private clients," said Asha. "That's all you need to know."

Tanya leaned over to her friends, a slow boil of frustration coming over her.

"We agreed to put our vigilante life behind us," she hissed. "If anyone found out what we used to do, Max and I would be out of a job."

"We're not here for vigilante work," Asha hissed back.

"*You're* happy to see us, aren't you, good boy?" said Katy, scratching Max's back. "Your mean mom wants to kick us out."

Tanya lowered her voice. "The chief has stationed a trooper on the island. If he finds out two PIs are nosing around, you'll have to leave. Don't ask me to justify your presence."

"Our client can speak for us," said Asha, thrusting her chin out.

"Where's Justin? At the big house?" said Katy, turning toward the manor. "Can't wait to meet him. Such a nice guy."

Such a nice guy?

"What did he sound like when he called?" said Tanya.

"Sweet. A little shy." Katy shrugged. "He sounded quite young, now that I think of it."

Tanya narrowed her eyes. Shy and sweet weren't how she would have described Stanley. If it was truly Justin who had hired her friends, he had to have known about Honoree Kensington's inheritance challenge.

That changes things.

"Did Justin call you within the past forty-eight hours?" asked Tanya.

"I've been trying to reach him to return his money transfer, but he hasn't called back," said Asha. She paused, her brow furrowing. "That's why we came. To make sure he had really sorted things out."

Tanya drew in a long breath.

"There's something you need to know."

Her friends looked at her with quizzical expressions.

"Justin passed away from a gunshot wound two days ago."

Asha stared at her, mouth open. "You *lied* to us?"

"I thought his brother had pretended to be him, to lure you over," said Tanya. "That's why I told you the case was already solved."

"Our client is *dead*?" said Katy in shock.

"Justin was a friend." Tanya blinked rapidly. "He was a junior paramedic who hung out with us. If I told you what really happened to him, I knew that would only push you to come."

"Are you sure it's not a different Justin?" said Asha. "Junior paramedics don't normally have fifteen thousand dollars lying around to retain a private investigation firm."

"It's a small town and I know of only one Justin." Tanya sighed. "We just found out he's a Kensington."

"How did you not know he was a member of the richest family in the region?" said Katy.

"His grandfather kicked him out when he was a teen. Stacey, our paramedic, and her husband adopted him, and helped him get his medic certification. He didn't tell anyone about his birth family."

"He told us none of that," said Asha, frowning.

"He probably took the money when he left his family, or someone gave it to him afterward. Stacey and George have a mortgage. Stacey kept her day job to pay the bills from her pub business, so I don't think your retainer came from them."

"So, who killed him?" said Asha.

"That's what I'm here to find out."

"It probably has to do with the estate," said Katy, looking at the manor, which glowered at them from a distance.

"Something tells me there's more here than a rush to find the will," said Tanya. "Stacey and George's pub burned down after an explosion yesterday. The fire department is still investigating but I'm sure it was a deliberate attack."

Katy's eyebrows shot up. "What on earth is going on here?"

"Why do you think I tried to keep you away?" said Tanya. "Two of the grandsons attacked me. One of them keeps a giant pet python in his room. This is a crazy family in a crazy house."

Everyone turned their eyes to the stately building on the grounds.

It felt like the forest had claimed more of the mansion, its branches crawling across the brick walls, just like the albino python had wrapped itself around David's body.

Tanya shuddered.

"Things are going to get worse. Go home before anyone sees you."

The crack of a dry twig made them whip around. Tanya spotted the silhouette of two people walking through the woods toward them.

"Too late," whispered Asha.

Chapter Thirty

A man and a woman emerged from the tree line.

They started walking through the cemetery, toward the wharf.

Their heads were bowed, like they were deliberating something urgent. There were so deep in discussion, they hadn't noticed the trio on the wharf.

Tanya scanned the open dock, but there was no place for Asha and Katy to hide now.

Veronika and Stanley gave a start as they spotted them. They hurried over while Tanya waited, her back muscles tensing more and more, the closer they got.

When they approached them, Veronika wrinkled her nose and scrutinized Asha, then Katy.

Stanley leered at Katy, his eyes traveling from her chest to her knees, then back up again. Tanya felt as grossed out as she had been when the python had crawled over David.

Veronika gestured to the newcomers and turned to Tanya.

"Who are they? What are they doing here?"

Asha whipped out a business card from her purse and offered it to the woman with a flourish.

"We're a private investigation firm from New York who manages civilian cases." She paused and gave a side glance at Tanya. "We hear one of your family members is missing. We're here to help find her."

Stanley smiled at them. "You gals are *private detectives*?"

"With the highest success rate in the state," said Asha. "We deliver on our promises."

Stanley stepped closer toward them, his smile broadening.

"Welcome to Kensington Island, ladies."

Veronika frowned, but he ignored her.

With a smug smile, Stanley ushered Asha and Katy away from the group. Tanya watched as he pulled out a card from his jacket pocket and offered it to Asha with a slight bow.

Whatever he was up to, Tanya was sure, it wasn't good. The man was a master manipulator, and he saw a benefit from her friends' presence.

I don't like this.

She turned to see Veronika was also observing the trio, her worry lines deepening.

"We'll find Monica," said Tanya. "Max is trained in search and rescue. We'll do everything we can to locate your niece."

Veronika turned to her, her face darkening.

"Monica's not my niece."

Her voice was so harsh, Tanya jerked her head back.

"I thought you—"

Veronika's eyes turned hard as steel.

"None of these ungrateful bastards are Kensingtons. They're all adopted."

With an irate hiss, Veronika spun around and marched toward the mansion, giving Stanley and his guests a wide berth.

Tanya stared at her disappearing back.

Chapter Thirty-one

Tanya's mind whirled.

So, that's why Mariposa said they hadn't "taken David back." She had been referring to his birth parents. Or an adoption agency.

"I'll give you forty grand up front."

She spun around to see Stanley beseeching to her friends, his hands spread out, in a subservient position she had never expected to see.

She stepped closer to the group.

"We've already made a commitment," Asha was saying.

"I bet your contract with the city is peanuts," said Stanley, not noticing Tanya behind him. "How much is it? Ten grand? Fifteen?"

Asha and Katy remained silent.

"Whatever they're offering, I'll multiply it by ten." He dialed his smarmy smile several notches brighter. "Let's say a one hundred grand retainer to find the document for me."

Tanya shook her head.

So, that's what he's after.

"We have our priorities," said Asha. "Sorry we can't be of more help."

Tanya watched as Stanley's face turned. He clenched his jaws like he was trying to control himself.

"Listen, ladies," said Stanley, putting on his smile again and transforming into the quintessential salesperson about to give them the best deal on a used BMW.

"How about the retainer plus a quarter percent of the estate?"

Katy gasped.

Tanya raised a brow.

A quarter of a percent of a billion-dollar inheritance is a lot of money.

"I'll cut you a check right now," said Stanley. "Screw the city. They're useless. They haven't even found out who killed that lousy-assed paramedic in the parking lot—"

"Justin was your brother," snapped Tanya, unable to keep silent any longer.

I'd give anything to see my brother alive again. And this knuckle-dragging Neanderthal talks about his brother like this?

Her blood boiled.

Stanley turned to her, his beady eyes narrowed. "Someone got rid of the golden boy, and now everyone's on the case."

"Golden boy?" said Asha.

"Grandfather treated him like he was everything under the sun." Stanley grimaced. "Justin was the chosen one."

"I heard your grandfather kicked him out," said Katy.

"It was Grandmother who threw him out of the house." Stanley made a face. "The old man loved him more than anyone else, and Justin sucked up to Grandfather. It was sick. I hated him."

Tanya stared at him, realizing none of these people were alive to corroborate his stories.

"Justin didn't talk to us after he left," continued Stanley. "He was dead to us and we were dead to him. He was a petty criminal. So, tell me again why I have to care?"

Tanya looked him in the eye. "Did you hate him enough to kill him?"

Stanley threw his arms in the air and whirled around to Asha and Katy. He pointed an accusing finger at Tanya.

"You see the stupid cops we have to deal with?"

Neither Asha nor Katy responded.

"This is why we need smart folk like you. If I had my way, I'd privatize the whole darn team. Get a proper police force. The ones we have now are a bunch of idiots."

He glared at Tanya.

Stanley turned around to Asha and Katy, his smile coming on again.

"Why don't we go inside and have a drink? You must be tired from your trip."

Asha's eyes flitted over to Tanya. She had been surveying the grounds, the house, and turning back to Stanley every once in a while, her brow furrowed.

Tanya knew that look. Her friend was scheming.

Stanley wouldn't open up to law enforcement, but he would speak to private investigators, especially those in his pay.

Maybe this wouldn't be such a bad idea, after all.

Katy saw the silent exchange between her friends and flashed a quick smile.

"Since you put it that way," said Katy, twirling around to Stanley and offering her hand, "we accept the deal."

A flicker of relief crossed his face.

"You've made the right decision. I knew you'd come around."

He shook Katy's hand, then Asha's.

"So, what's your favorite kind of poison, ladies?"

Tanya jerked her head back.

Poison?

Ignoring her, Stanley put his arm around Katy.

"Today's your lucky day. Grandfather kept a cellar full of vintage liqueurs and wines. We're going to celebrate our agreement by sampling the best of the best we have in the house."

Tanya leaned close to Asha and lowered her voice. "Watch your backs and report regularly."

"Roger that," whispered Asha.

Stanley turned around and extended his arm to her.

"Are you joining us?"

Tanya watched as her friends walked arm-in-arm with Stanley toward the manor.

She didn't know what would happen next on the island. She had dodged Ray Jackson's calls about her other job, but she couldn't hold off for too long, and the last thing she had time for was to watch over her friends.

Did I just make a big mistake?

Tanya cast her gaze downward at Max, who had been sitting by her feet. Her heart skipped a beat when she realized he was no longer there. Her eyes scanned the small quay, then the woods.

"Max? Where are you?"

She spun around, searching for a glimpse of his brown fur, the end of his furry tail, or the tip of his black nose.

"Max?"

She heard a bark. It appeared to come from the end of the cove, close to the cemetery, by the waterfall.

"Max!"

He barked, louder this time. And more urgently.

She spotted him. He was climbing onto a small rocky cliff that overhung the far end of the lake.

What's he doing there?

She leaped down from the wharf and onto the rocky shoreline.

Max barked again.

Tanya knew that bark.

He had discovered something.

Chapter Thirty-two

Max watched her come over, his tail wagging.

As soon as Tanya stepped onto the slab of rock he was on, he turned his attention back to the water.

"What is it, bud?"

Max barked, facing the lake.

Tanya kneeled next to her dog, one hand on his back. She surveyed the shore. At first, she noticed nothing amiss.

Stones of all colors had washed up around the boulders, their surfaces smoothened over decades, maybe centuries. That was when she noticed the human-made object stacked in between the boulders below her.

A rock cairn.

Most times they were created by kids for fun, but they were also built to give directions on a hiking trail or to mark a discovery in a forest or a beach.

Someone built a little rock tower. Tanya narrowed her eyes and scanned the area. *What is special about this spot?*

She bent down and gazed at the emerald waters below. The waterline was higher than when she had arrived on the island.

The tide is rising.

She realized how this small lake got its vivid color. A forest of bright green seaweed floated underneath the surface. Their broad leaves swayed back and forth as they got caught in the cross waves from the waterfall and the ocean currents.

Max barked again, and turned his snout to one spot, farther down the lake.

That was when Tanya saw the body.

The female corpse, still clothed, stood slightly upright in the water, her hair waving to the current. Her face was pallid, her eyes were closed, and her limbs were limp. Tangled in the submerged forest, she swayed with the seaweeds in a macabre underwater dance.

Monica was definitely dead.

With trembling hands, Tanya retrieved her phone and dialed.

"Found her."

"All good?"

"We might have a second homicide on our hands."

On the other end, Jack let out a weary sigh.

That wasn't like the chief. He was a stoic man who took his job seriously, rarely letting the events of the day affect him. Tanya wondered how she would feel running a precinct on a shoestring budget, with angry lawyers on her back and multiple murders coming at her.

"I'd bet someone killed her and dumped her in the lake, last night," she said.

"You didn't see her body when you got in today?"

"She's submerged on the other end of the lake, held down by the weeds. Otherwise, the ferry captain would've spotted her before any of us."

"How come Junior didn't report it?"

"He focused his search in the woods behind the house. He told me he checked the cove, but I don't think he looked close enough. Can't blame him. I only spotted her because Max led me here."

Tanya's eyes flittered down to Monica's watery grave. She knew it would be a matter of time before the body floated to the surface.

"You'll have to convince your state buddies to bring a dive team."

"Any signs how she died?" said Jack.

Tanya peered into the water.

Monica's face was visible a few feet below the surface. She looked like she was sleeping upright.

"Hard to say. But Rafael said he heard the front door open around midnight. If he's telling the truth, she was probably killed sometime between then and the time I got in. She could have been lured here, pushed in, and drowned. Or they could have killed her somewhere else, brought her here, then pushed her in."

"Dr. Chen can make the call for us." Tanya heard paper rustling on Jack's end. "Secure the crime scene. We'll get there ASAP. ETA in an hour max."

"I thought the ferry wasn't due back for a couple of hours."

"I just handed the captain a contract for exclusive use of his barge until this investigation is over." Jack sighed. "He complained as I expected, but as long as I pay him well, he'll keep trucking."

Tanya hung up when a gigantic wave swept through the cove and splashed against the rock she was on. She wiped the saltwater spray from her face.

A second and larger wave crashed against their boulder, spraying her and Max. Monica's arms and torso moved underwater, like an uncanny puppet master was twirling her strings. Watching her made Tanya feel queasy.

Max barked angrily at the waves. The tide was coming in, and it was coming in fast.

A loud bang came from the direction of the wharf. Tanya turned toward the other end of the cove, and her eyes widened at the sight. She slipped her phone in her pocket and called out to her pup.

"Come on, Max!"

Tanya scrambled over the boulders, hurrying toward the dock. Max leaped along with her, his face serious, like he knew something bad had happened.

By the time they reached the wharf, the sailboat was halfway down the lake, heading toward the inlet. Its sails had been secured, but it was getting buffeted by the wind, swaying to the big waves rolling in with the tide.

Tanya raced down the wharf with Max. When she got to the end where the sailboat had been tethered, she plucked her phone out and dialed the junior trooper.

"Get to the cove now!" she barked before he could say hello. "This is urgent."

She hung up and glanced back at the sailboat drifting in the middle of the lake. It was hard to know if anyone was in the lower deck. The boat tilted dangerously from side to side, but no one came out.

Soon, the waves would push it out into the ocean—if it didn't get smashed against the jagged rocks that lined the inlet first.

There's no one inside.

Tanya got to her knees and pulled out the rope that had tied the boat to the pillar.

"Someone pulled it loose," she said, as Max trotted up and sniffed the rope. "This was no accident."

Her eyes wandered down the dock and across the wooded tree line. It was hard to see if anyone was nearby.

Someone wanted to get rid of it.

Tanya's heart raced.

That meant only one thing.

The sailboat held evidence of Monica's murder.

Chapter Thirty-three

Tanya dropped the rope into the water and considered her options.

The yacht was out of the question. It was far too big and awkward to rescue the smaller vessel, plus she was sure the cockpit was locked.

She glanced at the speedboat moored next to it. Its outboard motors were tied to the quay with a steel cable and fastened with a marine lock. Even if she had the right tools to cut the cable, she might not be able to start it up.

That left the row of colorful kayaks bobbing up and down by the creaking pillars.

She shook her head.

There's a faster way.

She ripped off her jacket and kicked her boots and socks off. Max circled around her, whining, as if he was asking her what she was up to. Tanya pulled her cargo pants down and threw them on the dock.

She slipped her gun inside her tank top, glad it was a tight-fitting Lycra.

"Max, stay."

He sat dutifully next to her boots and clothes, his head cocked to the side.

In her underwear and tank top, Tanya dove into the water.

The seaweeds flapped against her thighs and face. She pushed through, in the sailboat's direction.

Her consolation was the multi-million-dollar yacht tied to the wharf. Its presence on the lake meant the water was deep enough and free of major underwater obstructions.

She swam faster and faster, pushing through the weeds. Behind her, she could hear Max bark from the dock.

She stopped when she got to twenty feet of the sailing boat. Its bow was almost at the rocky inlet, which connected the lake to the ocean.

She treaded water to catch her breath, bobbing up and down with the waves. The current was stronger than she had expected.

Tanya scanned all sides of the rogue vessel.

How do I get in?

If she didn't get in that boat in time, it would be lost to the ocean forever. That's when she saw it.

A rope ladder hung down the middle of the port side.

Taking a big gulp of air, Tanya dove back into the lake, and headed toward it. She grabbed onto the ladder hanging on the side of the boat and scrambled up, her heart beating fast.

When she got to the top deck, she collapsed, panting hard.

Wait. Max has stopped barking.

She spun around to see the junior officer next to her dog, peering at her, a hand shielding his eyes. He waved as he saw her look. Tanya nodded and pulled her Glock out of her tank top.

If someone was waiting for her inside this vessel, she would be ready.

She leaped to her feet and stepped toward the helm. A quick glance told her there was no one on the upper deck. She got on her knees and peeked into the porthole to the deck below.

All she could hear was the creaking of the boat.

With her weapon aimed forward, she lowered herself onto the wooden steps and climbed down, prepared to take on whoever would come at her.

But the deck below was empty.

She stepped around the tight corners, taking in the cot in the back, the minuscule sink, the toilet, the storage compartments along the wood-paneled walls, and what looked like a pullout table.

Part of the table was jutting out, like it hadn't been fully secured.

Someone was in a hurry.

Tanya pulled the table out.

Blood.

The red stain had splashed across the surface. It had blended so well with the dark wood, she hadn't noticed it at first.

Is this where Monica died?

A small piece of paper was stuck on a blood splatter at the end of the table. Tanya leaned across and plucked it out and immediately regretted her action. Her gloves were in her cargo pants pockets which now lay on the dock.

Too late now.

She unfolded the paper. Her eyes widened as she read it.

You're the biggest bitch. We all hate you.

A deep, drawn-out groan made Tanya jump. She whirled around, her heart racing.

She aimed her gun at the ladder to the top deck.

The boat tilted to the port side. Tanya dropped the note and grabbed on to the table to stop herself from falling. Waves crashed against the boat, and it tilted to the stern.

The wooden hull groaned as it scraped by a boulder. Then came a crash as the boat slammed against a rock. The entire vessel shuddered, like it was about to fall into pieces.

Tanya held on, her heart pounding.

I'm going to sink!

Chapter Thirty-four

Tanya scrambled up the wooden stairway, sliding on the wet steps.

The boat swayed wildly, now at the whim of the ocean tide.

When she reached the top deck, she glanced up at the sails. They had been secured well, and she didn't have time to unfurl them. Besides, the heavy winds would only make it harder to steer.

The junior trooper was jumping up and down on the wharf, hollering at her. Snippets of his voice carried through the wind.

"Watch... Out!"

Max released a barrage of barks to warn her.

I know, I know.

Tanya whirled around. If she didn't take control of the vessel now, it would crash on the rocks and sink, and take her down with it.

Think, girl, think.

She scuttled toward the stern, doubling over, grabbing on to anything solid so as not to get thrown off the boat. She stepped toward the outboard engine in the back and crouched low.

Please let there be fuel.

Tanya reached over and pulled the starter rope. The engine spluttered and died. Another warning yell came from the wharf.

She pulled the rope again.

Nothing.

She looked up, her heart pounding. The waves were pushing the boat toward the enormous black rocks at the mouth of the inlet.

Do I bail?

She pulled the rope once more.

The engine roared to life.

Tanya grabbed the throttle, but it took her a while to turn the vessel around. The waves slammed against the boat, rocking it back and forth, but she kept her grip tight and her eyes on the shore.

She knew the currents could easily dislodge Monica's body at the other end of the lake, and shuddered to think of what would happen then. She steered the boat across the turbulent water, toward the wharf, trying not to let her stomach get the best of her.

One thing at a time.

Max raced up and down the dock as he saw her approach, barking madly. As she got close, the officer kneeled and reached out to pull the boat in.

"Oh, man," he said, giving her a horrified look. "I thought you were gonna die."

Tanya didn't reply, her focus on securing the vessel. She was about to hand the rope to him, when she heard a peculiar sound.

She glanced up at the young man, her eyebrows raised.

He shrugged. "That's not mine."

That's not mine either.

Tanya handed the rope to him.

"Tie her up. Make it tight. This is a crime scene."

Letting him figure it out, Tanya stepped back toward the porthole. She climbed down the steps to the deck below.

The sound of the phone ringing got louder.

Following the sound, Tanya tiptoed toward the small cot in the corner. She threw the pillow to the floor and pulled back the sheets.

She stared at the mobile, ringing away at the bottom of the bed.

How did I miss it?

Chapter Thirty-five

Tanya felt around her waist for her gloves, when she realized she was still in her tank top and underwear.

She was dripping wet now. Wiping the water droplets from her forehead, Tanya bent over the cot to take a better look.

Whose mobile is this?

Monica's?

The killer's?

She squinted to read the name scrolling across the screen.

Craig Wood.

Tanya frowned. She had heard that name before, but where?

The cell went silent for a second, then rang again almost immediately. Craig Wood, whoever he was, was desperately trying to reach this number.

Who's Craig Wood?

Tanya racked her brain to recall the conversations she'd had with Veronika. She jerked her head back as she remembered.

Craig Wood was Monica's husband who had remained in New York. He had been held up in the city on business. At least, that's what Veronika had told her.

Using the bedsheet as a makeshift glove, Tanya plucked the mobile out of the cot and took the call.

"Where the hell have you been?" screamed a male voice on the other end. "I've been tryna get a hold of you all day!"

Tanya pulled the phone away from her ear. It seemed like every member of this family had a tendency to yell.

"Honoree is dead!" he shouted. "Now get your damn hands on the cash and send it to me!"

Tanya's eyebrows shot up.

"Do you hear me?" shouted Craig Wood. "Monica? Are you there? Talk to me, woman!"

Tanya placed the phone back to her ear.

"Good morning, Mr. Wood."

Silence fell on the other end.

"Who the hell are you?"

"Mrs. Wood's new personal assistant. She asked me to field her calls."

"She hired an assistant without telling me?"

"She's still grieving her loss here."

"What the heck do you mean, grieving?" He spluttered. "We should be celebrating. The bitch is dead, and we finally get the money. Get Monica on the phone now!"

Tanya's heart beat fast, feeling bad for lying to a dead woman's husband. But her need to know the truth about this family overcame her guilt.

"I apologize, Mr. Woods." She fought to keep her voice steady. "Mrs. Wood is occupied at the moment, but I'll let her know you called. May I take a message?"

"Occupied?" Monica's husband yelled. "Occupied with what? She needs to be occupied with me!"

Tanya swallowed a curse. Another self-important man with a grandiose ego.

"Tell her I need ten million wire-transferred today!"

Tanya gaped.

Did he say ten million?

"Yes, Mr. Wood."

"If I don't get it by the end of the day, I'm screwed. I said, screwed, do you hear me? Tell her the house is going up as collateral. It's my decision, and it's final!"

He sounded panicked. Tanya's brain whirred. Why would someone put their home on collateral and need ten million dollars in such a short period?

Is Monica's husband a member of the Mafia? Does he owe money to a dangerous gang? Or, was this a mega business deal gone sour?

"Did you hear me?" screamed Craig. "Stupid assistant!"

"I will let her know, Mr. Wood."

"She should fire you. You incompetent slob. Tell her if I don't get the cash by the end of the day...."

Tanya waited for him to finish, but it seemed like Craig was at a loss for words, all of a sudden. When his voice came back on the line, it was subdued, like he had come to terms with whatever was troubling him.

"If she doesn't get me the money today, I'll go to jail."

Tanya raised a brow.

That was what the millions were for.

Bail money.

Chapter Thirty-six

Craig Wood hung up.

Tanya stared at the now silent phone in her hands, her heart pounding.

The image of Monica dancing with the seaweeds rushed to her mind. She winced, as guilt flooded through her. She would have to tell Craig Wood what really happened to his wife.

"Hey, you okay in there?"

The junior officer was poking his head through the porthole from the upper deck.

"There's a corpse in the lake."

"*What?*"

Tanya paused as she realized she was being a tad unreasonable with the junior officer.

"Monica Kensington," she said, softening her voice. "I'm afraid she's no longer alive. The chief is coming over with the medical examiner shortly."

"Oh, man. I looked for her everywhere. How did that happen?"

"She was killed inside this boat and thrown overboard. That's my hypothesis, for now," she said, walking over to the steps. She looked up at the keen young man's face.

"Would you do me a favor, Trooper?"

"Yes, ma'am."

"Go back to the manor and make sure no one leaves the house. Can you do that?"

The officer saluted.

"Right away, ma'am."

He jumped to his feet and leaped onto the wharf, making the boat rock.

Tanya climbed to the top deck and stepped onto the quay, glad to be on more solid footing again. Max came over to welcome her back, whining, his tail swishing back and forth.

Tanya bend down and tussled his head.

"Happy to see you too, bud. See? I'm fine."

Max licked her face.

Tanya reached down and pulled her phone out of her crumpled cargo pant pocket on the floor.

Craig Wood, she whispered, as she opened the browser and punched his name into the search bar. *What have you done, Mr. Wood?*

Her eyes widened.

She hadn't expected this many search results. Craig Wood wasn't just any business executive. He was the CEO of one of the largest hedge fund firms on Wall Street, a company the FBI had had its target on.

Tanya scrolled through news article after news article.

Trouble had begun a year ago.

The company had let go of its employees in America, Europe, and Asia, hundreds at a time. Its stock prices had plunged. Finally, the FBI had confiscated its computers, and had rounded up Craig Wood and his associates for securities fraud.

A ten-million-dollar bail meant the charges were serious, and the courts considered him a flight risk. This family was in deeper trouble than she had thought.

Tanya turned around to survey the section farther along the cove, where Monica Wood was entangled in a forest of seaweed. Beyond those boulders and above the shoreline was the Kensington family cemetery.

I guess they'll bury her right here.

A pang of sorrow crossed Tanya's heart.

Everything she had heard about Monica repulsed her. The call from her husband told her he wasn't any better himself. Still, the woman was dead.

Was she murdered?

Why?

Did it have something to do with the challenge Honoree Kensington had given before she shot herself?

The smug face of Stanley Kensington popped to mind. He made her stomach turn, but she knew better than to take things at face value. What she needed was solid evidence.

Tanya double-checked the knot that tied the sailboat to the pillar and put her clothes back on.

She looked at her pup who was sitting next to her boots, his eyes shining, like he knew things had just got more interesting.

"Everyone's after Honoree's money," said Tanya, as she zipped up her jacket.

Max thumped his tail, seemingly in agreement.

"I'd bet Justin was the main beneficiary."

She picked up her holster and wrapped it around her waist.

"Otherwise, why would anyone want to get rid of him?"

Max yipped in reply.

Tanya felt something catch in her throat.

She hadn't had time to grieve Justin's death. His youthful face and his radiant smile flashed across her mind. She blinked away the tears welling in her eyes when she felt something wet and soft by the back of her hand.

She looked down to see Max was licking her, like he understood how she felt. Tanya flopped down to the deck and pulled him in for a nuzzle.

All of a sudden, she felt overwhelmed by everything she had to do. They hadn't found

Justin's killer yet, but she needed a minute to let the emotions run their course.

Get yourself together, she scolded herself, as she plucked her phone out and opened the message app. She pulled up the last group chat she had been in with Asha and Katy, and typed quickly.

"Stay away from Stanley. He could be our killer."

The chug of an engine came from the middle of the lake, followed by the strong smell of burning diesel. Tanya spun around.

The ferry was heading toward the dock, bouncing over the powerful waves. Even from where she was, Tanya could make out the grim face of Chief Jack Bold.

He's found something.

Chapter Thirty-seven

"Dumb cops!"

Peter slammed his fist on his armrest with so much force his soda cup fell to the ground.

The liquid foamed over the Persian rug. Max leaped back as the sugary spray flowed toward his paws. He sniffed the spill, then glanced up at Peter with a look that said, *Get yourself together, man.*

"I didn't kill my mother!" shouted Peter.

Tanya and Jack had been trying to persuade him to talk for the last half an hour.

They were in the living room of the Kensington Manor, interrogating a man who hurled curses, insults, and made rude gestures at anyone with whom he disagreed.

Tanya was thankful Jack had bought a small delegation to the island. If she had to guess, the chief had called in all his favors.

Dr. Chen had come with two of her interns, and four state troopers had jumped off the ferry with them.

Tanya had taken the doctor's crew to the opposite side of the cove to show them the submerged body. If it hadn't been for the forest of seaweed, Monica would have floated to the top and got swept away with the waves.

Two troopers had put on masks, gloves, and booties before stepping onto the sailboat to document the crime scene, while the remaining officers had hauled their diving gear off the boat and put on their wetsuits. They would have the difficult task of recovering Monica's body.

Leaving the teams to do their jobs, Jack and Tanya had hurried back to the manor.

After sending the junior trooper to find and bring in Stanley Kensington, they sat down with Peter. But Tanya wasn't sure if starting the interrogations with the most disagreeable person in the family had been a good thing.

Peter was toying with them, prolonging the discussion more than necessary.

Ignoring the spill around his wheelchair, he reached into the bag of chips sitting on his lap and stuffed a handful into his mouth. His laptop, which seemed to be permanently attached to his belly, wobbled as he moved.

"You're wasting time," he mumbled with his mouth full. "Go find the killer and leave me the hell alone. It wasn't me."

"No one's accusing you of anything," said Jack in a firm voice. He had been restraining himself for the past fifteen minutes, but looked like he wouldn't last much longer.

"Do you really think that by some miracle I started walking?" Peter pointed at his wheelchair. "What part of *disabled* do you stupid people not understand?"

"You can't deny the argument you had with your mother last night," said Tanya. "We have witnesses."

"Okay, here's a scenario for you." A smirk crossed Peter's face. "I miraculously started to walk again. I grabbed my mother, dragged her all the way from her room to the lake and pushed her in. Is that what you people think? Geez, they told me cops are idiots. But man, you're worse than I thought."

You could have paid or convinced someone to do the dirty deed for you, thought Tanya. *Was it Stanley?*

"All we want to know is what the argument was about," said Jack, in a strained voice. "If you would answer us, we can get this over quickly."

Peter glowered at him.

"Are you even listening to me? I told you I've nothing to share with you."

Potato chip bits flew out of his mouth and landed on Jack's face.

He didn't flinch. "We're only trying to find out who's harming your family," said Jack.

"If you want to search my laptop or get my handwriting, get a warrant," snapped Peter. "If you want to talk to me, get my lawyer."

He raised his hand in a one-finger salute.

"And now, you people can get the hell out of our home."

Tanya summoned all her patience and leaned toward him. "Don't you want us to find out how your mother died?"

Peter's eyes flashed in anger.

"I don't give a damn how she drowned like a rat."

Jack jerked his head back, and Tanya's eyebrows shot up.

"Yes, I wanted her dead. Yes, I would have done it if I could have," growled Peter.

There was pent-up fury behind those intelligent eyes. He pointed at his legs.

"I'm happy someone got to the bitch, because I sure couldn't."

He glared at them.

"You're never going to pin this on me."

Chapter Thirty-eight

Tanya wasn't a trained FBI profiler, but she had a pretty good idea of Peter's traits now.

Peter knew he was more intelligent than most people and liked to feel superior. Shocking others made him feel smarter. It was tied to his identity.

Tanya relaxed her shoulders and placed her palms up to look as non-threatening as she could.

"It must have been hard growing up with a hot-tempered mom like Monica."

"Is that what you call it?" Peter turned his blazing eyes on her. "She was a mean bitch."

"You're a very smart man, so I'm sure you see, hear, and know more than anyone else," said Tanya. "Can you tell us who might have wanted her dead?"

"Everybody. Everybody who was unlucky enough to meet her. Maybe even you people."

Neither Tanya nor Jack responded, but Peter was finally talking.

"She treated everybody like crap. Just like Grandmother used to. It runs through the Kensington bloodline. Like mother, like daughter, right?"

Tanya didn't reply, but her mind buzzed.

So, he doesn't know his mother, and his aunt and uncle, were adopted. Interesting.

Peter scrunched the potato chip bag and threw it on the ground, littering food bits all over the rug. He opened his mouth to say something, when the static on Jack's shoulder radio crackled to life.

Jack grabbed the speaker and turned his ear to it.

"We've recovered the body, sir," came a disjointed voice through the airwaves.

"Ten-four," said Jack, getting up. "Be there in five."

He turned to Tanya.

She nodded. *I've got this.*

Jack strode out of the room, but Peter's eyes were on Tanya, his expression dark and intense. It was like he hadn't even realized the chief had left.

"Do you know why I'm stuck in this stupid chair?"

Tanya shook her head.

"I was born with a congenital heart defect. Plus, I'm a type one diabetic. I've been in this since I was eight."

"That sounds really rough—"

"Do you think my mother cared? She was too busy trying to look good in front of the neighbors, the PTA, and those dumb bitches in her ladies-who-lunch club."

Peter was speaking fast.

"She forgot my medical appointments. She refused to feed me some days. She told me she wished I didn't go to school because I embarrassed her."

He waved his arms.

"I was at the top of my class, but that didn't matter. I was fat, ugly, and sick. She hated me."

The hurt lined on his face was clear for the world to see now. Tanya felt a pang of sympathy for him.

No wonder he turned out belligerent and anti-social.

"She even called the adoption agency in town to see if they would take me in. Can you believe it? She wanted to get rid of me, but no one would take a sick kid."

"That sounds awful. I can understand your pain."

He thumped his fist on his armrest. "You don't know what it's like. Don't tell me you understand me."

Tanya took a deep breath in. It was time to ask the question she had been dying to ask.

"Your father called today, about—"

"Bail money?" Peter nodded like he had known about it all along.

Tanya pointed at his laptop.

"You said you make more in a day than your grandmother's tobacco company. You can easily make his bail, can't you?"

He glared at her.

"Dad belongs in prison."

Tanya leaned forward and rested her elbows on her knees.

"How do you make your millions?"

Peter blinked, then looked away.

"I presume you're not running a charity from your laptop. Do you work for a hedge fund as well?"

He turned and glowered at her.

Tanya sat up, as she realized what he was up to.

"You're a day trader, aren't you?"

He didn't reply, but his face darkened, like she had discovered his secret.

"What was the fight with your mother about?"

Peter opened his mouth and shut it, but his chest heaved.

"She was overheard shouting *you think I have millions lying around,*" said Tanya. "What did she mean by that?"

His face flushed a bright purple.

"You were also overheard to say, *I will kill you.*"

He gasped, as if he was struggling to breathe.

"Peter, did you steal from your mother?"

He was hyperventilating now, like he had run a mile. She was getting close.

"She mistreated you," said Tanya, watching him closely, "so you thought she deserved to be stolen from. Plus, you needed the money."

"Day trading isn't a crime."

That wasn't the question.

If Peter was found guilty of stealing millions from his murdered mother, he would be a prime suspect for her death, regardless of his capacity to commit murder himself.

Tanya leaned in closer.

"You siphoned millions from her accounts to fuel your addiction, didn't you?"

Peter jerked up.

"I don't have an addiction!"

She had hit a raw nerve.

"It's like heroin. Or cocaine," said Tanya. "You think you're winning but you keep losing. Big time. You might make millions, but it all goes in a blink of an eye. But, once you start the game, you can't stop, can you?"

Peter grabbed his laptop and threw it at her.

"I'm not an addict!"

The laptop slammed against Tanya's shoulder and crashed to the ground. Max lunged at Peter, but Tanya grabbed him by the collar before he could snatch the man's arm.

Suddenly, Peter jerked in his chair and gasped out loud. He clutched his heart and doubled over.

Tanya jumped up from her seat. She reached over and shook his shoulder.

"Peter? Peter?"

His body remained still, like an immobile mountain of flesh and bones in his wheelchair.

Tanya placed her fingers on the side of his neck to feel his pulse, her own heart pounding.

Chapter Thirty-nine

"You killed him!"

Tanya swung around as Hazel rushed into the living room. She shoved Tanya to the side and kneeled by Peter's chair.

"It's Aunty Hazel." She shook Peter by the shoulders. "Are you okay, sweetie?"

"He needs CPR immediately," said Tanya.

Hazel whipped around to her.

"Stay away from my family!"

Tanya shot her a frustrated look. "He needs first aid."

Hazel's face flushed a deep red. "You murdered him!"

Tanya stepped away and plucked her phone out.

"Doctor, I need you at the house ASAP. A family member requires urgent medical assistance. Potential heart attack."

"My team's already on their way to the manor," came Dr. Chen's voice, calm and collected, down the line. "We need DNA swabs from all household members. Make sure everyone complies, including the staff. No one can wiggle out of this, you hear me?"

Tanya closed her eyes and sighed. That wasn't going to be easy. She hung up and turned to Peter in his wheelchair. Hazel had grabbed the young man's face in her hands and was shaking him.

"Peter! Talk to me!"

"Please don't move him," said Tanya. "The medical team is on its way."

Peter's left eye fluttered momentarily, or so Tanya thought. Her heart leaped to her mouth.

Please be alive.

"Oh, my heavens! What did she do to you?" cried Hazel, hugging her nephew tightly. "She tried to kill you!"

Tanya shook her head. If Peter had a heart attack, he was sure to be in a worse state now.

A timid knock on the door made Tanya turn. Relief flooded through her as she saw the two interns by the doorway, medical kits in their hands.

"Right here," she said, gesturing them in.

The interns' eyes widened for a split second, then they rushed inside the room. One pushed Hazel aside while another checked for Peter's pulse.

Tanya watched them work, praying to all the gods they would save the man.

She hadn't come to the island to make things worse, and the last thing she needed was a distraction from finding out who killed Justin.

"This is all your fault!"

Tanya looked up to see Hazel stomping toward her, her eyes fiery. At her feet, Max growled.

"Stay, bud," said Tanya.

Hazel stepped up to her and slapped her across her cheek.

Tanya snapped her head back in shock. She felt her face, as the stinging pain spread across her cheek like lightning fire.

Max lunged at Hazel, barking, but Tanya grabbed him before he did.

She stared at the woman's angry brown eyes. Her hands were curled into fists and her face was pinched, like she would beat Tanya to a pulp, if she could.

The petite woman who stood in front of her wasn't the frightened and grieving mother she had seen in the ferry. Hazel had transformed into a fierce bulldog ready to tear her limbs apart.

Tanya took a deep breath in to calm her nerves.

"I understand how frightening all this is. You just lost your son—"

"Someone killed him!" screeched Hazel.

"I'm doing everything in my power to find who—"

"And now you were going to kill Peter!"

Hazel's eyes burned into her.

"Stanley was right," she spat. "You're stirring trouble for all of us. You're nothing but a menace!"

A gasp from Peter made Hazel whirl around. She scrambled toward him, slipped to the floor by the wheelchair, and put her hand on her nephew's knee.

The interns continued administering CPR. Peter's eyes remained closed but his chest had begun to heave.

"Tanya?"

Tanya turned around to see Asha by the entrance, gesturing to her urgently.

What now?

With another glance to make sure the interns had the situation under control, Tanya stepped toward the doorway, pulling Max away. She could still feel her cheek throb from Hazel's slap.

Asha craned her neck over her shoulder. "What happened here?"

"Potential heart attack." Tanya narrowed her eyes. "Did you get my message?"

"You have to come," said Asha. "It's Stanley."

Chapter Forty

"I told you to stay away from him," said Tanya.

Asha grabbed her arm. "We need your specialized car skills."

"You need a driver?"

"We need you to break into a vehicle. We tried, but these are high end."

Tanya stared at her friend. "I can't believe you're asking me to break the law—"

Asha put a finger on her lips.

"Shh.... We don't have a lot of time."

Without waiting for her, Asha spun around and scurried along the corridor toward the front door. With Max at her heels, Tanya followed her, wondering what fresh hell was waiting for them next.

Rafael, who was changing a light bulb in the hallway, glanced at them curiously, but went back to his task.

"Where's Katy?" whispered Tanya once they were out of his earshot. "Is she safe? Are you both okay?"

"This way," said Asha.

She jumped down the front steps and pointed at the five-door garage attached to the manor. She scurried down the driveway toward a small side door.

Struggling to contain the low boil of frustration swirling through her, Tanya stepped through the garage door after her.

"Check these out," said Asha.

Tanya let out a low whistle.

Two new Land Rovers, a Cadillac, an Audi convertible, and a green Bentley, all polished to a sparkling shine, were parked in front.

So, this is what a tobacco empire family's fleet looks like.

But Asha was walking to the back of the garage. Tanya noticed Katy hovering by a closed door in the back, like she was on the lookout. Katy perked up and waved as she saw her.

Asha pointed at the three super sports cars parked in a row in the back of the garage.

"Check out *these* beauties."

A Lamborghini, a Ferrari, and an Audi R8 super sports car sat side by side. Tanya stopped to take it all in.

There's more than a million dollars of shiny European engineering in this corner alone.

"They're all Stanley's," whispered Katy.

Tanya turned to her friends, her brow furrowed.

"I told you to be careful—"

"He's eating out of our hands," said Katy, giving her a conspiring look. "The man's a big show-off. He's got the biggest ego in the world."

Asha pointed at the Ferrari. "He opened the trunk to show us his new golf set, but slammed it shut quickly, like there was something in there he didn't want us to see."

"He's hiding something," said Katy. "We sent him to get cocktails. He won't be back for another ten minutes."

Tanya shook her head. "Ten minutes isn't enough to—"

Max had left her side and was circling the Ferrari, sniffing the ground around it.

Did he pick up a scent? More contraband?

As she watched, Max sat next to the Ferrari and thumped his tail.

Tanya frowned.

When they were in Honoree's bedroom, Max had backed off from the chest of drawers, sneezing hard as the tobacco smell irritated his nose.

It couldn't be more Cuban cigars. There was something else in that car.

Tanya slipped her gloves on.

She stepped up to the vehicle and tried the doors, but it was locked. She turned to her friends who were watching her expectantly.

"Do you have the keys?" she said.

Asha shot her an exasperated look.

"That's why we brought *you*. Can't you do that magic trick you learned in Russia?"

"No."

Nudging her friend aside, Tanya navigated between the other cars, testing the Audi first, then the Lamborghini, in hopes of finding spare keys for the Ferrari, but both vehicles were also locked.

She took stock.

Stanley Kensington was a slippery character, and he had a phalanx of lawyers who would defend him. If he was the killer, they needed solid evidence to nail him.

There was no way she could break in to the cars, as any evidence they found had to be admissible in court. But she couldn't waste Jack or his new crew's time if whatever was inside the car had nothing to do with Justin's and Monica's deaths.

The sound of footsteps came from somewhere behind the garage.

Katy whirled around in panic. "He's coming!"

"Locate the keys," Tanya hissed, as she clicked her fingers at Max and hastened toward the side door. "Then, get out of here. I'll take care of this."

"When?"

"Tonight."

Chapter Forty-one

"She didn't mean it," said Veronika.

Tanya glanced at the glass of milk in the woman's hands.

Moments ago, Mariposa had come up to the second floor with a tray of milk, as part of the family's bedtime ritual. The housekeeper had presented one to Tanya, but she had refused, and now, Veronika was giving hers to her.

Is this a peace offering?

"Hazel's husband died in a car crash nine years ago." Veronika pressed the glass into Tanya's hand. "Justin was the second death for her. It's been very rough on her. I hope you understand."

Tanya took the warm glass of milk. "Thank you."

She had been about to call Asha and Katy about the car keys, when Veronika had accosted her in front of her new guest room.

"I hope you'll have a good rest tonight." Veronika's eyelids fluttered. "You'll be more comfortable up here."

Tanya had already forgotten Hazel's slap. She had experienced far more vicious encounters on the battlefield. What preoccupied her mind now was Veronika's sudden change in demeanor.

Tanya knew this was a facade, because the woman had forbidden anyone in the house to provide a handwriting sample or to answer her or Jack's questions.

Veronika had been apologetic, saying she was only following their lawyers' counsel, and was waiting for them to arrive on the island, but Tanya knew a delay tactic when she saw one.

What's her game? thought Tanya. *Are they all in on this?*

"Losing your child is the hardest thing for a mother to experience," said Veronika. "Poor Hazel."

Her blue eyes were steady. She was staring into Tanya's, like she was willing her to believe her words. Veronika was on a PR mission.

"We're a good family. We don't go around hitting people. These are unusual circumstances."

A whine from Max made them glance down. He was staring at the glass of milk. He licked his lips and wagged his tail.

"Would you like Mariposa to get a bowl for your pup too?" said Veronika, bending down to pat Max on the head.

Tanya shook her head. "He's on a strict diet. Rafael got him his raw meat ration for the day."

Though Max had been trained, he was still a dog, and a sucker for treats. If he could get away with it, he would lap up the entire glass of milk faster than any self-respecting cat.

"This will help you sleep better tonight," said Veronika, squeezing Tanya's arm. "I know you're here to help us."

With a motherly smile and another gentle pat on Max's head, Veronika turned around. Tanya watched her stroll down the corridor toward the larger bedrooms located farther along the floor.

Is she trying to deflect a lawsuit or a complaint? Or is she trying to avoid increasing scrutiny of her family?

A sense of unease came over Tanya.

She's hiding something.

At her feet, Max whined and cocked his head.

"No, bud," said Tanya in a firm voice. "You had your meals for the day."

She stepped into her room, ushered him inside, and closed the door. From one end, she heard the thump of heavy metal music.

She was sandwiched in between David's room and the spare guest room where Asha and Katy were staying.

She sent a silent thanks to Veronika.

Her hostess didn't know what her visitors had planned for the night. And now, getting the keys to Stanley's fleet of vehicles from her friends was going to be so much easier. All she had to do was knock on the next door.

An electric guitar wailed from the adjoining room.

Tanya shook her head.

A little boy trapped in a big man's body.

The music's volume increased as she stepped toward the bedside table and placed the glass of milk on it.

With a tired sigh, Tanya sank into an armchair at the foot of the bed.

Her clothes were still damp since she hadn't changed after her unexpected swim in the cove.

Dr. Chen and Adams had taken up most of her time that afternoon, as they'd secured the crime scene for the forensics team and prepared Monica's body to be taken to the morgue.

Tanya rubbed her face, thankful she hadn't had to fight to stay on the island. Jack had convinced Veronika that a greater police presence was necessary for the family's safety. She had been surprised at Veronika's new reception of her, and wondered if Monica's death had changed the tide.

A warning bark made her turn.

Max was sniffing at the glass of milk. The bedside table was low enough that he could lick its rim.

She was about to move it away from his reach when Max backed off in a hurry. He shuffled backward, bumping into her armchair.

With a curious expression on his face, he tottered all the way to the door, like he wanted to get as far away from the glass of milk as possible.

Goose bumps sprung up on Tanya's arm.

She leaped out of her chair and stepped toward the bedside table. She knew Max would never miss the chance to take at least one lick.

She picked up the glass and brought it to her nose.

Smells okay.

She examined it from all sides, then held the glass up to the light to scrutinize the bottom. It looked like an ordinary glass of milk to her.

She turned back to Max, who was watching her. Tanya set the glass on top of the highest chest of drawers in the room, away from his reach.

Max barked, a heightened urgency in his tone.

"It's okay, bud," said Tanya. "No one's going to touch that except for Dr. Chen's crew tomorrow morning."

She stepped up to her dog and squatted on the carpet next to him, coming down to his eye level.

"There's something in the glass, isn't there?"

As if in response, an electric screech came through the wall next door, followed by the thundering of heavy metal drums.

Tanya turned back to her pup.

"Is Veronika trying to poison me?"

Max whined in reply.

"Or is it Mariposa?"

Next door, the sound of the drums increased in volume, thundering to a crescendo as if to warn her.

A shudder went through Tanya's back. No one in this family was who they claimed themselves to be.

I can't trust anyone.

Chapter Forty-two

"You're not going alone," hissed Asha.

"Lock your door and stay in your room until I give the all-clear," said Tanya. "Don't touch anything, don't eat anything, don't drink anything."

Katy's eyes flashed.

"You can't tell us what to do."

"Get into your PJs. Go to bed and watch a cat video or something."

"We don't work for you," said Asha.

Tanya glared. "I'm speaking as your sister. The oldest in the family."

It was past midnight. Tanya had come over to her friends' room as soon as the coast was clear. Her eyes flitted over to their bedside table. She had already called them about her suspicions, and their glasses looked untouched.

"This place is a death trap," said Tanya, narrowing her eyes. "If you think we're immune to whatever's going on because we're not part of the Kensington family, you're kidding yourselves."

"That's exactly why we need to work together," said Asha. "If we team up, we can sort this out faster."

"I'm not jeopardizing your safety. It was a bad idea to come here. You need to get on that ferry first thing in the morning. Until then, you're staying in your room."

Asha pointed at the set of car fobs in Tanya's gloved hand. "We kept our end of the bargain."

"I had to distract Stanley," said Katy, "while she smuggled the keys from his office. It wasn't easy."

Tanya wondered how she had stayed sane this long given her stubborn family members. She had pleaded with them to get on the ferry that afternoon, but they had blithely ignored her, staying out of sight till the captain's last trip out.

She turned toward the door.

"I appreciate your help."

"You need backup," said Asha.

"I've got Max."

Just as Tanya yanked the door open, Katy pushed past her and stepped into the corridor. She hurried toward the stairway without looking back. With a shrug, Asha followed her out.

Tanya shook her head. It wasn't like she could grapple these two to the ground and tie them up.

"Let's go, Max." She looked down at her dog who had been waiting by her feet, while his family bickered around him. "At least you listen to me, bud."

Closing the bedroom door behind her, and double-checking the hallway to make sure no one had seen them, Tanya tiptoed down the corridor.

The four of them walked in single file, with Max in front and Tanya keeping guard in the back, her Glock in her hand. She swiveled her head back and forth as she walked. She peered into the nooks and crannies of the darkened house, expecting to see shadows everywhere.

It was eerie to walk through the corridors of the large manor in the dim light. A handful of night-lights lit their path to the main entrance, but Tanya could feel her friends' nervousness, and hoped they didn't feel hers. Still, Max was trotting along quietly, and nothing in his deportment told her they were being watched or followed.

When Asha got to the front door, Tanya put a hand up to stop her.

"Wait."

She scanned the foyer and the corridor before giving the go-ahead. Asha pried the front door open a few inches and peeked out.

"Clear."

Tanya nodded.

The junior trooper had been stationed on the yacht that evening. Jack had got Veronika's agreement to place him inside the big boat's cockpit for the night with all of its spotlights switched on. That way, he could have a bird's-eye view of the entire lake.

If Tanya knew the young man, he was dozing off in the luxurious surroundings where he'd found himself. He hadn't had a break all day and needed sleep like the rest of them. Still, she doubted anyone would come over to the island, especially with the cove lit up like Christmas.

Her gut told her the killer was already on the island.

In front of her, Katy hugged herself. "It's super chilly."

"I told you to put a jacket on," grumbled Asha from up front.

"I didn't know it was going to be this windy."

"Keep it down," whispered Tanya, as she surveyed the dark forest surrounding the house.

Though she had a flashlight in her pocket, she had insisted on using the waning moonlight as their illumination. The moon cast bizarre shadows by the woods, making the trees look like monsters swaying to the night ocean breeze.

The ominous call of a night owl came from behind the manor, followed by a shrill squeak of an animal. Katy shuddered and hugged herself tighter.

"It's pretty dark," she whispered.

Tanya gritted her teeth, swallowing the words that came to her throat.

You two should have stayed at the house.

"Are you sure Stanley's in his room?" she said as they approached the side door of the garage.

"I tucked him in," said Katy, turning around with a nervous giggle.

"How do you know he hasn't come out?"

"We had a few drinks with him, then said goodnight, and closed his door behind us," said Katy. "Ours was open so we could keep an eye out on the second floor. We only saw Mariposa come up with the milk, then you and Veronika chat in the hallway."

"Can we go in already?" said Asha in an impatient voice.

Before Tanya could reply, she pulled the garage door open and stepped inside.

Chapter Forty-three

The side door creaked as it opened.

"Sorry," came Asha's voice in the dark.

Katy pushed through the narrow opening and followed her inside the garage. Tanya walked in and took her flashlight out of her pocket.

"Don't move."

Tanya turned on her light and shone it around the open space. Asha and Katy stood frozen. The vehicles were in the same places as she had seen them earlier in the day.

Tanya glanced down at her pup. Max was looking at her expectantly, his head to the side, waiting for a command. He knew they were on a mission and was alert, but he wasn't barking, growling, or making any warning movements.

Tanya nodded to her friends.

"We're alone."

"Who did you think would be here?" said Katy, strolling to the back. "A ghost waiting to pounce on us?"

"We'll check the Ferrari first," said Tanya, ignoring her. She treaded in between the Mercedes and a Land Rover, making sure not to touch either vehicle.

She walked to the back of the garage, to where Stanley's fleet of luxury super cars were parked in a row. They sat right in front of a large metal shelving unit on which were bottles of windshield wiper fluid and antifreeze.

She passed her flashlight to Asha and stepped up to the red sports car.

She clicked the unlock button on the key fob with the Ferrari logo, and braced for an alarm. The vehicle beeped twice to indicate it was now open and promptly fell silent.

"Let's see what's in the trunk," whispered Tanya, stepping to the back of the car.

"It's a frunk," said Katy.

"A what?"

"New super sports cars have the engine in the back," said Asha. "The cargo space is up front."

"How did you *not* know that?" said Katy.

"Ask me about storage in a heavy armored battle tank, and then, we can talk," said Tanya as she walked over to the front of the vehicle.

The frunk of the Ferrari opened automatically with a click of the fob.

Tanya turned to Asha.

"Flashlight, please."

Asha squeezed in between Katy and Tanya, and shone the light inside the cargo space. Tucked in a row in the small storage compartment were two backpacks with the Ferrari logo.

"I was expecting golf equipment, to be honest," said Asha, reaching over to one bag.

"Don't touch that," said Tanya. "Don't you guys use protection?"

Neither Asha nor Katy replied. Tanya reached toward the closest bag with her gloved hand, and pulled the zipper open.

Katy gasped out loud.

"So that's why he didn't want us to see inside," said Katy in an awed voice.

Tanya pulled the zipper open all the way and rummaged around the bag. She picked up a wad of neatly packed hundred-dollar bills and placed it on the bumper.

"Cash, cash, and more cash," she whispered, as she pulled out more packages of greenbacks.

"There must be one hundred thousand dollars in here," said Katy. "At least."

Tanya ripped open the second bag's zipper.

"One hundred? I think we have four to five times that in here."

"Why would anyone hold a cool quarter of a million in their car's frunk?" said Asha.

A whine from Max made Tanya glance back at her dog. He had been sitting behind them, but got up when he saw her look. She followed his movements with her eyes. Max did two rounds around the Ferrari, came back and sat down by the front, his muzzle up and his eyes beady.

"The money," said Katy. "That's what he smelled earlier."

Tanya shook her head. "He's not trained to sniff out dollar bills."

Taking the flashlight from Asha, she scrutinized the bills, one by one.

"What's that stuff on them?" said Katy, peeking over her shoulder.

Asha leaned in to inspect.

Tanya pulled her back by the shoulders. "You don't want that up your nose."

"Is that what I think it is?" said Asha, frowning.

Tanya plucked a white plastic bag she'd spied hidden among the bills. She pried it out and held it up.

"Drugs," she whispered. "This is drug-laced money. That's what Max sniffed out."

Chapter Forty-four

"Stanley's a lowlife," said Katy. "And to think he accused *Justin* of being a petty criminal."

"Meanwhile he's got oodles of cocaine-dusted cash in his car with a full bag of coke," said Asha, shaking her head.

Katy sighed. "I can't believe we signed a contract with a drug dealer."

Tanya gave a side glance at them. "If it walks crooked, talks crooked, it's crooked. Period."

Her friends fell silent.

Tanya knew why.

They had known the type of person they were getting involved with. They had only signed up with him to legitimize their stay on the island to uncover the secret of Justin's odd inheritance request.

The irrefutable allure of a treasure hunt. They couldn't escape it.

Tanya let out a resigned sigh.

But I'm no better. I encouraged them.

The three of them were walking back to the manor, stunned at their discovery.

"The good news is we have more than reasonable grounds for an arrest," said Tanya grimly. "But until we have the forensics team here, we have to keep quiet. The family can't know we rooted around their private property without a warrant."

She had left the illicit items exactly as they had found them, but had taken photos and locked up the car, so no one would notice their presence that night.

She had also checked the other vehicles in the garage. The Mercedes sedan and one of the Range Rovers had been unlocked, but Max had sniffed the remaining cars with no interest.

He kept returning to the red Ferrari, his pointy face focused on the bags, like he was trying his best to tell his human friends to stop searching elsewhere.

He had known the truth all along.

Tanya had notified the officer in the yacht to make sure he was keeping an eye out, before stepping out of the garage with her friends.

"Justin was a good kid," said Tanya, sadness creeping into her heart. "He brought everyone coffee in the morning, even for us at the precinct, though we weren't part of the same team. He didn't have a mean bone in his body. I can't imagine how he could have been part of this clan."

"That's why he never spoke to them after he left," said Katy.

"Why don't we interrogate Stanley right now?" Asha screwed her eyes. "Just Katy and me. This is the perfect time. He'll be confused, groggy, and invariably slip up. We'll have our phones turned on in our pockets, so you can listen in."

"That won't be admissible in court," said Tanya.

"But you'll have new intel," said Asha. "You'll get further ahead in your case."

"How are you going to explain the car keys you stole from his office?" said Tanya. "And us breaking and entering the garage?"

"The garage wasn't locked, so technically, that wasn't a break and enter," said Katy.

"I'll bet you anything, he'll pay us to keep quiet," said Asha. "What better way to admit guilt? And then, Special Agent Stone, you'll have your man."

Tanya shook her head.

"He's going to defend, deflect, and call his lawyers before I can get reinforcement. It will tie our hands. We need to be more strategic."

Tanya had called Jack who had been at the hospital, visiting Stacey and George. Stacey had been discharged that night, but her husband was still under intensive care.

Jack hadn't been too happy to hear the news about Stanley and his stash of cash, but he had hung up to get a search warrant.

Tanya stopped and turned to her friends.

"What if they're all in on this together?"

"Having met them, I doubt it. This isn't a loving family, by any definition." Asha shook her head. "They're all scrapping for the inheritance, and are ready to pull each other's eyes out for it."

"Peter cornered us in the kitchen when we were having lunch," said Katy. "He said he'd pay double what Stanley offered to find the inheritance for him. He wanted exclusivity."

"Why didn't you tell me this before?"

"You were busy by the lake with the chief and the doctor," said Asha. "The only time we got you alone was when you called us about the poisoned milk."

"*Potentially* tampered," said Tanya.

They had arrived at the mansion's front door. She stopped and scanned their surroundings.

Except for the security lights on the façade and the dim wrought-iron lights lining the driveway, it was dark. There weren't any lights switched on in the house, on this side of the manor, anyway.

Tanya turned to her friends.

"If anyone is up, I took Max out for a potty walk."

"And us?" said Katy.

"We couldn't sleep," said Asha, "we heard Max in the hallway, and joined them for a midnight stroll."

Tanya pushed down the front door handle, hoping Rafael hadn't woken up during the night and locked them out. Max trotted in confidently.

Tanya let out a relieved sigh.

They tiptoed after Max, but remained alert. They climbed the main staircase and walked down the second-floor hallway toward their rooms.

The heavy metal music had stopped, and the floor was deserted. Or, at least, it looked like it was.

"Everyone's asleep," murmured Katy as she approached her guest room door.

Tanya followed her pup to her room. It was only when Max got to their door he started growling.

She whipped out her Glock.

Is someone in my room?

Chapter Forty-five

Asha spun around.

"What is it?" she whispered.

"What's going on?" called out Katy, peeking out of her door.

Tanya put a finger to her lips.

She placed an ear to the bedroom door and listened for a few seconds, but heard only silence. She placed a hand on the doorknob, keeping her Glock aimed in front of her.

Behind her, she felt her friends' anxiety, palpable in the air. She glanced around to see Asha and Katy, ready to back her up.

She turned back to the door, hoping she didn't need to use her gun.

By her heels, Max growled again, this time deeper and louder. Tanya turned the doorknob and pushed it an inch. Max was on all fours, his ears pricked and his eyes focused, ready to attack.

She peeked in and listened.

It was dark inside but deathly quiet.

She opened the door another inch and peered through the narrow opening.

There didn't seem to be anyone inside, but her heart was racing, and her gut was sending warning signals. Her eyes scanned the darkened room before landing on the chest of drawers against the opposite wall.

She realized what was bothering her.

A narrow beam of light from the corridor had fallen on the chest of drawers. The glass of milk she had placed on it for safekeeping now lay on its side. Its contents were spilled over the wooden surface and on the floor.

Another growl came from Max.

Keeping a tight grip on her Glock, Tanya pulled the door open and switched on the light.

The room was empty.

If someone had come in while she was away, they weren't in the room anymore.

Signaling to her friends to remain by the doorway, Tanya stepped inside and checked under the bed.

Nothing.

She jumped to her feet and stepped toward the small armoire next to the bed. Only a child would fit inside, but it was worth looking.

Again nothing.

The guest bathrooms were at the end of the hallway, so there was no other place to hide in this room.

Tanya treaded across the room and back, looking behind every piece of furniture and in every corner. The windows were closed, and the curtains were still drawn. Her overnight bag on the bed was in the same position she had left it. Other than the spilled glass of milk, nothing else looked disturbed.

"What am I missing?" said Tanya, as she spun around the room.

"Max smelled the scent of whoever came in," said Asha from the doorway. "He's trying to tell you there was an intruder."

As if in reply, Max barked.

He trotted inside and positioned himself in front of the bed. For the thousandth time, Tanya wished her K9 partner could talk.

With a heavy sigh, she plopped at the edge of her bed.

Max barked again.

Katy cringed at the noise.

"The entire house is going to wake up now," said Asha.

"What is it, bud?" said Tanya, lifting her tired eyes to her pup. "Tell me where to loo—"

"Oh, my goodness!" screamed Katy.

Tanya looked up. Her friends' faces had turned white. Katy stood frozen and Asha was staring at something behind her.

"Get out!" hollered Asha.

Tanya leaped to her feet, her heart pounding.

What is it?

The head of the albino python pushed out from under the bed covers, inches from where she had been sitting. It hissed at Tanya.

"Get out now!" yelled Asha.

The snake opened its massive mouth, showing a slimy mass of pink muscles, large enough to snap an adult human in two.

It raised its head.

"Watch out!" screamed Katy.

It lunged at Max.

Chapter Forty-six

Tanya yanked Max by the collar.

She dove headlong toward the open doorway with him.

She pushed her friends back and slammed the door shut. The three of them stared at each other in shock, while Max barked angrily at the door.

"What's that doing in my room?" said Tanya, panting hard.

Katy turned to her, her eyes wide. "Did I imagine the biggest snake in the world on your bed?"

Keeping a tight grip on her dog, Tanya opened the door an inch and peered inside.

The python was crawling across her coverlet. Its head darted to the right and left, its forked tongue feeling the air like it was searching for something.

Tanya's stomach churned. She banged the bedroom door shut.

Max was barking his head off now, struggling to wriggle out of her grasp, but she held on.

All of a sudden, chaos erupted in Kensington Manor. Doors banged along the hallway. Someone shouted. Then, came a roar that made the hair on the back of Tanya's neck stand.

Soon, heavy footsteps came running down the corridor.

"She kidnapped Xena!"

Tanya whirled around to see David, still in his wife-beater shirt and stained pants, with his hair frazzled like someone had electrocuted him. He started jumping up and down in front of her, his face red with fury.

"You were going to shoot Xena! You murderer!"

Tanya holstered her weapon.

"What's going on?" said Veronika, stumbling down the corridor, tying up her bathrobe.

Hazel opened her door and peeked out.

"What happened?" she called out, blinking sleepily. "David? Are you okay?"

"It's his snake," shouted Tanya, trying to get heard above the melee. "The python is in my room."

Veronika stared at her, her eyes bulging. "She got out? How?"

"That's what I'd like to know as well."

Veronika shook her head. "She's probably starving."

"She tried to eat my dog."

"She was going to kill Xena!" David pranced around Tanya, his fists punching the air. "She was going to shoot her! She's a witch!"

Max lunged at him. Tanya put both hands on his collar, knowing the last thing she needed was for her dog to attack this man.

She watched warily as David danced around her in fury. If she had to guess, he wanted nothing more than to beat her up, but he remembered what had happened the last time he did.

Tanya glanced over his shoulder at Veronika and Hazel. They were both in their bathrobes, hair disheveled, eyes widened, staring at her like she was an alien.

"His pet snake tried to snatch my dog. We barely got out before it attacked."

Neither woman said a word, but Tanya could feel their accusing eyes, like laser beams pointed at her.

David twirled around and spotted Asha and Katy by the wall.

"You!" screamed David, pointing a trembling finger at them. "Mean nasty witches. All of you want to steal my Xena! You were going to take her from me!"

They glared back at David.

"We didn't touch your snake," said Katy. "We don't want it."

"My question," said Asha, her voice rising, "is how did your pet python get in Tanya's room?"

David glowered.

"Were you trying to hurt Tanya? Were you planning to kill Max?"

David took a step toward Asha.

He raised his fist.

"Asha!" Tanya hollered.

Chapter Forty-seven

David swung his fist.

Asha moved.

He roared as his hand hit the wall.

Asha stomped on his foot and blocked his next punch.

David doubled over, screeching. Tanya let go of Max and grabbed him by the shoulders. She pulled him away from her friend, with Max's jaws latched on to his trouser leg.

"Stop it!" called out a woman's voice. "Don't hurt him!"

Tanya turned around to see Hazel stomp toward her, coming to the defense of her family once again.

Hazel glared. "Leave our boy alone."

Tanya pushed David toward his aunt. Her blood boiled inside of her. She'd had enough of this eccentric family.

"Take him to his room," she snapped. "And get that snake out of my bed."

David stumbled toward Veronika and sank into her shoulders, sobbing.

"She won't let me have my Xena," he cried.

"You're more than welcome to take your pet back," said Tanya.

David spun around, his eyes blazing. "You took Xena!"

"You're a terrible person," hissed Hazel at Tanya. "What were you doing with his pet?"

Tanya stared at Hazel and Veronika, their accusing eyes glowering at her.

Do they seriously think I would smuggle a live python into my bedroom? On what planet do these people live?

"Who else in this house knows how to handle that snake?" asked Tanya, eyeing the women.

The sound of someone running up the stairs made everyone turn.

"Is everyone okay?"

"Ah, Rafael," said Veronika, relief flooding her voice. She turned to Tanya. "David only allows Rafael to handle Xena. No one else."

Hearing his name, Rafael scurried over, rubbing his eyes. Mariposa trailed behind him, her eyes wide in surprise to see everyone gathered in the hallway.

"What's going on here?" she asked.

"Can you please get Xena back into her aquarium?" said Tanya.

"No!" shouted David, trying to wriggle from Veronika's grasp. "I'll get her out! That nasty woman was going to shoot her!"

Veronika held on to his shoulders.

"Xena's going to be fine, honey. Rafael is here to help. Don't you worry. Let's get back to bed, okay?"

She led the sniffling David back into his room. With an annoyed hiss, Hazel swung around and followed them in. Tanya could hear the low voices of the women as they consoled David.

Rafael turned to Tanya in confusion. "Where's Xena?"

Tanya pointed at her closed door.

"Strange." Mariposa frowned. "David never lets her outside his room."

"She hasn't eaten in a month." Rafael shook his head. "She gets real nasty during this period. Must have come out looking for food."

Asha stared at him. "Why didn't someone feed her, then?"

"I was going to," said Rafael, rubbing his forehead. "Tomorrow is feeding day."

He opened the bedroom door and peeked inside.

"When did she get in here?"

Spotting the serpent through the opening, Max started barking again. Tanya grabbed him and moved him away from the scene, and toward her friends.

"I think the more appropriate question," said Tanya, "is *how* did she get into my room."

Rafael shrugged and turned back to the open door. "Xena?" he said in a soft voice. "What are you doing in there? You almost gave David a heart attack."

"Be careful, Mi rey," said Mariposa, clutching her robe.

Rafael closed the door and turned back to the small crowd gathered outside.

"I'm only supposed to feed her once a month." With another resigned shrug, he turned around and lumbered down the corridor.

"Hey, where are you off to?" called out Tanya.

"To warm up some chicken meat. Once she smells that, she'll be back in her cage in no time."

Tanya turned to her friends, who were still gaping at her in shock. She scanned the hallway and the darkened stairway at the other end.

"Where's Stanley?"

Asha and Katy turned around as if they also realized what she had noticed.

"And Peter," said Asha.

"Still sleeping?" said Katy.

Tanya raised a brow. "Through all this racket?"

Chapter Forty-eight

A cold hand clutched Tanya's arm.

Tanya flinched and glanced down to see Mariposa looking up at her. Her eyes were dark.

"That wasn't an accident," whispered the housekeeper. "Someone knew she was very hungry, and was going to attack you."

Tanya raised her brows.

"Do you know who did this?"

Mariposa pulled her robe tighter around her shoulders.

"They want to scare you off."

"Tell us who it is," said Katy, coming closer.

Mariposa looked away and blinked, like she wasn't sure whether to say more.

"Just be careful, girls."

Mariposa turned away quickly and shuffled down the corridor, following in her husband's footsteps. Tanya and her friends watched her scurry off, their brows furrowed.

"David wasn't acting," said Tanya quietly. "He genuinely thought I was going to harm his pet. She can't be referring to him."

"That man needs professional psychiatric help," said Asha. "I can't see him orchestrate a snake attack, either."

"Rafael is supposedly the only other person who handles that python," said Tanya.

"No, she wasn't accusing her husband." Katy shook her head. "I've seen them together. They're very close. It has to be someone else."

Tanya turned to her friends.

"I'm sure that snake was as scared as we were, but Max could have got *killed*."

Katy put a hand on her arm.

"When was the last time you got a few hours of sleep, hun?"

Tanya blinked. Her mind was buzzing too fast to contemplate rest.

"You're not getting in that bed with snake slime all over your sheets," said Katy.

"Pythons have scales, not slime," said Asha.

"Scales, slime, same icky stuff," said Katy, pulling Tanya by the arm toward their guest room.

"You and Max can take the couch," said Katy, as she ushered them inside. "We got a suite. I think Stanley convinced Veronika into giving us the best guest room in the house."

Tanya let her friends lead her into their room, her mind still reeling from the incident, trying to figure out what she needed to do next.

Max trotted past her and jumped on the couch. With a heavy groan, he laid his head on his paws.

"See?" said Katy, as she closed the bedroom door behind them. "You think you don't need downtime, but he does."

Tanya plopped down on the couch next to her pup and put her head in her hands.

"This place gets crazier by the hour."

"They're treating *us* well," chirped Katy as she stepped over to the walk-in closet in the corner.

"No snakes in here. Mariposa left us bathrobes and slippers. It's almost like staying at a five-star hotel."

Tanya looked up and glanced around the spacious suite.

"Mine's one tenth of this size." She shook her head. "I guess I'm a little low on the totem pole compared to the detectives searching for the family's prized possession."

Katy disappeared into the walk-in closet. "I thought I saw some slippers in the back...," she mumbled from inside.

Asha patted Tanya's shoulder. "You need a clear head. Get some sleep and we can discuss strategy tomorrow."

Tanya frowned. "There's nothing to discuss. You will head back home."

A thud made them turn around.

"You okay?" called out Asha.

Another thud came from the closet.

"Hey, you guys?" came Katy's muffled voice.

Tanya leaped from the couch and dashed toward the closet, with Asha and Max right behind her. Katy disappearing into a wardrobe was a ludicrous idea, but right now, Tanya was prepared for anything.

Katy popped her head out of the closet doors.

"You won't believe this," she whispered.

Asha shoved her aside and stepped in. Tanya put one hand on her holster, and followed them inside.

Katy had pushed the hanging dresses and bathrobes all the way to the end of the rod. She pointed at the back of the closet. "Check this out."

Asha and Tanya stared at the goblin-sized wooden door in the back.

"Where does this go to?" said Asha. "Narnia?"

A man's trembling voice came from the other side, and the three of them fell silent.

"Xena?" came the voice. "Come on out, girl. Don't make this hard on both of us."

Rafael, mouthed Katy.

Tanya leaned closer and examined the frame.

"This is a connecting door," she whispered.

Katy nodded. "Just like in a hotel."

"When was the last time you saw a connecting door inside a closet?" whispered Asha. "This is a secret entrance."

"This is how Xena came to my room," whispered Tanya. "There must be a door between mine and David's."

"Have you looked inside your closet?" said Katy.

"Haven't even opened it. My clothes are still in my bag."

"Xena?" came Rafael's shaky voice. "Let's go back to David. Come on, now. Please. You need to go back to your home. David is waiting for you."

Tanya, Asha, and Katy exchanged glances.

"Tomorrow's your feeding day," continued Rafael, louder this time, but still shaky. "I'll bring your favorite mouse treats if you go into your aquarium. Did you hear me, Xena?"

Asha shook her head. "Gosh, I hope she doesn't eat him alive."

Day Four

Chapter Forty-nine

"Open up!"

The intense banging on the manor's front door grew louder.

"I said, open up, you murderers!"

It was an infuriated female voice, but a familiar one.

Rafael stumbled down the hallway, a troubled frown on his face. Tanya followed him toward the main entrance, one hand on her holster.

She had just sat down for breakfast with Asha and Katy in the kitchen. Mariposa had served muffins and coffee, too frazzled to do anything more, and Rafael had been chopping up a plate of raw meat for Max while Tanya watched.

The couple had adamantly refused to talk about the snake incident of the night before. Tanya suspected the housekeeper and handyman were hiding their own secrets, though they seemed like they wanted to help.

No one had slept well.

And none of the Kensington family had come down for breakfast that morning.

The only silver lining was the ferry would be arriving at the island within the hour. Jack was due with the undertaker who was bringing Honoree's body to the family. What Tanya hadn't expected was the extra passengers who had come with them.

"Open the door, you hear me!" screamed the woman. "You killers!"

More banging.

Rafael stared at the front door, a numb expression on his face, like he was too afraid to touch it.

"I'll get it," said Tanya, nudging him aside.

If this was who she thought it was, things were going to get ugly fast.

As soon as Tanya turned the bolt, the door slammed open, hitting her face. An angry tornado barreled through the doorway. Tanya and Rafael jumped back in alarm.

"Where are they?" shouted Stacey, whirling around. "Where's everyone?"

They stared at her. Stacey's eyes seemed to be consumed by fire. The bruises on her neck and the blood-soaked bandages on her arms made her look like a survivor of a zombie attack.

Stacey whipped around to Rafael.

Tanya's eyes widened as she saw the small gun in her hands.

"Whoa," said Tanya. "What are you doing? Hand that to me."

Stacey didn't look at her, her barrel focused on the trembling Rafael.

"Show me where they are," she shouted. "I won't let them get away with this. They murdered Justin!"

"Hey," said Tanya, stepping closer to Stacey. "This isn't how we're going to find answers to his death."

"They killed him!" shrieked Stacey, her eyes still on Rafael. "That's what happened. They conspired to murder him!"

Rafael took a shaky step back, his hands high in the air.

"Where are they?" shouted Stacey. "They tried to kill George too!"

Tanya reached out and put a hand on Stacey's shoulder.

"How is George doing?"

Stacey jerked around.

She stared at Tanya like she was seeing her for the first time. Her eyes welled up with tears. The hand holding the gun slackened.

"He's still in intensive care." Stacey croaked the words, as if it hurt her to speak. "He's... he's... in so much pain...."

She swayed on her feet and reached over to Tanya to steady herself. Tanya caught her in her arms, and gently pried the weapon from her hand, but Stacey didn't seem to realize it.

"First Justin, then George...," sobbed Stacey. "They're trying to kill us."

Tears rolled down her cheeks.

Tanya pulled her in for a hug, while she quietly pocketed the gun in her cargo pants.

"It's okay, hun. It's going to be okay." She held on to Stacey.

The sound of gravel crunching made Tanya look up. She peered over Stacey's shoulder.

The hearse was meandering up the manor's driveway. Honoree's body was arriving.

A blue utility van was behind the hearse, and the woman at the wheel frowned as she saw Tanya by the open doorway.

Dr. Chen. What's she doing here?

Chapter Fifty

Crawling up the path, behind Dr. Chen's van, was a Black Rock squad car.

Jack.

"You look like you could do with a cup of tea," came a voice from down the hallway.

Tanya turned to see Asha and Katy walking toward them. She wondered if they had been watching the scene all along from the shadows.

Katy stepped up to Stacey.

"Come. We need to have a chat about Justin."

Stacey shook her head.

"I came here to talk to the people who killed him and almost tried to kill my husband."

Asha took her arm. Tanya let go of Stacey, and for the first time felt grateful for her friends' presence.

"We have questions for the family too," said Asha. "Why don't we sit down and figure out a plan together?"

Stacey's brow furrowed. "Who are you?"

"We're a private investigator team," said Asha, bringing out her business card.

Stacey took it with a frown.

"Justin called us a week ago," said Katy. "He invited us to Black Rock to help him."

Stacey's shoulders dropped. She stared at the two women, her face scrunching in sorrow. She stepped toward them and clutched their arms.

"You talked to Justin?" she whispered. "What did he say?"

Linking their arms with hers, Katy and Asha led her to the kitchen.

Rafael hadn't budged from his spot by the wall, frozen like a statue. It was like he was pretending he wasn't there, traumatized by having a gun pointed at him.

Tanya shifted her gaze back to the vehicles driving up to the manor. The ferry must have been full that day. It seemed like everyone was arriving on the island.

The hearse stopped at the top of the driveway, and Jack parked his cruiser several yards behind it. Dr.

Chen parked next to the hearse and waited inside, watching the undertakers take Honoree's coffin out and carry it toward the manor.

Jack was having an animated conversation on the phone in his car. The frantic manner in which he was gesturing told Tanya whatever he was discussing wasn't good news.

Dr. Chen stepped out of the driver's side of the van and marched toward the front doors.

Though the physician was no longer in her clinic, she still had her white lab coat on. It made her look more officious and commanding, despite her petite stature. Tanya watched her approach the house, noticing the dark look on her face.

The doctor usually had on a stoic expression that it was hard to say if she was happy or sad, but now, a sinking feeling came over Tanya's stomach.

Something's wrong.

Dr. Chen stomped up the front steps behind the undertakers who were struggling to bring the heavy coffin up the steps.

When they were safely inside the house, she marched over to Tanya with a glare.

Tanya braced herself.

"I don't care for Mr. Wood at all," snapped Dr. Chen when she approached her.

"You talked to Monica's husband?" said Tanya, relieved it wasn't worse news than that.

"I called him to inform him of his wife's death. That man has no manners at all. He swore at me."

"Well—"

"He told me he's happy she's dead."

Tanya sighed. "I would have considered him a primary suspect if he wasn't incarcerated at the moment."

"Did you know they were finalizing a divorce? Guess what their biggest bone of contention was?"

"Money," said Tanya.

The doctor shook her head.

"Peter."

Tanya raised a brow. "I didn't realize he was the prodigal son."

"Quite the opposite. They were trying to get rid of him. Each wanted the other to take him."

"Wow. When your own parents reject you, that's saying something."

"Sometimes, I meet the worst of humanity in this line of work," said Dr. Chen. "I can't say I like any of them."

You can say that again.

They stepped back as the interns passed them with Honoree's remains, following Rafael who seemed to have come alive again. He ushered them toward the living room.

As soon as the small group disappeared down the corridor, Dr. Chen leaned over and tapped Tanya's arm. Tanya looked down at the physician's dour face.

"You've found something."

The doctor nodded. "There's something you must know about Honoree Kensington's body."

Chapter Fifty-one

"She was *poisoned*?"

Tanya stared at Dr. Chen.

The physician had pulled her by the arm, out of the manor's front entrance, and down the steps. She didn't talk until they were huddled behind a pillar on the side of the building, where they had more privacy.

"I thought Honoree Kensington died from a self-inflicted gunshot wound," said Tanya.

"Yes, yes." Dr. Chen waved an impatient hand in her face. "But there were extenuating circumstances. Alice ran the toxicology tests yesterday, and we can say with some certainty she had been ingesting a poison. Her kidneys were in terrible shape."

"What kind of poison?"

"Ethylene Glycol."

Tanya's eyebrows shot up.

"Antifreeze?"

"Garden variety. Mild and sweet. Perfect for the everyday killer who wants to knock off a family member."

Tanya stared at her, her brain stirring.

Antifreeze? Where did I see a box full of that stuff?

Her head cleared.

In the garage. On the rack behind Stanley's super cars.

"A few drops into a glass of ice tea or a can of soda, and no one would know," the physician was saying. "It's been done before. All you need is a sweet drink."

"What about milk?" said Tanya. "A warm glass of milk every night?"

Dr. Chen nodded.

"It would have to happen over the course of a few weeks or months. The effect isn't immediate, especially if the poison was being fed by the spoonful. But I can assure you it would impact the victim's physical and mental health."

"So, someone was trying to kill her slowly."

"I said we discovered traces of Ethylene Glycol in her blood. That is all." Dr. Chen shot her a stern look. "If someone was trying to kill her, that's *your* job to figure out the who's and the why's."

"How else would she get antifreeze in her body?" said Tanya, spreading her hands. "She wouldn't drink it herself unless...."

She stopped as she realized what she had been about to say.

Dr. Chen nodded.

"If she hadn't turned that gun on herself, this would make your job a lot easier."

Tanya sighed.

"But now, anyone can argue she had tried to poison herself, and when the first attempt didn't work, she shot herself. An easy defense even a mediocre lawyer can make."

"One thing I'll say," said the doctor, "is that Honoree wasn't in her right mind for the last few months."

"Was the antifreeze messing with her?" Tanya narrowed her eyes. "You were her family physician, weren't you?"

"I used to visit her every three months for the past two years. I did regular checkups, blood tests, heart monitoring. The usual stuff. She was a healthy woman for her age. Unlike her husband, she never smoked. She ate healthy and stayed active."

Dr. Chen shook her head.

"But she stopped me from coming to the island four months ago."

"Any idea why?" said Tanya.

The doctor glanced up at the mansion, her eyes flitting from window to window.

It was quiet inside the manor, despite the horror and chaos that had reigned inside over the past few days. Tanya wondered if the family members were still closeted away in their rooms.

"Hard to say what's going on in this house." Dr. Chen sighed. "I wanted to keep Honoree's body in the morgue for longer. I could have carried out more tests, but the mayor knows the Kensington family, and they're pulling strings."

"Mayor Bailey is sticking his nose into this investigation?"

"He barged into my clinic and threatened to sue me." Dr. Chen narrowed her eyes. "I don't like it when stupid politicians meddle with my work, but I want to find out who's behind all this."

She leaned close and tapped Tanya's arm.

"I came to warn you," she whispered. "There's a killer in this house. Watch your back."

Chapter Fifty-two

Without another word, Dr. Chen turned around and marched back to the main entrance.

Tanya watched her stomp up the front steps and disappear inside the manor. She squeezed her eyes shut. Her headache was coming on again.

A murderer in the mansion? Tell me something I don't know, Doctor.

Someone hollered her name. Jack was striding up the driveway toward her.

"You look like you've been sleeping on your office floor," said Tanya, taking in his crumpled uniform, and the growing five o'clock shadow on his face.

Jack stopped in front of her and placed his hands on his belt, his eyes traveling to her creased pants and jacket.

"You're one to talk."

"Who were you arguing with on the phone?"

"Bureaucratic muck up," said Jack. "Just learned forensics hadn't got the murder notes. They got lost in a shuffle, but they finally found them in an evidence bag in a truck."

"You must be joking," said Tanya, shaking her head.

Jack waved a paper in the air.

"We got the warrant. I also negotiated a few more volun-tolds. They'll go over the cars with a fine-tooth comb as soon as they're on the ground." He sighed. "I'll owe every WSP employee a keg of beer before this case is over."

"The stack of cash in that Ferrari should give us some leads," said Tanya.

Jack rubbed his forehead. "Thing is... Stanley Kensington should have a record, but he doesn't."

Tanya frowned. "Either he has one or he doesn't. Which is it?"

"He racked up a series of charges while in university. Sexual assaults against co-eds."

"Don't tell me he got away with that," said Tanya.

"Each and every one was dropped." Jack sighed heavily. "That's what happens when you have a powerful father."

"I should have arrested him when he attacked me." Tanya grimaced. "That would have taught him a lesson. People like that should get double time."

"Took me a bit of digging to find the dropped charges," said Jack.

"The Kensingtons' legal team is skilled in the art of lobbying. They have a roster of paid unscrupulous scientists lobbying policymakers to convince them tobacco is good for our health. That's how the company survived this long. You can bet your bottom dollar they rallied around their grandson when he got in trouble."

"So, while Veronika is trying to keep up good family appearances here," said Tanya, "their high-powered attorneys in Seattle are working behind the scenes, pushing all the buttons they can?"

Jack nodded. "They've lobbied the Black Rock mayor to get on their side too."

"That's why he had the gall to bully Dr. Chen today," said Tanya.

"I didn't think I'd live to see the day anyone intimidated our doctor and got away with it."

"He won't," said Tanya, narrowing her eyes. "If I know her, she'll scheme up a nasty surprise for when he comes asking her for a vote or a favor."

"I hate politics." Jack shuddered.

"I've some good news though," he said, slightly brightening. "The lab found a print on the Cuban cigar boxes."

Tanya straightened up. "From a staff member?"

"Honoree Kensington. There's a possibility she was the only one who knew about the contraband. But figuring out how those boxes got here might expose more culprits in the house."

Tanya pointed at the paper in his hands. "Maybe Stanley will start talking once we nab him on illicit drug charges, and perhaps money laundering."

"He could say the cash was from a business deal and blame the drugs on someone else. We'll need conclusive watertight evidence or his high-priced lawyers will do everything to wiggle him out."

"Could we add attempted murder with a python to the list?" said Tanya, giving a pointed look at the chief. "If I have to guess who placed the snake in my room last night, I'd say it's our boy."

Jack looked at her with interest.

"Do you have any proof?"

"Circumstantial." Tanya sighed. "Everyone came running when they heard the commotion, except for him and Peter. Peter's in a wheelchair, unless he's faking the whole thing. That leaves Stan—"

"Hey, guys!"

Tanya and Jack spun around.

Asha and Katy were racing down the front steps with Max at their heels.

"Who are they?" Jack frowned. "Wait, I know the short one. Isn't she that PI friend of yours from New York? What's she doing here?"

Tanya put her arms up in defense. "Long story—"

Max darted over to the chief, tail wagging and his tongue lolling like he hadn't seen him in years. He licked Jack's hands before twirling around his legs.

"We found it!" cried Asha as she hurried over, panting.

Katy grabbed Tanya's arm.

"We found the will!"

Chapter Fifty-three

Jack's eyes bulged.

"You found Honoree Kensington's last will and testament?"

Asha gave him a startled look, like she hadn't realized the police chief was standing right next to their friend.

"Hey, you look different," said Katy, peering at him. "Oh. You're growing a beard."

"What are you two doing here?" said the chief.

"We're on a private job," replied Asha in a crisp voice.

Tanya let out an exasperated sigh. "Are you going to tell us about the will?"

"We went to the kitchen, so Mariposa could make Stacey a cup of tea to calm her down," said Asha. "Stacey started crying about Justin and how this family had betrayed him, when—"

"Mariposa told us about the new will," piped up Katy.

Jack and Tanya stared at them.

"The day before Honoree killed herself, she came down to the kitchen and asked Rafael and Mariposa to witness her new instructions," said Asha. "According to them, she sat down at the kitchen table and wrote it out on the yellow pad which Mariposa uses for her shopping lists."

"Did she tell you what's in the new document?" asked Tanya.

Her friends' faces fell.

"Honoree covered the top part and showed them only the signature portion," said Asha. "She signed the paper. Then, they signed beneath hers, as witnesses to her signature."

Jack shot them an impatient look.

"So, where's this new will?"

"Honoree ripped the sheet off the pad and took it with her upstairs," said Katy. "But we have some of it."

Asha whipped out her phone and opened her photo app. Tanya and Jack squinted at the image of a blank yellow pad.

Jack furrowed his brow. "I don't see anything."

"Honoree used Rafael's old ballpoint pen," said Asha. "You know the kind you have to push extra hard and gives you calluses? Well, we can make out a few words."

"That's Justin's name," said Katy, pointing at a faint mark embedded into the paper.

"Did you glean anything else?" said Tanya, trying in vain to make out the letters.

"Not full sentences, but we read a few words like *game, idiots.* It's like an angry letter to her family."

"See that line at the bottom?" said Asha. "We think it reads *I hate you all.* She pressed super hard on that one."

Jack plucked the phone out of her hands and brought it closer to his eyes.

"How do you even see anything?"

"Zoom on it," said Katy. "We think she may have left everything to Justin. Our hypothesis is that another family member found out and targeted him."

"But we don't have the document," said Jack, handing the phone back to Asha. "This is speculation at best."

"We're going to find it," said Asha, looking him in the eye.

Jack crossed his arms and was quiet for a few seconds. Asha narrowed her eyes and kept her gaze steady, like she was challenging him. Tanya felt the tension rise in the air.

"Who hired you?" said Jack, finally.

"Justin," said Asha. "He called us a week before he got killed."

Jack frowned. "How can you work for someone who is now deceased?"

"He retained our services. Paid fifteen thousand dollars for the job and we plan to finish it."

Jack looked at Tanya. "You knew about this?"

Tanya sighed.

He turned back to Asha and Katy. "How long have you two been on the island?"

"Just a day... or so," said Asha. "The point is, we'll find the will. That's a promise."

"Stanley's the perfect cover for us," said Katy. "He invited us to stay because he wants us to hunt down the document too. Peter also wants us to work for him, but our promise was to Justin."

"And you'll be the first to know when we find it," said Asha.

"I can't permit this." Jack shook his head. "Things never go well when civilians get involved. You need to get on the ferry and fly back home."

Asha crossed her arms. "You can arrest us, Chief, or you can let us do our job."

Jack looked at Tanya, exasperation etched on his face. Tanya knew he had no justification for restraining them, and partly sympathized with him. She shrugged.

"I'd give you a medal if you can get them to change their minds."

Asha's eyes flashed.

"A client pleaded with me to find a will that might be rightfully owed to him. I'll donate his entire retainer to an orphanage, but darned if I'll break my promise to a dead man." She paused. "*A murdered man.*"

She turned to Tanya. "You know I never opt out for convenience or for safety. I'm doing this for Justin. You would do the same in my position."

Tanya didn't reply, but knew that was true.

No one spoke for a minute.

Jack shot Asha a steely look.

"I'll be watching you like a hawk. If you give me one excuse to boot you out—"

"Sir!"

Max barked as the newcomer approached them.

Everyone turned around.

The junior officer, who had been stationed on the yacht, was stumbling their way. With his hair askew, creased shirt, and tie askance, he looked like he had spent the night in a ditch. A pang of guilt crossed Tanya for having thought he would have taken advantage of his luxurious accommodations.

"Your replacement's coming in the next ferry," called out Jack. "You can go home soon."

"That's not it, sir," said the officer as he headed over, a worried expression on his face. "Something super weird's going on at the cemetery."

"Weird?" said Tanya, her gut tightening. "Like what?"

The officer pushed his ball cap back and scratched his head.

"Someone tried to dig up one of the graves last night."

Chapter Fifty-four

"Good morning!"

The group turned toward the house.

Jack frowned.

Stanley Kensington was sauntering toward them in a stylish linen suit. His face was fresh, and his arms swung confidently. Unlike everyone else in the house, he looked like he'd had a good night's rest.

Tanya glared at him.

Did he sleep through the whole snake incident?

459

She wished she had put the guy behind bars the last time he had tried to attack her. Ignoring the chief and Tanya's dark looks, Stanley turned his bright smile on Asha and Katy.

"I was looking for you at breakfast. We have work to do today, ladies."

"We're ready," said Asha, her voice unusually chirpy. "But you promised us a ride this morning, didn't you?"

Tanya turned to her friend, her eyes narrowed.

Didn't I tell you to stay away from him?

To her chagrin, Katy put a hand on Stanley's arm.

"I've never been inside a Bentley," she said breathlessly. "I can't wait to go for a drive."

Stanley rubbed his palms together. "Whatever it takes to get you to find Grandmother's legacy."

Jack leaned toward him.

"Mr. Kensington, your grandmother's last will and testament is considered potential evidence in a murder investigation. We'll be taking it to custody as soon as anyone finds it."

"Man, you look nasty." Stanley grinned and slapped the police chief on the back. "You're working too hard, Chief. You and your gang here look like a bunch of refugees."

He gestured at Asha and Katy, and turned toward the garage.

"Come on, ladies. A short jaunt down the driveway and back, then you two need to get to work. I'm paying you big bucks for the job."

Tanya watched as her friends strolled with him toward the garage, their fake smiles intact. She pulled out her phone and opened her messaging app.

"Danger," she typed. *"Stanley has a history of assault."*

Asha stopped on her tracks and glanced at her phone. She looked up at Tanya and nodded.

Gritting her teeth, Tanya turned back to her phone.

"Go home. Now!"

The garage doors rolled up as Stanley clicked a fob on his key chain. With a grand gesture, he showed off the green Bentley parked in the corner while Katy giggled and clapped her hands in fake glee.

"Your ride awaits, ladies."

Standing a few steps behind them, Asha typed on her phone.

"Must distract him. Plan to find will today."

"No."

"Give us 4 hrs."

"No."

"We've stopped gangsters before."

Tanya could almost feel her blood pressure rise. She wrote back, trying hard not to punch through the screen.

"Next ferry in 1hr."

Asha's reply came back.

"3 hrs."

With a quick wave at Tanya, Asha twirled around and entered the garage to join Katy and Stanley. Tanya watched them walk toward the Bentley, the sense of alarm growing inside of her.

"I don't like this." Jack shook his head gravely. "They're playing with fire."

Chapter Fifty-five

"They used a small shovel," said Jack, peering at Charles Kensington's tombstone.

The stone was tilted, like someone had tried to pull it out.

Tanya examined the freshly dug up soil at the top of the grave. "What scared them off?"

"Our junior trooper didn't see a thing," muttered Jack. "His eyes were on the cove, watching for intruders coming into the island."

"What we need are cameras," said Tanya, glancing around the cemetery.

"This is private property. According to the family lawyers, we don't have the right to be here. The only reason we are, is because we have one judge who supports procedure versus politics."

The junior officer was now scouring the grounds in search of the shovel, or any tool that could have been used for the task. Realizing they were on a search mission, Max had trotted importantly after him, and was sniffing everything the officer glanced at or touched.

"If this digging expedition happened during the snake escapade," said Tanya, "the only two people missing from the second floor were Stanley and Peter."

"This could have happened after you all went to your rooms," said Jack. "That means, any of them could have come here to dig this up in the middle of the night. Except for Peter, that is."

"Are we giving him too much benefit of the doubt?"

"What do you mean by that?"

"Mariposa said he stopped walking at nine years old," said Tanya. "Veronika said he was ten, and Peter told me he got his wheelchair when he was eight."

A thoughtful expression came over Jack's face.

"It's hard to remember lies. Did they slip up?"

"Veronika dismissed the discrepancy saying it was a long time ago," said Tanya. "I kept my questions casual, but she made it clear she didn't like me probing into her family's past."

"Secrets, and more secrets," said Jack, shaking his head. He hunched down to examine the broken ground around the tombstone.

"Whoever came last night wasn't prepared. If it was a fit adult, I'd say they put a good ten minutes of effort before giving up."

"Or running off," said Tanya.

She kneeled at the foot of the mound to examine the grass around the desecrated grave. Something strange caught her eye.

She stared at the perfect rectangle patch in front of her. Charles's grave was easily demarcated from the cemetery lawn surrounding it.

"If they weren't fit or healthy," Jack was mumbling to himself at the other end, "they probably spent twenty or thirty minutes—"

"Jack?" called out Tanya. "There's something not right about this."

Jack looked at her, then lifted his head, focusing on something or someone behind her.

Tanya spun around.

"Dr. Chen?" said Jack.

The physician was treading toward them, a curious expression on her face. Tanya wished she would show her emotions more, because she never knew when the doctor had bad news or good.

Dr. Chen stopped at a distance from Charles Kensington's tombstone.

"Alice said you found more, er, clues at the cemetery."

"Nothing for you at the moment, Doctor," said Jack. "If we find anything, we'll notify you asap."

"Given the circumstances, and since I'm here anyway, I er, thought I'd... er, give you a hand."

Jack stared at her for a second. "I wouldn't dream on imposing on your time."

Dr. Chen didn't move. She kept her stance, a few feet away from Charles Kensington's grave, her hands by her sides.

Tanya straightened up.

Dr. Chen evoked terror among city employees, local deputies, even Chief Jack Bold. Tanya never imagined seeing this formidable force of energy behave this tentatively or speak this softly.

Something wasn't right.

"That's very good of you, Doctor," Jack was saying. "But I'm not sure you can help us with this."

"Try me."

"Someone tried to dig up this grave last night."

Dr. Chen raised a brow, but other than that, remained expressionless.

"Interesting."

Interesting?

Tanya turned to her. "How long ago did Charles Kensington die?"

"Almost three years ago," said the doctor.

"Did you know the family then?"

"My father was their personal physician for decades. Charles and Honoree wouldn't see anyone else, not even me, until Father retired, and I took over the practice."

"Your father knew them well?"

"He was here for every birth, death, funeral, wedding even. He retired three years ago, soon after Charles died, but they kept calling him whenever they had an emergency or a health issue. It was only about two years ago they let me come over."

Dr. Chen paused as if she was searching for the right words, unusual for her.

"I don't think they're happy with me. They used to treat Father like family, while I'm still a stranger."

"How did Charles Kensington die?" said Jack.

"Lung cancer. Tobacco was prominent in his business and his life. My father was quite unhappy about it and repeatedly advised him to stop, but Charles never did."

"Who signed his death certificate?" said Tanya.

"My father, of course."

"What about their granddaughter, Lisa? Didn't she commit suicide about six months after her grandfather died?"

Dr. Chen screwed her eyes and stared at Tanya.

"The poor girl hung herself, but you knew that."

Tanya nodded. "Yes, but what made her do it?"

Chapter Fifty-six

Dr. Chen looked away and blinked.

"I heard she had major mental health issues."

She sighed, still not making eye contact.

"It was pushed under the rug. They buried her at the edge of this plot, and the whole incident was never spoken of again."

Tanya observed her carefully.

She looks guilty.

"What are you not telling us, Doctor?"

Dr. Chen gave her a startled look, like she hadn't expected such a direct question.

"I know as much as you do, Detective."

"I'll tell you what I suspect," said Tanya, "and you can tell me what you think of my hypothesis."

The doctor didn't reply, but was watching her with interest.

"Everything happening on this island," said Tanya, "has something to do with Charles and Lisa Kensington's deaths."

A heaviness came over the physician's face, like the weight of the world had all of a sudden landed on her shoulders.

"I thought this was an inheritance game gone bad." Jack sighed. "Are you telling me I'm wrong?"

Tanya turned to him. "If this was merely a race to find a document that was signed only four days ago, why would someone try to dig up the grandfather's grave?"

Jack shrugged.

The physician remained silent.

"The puzzle goes much deeper," said Tanya.

"This is beginning to feel like a whack-a-mole game," said Jack, shaking his head. "We answer one question, when another one pops up, then another, and another."

"I er... I must..." Dr. Chen stopped and swallowed.

Tanya and Jack watched her, waiting.

"My father never...," stammered the doctor. "His generation didn't talk about such things as suicide. It was taboo. He was protective about his patients. He didn't share their medical files with me after I took over the practice. I'm starting from scratch."

Dr. Chen looked down at her feet.

"I came here because I felt an obligation to my father's patients."

Tanya stared at the physician who was usually blunt with her words. She had never seen her being sentimental until now.

The doctor turned to Tanya, her eyes narrowed.

"You said something when I walked over."

Tanya frowned as she tried to recall her words. Her head was swimming with so many theories, ideas, and potential suspects, she felt like she was getting lost in a sea of explanations.

"You said, *something's not right about this?*" said the doctor.

Tanya jerked up as she remembered. She pointed at the mound they were standing next to.

"Do you notice anything different between Charles' grave compared to the others?"

Dr. Chen and Jack craned their necks and scanned the cemetery. Tanya pointed at a small tombstone near the edge of the plot.

"That's Lisa Kensington's grave. They buried her six months after her grandfather. See how the color of the grass is the same all around?"

Jack's brow furrowed.

"Where are you going with this?"

Tanya got down on her knees and traced her finger along the border of Charles's grave. "This is an older grave. It shouldn't be so clearly demarcated like this."

Jack kneeled and scrutinized the grass. Dr. Chen took her glasses off, wiped them, and put them back on, before peering at the ground.

"The grass on top of this grave is lighter than the grass everywhere else," said Tanya. "That means someone had dug up or had tried to dig up this grave previously. The grass grew back, but it's younger."

Jack rubbed his eyes. "You've got to be kidding me."

"I'd say this happened maybe eight or ten months ago. Probably in the fall." Tanya ran her hands through the grass blades. "Then, last night, someone tried to dig it up again. What does that tell us?"

Jack's face cleared. "Something's down there, something someone wants to take."

"Or hide," said Tanya.

"The body," came Dr. Chen's voice.

Tanya and Jack turned to the doctor. She was staring at the grave, her eyes hard.

"What about the body?" said Jack, narrowing his eyes.

"We must exhume Charles Kensington," said the doctor, speaking fast. "He may have been poisoned as well. We must confirm his death wasn't suspicious."

"The death certificate said lung cancer," said Jack.

"That's not the point."

"But Doctor, it was your father who signed the death certificate."

"It doesn't matter!"

Tanya and Jack exchanged a surprised glance at her outburst.

"It is my recommendation as your medical officer." Dr. Chen glared at the chief, returning to her usual no-nonsense self. "Given what we discovered in Honoree Kensington's corpse, this is the judicious thing to do."

Jack pulled his phone out with a groan.

"The family will never allow it. I'll have to make a strong case to the judge, but that's not going to happen overnight. Plus, the mayor's on my back, goaded by the family lawyers."

"Maybe we don't need an order for an exhumation," said Tanya.

Jack looked at her, his eyes hopeful. "Anything to make things go faster." He paused. "As long as it's legal, Stone."

Tanya turned to the doctor. "Take me to your father."

Dr. Chen stiffened, then her face went pale.

"I was afraid you'd ask me that."

Chapter Fifty-seven

"How dare you ask me to violate my professional ethics?"

Senior Dr. Chen banged his cane on the floor.

He was ninety-one, slightly bent and with a thinning head of white hair, but he looked like he had enough willpower to whack them both with his walking stick.

"I'll never breach the privacy of my patients," he shouted. "You know better than to ask that!"

The younger Dr. Chen had retreated to the doorway the minute he had raised his voice. She now stood there, blinking uncertainly, like she had reverted to her nine-year-old self.

"We're investigating multiple murders, sir," said Tanya.

The older physician had been pointedly ignoring Tanya and Max all along. She wondered if he had gone deaf and blind in his old age as he didn't look at her.

"Dr. Chen," Tanya called out again. "There have been two homicides and there might be more. We need your help."

But he continued to shuffle toward his daughter, whipping his cane in the air.

Max, who had been sitting by her feet, growled. Tanya gestured for him to settle down. The old man wasn't a threat. Not a physical menace anyway, despite his attempts to weaponize his walking stick.

"Stay, bud," she said in a hushed tone.

With a soft groan, Max settled on the floor and placed his head between his paws. But his eyes remained on the senior Dr. Chen, like he was ready for him if he ever attacked the other humans.

The old man didn't seem to notice the massive canine in his study. His livid eyes were on his daughter, like laser beams that could burn her into a cinder.

"What were you thinking, coming here like this?"

He whipped his stick, inches from his daughter's face.

"How dare you try to pry information about the Kensington family from me?"

"Sir," called out Tanya, hoping she wouldn't have to arrest an elderly man for threatening their medical examiner. "Please put your cane down."

He didn't turn to her, his focus on his daughter.

"You have disappointed me. I expected more from you. What have you done with your life?"

Tanya swallowed the angry words that came to her throat.

She's the highly respected medical examiner for her county. What do you want? A freaking Nobel prize in medicine?

"Your mother and I tried so hard to have a son. We tried for years. We wanted a smart boy who'd make us proud." He scoffed. "And look what we got."

Tanya's ears burned.

How could you say something like that? She's your only child!

Tanya curled her hands into fists and suppressed the urge to punch his face.

If you were a few decades younger, I'd....

The junior Dr. Chen gestured to her with her hand as if to say, *it's okay.*

"Please, Father," she said in a meek voice. "We're only trying to help the family."

Tanya stared at her colleague wordlessly, unsure if she could believe her ears and eyes.

The younger Dr. Chen turned to her.

"Maybe we should go."

"He has information that will help us," said Tanya, shaking her head. "If we don't figure this out, more people are going to die."

The old man waved his cane at his daughter. "I don't want to have anything to do with you any more. Get out and don't come back."

His daughter's shoulders dropped. She turned to Tanya.

"I told you this wasn't a good idea."

Only half an hour ago, Tanya had pulled the doctor onto the ferry to Black Rock.

It had taken a lot of talking from Jack to convince the medical examiner to help them, but something told Tanya that the doctor was also yearning to learn more, despite the peculiar fear in her eyes.

Dr. Chen's childhood home wasn't as imposing as the Kensington Manor, but it was what Tanya would have expected for a wealthy family's personal physician.

The senior Dr. Chen had done well for himself.

Set in a quiet suburb of Black Rock, and overlooking the blue bay, the stately home had looked deceitfully welcome from the outside.

Tanya had followed her colleague inside the house and through the many hallways to the back, where large bay windows gave way to ocean views. They had discovered her father in his home library on the second floor, seated in a comfortable leather chesterfield in front of a roaring electric fireplace, though it was the middle of summer.

An empty cup of tea had sat by his side and a yellow tabby had curled up on his lap. He had been reading when they had walked in. From the threshold of the study, Tanya could make out the title of the book.

Endless Night.

A brooding Agatha Christie novel about ancient curses and evil deeds in paradise, a book Asha had recommended to her, a while back. *Fitting*, Tanya had thought, given what she had experienced over the past forty-eight hours.

Endless Night in paradise, indeed.

As soon as the older physician spotted his daughter by the doorway, he had thrown his book down, pushed the cat off his lap, and grabbed his cane with a huff.

That was when Tanya had understood Dr. Chen's apprehension about returning home. This father held no love for his daughter.

"We found poison in Honoree Kensington's body," said Tanya, trying one last time to get the older physician to talk. "Don't you want to know how it happened?"

The senior Dr. Chen put a hand behind his ear. "What did you say?"

He turned his glare on Tanya for the first time.

"What nonsense are you talking about?"

"Our medical examiner, your daughter here," said Tanya, giving him a pointed look, "did an autopsy on Mrs. Kensington. She suspects Honoree had been ingesting Ethylene Glycol in small doses over a long period."

"Ethylene Glycol?" The senior Dr. Chen snapped around to his daughter. "Is this true?"

Dr. Chen nodded but took another step back to safety, just in case.

Her father's eyes widened.

"Why didn't you tell me?"

Chapter Fifty-eight

"Sorry, Father," said Dr. Chen.

Tanya stared at the senior physician.

What did you think we were doing for the past ten minutes? While you were trying to behead us with your cane?

She saw where their medical examiner had got her bulldog personality. She was an echo of her father in public, but crumbled to a humbled wreck in his presence.

Tanya sighed.

Families. If they don't kill you....

"My fault, sir," she said. She gave her colleague a subtle wave to say, *I've got this.* "I forgot to bring it up at the beginning, but here we are now. So, can we chat?"

The old doctor stopped in the middle of the room and turned around toward Tanya. He stood quietly for several seconds, leaning on his cane, his eyes lowered to the rug, like he was contemplating whether to talk to her.

Gosh, I hope he doesn't have dementia, prayed Tanya.

She looked at her colleague, who shrugged like she didn't know what her father was up to either.

Suddenly, the senior doctor jerked his head up like he had just woken up.

"You!" He pointed his cane at his daughter. "Get me my tea."

Junior Dr. Chen backed out of the living room and disappeared down the hallway.

"You," he said, with a glare at Tanya. "Go help her."

Tanya didn't budge from her spot.

Ignoring her and Max, the old physician shuffled over to the antique table by the bay windows. It was a dark walnut secretary desk, with a pull-out writing ledge and a built-in bookshelf in the back.

He picked up a stack of faded yellow documents from the desk, opened a drawer, and stashed it inside. Tanya watched him try to close the full drawer with trembling hands. Whatever those papers were, he didn't want anyone to know they were here.

Once done, the senior Dr. Chen turned around, and gave a start as if he hadn't expected to see her.

"Who are you?"

Tanya sighed. "I'm with the Black Rock police precinct, sir. I came with your daughter to ask a few questions."

"Didn't I tell you to make me my tea?"

"Dr. Chen, we came here to talk about the Kensington family."

He narrowed his eyes and shook his head.

"So, I won't get rid of you easily, will I?"

Tanya suddenly realized his senile act was a way to avoid answering her questions. *He's sharper than he pretends to be.*

"The Kensington family seems to have had their fair share of tragedy, haven't they?" she said, taking a step toward him.

"Every family has tragedy at one point or the other. Everybody grapples with sorrow and heartbreak. It's the human condition."

He grimaced, like something gave him a foul taste in the mouth.

"Didn't they teach you basic psychology, Detective? Why are you asking me these stupid questions?"

Tanya didn't take the bait. He was goading her, trying to get her defenses up, looking for an excuse to throw them both out.

"Three years ago, the Kensington patriarch passed away from lung cancer," said Tanya, watching him as she spoke. "Then, about six months later, his granddaughter committed suicide. Is there a connection between those two deaths, and what's going on right now?"

"I thought you were the investigator."

"What do you know about Lisa Kensington's death?" said Tanya. "Were you there when she died?"

The doctor's face turned ashen. He stared at her without speaking.

"Did the family lock her up in her room, Doctor?" Tanya watched him carefully as she spoke. "Was it because she was ill? Or was it something else?"

He didn't reply. He didn't even look at her, so that she wondered if he had heard her.

"Dr. Chen? Please answer my questions."

The physician swayed on his feet and clutched his walking stick to stabilize himself. Tanya lunged over to catch him in case he fell, but he waved her away with an annoyed hiss.

"Stop treating me like an invalid. I'm in perfect health."

"What do you know about the adult Kensington children?" said Tanya, undeterred.

"They're adopted," he spat out. "That's all you need to know, okay?"

Tanya remained silent. She was no longer sure what would trigger him. *The less said, the better.*

"Except for David," he muttered under his breath.

Tanya's brows shot up. "Pardon?"

"You heard me," he said with an irritated hiss.

Tanya frowned. "So, who are David's parents, then?"

"You're useless." He glowered at her. "You call yourself a police detective?"

Chapter Fifty-nine

"Charles was a cruel man," said the senior Dr. Chen.

Tanya frowned. "Can you elaborate?"

The physician looked down at his cat, a grave expression on his face, the wrinkles on his forehead deeper than before. His pet was by the electric fireplace, sitting on the discarded Agatha Christie novel, one wary eye on Max.

"Charles always got what he wanted. No one could stand up to him." The doctor's voice was low, like he was talking to himself. "Even me, and he considered me his friend."

"About David," tried Tanya again. "Who are his parents?"

But the senior Dr. Chen had fallen silent again. He was staring at his cat, but the faraway look on his face told Tanya his mind was buzzing with memories, memories he may not want disturbed.

She remained in her spot, wondering if interrupting his reminiscences would make him clamp down, or if he would become more hostile.

A crash made her jump. Max got up and turned toward the open doorway.

"Sorry," called out the daughter's faint voice from somewhere in the bowels of the house.

Tanya wondered what the junior Dr. Chen was up to. Never in a million years had she imagined their medical examiner in a kitchen, let alone making tea. *Does she even know how?*

Max barked urgently.

Tanya spun around, just in time to see the senior physician sway on his feet. He staggered back, clutching air. She lunged forward and grabbed him by the arm.

This time, Dr. Chen didn't object to her holding on to him.

Tanya noticed a tear rolling down his cheek, but looked away, knowing he would be too proud to admit to his emotions. *A man from another era,* she thought as she helped him back into his recliner, and settled his cane against the coffee table.

The cat ambled over and jumped on his lap. He bent down and stroked its fur.

"Dr. Chen?" said Tanya. "Are you feeling okay?"

"Charles knew I was addicted to Temazepam," he said in a soft voice, his eyes on his pet.

Tanya's eyebrows shot up.

"Sleeping pills?"

"Started when I was an intern. We all took it. Helped us cope with long shifts and short sleep cycles." He looked up, his eyes reddened. "Do not judge me, Detective. Fifteen percent of physicians are addicts. I'm not an anomaly."

Tanya nodded.

"He used it against me," he continued, as if he didn't care for a response from her. "It was either be part of the plan or lose my medical license."

"What plan?"

"David," he said. "He's the one you need to follow."

"May I ask why?"

The doctor turned to the crackling fireplace and stared at it for a long time, like his mind was lost in the mists of time again. Tanya waited patiently, but he seemed to have fallen into a sullen trance.

When she realized he wouldn't answer, she stepped over to the empress chair next to the fireplace, moving slowly so as not to startle him.

Max trotted over and settled by her feet. The cat hissed, but pulled back as the doctor patted it on the head. It started purring, which seemed to relax him.

Tanya leaned toward the doctor and softened her voice.

"Do you know if the adoptions of the Kensington children have anything to do with the recent homicides?"

He lifted his weary eyes to her, but didn't reply.

She leaned in closer.

"Can you tell me anything about the family's history that could point to—"

"You need to send David to a psychiatrist," he snapped. "The man needs help. Why won't you listen to me?"

Tanya bit her lip, feeling like she was Alice in Wonderland attempting to glean words of wisdom from the elusive Cheshire Cat.

A rustle by the entrance made her turn. Junior Dr. Chen appeared at the doorway, holding a tray.

"Ah, my tea," said her father, his face clearing. "What took you so long?"

Chapter Sixty

J unior Dr. Chen stepped across the study, like she was approaching an angry lion.

Keeping her head bowed low, she poured the tea into her father's cup and set the pot down. Then, she took the empress chair next to Tanya's and shrank into it.

Tanya couldn't help but marvel at this sudden reversal of power.

She wondered what the doctor's childhood must have been like under her austere father. All she had known was that Dr. Chen's mother had died at childbirth and she was their only offspring.

Everyone has a story.

Tanya made a mental note to never judge the medical examiner again. She took a deep breath in before making another attempt to extract information from the father. A sage piece of advice from the cranky Ray Jackson sprang to mind.

To get information, give information.

While the senior doctor sipped his tea, his eyes on the fireplace, she told him everything that had happened so far. His daughter sat next to her, not uttering a word. Soon, the elderly man leaned back in his chair and closed his eyes, the empty teacup on his lap.

Did he even listen to me?

Tanya gritted her teeth and tried not to take it personally. She was about to ask her colleague what they should do, when the father's eyes flickered open.

"They're all mad!" Dr. Chen banged his cup on the coffee table, making his daughter jump.

Tanya sighed in relief.

He's awake.

Max raised his head, stared at the old man, then at Tanya as if to ask, *Should I do something?* She shook her head and turned back to the physician.

"How well do you know the Kensingtons' adult children and grandchildren?"

Dr. Chen sat up so quickly, his cat tumbled to the floor with an annoyed meow.

"You want to know who hates everyone enough to kill?"

"Tell me," said Tanya.

"Peter would murder his mother and sell his grandmother's liver if he could make a buck."

"He's an invalid."

"Behind that obese physique, he has a highly intelligent mind. Charles was a cunning fox, almost Machiavellian. Peter learned a lot from his grandfather."

He raised his hardened eyes at her.

"Peter will die soon."

Tanya gasped out loud.

"What do you mean by that?"

"Mark my words. He'll keel over in his wheelchair one of these days."

The doctor narrowed his eyes.

"He'll be six feet underground before we know it. He needs to be up and about, socializing, moving, and eating healthy. Not stuck in a wheelchair, scarfing down cheeseburgers and chips, all day and night."

"Is the wheelchair legit?" said Tanya, thankful he was finally talking, and praying he wouldn't stop now.

"His mother ordered it for him. He was getting so heavy, she thought his bones couldn't take the weight, but I fought back. He was a sick child, but could have recovered with proper care. She should have enrolled him in school activities, not stuck him at home. He only got worse and worse. Stupid woman. She never listened. He hated her for it."

"Do you think he killed his mother?"

The doctor grimaced. "All Peter has to do is sit on her, or anyone for that matter, and they'd suffocate within minutes."

"Monica was stabbed to death and drowned."

"He knows how to make others do what he wants. Except for his mother. He held no power over her."

"If he's behind this, he has to have an accomplice. Who would work with him?"

No answer.

"Is it his cousin, Stanley?" said Tanya. "We know he's a criminal. But is he a killer?"

Dr. Chen jerked his head up and glared at her.

"That donkey-brained imbecile? He wouldn't know how to follow instructions if you told him a thousand times and shoved them down his throat."

He shook his head.

"Stanley's a useless excuse for a human. Always running after girls and spending money. He's the biggest liar in the world, too. His grandfather did everything for him when he was alive. Without his family name, Stanley would be nothing today."

"Who do you think shot his brother, Justin? It can't be Peter, because whoever it was made a fast getaway. Was it Stanley?"

Senior Dr. Chen stared at the fire for a long time. When he looked up, his face was pinched and his shoulders were tight, like the past had finally caught up to him and was strangling him.

Tanya couldn't help but feel like he was shielding someone. It couldn't be Stanley, from the way he spoke of the man. But if not Stanley, who?

"Can you tell me why all this is happening?" she said, hoping one of her questions would resonate with him. "What is the purpose of killing Justin and Monica?"

The doctor remained tight-lipped.

"I can only assume they've all taken up Honoree's challenge to find her final testament first," she said. "Except, one of them is on a deadly endeavor. Who do you suspect, Doctor?"

The doctor's voice was hoarse when he replied.

"That's your job, Detective."

A heaviness settled in the air. His daughter shifted uncomfortably in her chair, but Tanya sat still, her eyes focused on the father.

"You know who the killer is, don't you, Dr. Chen?"

Silence.

Chapter Sixty-one

Tanya's phone vibrated the second she stepped on the island.

Dr. Chen had been quiet on their drive back to the Black Rock's pier. She had kept her face turned away from Tanya throughout the ferry ride, like she hadn't wanted to talk to her.

Tanya hadn't spoken either, because every word that had come to her throat had been fueled with frustration.

She hadn't told the medical examiner how much she had wanted to shake her father. He had refused to answer any further questions, pretending not to hear. In the end, he had picked up his cane and slammed it on the coffee table, almost breaking it.

"Get out!" he had hissed.

His daughter hadn't hesitated.

She had grabbed Tanya by the arm and propelled her out of the study with more force than Tanya thought the small woman possessed.

One thing was for sure. It was going to be a long time before Dr. Chen visited her father again, if ever.

Leaving the doctor to unload her van from the ferry, Tanya got out to walk to the Kensington Manor. Max darted down the quay, like he had an important job to attend to.

Tanya stood on the wharf, her immediate focus on her phone.

It was her public cell, the one she gave to everyone in town. The newest text message had come from Asha, except it contained only a single emoji of a blue gemstone.

Tanya frowned. Asha hated emojis with a passion and considered them to be juvenile. Katy was the emoji lover and sprinkled them all over her messages.

Tanya typed into the small box underneath it.

"Where are U? Are U OK?"

She hit send and waited for Asha's reply.

A thumbs up emoji appeared.

Tanya typed again, gritting her teeth.

"This isn't a game. What are you up to?"

She tapped her foot on the wooden dock as she waited for a reply. Dr. Chen revved her vehicle up the ramp and onto the island path, without a glance at her. In the distance, Max barked.

Tanya looked up to see Jack with two men in state trooper uniforms in front of the manor. Max rushed over to them, wagging his tail furiously. He started frisking around, licking Jack's face, while the chief tried not to get dog slobber all over him. The other two men bent down to pet her pup.

Tanya turned her focus back to the phone.

The gemstone emoji mocked her.

Did Asha type these by mistake? She couldn't have done it twice. Does someone have her phone? Has Stanley taken them....

Tanya shook her head.

Katy and Asha had trained in Krav Maga defense. Asha's fiancé, an expert on the martial art technique, had learned it directly from the Mossad, Israel's intelligence agency. If Stanley wanted to subdue her friends, he would have a bloody fight on his hands.

Tanya shook her head to clear the cobwebs.

Should have sent them packing to New York the second I saw them.

She clicked on Asha's number but her voice mail came on. After several more tries, Tanya left a stern message and slipped her phone into her pocket.

I have work to do.

She marched down the wharf and toward the driveway, where Jack was now conferring with his new team members. They had made space for

Max in their circle. He sat by their feet, tongue lolling, as if he understood every word they were saying.

About time, thought Tanya as she marched toward them. *We need reinforcement.*

Her first task was to interview Peter.

The senior Dr. Chen had been adamant about him. She didn't know how much she could rely on the haphazard chat she'd had with the retired physician, but something told her he knew who the culprit was. He had dropped clues, without saying the name outright.

She picked up her pace, her mind whirring over the strange conversation, trying to think of anything she had missed.

A loud screech made her look up. The front doors of the manor swung open. Veronika scrambled down the front steps, her arms flailing.

What's happened now?

Screaming at the top of her lungs, Veronika ran toward the officers on the driveway. Tanya sprinted over, her heart beating fast.

Is it Asha? Katy?

Max spotted her and barked as if to say, *hurry*. He cantered over to greet her, twirled around, and darted back to the group on the driveway.

Tanya ran up, as the two troopers leaped up the steps and disappeared inside the house. Max followed them, barking.

Veronika had latched onto Jack. She was sobbing on his shoulder, her face buried in his chest, holding on to him for dear life. Tanya glanced at Jack and raised a brow.

First, they chase us out, and now they want our help.

Jack patted Veronika awkwardly on her shoulder.

"It's okay, ma'am. We'll get to the bottom of this."

Veronika clutched his arms tighter.

"What's going on?" whispered Tanya to him.

"Our family's cursed," cried Veronika, through her sobs. "We're all going to die!"

"That isn't going to happen," said Jack with another awkward pat.

"Sir?"

One of the officers had rushed out again. He stood on the top of the steps, his face grim.

"We have a ten-forty-five-D."

Tanya jerked her head back. A sinking feeling came in her stomach.

Another dead body?

Veronika lifted her tear-stained face and pointed a trembling finger at Tanya.

"You! You did this!"

Tanya's stomach hurled.

Oh, my goodness, please don't let it be Asha and—

"Now, now, ma'am," said Jack, patting her back.

Veronika's face scrunched with anger, her venom aimed at Tanya.

"You killed him!" she screeched. "You killed Peter!"

Chapter Sixty-two

"Myocardial infarction."

Dr. Chen's voice was crisp and confident again.

She seemed to have recovered from her unpleasant reunion with her father. It was either that, or she was powering through her feelings to get the job done. Tanya suspected the latter.

"That's my preliminary diagnosis," said the doctor with a firm nod. "We'll find out more during the autopsy."

She was standing next to Peter's slumped body. He was in his wheelchair, with one hand glued to his laptop, like he wasn't ready to give that up, even at death.

A chill went through Tanya as she recalled the conversation with the doctor's father.

"Heart attack?"

It made sense, given Peter's health issues. Cardiovascular disease was the most common cause of natural death in the country, the highest at risk being those who were overweight like Peter had been. But she hadn't expected it to be this soon.

Tanya wasn't close enough to notice if there were cuts, bruises, or gunshot wounds on the corpse. From where she stood, it looked like Peter had merely keeled over and died, like how the older Dr. Chen said he would.

She turned to the medical examiner. "Your father's prediction was correct."

"I said preliminary," snapped Dr. Chen. She spun around to her interns. "Prepare to take the body to the morgue."

"What the heck's going on in this house?" said Jack in a low voice. "I asked Veronika to put security cameras up, but she refused."

"Privacy is more important than murder," said Tanya, shaking her head.

"I offered to set them up myself too," grumbled Jack.

He and Tanya had put on the booties and gloves Alice had handed to them earlier, but Dr. Chen's instructions had been clear.

Until they completed their examination, only the medical team was allowed near Peter's body, or inside the living room. The doctor had permitted Tanya and Jack to stand by the door, but had banished Max and the state troopers.

"Dr. Chen!" a young female voice called out.

Tanya looked up to see Alice, one of the interns, lift Peter's right hand off his laptop.

"There's something stuck in here."

"Get it out then," barked Dr. Chen.

Alice pried the piece of paper out and unfolded it with trembling hands, like she could feel her boss's dictatorial eyes on her.

"What does it say?" called out Jack.

Alice adjusted her glasses and read the note out loud.

"You liar. Cheat. Thief. Shame on you."

A hushed silence fell in the room.

Jack and Tanya exchanged a curious glance.

"Another death note," muttered Jack, shaking his head.

"Justin, Monica, and now Peter," said Tanya in a low voice. "They were all targeted."

"Peter!"

Everyone turned around to see the source of the anguished scream.

Veronika and Hazel were standing by the doorway. Their faces were flushed, and Hazel was crying.

"What's happening to us?" said Veronika, her eyes red with stress. "Someone's taking us out, one by one."

"You and your stupid questions!" shouted Hazel, pointing at Tanya. "You did this to him! You killed him!"

"She wasn't even on the island for the past hour," said Jack, turning to them.

"She stressed him out with her heavy-handed interrogation. I saw her. Like a Gestapo. She gave him a heart attack!"

Jack didn't move but his face turned stern.

"I think we need to look for the culprit closer to the family."

The two Kensington women fell silent, but Tanya caught a shadow behind them. Mariposa was on her tiptoes, peering over her employers' shoulders.

Tanya's brain whirred. Their list of suspects were diminishing, but the disparate pieces of evidence were growing.

The illegal cigars. The vanished jewelry. The ransacked rooms. The housekeeper and handyman's access to the entire mansion. Their nervous glances and anxious faces.

Tanya had put the Kensington family members on top of her list of potential culprits. Now that her most recent suspect had died, she wondered if she should push the staff members up.

She slipped in between Veronika and Hazel, ignoring Hazel's furious glare. Mariposa stepped back as she saw her approach, almost bumping into Rafael. He had been hovering behind her, not visible to anyone from the living room.

Tanya ushered the couple to a quiet corner.

"Did you see what happened?"

Mariposa and Rafael shook their heads.

"Did anyone come inside the house in the last couple of hours?"

"It was pretty quiet," said Mariposa. "I was in the kitchen and Rafael was in the garden. Peter was in the living room on his laptop, but I didn't talk to him...."

She blinked rapidly.

"I was too scared."

"Why do you say that?" said Tanya.

"He didn't like anyone interrupting him when he was working. I usually ask the others if they want tea, coffee, or invite them for lunch, but I always left Peter alone. He got really mad if we talked to him when he was on his computer."

"Who found the body?" said Tanya.

Mariposa gestured in Hazel's direction.

"I heard her scream," she said, lowering her voice. "I came running. That's when I saw Peter. I thought he was sleeping, but she said he... was dead."

"Where was Stanley during all this?"

"He... he was with the two detective ladies...," said Rafael, stumbling over his words. His face was pale, and he seemed more jittery than usual. "I saw them drive the Bentley down the driveway."

"Did you see them after that?"

Mariposa and Rafael exchanged a nervous glance and shook their heads. Tanya stared at them, unable to shake the feeling they weren't telling the whole truth. But they didn't set off alarm bells in her gut.

Who are they protecting?

Tanya took out her phone and checked her message app. There were no new texts other than those unusual emojis.

She typed another note to her friends. *"New development @ house. Come ASAP."* She hit send.

When she looked up, Rafael and Mariposa were walking toward the kitchen, holding hands. Veronika and Hazel had their backs to her, both focused on Peter. Inside the living room, the interns were getting ready to take his body away in a stretcher.

Tanya felt a finger jab her lower back.

"He thinks I'm a murderer," came a low voice behind her.

She spun around to see who was speaking.

Chapter Sixty-three

D r. Chen's eyes were dark, like something deeply troubled her.

"*You* killed Peter?" gasped Tanya.

Just when she thought she was pulling all the disparate lines of thread together, something unexpected blew up in her face.

"Not Peter," snapped the doctor.

Tanya's mind raced. *Is our medical examiner part of this inheritance game?*

"Who are you accused of killing?"

Dr. Chen grabbed her arm and pulled her away from the crowd.

"My mother," she whispered hoarsely, her dark brown eyes penetrating into Tanya's. "My father believes I killed her."

Tanya half wondered if everyone who entered the Kensington manor started to lose their minds.

"What do you mean?"

"He loved her," said Dr. Chen. "He would've given her his life if it had come to that."

Tanya nodded politely.

Shouldn't we be focused on Peter's sudden and much more recent death?

"He said I disappointed him, that he wished he had a son who would have made him proud," said the doctor, holding on to Tanya's arm in a vice grip. "But that's all an excuse."

Tanya blinked. "An excuse for what?"

"My mother died the day I was born, and he never lets me forget it." Dr. Chen shook her arm, like she was frustrated Tanya didn't understand.

"That's completely unreasonable," said Tanya. "He can't—"

"Oh, yes, he can blame me. And he does."

"He's a physician. He should know better."

"When it comes to her, he reacts from his emotions. She wasn't just his high school sweetheart, she was his childhood sweetheart. He thought they would be together, forever."

Dr. Chen closed her eyes and sighed.

"Until I came along."

"I'm sorry Dr. Chen, but—"

"He's the only living family member I have," continued Dr. Chen. "You don't know what it's like to be alone in this world."

Tanya bit her lip.

You're wrong, Doctor. If there's one thing I know, it's that. We're more alike than different.

Dr. Chen's eyes turned hard again.

"The Kensingtons confided in my father. He was part of this family. He never spoke openly in front of me, because I was the outsider. The black sheep."

Tanya knew what that felt like. It had been the story of her own life until she had met Asha and Katy a long time ago.

"Charles Kensington and my father were good friends," Dr. Chen was saying. "They played golf and visited each other for whiskey and cigars every weekend."

Tanya raised a brow.

"Cuban cigars?"

"You must speak with him alone," hissed the doctor. "He'll open up to you."

She pushed Tanya's arm away and marched back into the living room to join her team.

Tanya stared at her back, wondering how much their medical examiner was involved in this multiple murder case.

Chapter Sixty-four

"Out of the way!"

Dr. Chen beat everyone back.

Her interns brought out the stretcher, where Peter now lay covered in a white cloth.

The team followed Alice, who was rolling his empty wheelchair in front. The chief was still inside the living room, waiting for Dr. Chen's crew to depart, so he could cordon off the scene.

Tanya stared at the laptop on the wheelchair as Alice rolled it by her.

"Jack?" she called out. "We need to look at his laptop."

"They'll take it to the precinct," he said. "I've already notified the forensics lab."

Tanya stepped back to give way to the stretcher. She was itching to pick up the laptop, but she couldn't disobey the police chief's request in front of the family and the medical team.

She was debating whether to snatch it from the wheelchair, when a miserable wail rose from Hazel.

Veronika pulled Hazel in and held her. The two women huddled by the living room's doorway, as they watched one more member of their family being taken to the morgue.

"Chief?"

A trooper was running down the hallway with Max dashing alongside him. Spotting Tanya, Max rushed up to her to greet her with whines, his tail whirling back and forth.

The officer signaled to Jack.

"Backhoe got offloaded from the ferry, sir."

Veronika spun around, her face flushing.

"Backhoe? What are you doing now?"

Jack pulled an envelope from his jacket pocket. "We have the exhumation order, ma'am. I've already shared this with you and your attorneys. I'm—"

"You're going to dig up Charles? How dare you?"

"We've taken meticulous effort to adhere to procedure. Please understand—"

"Look what your procedures did!" Hazel pointed at the living room where Peter's body had sat, only moments ago.

Jack sighed. "Ladies, I must—"

"We don't care about your procedures!" screeched Hazel.

"I'm calling our lawyers!" cried Veronika. "How many have to die before you show us some sympathy, for goodness' sake!"

"That's what we're trying to—"

"Get out!" screamed Veronika. "All of you! Get out of my house!"

The interns hurried toward the main entrance with the stretcher. Jack followed the trooper and the doctor out, one hand on his radio.

Tanya watched everyone scurry off, her heart ticking faster. She slipped into the shadows, knowing she would be next to be kicked out.

She scrambled up to the second floor and into her room. She ushered Max in and closed the door, hoping no one saw her slip upstairs.

While it sounded like all hell had broken loose on the first floor, the second floor was quiet.

She checked her phone but there were no further texts from Asha or Katy.

Where are they?

The only missed call she had received in the past hour had been from Ray Jackson, but he hadn't left a message. She blew a raspberry, knowing she could only hold her real bosses off for so long.

How am I going to find Justin's killer, get Asha and Katy off the island, and start on my real mission without losing my mind?

She felt her chest constrict, and the migraine coming on again.

Tanya inhaled deeply and let it out, as the feelings of overwhelm flooded through her. She pocketed her mobile, kneeled, and pulled Max in for a hug.

"I have an important job for you, bud," she whispered in his ear. "We need to find Aunt Asha and Aunt Katy. Do you understand?"

Max licked her face and whined as if to say yes. Tanya patted him on the head and got up.

"Come on, bud."

Using the secret entrance inside the closet, she slipped into her friends' guest room next door.

She grabbed the first things she found on their beds, a scarf belonging to Katy and a ball cap Asha wore. She called Max over and held the cap and scarf to his nose.

"Go, search, bud."

Max sniffed the items and trotted around the room twice. Tanya watched him as he investigated the corner by the closet, then retraced his steps toward the door. He turned his head around and whined as if to ask her to open it.

Tanya put her hand on the handle, when her eyes fell on the note on the floor. Someone had slipped it under the door. She swooped down to pick it up, and her eyes widened at the terse message.

She pocketed it and pushed the door open an inch.

The second-floor hallway was empty. Whoever had pushed that note under Asha and Katy's door was nowhere to be seen. After all the commotion only moments ago, the house had fallen into an eerie silence.

It must have been lying there for a while, thought Tanya. Max would have heard if someone had slipped it through while they were in the room.

She opened the door fully and gestured for Max to follow her. He nudged her aside and darted out. She raced along the corridor and down the stairway after him, her heart racing.

Max headed straight to the front entrance. Tanya could hear inaudible murmurs from somewhere in the house, but the hallways were empty.

She leaped down the front steps after her pup and ran across the driveway, her mind swirling.

So Asha and Katy aren't inside the house. They're not junior college co-eds. They're smart women who will fight back. Plus, it's two against one.

She gritted her teeth.

When I find them, I'll....

Tanya stopped to scan the driveway and the woods behind the manor. She thought she spotted a silhouette by the darkened doorway of the mansion.

Mariposa? Or is that Rafael?

The interns were now loading Peter's body onto the clinic's van, with the doctor supervising the operation from the side.

Max was sniffing around the garage's side door. After another apprehensive glance back at the house, Tanya hurried toward the garage. She opened the side door and stepped inside, with Max at her heels.

She didn't have to use her flashlight as natural daylight was streaming through the high windows. She walked toward the back, while Max investigated all the corners.

The Bentley was parked in its spot, and so were all the other vehicles. She threaded around the garage, checking the undercarriages of each vehicle and behind the shelves. Other than the cars, the garage was empty.

Worst-case scenarios swirled through her head like a tornado.

Maybe they're stuffed in the trunks!

A bark came from outside, like Max was calling to her.

She was about to follow him out of the garage, when her phone pinged. She pulled it out of her pocket and checked the screen.

Asha.

Her heart thudded as she squinted at the message.

"Found a clue. Getting warm."

Chapter Sixty-five

Tanya clenched her jaws.

What clue? Tell me!

A bark made her look up. Max was trotting along the pathway that led to the cemetery.

Tanya closed the garage door and hurried to catch up with him.

It had been a relief to hear from her friend, but her gut signaled danger. Neither Asha nor Katy had taken her calls or replied to the messages she'd typed furiously in the garage.

If anything happens to them, I will strangle you, Stanley, till you choke to a slow and painful death.

Max stopped in his tracks and glanced back, as if to confirm she was following him.

"Keep going, bud." Tanya scurried after him. "Let's find them."

Max placed his snout back on the trail and trotted in the direction of the cove. Tanya could hear the backhoe in operation, occasionally drowning out the hollers of the police crew.

Max moved rapidly, heading toward the crowd gathered at the cemetery.

Tanya frowned.

Is he following the right scent?

The backhoe was hauling dirt out of Charles's burial plot, while two workers shoveled the excess soil away from the tomb.

The backhoe's claw lowered deep into the hole and scraped at something.

The police officers, who had been standing around watching the operation, leaped into action. Shouts and commands filled the air as the backhoe reversed and people jumped into the pit with shovels.

Max weaved in and out of the crew and around the machinery, stopping to sniff something on the ground before taking off in another direction altogether.

Tanya frowned.

"He's going in circles," she said out loud.

Jack walked over. "What's he looking for?"

"Asha and Katy."

"They're not here."

Tanya surveyed the wharf and the cove. The doctor's van was parked by the ramp next to the wharf, waiting to be transported back to their clinic in town. Max hadn't gone near the dock, so they couldn't have been there.

"He's caught a scent, but something's muddled him. He doesn't usually run around like this." Tanya swallowed hard. "They're with Stanley. I don't like this."

"I've already started a search for him and your PI pals. Two troopers are scouring the house and the woods."

"They're not there."

"How can you be certain?"

"Max wouldn't bring me to the lake if they're in the manor or the woods."

Jack pulled his phone out of his pocket and dialed.

"Ferry left fifteen minutes ago. Maybe they took my advice and got on the boat."

He spoke into his phone. From the gravelly barks on the other end, Tanya deduced he was talking to the ferry captain.

"Wishful thinking," said Jack, hanging up. "No passengers, other than the crew."

Max was circling the lake now, his nose down, a confused expression on his face. He kept looking up, then swiveling his head back and forth, like something was stopping him from following the scent.

"My guys will find them," said Jack. "There's only one way out, and this isn't a vast area for a search operation."

Tanya turned to him. "But there are many places to hide on this island." She scanned the grounds. "They're here. I know it."

"Sir!"

They turned to the crowd standing around the open grave.

An officer was hurrying over, gesturing urgently.

"You won't believe this, sir."

Chapter Sixty-six

Jack marched over to the open grave.

He stopped and stared, then whipped around to his team.

"Get Dr. Chen!"

Tanya stepped up to him and peered over the edge of the pit.

Two of the officers were still down there. They had loosened the soil around the metal coffin and had jacked it open.

Tanya's eyes bulged at the sight. "How did this happen?"

The metal casket looked almost new inside, like no dead body had touched this box. Or, if there had been one, it had only been inside for a small period of time.

Jack shook his head. "This is nuts."

"There's nothing here, sir," called out one man from the pit, in case they'd missed the glaring absence of a corpse or even a skeleton.

"It's been three years, right?" said the second man, looking up at the chief.

"But wouldn't there be like pieces of his skull and bones and stuff like that?" said another officer.

"Looks like he disappeared into the Twilight Zone," said an older officer, standing across from Tanya and Jack. "Poof. Just like that."

"What's going on here?" came a cranky female voice from behind them.

Jack spun around, relief crossing his face.

"Can you give us your expert opinion, Doctor?"

Silence fell among the crew as Dr. Chen pushed her glasses up her nose and stepped up to the edge.

"Would there be any circumstance where a body inside a metal coffin could have disappeared?" said Jack. "Like insects devouring the remains, for example? Something that could eat through bone?"

Dr. Chen shook her head, her eyes still on the open pit.

"They buried an empty coffin."

Chapter Sixty-seven

"We checked the whole house, sir," said a trooper.

"Didn't see any decomposing bodies lying around, anywhere," said another officer. "We would have smelled it for sure."

"What about the woods?" said Tanya.

The crew shook their heads.

"We may have to dig up the entire estate," said Jack in an exasperated voice.

"We'll need the dive team too, sir," said the older officer. "They could have dumped the body at sea."

"If that happened three years ago, then, it's gone for good." Jack shook his head. "But why would anyone do this?"

Tanya spun around to the doctor.

"Do you think your father knew about this?"

Dr. Chen stared at the open coffin quietly, like she didn't want to contemplate the question.

Jack let out a heavy sigh.

"The family's not cooperating. They're either lying or withholding information. And your father's pushing back. Is there anyone who knows the history of this island we can talk to?"

"Good luck with that," mumbled the doctor.

"Your father was leery about Lisa," said Tanya. "He turned pale when I asked if she'd been locked up. There's something about that granddaughter no one is telling us." She paused. "Do you think her coffin's empty too?"

Dr. Chen blinked and a pink flush crept up her neck.

Jack turned to Tanya.

"What do you know about the granddaughter?"

"She committed suicide by hanging in her bedroom when she was eighteen," said Tanya. "It happened about six months after her grandfather died."

"Any idea what led to that incident?" said Jack.

"The family kept quiet about it, and everyone I talk to tells me she had mental health issues."

Tanya paused. "But I feel like no one is telling me the complete story."

"Welcome to my life," muttered Dr. Chen.

As if a sudden thought struck her, the doctor lifted her chin, and a determined expression came over her face. She pointed at the other end of the cemetery.

"Chief? That one, over there."

Jack squinted in the direction she was pointing. "What is it?"

"The only way to answer your questions," said Dr. Chen, whirling around to face him, "is to dig her up."

"You know I can't do that."

Dr. Chen glared at him through her thick glasses, which made her eyes look larger than normal.

"Do you want to solve this case or not? You might even stop the next murder."

Tanya's heart skipped a beat.

"This is a bureaucratic nightmare," muttered Jack, pulling out his phone. "Their lawyers are going to jump down my throat, and the judge will be mad as—"

"Don't waste time. Just do it," said the doctor.

"That's a serious breach you're asking of me."

"These tombs are hiding family secrets," said Tanya. "Honoree's suicide has triggered the past. Why else would anyone try to dig up Charles's grave last night?"

"A request for a second exhumation is going to take more time." Jack wiped the sweat off his brow and turned around to make the call, mumbling to himself. "I'm using up all the favors I've got."

Tanya stepped closer to the doctor and lowered her voice.

"Can *you* give the order?"

Dr. Chen shook her head. "I have no jurisdiction."

Tanya snapped around and marched toward the backhoe parked in the middle of the cemetery.

The driver was still seated inside the cab, his head bowed over his phone, ignoring the turmoil around him. The sound of laughter came from his cell, followed by an advertisement for a popular fast-food restaurant.

YouTube videos, thought Tanya as she stepped up to the cab. She knocked on the glass door.

"Hello, there."

The man jerked his head up and quickly pocketed his phone.

"Just taking a quick break, ma'am."

Tanya pointed at Lisa's grave in the far corner.

"Your next job got lined up. Start digging."

"Yes, ma'am."

He started the backhoe and rolled toward the edge of the cemetery. Tanya followed the machine with Max in tow. The driver let the backhoe's claw crash on top of the tomb. He pushed a lever to scrape the claw back and bring it down again.

The ground broke.

"Hey!" came a holler from behind Tanya. "Stone!"

She turned to see Jack stomp over.

"You can't do that," he yelled.

"I just did."

Chapter Sixty-eight

Tanya stood by Lisa's grave, supervising the backhoe driver.

A call from the judge had taken Jack to the side, where he was having an animated conversation. Tanya felt bad for him, but the grave was half dug up now.

Once the backhoe had loosened the top soil and hauled most of it out, two junior officers started shoveling the remaining dirt. They worked quickly as the rest of the crew watched from above.

"It's another metal coffin," called out one trooper, banging his shovel on the partially buried casket. "Bet you this one's empty too."

"Show some respect," snapped Dr. Chen.

Her own team had left the van parked on the ramp by the wharf and had come over to see what the excitement was about. They stood huddled by their boss, eyes wide as they watched the scene unfold.

Soon, the crew hauled the intact coffin to the surface. It took three officers to pull it open.

"This one's occupied," one called out, as they laid the lid to the side.

Tanya put her hand over her nose as a rotting smell wafted over to her. Dr. Chen bent over the open casket, while her interns stared in fascination.

Lisa's youthful body had partially decomposed, having been protected inside the metal container. But it was what was between her legs that made Tanya nauseous.

A shiver went through her. She looked away quickly and took a breath in before turning back to the casket.

This is the stuff of horror movies.

An officer who had been standing next to her stumbled toward a tombstone, gagging. Another staggered back and grabbed a tree to steady himself, then doubled over and vomited.

Jack came over, his brow furrowed. He stopped by Tanya and stared at the coffin in shock.

"What in heaven's name...?"

"How did the baby die?" said Tanya, finally making her tongue work again.

Dr. Chen turned to her team. "Take a good look, kids. It's not every day you'll see something like this."

"Poor girl," said a junior officer. "This is horrible."

"She used to work at the adoption agency in town," said an older officer with a sigh. "She was the nicest one out of the Kensingtons, but a little strange."

"My husband told me the story," piped up another trooper. "She disappeared from her job and wasn't seen in town for about six months before she hung herself. The rumor was she had gone a little cuckoo..." She tapped her head.

The doctor grimaced, but didn't reprimand her.

"Maybe she wasn't sick," said Tanya, speaking slowly. "Maybe the family was trying to hide her pregnancy."

"Her death certificate said she died from self-inflicted strangulation, but I would like to confirm it." Dr. Chen turned to Jack. "I'm not waiting for approval this time. The autopsy will get done today."

Alice, the intern, snapped a series of photos. "Did they bury the baby and the mother together, Dr. Chen?"

"That's not common practice these days, is it?" asked another intern, getting closer to take more pictures.

Dr. Chen shook her head. "That's not what happened here."

"No?" Tanya frowned. "Then, what?"

Everyone, including the backhoe driver, fell silent and turned to the physician, like they wanted to know as well.

"This is what we call," said Dr. Chen, speaking slowly like she was choosing her words carefully, "a postmortem fetal expulsion."

"What on earth does that mean?" said Jack.

"A coffin birth is the common vernacular."

Shocked gasps rippled through the crowd.

"Coffin birth?"

"Never heard of such a thing in my life."

"Geez. This is wild."

The medical team grimaced but stepped closer, keen to observe this rare phenomenon.

A few brave souls from the police crew stared, like they couldn't take their eyes off the macabre sight.

Others averted their faces but didn't move, like they were eager to hear the story but unable to look.

Dr. Chen shook her head at the sad little shriveled-up body lying in between Lisa Kensington's thighs.

"I thought as much. Lisa was pregnant when they buried her."

"Are you saying Lisa gave birth inside the coffin?" said Tanya, feeling sick with the thought. "While she was six feet underground?"

More shocked gasps rippled through the crowd.

"My good Lord. Does that mean she was buried alive?" said Jack.

"Gas buildup inside the dead mother over a few days is what pushed the unborn fetus out."

Dr. Chen pushed her spectacles up her nose.

"Lisa Kensington couldn't have been alive at that point. She was most certainly dead."

Chapter Sixty-nine

"We found Stanley!"

The junior officer, who had been first stationed on the island, was dashing over to the cemetery.

Tanya's heart skipped a beat. She whirled around.

"What about my friends? Are they safe? Where was he?"

"He was down in the cellar," said the officer, stopping next to them, panting from the run.

Tanya's throat went dry.

"In the cellar?" said Jack.

"He was alone, sir. We didn't see anyone else inside the house, other than the two older ladies, that weird dude with the snake, and the staff members."

"What was Stanley doing in the basement?" said Jack.

The officer made a face.

"He was sleeping in a dark corner, when we found him."

"What did he have to say for himself?"

"Nothing much, sir. I, er, don't think we'll be able to question him for a while."

"Why's that?"

"Drunk as a skunk. There were two opened bottles of whiskey by him. He had a half-empty tumbler in his hands. I'd say he had been drinking for a while. He's completely smashed."

A flag went up in the back of Tanya's head.

"How many glasses did you see near him?"

The officer scratched his head.

"Other than the one he was holding? There were a couple more on the wine barrel next to him. They were full, so we thought he poured himself a few, in his state."

The officer looked at her, suddenly realizing what she was saying.

"You mean, the ladies we're looking for might have been drinking with him?"

"Did you see any lipstick marks on the other glasses?" said Tanya.

He stared at her for a second, then tapped his shoulder radio.

"Blake, you still at the scene?"

"What do you need?" came a crisp female voice through the air.

Tanya and Jack listened in as the two officers chattered with each other.

"No lipstick marks," said the officer on the other end. "We're gathering prints. Almost done dusting."

"Where's Stanley Kensington now?" said Jack, leaning into the radio. "Still in the cellar?"

Both officers fell silent, but Tanya could hear snores in the background, through the speaker.

"Dead to the world, sir," came the second officer's voice over the airwaves. "He's going to have a hell of a hangover."

"Don't stop looking for the two civilians," barked Tanya. "They're on the island, somewhere."

She was in no position to command the crew helping the chief, but Jack nodded.

"Double-check the area surrounding the cove," he said. "We have a dog here who has picked up their scent in the vicinity."

He turned to Tanya.

"I expect to get a warrant for Stanley's arrest shortly. It's been like pulling teeth, but I think we can at least put him away for assault charges. Drug charges might get added on later."

Tanya let out a sigh of relief.

Using the plastic glove she kept in her pocket, she dug out the mysterious note she had discovered in Asha and Katy's room.

"Found this in my friends' room."

Jack took it from her and read it out loud.

"Please help. I've been framed. I didn't do it."

"If I know my friends, they're on this trail."

Chapter Seventy

J ack flipped the note over.

"No signature?"

"They were careful," said Tanya. "All caps makes it harder to identify the handwriting."

Jack furrowed his brow. "The current residents are still suspects. So, what do they mean by being framed?"

"My question exactly," said Tanya. "Who's framing who?"

"There was no sign of your friends in the house?"

"Max is thorough."

Jack scanned the cove. "If they're here, we should have found them. We even checked the yacht."

"I asked Stanley about the two ladies," said the junior officer. "He said they were right there, next to him in the cellar. He was so drunk, he couldn't see straight."

Tanya pulled out her phone and clicked on Asha's most recent message. She turned the screen toward Jack and the officer.

Jack read Asha's last text out loud.

"Found a clue. Getting warm."

"I'd bet anything they convinced Stanley to go into the cellar after their Bentley ride, and they piled him with drinks," said Tanya. "That way he wouldn't bother them as they searched for the final will."

Jack waved the note in the air.

"What about this? Is this some game your friends are playing with us too?"

"They wouldn't do anything like this," said Tanya. "This isn't their handwriting. It could have been from someone trying to lure them, pretending they need their help."

"Send this to the lab for a print check," said Jack, handing the note to the officer.

The trooper took the letter and placed it inside a plastic bag and zipped it. "It will be on the next ferry out, sir," he said, before stepping away.

The sound of an engine came from the inlet.

"Speaking of the devil," muttered Jack.

The ferry barge was chugging into the lake.

"Make way!"

Tanya and Jack turned to see Dr. Chen's team carrying Lisa Kensington's coffin, heading toward their van by the wharf.

The doctor was urging them to hurry, and Tanya knew why. The family wasn't here to protest, but if they ever found out, every one of them would be in major trouble.

"I will lose my job over this, Doctor," said Jack.

Dr. Chen turned to him, her eyes steely.

"I'm going to find out what happened to Lisa. And I'm going to find out who fathered that fetus."

Tanya frowned. "How? It's not like you have the entire town's DNA."

"I have my means—"

Dr. Chen stopped as a loud ring came from somewhere. Everyone started checking their pockets. Dr. Chen pulled her mobile out and clicked on the screen.

"It's mine."

Her eyebrows shot up.

"Why on earth would he...?" she mumbled.

She brought the cell to her ear slowly, like she was dreading to take the call. Tanya watched the doctor's face change from her normal fierce bulldog expression to that of an obedient poodle.

I have a hunch who that is.

No one spoke as Dr. Chen listened quietly. Without saying a word to the caller, the doctor turned to Tanya.

"My father wants to see you now."

"I need to find my—"

"He has information on the killer. He'll only speak with you. Alone."

Chapter Seventy-one

Tanya jumped onto the ferry.

Dr. Chen's van had been stabilized on the barge, with wooden blocks placed against its tires. The medical team had elected to stay inside their vehicle for the boat ride to town.

Given the blustery ocean wind, Tanya couldn't blame them.

Max pranced around the deck, his tongue lolling. He leaped onto his favorite seat by the cockpit.

The captain flashed a rare grin at the pup and placed his peaked cap on the dog's head.

Tanya sat on a wet bench in the back and took her phone out to text Asha and Katy one more time.

"Search party looking for you."

She grabbed the railing as the engine revved and the barge rocked with the waves. The boat was reversing, pushing away from the wharf. Soon, the smell of burning diesel prickled her nose.

Max barked again, this time at Jack. He was on the wharf, watching the ferry depart.

He had promised to not let up the search for Tanya's friends. It was the condition on which she had agreed to return to the senior doctor's house. With a heavy sigh, she made a silent vow to never allow Asha and Katy near any crime scene.

A ping from her phone made her look down.

"Call them off," read the message. *"We're busy."*

An angry rush of blood came to Tanya's face. She texted back. *"Tell me where you are!"*

"So they can kick us out? No thx. Pls stop looking."

"Like hell I will. You SHOULDN'T be on the island. PERIOD."

The boat ride back to Black Rock was excruciatingly long, as Tanya kept checking her phone. But Asha and Katy were now giving her the cold shoulder.

Tanya gritted her teeth.

When we find you, I swear I'm going to.... I don't know what I'm going to do, but you'll never push your way into one of my cases like this, ever again—

The grating sound of the boat's engine jerked her back to reality. They were docking at the loading ramp of the Black Rock pier.

Tanya twisted her neck to see the charred remains of Stacey and George's pub. Her stomach fell, realizing they could have lost their lives to that fire.

A quarter of the quay had been cordoned off with yellow tape, and two security guards stood by the perimeter, keeping the tourists and curious onlookers at bay.

Tanya messaged Stacey, promising to visit her and George as soon as she got a few minutes to breathe.

When am I going to get a break?

This case had become convoluted, and she was sure this trip was only going to create more tangles she would have to unravel.

My combat days were straightforward. I always knew the bad guys from the good guys. Not like this.

She jumped out of the boat and onto the docking ramp. She and Max strode down the pier and onto the adjacent city parking lot where she had left her Jeep.

A loud rumble made her spin around. Dr. Chen's van was trundling out of the barge and onto the ramp. It pulled onto Marine Drive before heading in the direction of the clinic.

"Let's go, bud," she called Max, as she unlocked her Jeep.

Max hopped into the backseat and thumped his tail, ready for a ride. Tanya scratched his neck before closing the door. *Glad one of us is having fun*, she thought, as she jumped in and put on her seat belt.

Using the GPS on her phone, she retraced her path back to senior Dr. Chen's residence, her focus on the road, but her mind buzzing a million miles a second.

"Where's Charles Kensington's body? What do you think, bud?"

Max barked at her in reply.

Tanya wound around the town's only roundabout, and headed toward the wealthy suburbs of Black Rock.

"Did someone kill him and throw him into the ocean to hide the evidence? Or, is he still alive? Is he living somewhere, pretending to be dead?"

In the back, Max thumped his tail and whined.

Tanya gasped, as she realized another possibility. She turned around to her pup.

"Is *Charles Kensington* our killer?"

Chapter Seventy-two

"Justin, Monica, and Peter are dead."

Tanya thought out loud.

"Lisa died more than two years ago, and Hazel's husband was killed in a car crash a decade ago. Craig Wood is in prison, which leaves..."

She started counting with one hand.

"David, who seems incapable of taking care of himself. Honoree's sixty-something-year old sister, Veronika, and Honoree's remaining daughter, Hazel."

Tanya shook her head to clear the migraine fog that was threatening to cloud her mind.

"Stanley stinks to high heaven, but something tells me he's a red herring. What did the older Dr. Chen call him? Donkey-brained imbecile...."

She stopped. There were two more people who were as important as the family members.

"Mariposa and Rafael might be loyal to the family for helping with their immigration papers, but they might be hiding secrets of their own—"

A car honked behind her and passed her on the left. The driver flipped her a finger. Tanya hadn't realized she had slowed down. She pressed the accelerator to speed up and kept her eyes on the road.

She was almost at her destination, but the thought of trying to have another conversation with the senior Dr. Chen made her shoulders tight and her back stiffen.

Tanya had interrogated terrorists and gangsters, but they hadn't required kid gloves. The force of a palm slammed against the table, or a strategic threat of being imprisoned with their rivals usually loosened their tongues.

Dr. Chen had his wits and intelligence about him, but he was a frail old man. And not one to speak freely.

Why does he want to talk to me alone? Is it something he doesn't want his daughter to know?

The tension in Tanya's back rose, like a foreboding of things to come.

"Here we are," she said, as she turned to the expansive brick driveway of the Chens' residence.

A tight knot had formed in her stomach now. It was like her entire body was signaling to her.

"Something's wrong," she whispered to herself as she parked next to the Lexus sedan on the driveway.

She turned off the engine. In the back seat, Max leaped to his feet and rumbled around, waiting impatiently for her to open the door for him.

Tanya would have expected an empty home if the doctor's car hadn't been parked in front. She sat still for a second, glancing at the house, taking stock.

Her eyes flittered across the first-floor windows, and up to the second floor. The curtains had been drawn back in the room at the end.

Tanya froze.

Through the large bay windows, she spotted the body.

It was hanging from the ceiling.

Chapter Seventy-three

Tanya leaped out of the Jeep, her heart pounding.

She gripped the phone to her ear.

"I'm going in!"

"Wait for the crew," snapped Jack.

"Max is with me."

Hearing his name, Max pawed at the door. As soon as Tanya yanked the back door open, he jumped out and darted toward the house, barking. It was like he knew something was going on inside.

Tanya raced after him.

"If he's still alive," she shouted into the phone, "I've got to get him down."

"If that's murder dressed as suicide, the killer could still be inside," said Jack. "Wait for backup, Stone!"

Tanya hung up.

She squinted at the second-floor window, where the figure swung from the ceiling. A bitter taste came to her mouth. In her heart, she knew this wouldn't be a rescue operation, but a recovery one.

It would be a miracle if he's still alive.

She scanned the front yard and the tree-lined boulevard. It was the quiet kind of neighborhood with massive homes and enormous front lawns, built so far apart that no one could look inside the house across the street.

She pulled out her Glock and stepped toward the front entrance of Dr. Chen's house. She treaded up the steps, her senses heightened, while Max whirled in circles by the door.

She was about to scrutinize the entrance to find out if it had been broken into, when Max nudged it with his nose. The door inched open silently.

Tanya's heart jumped to her mouth.

It's unlocked.

She examined the doorframe and the metal plate behind the bolt. They were intact. If someone had come in, they either had a key to the house, or the senior Dr. Chen had let them in.

Is the killer waiting for me?

Max cocked his head, as if to ask if he could go in.

"Heel, bud," she whispered.

With her weapon aimed forward, she pushed the door open with her boot. She scanned the foyer and the open living space.

It was empty.

She stepped across the threshold and listened, her eyes darting back and forth to check for signs of an intruder or a struggle. But an uncanny silence had settled in the house.

At her feet, Max whined softly, as if to say, *Let's go.* She shushed him and threaded through the foyer and into the living room.

Max trotted confidently across the room and halted by the coffee table. He sniffed at something on the center rug. Tanya's intuition told her that her dog's instincts were correct, despite the front door being open. This wasn't a break-in.

She now knew why Dr. Chen had summoned her alone. He didn't want his daughter to be the first to find him.

But she also knew from combat experience that making hasty assumptions was the fastest way to get killed. After glancing around to confirm there was no one else in the room, Tanya stepped over to Max.

"What did you find, bud?"

She stared at the torn piece of paper by his paws. It was a page from a book—a book she had seen recently.

She kneeled to scrutinize it. There was a message written over the printed words in large, shaky black letters, like someone had used a felt pen. She took a sharp breath in as she read the note.

Thank you for coming, Detective.

She pulled a glove out of her pocket and slipped it on before picking up the paper. She glanced at the printed header on top of the page.

Endless Night.

It was the Agatha Christie book Dr. Chen had been reading in the study when she had visited earlier that day. Her eyes skimmed the first words of the first chapter.

"In my end is my beginning...."

Tanya's heart beat faster.

Why did he do this?

An urgent bark from Max made her look up. He was by the stairway now, wagging his tail, urging her to come over. As Tanya straightened up, he lowered his nose and sniffed at something on the bottom step.

Another note?

Before picking it up, she surveyed the darkened landing on the second floor, but that eerie silence persisted. All she could hear was the thudding of her own heart.

She scooped up the second ripped page and read the message scribbled over the printed words.

Everything you're looking for is in this house.

Chapter Seventy-four

A chill went down Tanya's spine.

Dr. Chen left these for me.

Clutching the ripped pages in one hand, and her sidearm in the other, Tanya followed her dog up the stairs to the second floor.

So far, Max hadn't demonstrated any nervousness. He wasn't in attack mode, but search mode. Her weapon might have been overkill, but she wasn't about to put it away.

She whirled her head back and forth as she weaved through the second floor, taking in the long hallway and the bedrooms on both sides. The doors were open, some halfway, some all the way. Everything looked just as it had during her last visit to this house.

Tanya stepped up to the nearest room and peeked inside.

Empty.

She swept each room, working fast, as she approached the end of the hallway. With every step she took toward the study, her heart felt heavier, and her stomach tighter.

Max was already at the entrance of the library, staring at something inside. He whirled around, barked at her, and twirled back, but didn't enter the room. It was as if Max knew the space would be restricted.

Tanya stepped up to the threshold of Dr. Chen's study, and her throat went dry.

Hanging from the rafters was the senior Dr. Chen. His pallid skin and bulging eyes told her he was no longer alive.

Goose bumps sprang up on her arms.

Max barked at the cat who was asleep on the leather recliner by the fireplace. It jumped awake, its hair standing up. It hissed at Max and glared, as if challenging him to come close, but Max's focus had shifted.

He was looking up at Tanya. He thumped his tail as if to say, *We've found what we've been summoned here for.*

Tanya holstered her weapon and stepped inside the room.

She walked toward the body, a sadness overcoming her. She placed her hand on the doctor's right wrist, then the left, praying to feel something, anything, but she knew it was over.

A lump came to her throat as she felt his soft hands. His skin was still warm to the touch.

She had been expecting to find him dead since she had spotted his silhouette through the window. Still, seeing him this way so soon after speaking to him broke her heart.

She stepped away from the body with a heavy sigh, wondering how she would break this news to his daughter. Though they'd had a troubled relationship, the younger Dr. Chen cared for her father, her only living relative.

Well, no longer.

Something crinkled under her boots as she stepped back.

She glanced down to see a third page from the Agatha Christie book under her foot. She bent down and picked it up, her eyes scanning the shaky handwriting over the printed words.

I have done terrible things. Please forgive me.

Chapter Seventy-five

"We need a medical examiner," said Tanya.

"I'll call the sheriff in the county over," said Jack, in a heavy voice. "But I have to tell Dr. Chen first."

"Leave that to me," said Tanya, as she paced the second-floor hallway. "I found him. I have to break the news to her, personally. I'll go to the clinic as soon as the team gets here."

"She's gone incommunicado. You can't reach her for another couple of hours."

Tanya frowned. "Is she okay?"

"She's carrying out the autopsy on Lisa Kensington. No one's allowed to bother her when she's in surgery. That's her usual policy." Jack sighed. "But nothing about this is usual, anymore."

"Why do you say that?"

"She's hell-bent on finding out her father's involvement—"

Tanya heard someone holler urgently to the chief in the background.

"Wait, Jack," said Tanya. "Before you go, have you found Asha and Katy?"

"We're looking." His voice was strained. "I don't know if this will make you feel better, but I've asked the divers to go back in the lake."

Tanya's heart leaped.

"But they can't have...," she stammered. "They can't be...."

"It's a precaution," said Jack. "I still think they're hiding, trying to outwit us, to find the will." He paused. "The guys are here, anyway. No harm in asking them to have another look."

Jack hung up saying he had to take a call from a local sheriff who had promised to send help. Tanya slipped her phone into her pocket and walked back into the library, her mind in a daze.

She stepped into the study and stared at Dr. Chen's body. If she had felt low before, she felt worse now. There was one thing she hadn't told the chief.

The doctor was no longer hanging from the ceiling.

She had taken several photographs of the corpse and the room, including the pages she had discovered along the way up. Then, she had brought the body down and laid him on the floor, before placing a blanket over him.

She knew she would get reamed out for this, if not from the new medical examiner, then Jack himself.

It would be another black mark on her personal files, but leaving the doctor dangling like a mindless puppet from the ceiling felt so wrong. It was undignified for a physician and the father of her colleague.

This family had had enough tragedies of their own, and the last thing Tanya had wanted was for the junior Dr. Chen to see her father like this.

But that was before she had learned Dr. Chen was locked away in her surgery.

Too late now.

Tanya sighed, trying to straighten out her muddled thoughts.

Working on this case felt like getting whiplashed every few hours. Another turn. Another twist. She wasn't sure what the final puzzle looked like, or if she even had the right pieces to put it together.

But there was one thing she knew for certain.

She had seen enough during her stints in combat and law enforcement around the world, to know the senior physician had committed suicide.

This wasn't murder.

Tanya stepped toward the writing desk by the window and put on her gloves again.

He hid a stack of papers here.

Senior Dr. Chen had been a meticulous man. The books on the back shelves had been arranged according to height. A green banker's lamp and a Montblanc pen were the only items on the desk, placed methodically.

Tanya's hand swooped toward the top drawer.

She tugged it open a few inches before something caught it. She got on her knees and peered inside to see a large rectangular object was preventing it from opening.

She wiggled the drawer up and down until it got unstuck, and pulled it open all the way. That was when she realized what had blocked the drawer.

It was a diary.

Chapter Seventy-six

Tanya reached into the drawer and pulled the journal out.

With her heart ticking fast, she flipped through the book, her fingers tracing the shaky words of each journal entry.

The handwriting on the torn Agatha Christie book pages, and that in the diary were the same. They confirmed Dr. Chen wrote those suicide notes.

She read the entries for the past three months, one by one.

He hadn't journaled daily. His musings covered his cat's health, books he had been reading, and complaints about the incompetent medical staff at the local hospital where he went for regular dialysis.

So, he had kidney problems.

She placed the journal back in the drawer and reached in to look for the stack of papers he had shoved inside that morning. Something told her those documents held the answers she was seeking.

She rummaged through the desk several times before giving up. With a resigned sigh, she closed the drawers and stepped away.

What did he do with them?

She walked over to the fireplace, which was still roaring. She switched the main button off, killing the LED simulated flames. It sprang to life quickly when she switched it back on. Electricity fueled it, not wood or coal. This fire wouldn't burn a thing.

She switched the machine off and turned around, her brow knotted.

Where did he put those papers?

Her eyes fell on the bookshelf attached to the secretary desk. She scanned the tomes.

The top shelf contained medical journals on human ailments of all types, but the remaining shelves held murder mystery classics. She gazed at them, feeling them tug at her. It was like they were calling out to her, desperate to tell her what had happened in this room.

A hardback with a dark purple cover looked familiar. Without thinking, she plucked it out and turned it in her hands.

Endless Night by Agatha Christie.

Chapter Seventy-seven

Did he leave more messages in this book?

Using her gloved fingers, Tanya opened *Endless Night.*

The first page of the first chapter had been ripped out. It had contained the first message she'd found downstairs.

She flipped through the rest of the book, noting the two other torn pages Dr. Chen had scattered like breadcrumbs for her to follow. But there were no secret memos in here.

She was about to slam the book shut when she noticed the last page was missing.

It was the page with the printer's address and bar code, not listed in the table of contents. She felt the scraggy edge on the inside spine. He had ripped it out.

Tanya whirled around, her heart thudding.

There's a fourth message.

Dropping the book on the desk, she scoured the room. She pulled out every drawer and peeked behind every piece of furniture. She even lifted the sleepy cat on the recliner to see if it was sitting on it.

Finding nothing, she stepped toward Dr. Chen's body on the floor. A pang of guilt crossed her as she sank to her knees and removed the blanket.

She slipped her hands into his shirt and pants' pockets and felt for the contents.

Nothing here.

With a sigh, she sat back on her haunches.

Where is it?

A sinking feeling came over her, as she realized she would have to search the entire house. A mansion with ten bedrooms, a half a dozen bathrooms, two living rooms, a kitchen....

Better start looking, then.

Tanya got to her feet.

She stepped toward the desk, picked up *Endless Night* again and shook it with vigor, to make sure the torn page wasn't stuck between the others.

Nope.

Disappointed, she reached up to place the book in its place, when she spotted the light brown cardboard-like object in the back.

What's that?

She pulled all the books from the shelf to see what was sticking out from behind the tomes.

A manila folder.

Her heart thumped louder.

The doctor had stashed it behind the Agatha Christie book for a reason. She took down the folder, placed it on the desk, and pulled up a chair for herself.

Max was guarding the front door. Soon, the medical examiner from the next county, and the rest of the crew would be swarming this house, bagging evidence to hand it all to the state forensics lab.

She didn't have much time.

Chapter Seventy-eight

T anya opened the folder.

Found them!

The faded yellow documents stared back at her. It was the same stack of papers the doctor had shoved into the desk drawer that morning.

Tanya wondered why he would play such games, then kill himself.

But something pulled at her attention.

The first document that lay face up on the folder was frayed around the edges. It mocked her, telling her, *You didn't expect to find me in here, did you?*

It was a birth certificate.

"David Kensington," said Tanya out loud.

She traced her finger along the rows of printed boxes, with the handwritten notes scribbled inside. The ink was faded and hard to read, so she pulled her phone out and snapped a picture.

She scrolled to the two boxes that named his parents and zoomed in to make sure she had read them correctly. Then, she plopped back in her chair, her mind whirling.

Old Dr. Chen had been telling the truth.

David hadn't been adopted. But his parents weren't Honoree and Charles, the matriarch and patriarch of the Kensington family.

"Veronika," whispered Tanya to herself, reeling from the discovery. "David is Veronika and Charles's son."

Did Veronika and Charles have an affair? Or did this happen before Charles married her sister, Honoree?

She scoured the certificate again, feeling like this was the crux of the matter.

"Didn't the doctor say David was the thread I needed to follow?" she said out loud.

But what does this have to do with the multiple murders in that family?

She glanced around the room.

Those suicide notes.

She sprung out of her chair and advanced toward the coffee table, where she had stacked the torn pages of the Agatha Christie book for the crew to bag and take away. She picked the one she had found under the doctor's dangling feet and squinted to read the words.

I have done terrible things. Please forgive me.

Tanya frowned.

If Veronika and Charles had a secret baby, even an illegitimate one without Honoree's knowledge, it wasn't the doctor's fault.

So, what were these terrible things the doctor did?

Tanya walked back to the folder on the desk.

What else is in here?

She removed the birth certificate from the stack and laid it on the table. Then, she rifled through the next set of documents held together by a rusty paper clip.

They were adoption papers.

She bent down to read the faint handwriting and made out the names of Monica and Hazel. There wasn't anything amiss in them, but something niggled in the back of her head.

She sat up as she realized they had been fostered at the same agency Lisa Kensington had worked for, prior to her death.

Coincidence?

Tanya pulled out her phone and searched for child fostering and adoption organizations in the area. She found only one.

The Black Rock Adoption Agency.

Did Lisa discover the truth about David's parents and was killed for it?

Tanya stacked the adoption papers on top of David's birth certificate, when a sudden notion struck her.

Though Monica and Hazel were adopted, they could still legally claim part of the inheritance, unless Honoree's last decree said otherwise.

She gazed at the remaining documents that lay innocently in front of her.

Her heart raced.

Is Honoree's will right here, under my nose?

Chapter Seventy-nine

The desire to find the elusive will pulsed through Tanya like an electric current.

Her fingers and eyes moved through the remaining documents at lightning speed.

This will was the specter that had been haunting Kensington Island for the past three days. It would finally shine a light on this riddle.

But all Tanya found were various property deeds, inconsequential medical records, and ancient stock and bond certificates.

She went through the folder a second time, trying to ignore the worry gnawing at her. The state troopers and the new medical examiner would be here soon, and that would be the end of her solo detective work.

It has to be here.

One more time.

Tanya flipped through the files so fast, the manila folder tilted over the edge of the desk. She grabbed the folder before it spilled its contents to the floor, but just as she did, something fluttered down and landed on her foot.

She thrust her chair back and stared at the beige envelope that lay on top of her boot. She picked it up, opened it, and pulled out the folded piece of paper.

It was a handwritten letter addressed to senior Dr. Chen. The ink was faded but readable. Her eyes went to the date on the top right-hand corner.

This was sent forty years ago.

Tanya scanned to the bottom and almost stopped breathing to see the sender's signature.

Her pulse quickened as she read the letter.

"Dear Dr. Chen,

Thank you for taking care of the boy.

You have been a tremendous assistance to the family. I knew I could entrust you with this arduous task.

Honoree has finally agreed to adopt three children. We need to ensure David is one of them. I trust I will have your assistance here, as well?

Rest assured, they will become part of the family, and David will have two siblings and a mother and a father, like he is supposed to. We will give him a good life.

I understand Veronika is unhappy with my sudden breakup, but this is best for everyone. She is still in tremendous pain from what she thinks was a stillbirth, but she trusts you and believes everything you have told her.

David must never know who his mother is. And Veronika must never know that David lived. She can be hysterical, as women tend to be, but she has been particularly trying of late.

What I am doing is best for the good of the entire family. I appreciate you respecting the confidentiality of our arrangement.

Please know that I am forever in your debt. You have been a good friend to me.

Thank you for following my wishes.

With eternal gratitude,

Charles."

Chapter Eighty

Tanya read the letter several times, her mind swirling.

The penultimate line stood out.

"Thank you for following my wishes."

She glanced at the physician's body on the floor. She recalled how Dr. Chen had described the billionaire.

"Charles was a cruel man. He always got what he wanted."

Charles Kensington had been the mastermind who had coerced his physician into doing a deed he hadn't wanted to, one that had racked the doctor with guilt for the rest of his life.

Senior Dr. Chen had lied to a mother about her newborn, snatched him away, kept him under wraps, then orchestrated his adoption back to the father and his new wife. The victim's sister.

Charles had been a diabolical megalomaniac who thought he could play with lives. Tanya now understood why the senior physician had been tormented.

It sounded like something out of a bad daytime soap, and she wondered if things could get any more twisted. There were still several unanswered questions.

Was Veronika still in the dark about David?

Did David know who his actual mother was?

Did Lisa, Justin, Monica, and Peter discover the truth? Was that why they were killed?

Charles's reputation would have been destroyed by this family secret coming to light, but he had died three years ago.

Or, so everyone said.

Honoree would have been horrified to find out she had been tricked. Discovering her adopted son had resulted from a torrid affair between her husband and her sister could explain her violent suicide.

Then, there was Veronika.

The image of the blonde middle-aged woman wearing the sunflower necklace swam through Tanya's mind. A woman who remarkably looked like her own dead mother. Tanya instinctively reached up and touched the pendant on her neck.

Was Veronika behind all this?

An impatient whine from Max jerked Tanya from her spinning thoughts. She turned around to see him sitting at the open doorway. He thumped his tail when she looked.

"I'll be done soon, bud," she said, giving him a sympathetic smile.

Max loved to chase suspects, search for missing persons, guard children, and take rides in anything that moved. Hanging around with nothing to do wasn't his forte.

"Give me a few more minutes, would you, bud?"

Max let out a loud doggy sigh and settled down by the doorway.

Tanya wondered what had delayed the medical examiner and the rest of the team. They should have been here half an hour ago.

Working quickly, she put the documents back in the manila folder in the order she had found them. She placed David's birth certificate on top of the stack and snapped the folder shut.

She stared at the small pocket in the back.

So, that's where Charles' letter had fallen out of.

She reached inside. Her heart ticked faster as she felt loose papers. She pried one out and dropped to her chair.

It was the last torn page from the Agatha Christie book. She unfolded it with shaking hands, wondering what more Dr. Chen had wanted to tell her.

Please don't share this with my daughter. Promise me, Detective.

Tanya stared at the shaky words, written by a man who was about to take his last few breaths.

Dr. Chen's errant behavior now made sense. If the doctor had had any conscience, the part he played in this perverse arrangement had probably eaten into him.

Tanya felt tears well up in her eyes.

He had cared for his daughter. He hadn't wanted her to know what a monster he had been.

Chapter Eighty-one

Max jumped to his feet and barked.

The sound of a vehicle screeching to a stop came from below.

Max raced down the stairs, barking.

Tanya leaped to her feet and peeked out of the window. A Black Rock police cruiser had turned into the driveway and had parked next to her Jeep. The driver's side door opened and a uniformed officer got out.

Jack.

Tanya froze.

In the library, only a few feet behind her, lay the senior Dr. Chen's body.

"Hey there, big boy." She heard the chief address her pup. "What a good guard dog you are. I should promote you to a deputy."

Max sneezed and whined a happy whine.

"Where's your mom gone off to now?" said Jack.

Soon, heavy footsteps pounded the stairs.

"Stone?"

Tanya turned from the window and braced herself.

Jack appeared at the threshold, with her dog at his heels. Max sat down by the door and cocked his head. The chief stared at the body on the floor, then looked at Tanya, a quizzical expression on his face.

"I was expecting Dr. Chen," said Tanya, steeling herself.

"She's in surgery. I told you."

"I thought the news would get around to her and she'd come running over."

"So, you unilaterally took down the body?" Jack stared at her. "You realize we're in the middle of a multiple homicide investigation in which the deceased could have played a role?"

"I didn't know Dr. Chen was occupied." Tanya kept her gaze steady and her voice firm. "I didn't want her to find her father like that."

"You're supposed to make my job easier, not harder."

"This was a suicide," said Tanya.

"Not your call. The ME from the next county is on his way. He's going to be asking questions."

"And I'll give him my answers. I'm ready for the consequences."

"This is grounds for termination."

"Fire me, then."

Jack closed his eyes like he wished he was elsewhere.

"I'm familiar with the feeling of losing a family member to a violent death," said Tanya. "Finding her father the way I did would have haunted her for the rest of her life. I just couldn't...."

"Why didn't you call me?"

Tanya indicated the folder on the secretary desk.

"There's something you need to see. It might be the breakthrough we're looking for."

With an exasperated sigh, Jack stepped in and walked along the perimeter, toward the table by the window.

Tanya opened the folder and went through the documents, one by one. When she was done, Jack wiped his face.

"What we need is a psychiatrist, not a medical examiner," he said. "Don't mothers normally recognize their estranged children? Or, is that an urban myth?"

"Veronika hasn't shown any special feelings toward David, at least when I was around," said Tanya. "She could be suppressing the truth because it hurts too much. Or she could be pretending not to know."

"This still doesn't answer who's behind the homicides. Who benefits from their deaths?"

"We need to find Honoree's last testament," said Tanya. "The adoption agency must keep archived records, too. If we follow the paper trails, we might find the answers to the family secrets."

"Secrets," said Jack, shaking his head. "They will eat you up from the inside, which is exactly what has happened to this family."

Tanya's heart skipped a beat. Her hand went to her pocket where she kept her FBI burner phone. She had been ignoring Ray Jackson's calls all day.

And I'm keeping the biggest secret of all from you, Chief.

Chapter Eighty-two

Tanya crossed her arms, to stop her nervous movements.

"Have you found Charles Kensington's body yet?" she asked.

Jack narrowed his eyes.

"The crew has kept the family away from the cemetery. We haven't told them yet, but I think it's time to make inquiries."

"Honoree could be the killer," said Tanya.

"She's dead."

"I mean she could have killed Charles. For all we know, the affair between him and Veronika continued for decades."

"What are you getting at?"

"If Honoree found out about the affair, that would have been solid motivation to kill her husband. She could have orchestrated a burial without the body, to hide the evidence. She was the matriarch and pulled all the strings after her husband died."

Jack rubbed the back of his neck. "Why did she let Veronika live?"

"It's one way to torture a cheating sister."

"Insidious games like that would drive anyone insane. No wonder she shot herself in front of the family." Jack pointed at the folder on the desk. "But this doesn't solve our most recent murders."

"The man who's most capable of killing all these people is Stanley Kensington," said Tanya. "He has the capacity and the motivation."

Jack sighed with frustration. "But we have no evidence."

"You're right. This is all speculation."

"Want to speculate where Charles's body is?" said Jack, turning to leave. "Because I'm ready to dig the whole darned island up right now."

His phone rang before Tanya could reply.

"I've gotta take this."

"Wait," called out Tanya. "Any sign of Asha and Katy?"

"Nothing in the lake. They're not in the woods either. The watercraft by the wharf are accounted for, and we're sure they didn't get on the ferry."

He shot her a steely look.

"When we find them, I'll cuff 'em and jail them for twenty-four hours, so they'll never play hide-and-seek with me again."

Tanya watched Jack stride down the hallway, toward the stairway. Max trotted after him, as if it was his duty to walk the police chief out.

Tanya swallowed.

Are they hiding or are they in danger?

She pulled her phone out to check for messages, but there were none. She tried her friends again, but they didn't pick up or reply to her texts.

A whirlwind of worries surged through her.

She had to break the news to Dr. Chen soon, but her father's death plea only made that job a hundred times more complicated. His last words swirled through her head.

Please don't share this with my daughter. Promise me, Detective.

Tanya turned around with a sigh, when she spied the loose paper on the floor, under the desk. She hadn't noticed it before.

Was that in the folder?

She stepped over to the desk and picked it up, but almost dropped it immediately.

Her heart jumped to her mouth.

"The will!" she yelled. "Jack! I found it!"

Chapter Eighty-three

"Honoree's will!" hollered Tanya, racing down the second-floor corridor.

Max barked excitedly downstairs.

By the time she got to the front entrance, Jack was already driving off, talking animatedly to the phone on his dash.

Tanya sank down on the front step, the will in her hand. Max trotted over to her and sniffed the paper.

Tanya read Honoree's last will and testament, word by word. She was so focused, she didn't hear the sirens coming down the street.

Honoree Kensington's instructions were brief. At her death, her estate would be equally divided among her successors, the three adult children.

That was it.

This meant Hazel, Monica, and David would each get a third of the estate. Since Monica was now dead, her incarcerated husband in New York could claim her portion, once he gets out.

Tanya rubbed her face.

That would only be true if the two women had planned to leave their estates to their respective spouses. They could have bequeathed it to their offsprings instead, or to a charity or two.

Is that why Stanley killed Justin? Tanya shook her head as she realized if he had wanted the money for himself, he would have killed Hazel first.

I need to find the adult children's wills.

Exasperated that she still didn't have the answers yet, she threw the paper on the floor. It landed gently on the step, face down.

She gasped and scooped it back up.

The flip-side had the signatories. The witnesses to Honoree's signature were the senior and junior Dr. Chens. But written in the father's now familiar shaky handwriting was one word that cut across the document.

Obsolete.

Another document superseded this one.

Tanya wanted to crumple the piece of paper and throw it in the trash. Just when she thought she was figuring things out, more threads had come loose.

She got up and stomped up to the second floor, feeling the blood pounding in her head. Her migraine was back.

Maybe Mariposa and Rafael weren't lying. Maybe they witnessed Honoree's last will, after all.

She marched into the study.

She flung the old will on the desk and leaned across to the bookshelf in the back. One by one, she hauled the books off the shelves, making them tumble to the ground.

"Where's the final will?" she hissed in frustration, as she threw the books on the floor.

Once she had cleared the shelves, she searched the back for stashed envelopes or secret compartments. She was knocking on the wood of the middle shelf when she heard the strange voice behind her.

"Excuse me, ma'am?"

Tanya whirled around.

Two uniformed officers were by the threshold, staring at her. Standing in between them was a bald man in a tweed jacket, corduroy pants, and thick black glasses. He was carrying a briefcase, and looked like a university professor on his way to a classroom.

The medical examiner.

"I was informed this was a suicidal hanging," he said, turning to Dr. Chen's body on the floor. "How did the corpse get down?"

Chapter Eighty-four

"There's something I need to tell you," said Tanya.

"No, you listen to *me*." Junior Dr. Chen stabbed an angry finger in Tanya's face. "I'm furious. I'm livid as hell, you hear me?"

Tanya breathed in deeply to settle her nerves. This was more difficult than she had anticipated. The tongue lashing she had got from the new medical examiner hadn't helped.

Dr. Chen had completed Lisa Kensington's autopsy, and had finally got out of her surgical scrub suit, and washed up.

Tanya had handed her father's yellow tabby to a nurse, while she waited for the doctor in the clinic's reception area. The cat had immediately taken over the front desk, and had sprawled itself across a keyboard, while it watched Max with a wary eye.

When Dr. Chen had come out of the surgery, she hadn't even noticed the cat. To Tanya's surprise, the doctor had grabbed her by the arm and hissed.

"Why haven't you jailed him already?"

Before she could reply, the small woman had pushed her into her office and slammed the door shut. Tanya watched the angry doctor, wondering how she was going to share the disturbing news.

Tanya reached over to touch the doctor's shoulder, but she drew back with a grimace. The physician sat ramrod straight in her chair, glaring at Tanya like she had dared to slap her.

"I told him what he's doing was harmful," snarled the doctor. "He never listens to me!"

Dr. Chen's cheeks were flushed, and every nerve on her face seemed to pulsate in anger. It was an unusual display of emotion for her.

Does she already know?

Tanya tried again. "I'm so sorry—"

"*You* are sorry?" snapped Dr. Chen. "How do you think *I* feel?"

Tanya sank into her chair.

"I warned my father about this," continued the doctor, oblivious to the hurricane rolling through

Tanya's head. "I tried, but it wasn't enough, was it?"

Tanya nodded cautiously.

"He thinks he's doing the right thing," spat Dr. Chen. "He believes he's protecting them, but he's only hiding toxic secrets. He's wrong. Dead wrong!"

Tanya stared at her.

Wait, she's speaking about him in the present tense. She doesn't know he's dead yet.

Dr. Chen slammed her palm on the desk. "I should have taken over. I should have done something!"

Tanya sat up. "Done something about what?"

"Lisa!" yelled the doctor, though they were the only two in the small office. "Do you know who the father is?"

Tanya raised a brow. "You got the DNA results already?"

"My team works hard and fast." Dr. Chen scoffed, like she didn't have time for insignificant questions. "We're not a stupid bureaucratic hospital."

Something bitter came to Tanya's mouth, as she realized what she was getting at.

"He's a disgusting man!" shouted the doctor.

Tanya felt sick to her stomach. *Just when I thought things couldn't get worse, they do.*

Charles Kensington had an affair with his wife's younger sister, Veronika. Who was to say he hadn't been abusing other women in the family too?

"Did Lisa's grandfather rape her?" said Tanya.

Dr. Chen glared at her. "What are you talking about?"

Tanya felt even sicker.

Please don't say it's senior Dr. Chen.

She took a deep breath in. "Is it—"

"Stanley is the father!"

Tanya sat up in shock.

"Stanley Kensington?"

Dr. Chen pushed her chair back and stood up with her hands clenched, like a small military general, ready to declare war on a country.

"He's Lisa's first cousin and a decade older," she growled at Tanya, as if this had been all her fault. "He's a pedophile. A predatory hyena."

She paced her office while Tanya sat in her chair, wondering if things could get any crazier.

"The family was trying to hide this incestual pregnancy," said the physician, gesticulating wildly. "That's why they didn't talk about Lisa's suicide. That's why they kept her locked up after they found—"

Tanya sat up. "So that's what the electric keypad on her door was for?"

Dr. Chen glared at her.

"I overheard my father talking on the phone one day. He had medication for Lisa and asked if she was still locked up in her room." She paused. "I could see he was angry about it, but he never said anything."

Tanya tried to get a grip on her thoughts, but they were burning like a wildfire gone out of control.

"The family didn't want anyone asking questions," spluttered Dr. Chen. "All for what?

To protect their reputation. In the meantime, Stanley got away with rape."

She whirled around in fury.

"My father knew all along what was going on and he said nothing. Nothing. Do you understand the gravity of my anger?"

Tanya stared at the doctor.

"Are you saying the family conspired to kill Lisa Kensington?"

Dr. Chen shook her head violently.

"The autopsy doesn't lie. That girl committed suicide. She probably killed herself from shame."

"We need conclusive evidence to—"

"No more questions!" shouted Dr. Chen. "You must arrest Stanley and put him in the worst prison in the country and throw away the key."

Tanya got to her feet. "I want that more than anything else, but—"

"I will have a good talk with my father," snarled the doctor. "He can't throw me out this time. A good doctor doesn't look away when a young patient is being terrorized and subjugated. He's going to hear what I really think of him."

"Dr. Chen, I don't think—"

"Stop stalling! If you won't do your job, I'll take care of it myself."

Dr. Chen yanked open the medicine cupboard in the corner and pushed out a dozen glass bottles. Tanya sprang to her feet to catch them before they tumbled to the ground.

When she looked up, the physician was brandishing a pistol.

Chapter Eighty-five

Tanya gaped at Dr. Chen.

"What are you doing with that?"

The doctor glared at Tanya, like she would shoot her first.

"It's my father's old pistol. He used to go to the range with Charles. This will be poetic justice."

Tanya let the medicine bottles fall to the ground.

"Please put that away."

"You people will mollycoddle Stanley and make sure he gets treated well, while Lisa lies cut open on my surgery table with the child from her own cousin." Dr. Chen's face turned purple. "Lisa was eighteen. She killed herself. I can't ignore that."

"You took a Hippocratic oath, Doctor. You save lives, not take them."

"Stanley Kensington has to pay. And so does my father."

"Stanley won't get away with it," said Tanya. "I'll do everything in my power to make sure Lisa gets the justice she deserves."

Dr. Chen only gripped her gun tighter.

"Stanley's on top of our list of culprits now. From everything I've seen, he looks like our man. He's behind all these murders." Tanya spoke fast, one eye on the gun, waiting for the right time to snatch it away. "These are serious charges. He'll be fighting against multiple life sentences. I assure you, he'll get his just desserts."

Dr. Chen didn't reply.

If it had been anyone else, Tanya would have twisted the woman's wrist, kicked her in the shins, knocked the gun out of her hand, and slammed her to the ground before handcuffing her.

Instead, she leaned toward the doctor and reached for the weapon. Knowing she was taking a risk, Tanya clasped her hands around the doctor's and squeezed tightly.

"Listen to me. I have terrible news about your father."

Dr. Chen's eyes widened. She stared at Tanya mutely, but she was listening at last.

"I don't know how to say this, but I know you would want it straight."

Tanya took another breath in to steady her nerves.

"Your father died today."

Dr. Chen's hand slackened.

"He killed himself." Tanya swallowed. "He left a message for you. For all of us."

Dr. Chen stared at her, frozen. Tanya removed the pistol, placed it back in the cabinet, and clasped the woman's hands again.

"He asked for forgiveness."

The doctor's shoulders dropped, and her hands went limp, but Tanya held on to her. Dr. Chen bowed her head.

"I'm so sorry for your loss," croaked Tanya.

She held Dr. Chen while she wept into her shoulder.

Chapter Eighty-six

Tanya's phone vibrated.

Dr. Chen sprang back like she got an electric shock.

The doctor wiped her cheeks with the back of her hand. She pushed her spectacles up her nose and wrapped her arms around herself, an uncommonly vulnerable gesture for her.

Tanya turned away, realizing how embarrassed she must feel after that emotional outburst. This was a woman who hated to shake hands, let alone cry on someone's shoulder.

She stepped away from the physician and plucked the phone out of her cargo pant pocket.

"Are you with Dr. Chen?" came a male voice.

Jack.

"At the clinic," said Tanya in a terse voice.

"I need you both at the Kensington Manor ASAP."

"Is it Asha and Katy? Are they okay—"

"It's David." Jack hesitated, like he was having a hard time finding the right words. "Come quick."

It took Tanya half an hour to corral the ferry and get to the island with the doctor.

It seemed like the ferry captain got more ornery with every trip they took to the Kensington residence. He was no longer speaking to his human passengers.

Tanya sat inside Dr. Chen's van in silence, as the ferry carried them across the open sea. Max had whined and pawed so hard at the back door, Tanya had let him out as soon as the captain had stabilized the van on the barge.

Her pup was now sitting up front by the cockpit. His frequent glances at the captain, and the thumping of his tail on the bench told her they were having a great conversation.

Dr. Chen hadn't said a word since Jack's call. She had gathered up her doctor's kit when Tanya had told her they were expected on the island immediately. They now sat next to each other without speaking, as the ferry rocked the vehicle.

Despite the silence, Tanya's mind was buzzing like a swarm of bees.

She desperately wanted to hash out the recent discoveries with someone close to the case. She had so many questions and only a few answers, and talking things out always helped to clear her mind.

As soon as the ferry docked on the wharf, Dr. Chen switched on the van's engine. She pressed her hand on the van's horn, startling Tanya.

The ferry captain turned around slowly, his face scrunching in irritation. He shuffled toward the van, grumbling, taking his sweet time. He shot an annoyed look at Dr. Chen, before bending down to remove the wooden blocks he had placed against the wheels.

Tanya peered out of the windshield to see Jack was waiting for them on the wharf.

"I'll see you inside," she said, jumping out of the van. With a joyful bark, Max leaped onto the dock, his tail wagging as he greeted the chief.

Tanya joined her dog on the pier.

"I got an arrest warrant for Stanley Kensington," announced Jack as she approached him. "We're holding him in the house till we sort things out. He's under guard, so he can't do anything fishy."

"Do we have multiple murder charges?" said Tanya, surprised he had worked things out so quickly.

Jack winced. "We're going to nab him for aggravated sexual assault of a minor first."

Tanya's throat went dry. "Did you find my frien—wait, did you say a *minor*?"

Jack nodded.

"All those calls I've been making finally got a bite. It's an older incident but within the statute of limitations."

Tanya wiped the beads of sweat that had gathered on her forehead.

"Who did Stanley assault?"

"Stacey told me a young server worked at the pub during spring break this year. One day, she mentioned Stanley Kensington had asked her on a date."

Tanya grimaced. "How old was she?"

"Seventeen." Jack's face turned grim. "Stacey said the girl quit her job the next day and disappeared. I got the number from her and tracked the girl at her parents' home. As soon as she heard we were investigating Stanley, she opened up."

He sighed.

"The man's a psychopath. That poor girl went through a lot that night."

"And she never told anyone?" said Tanya, shaking her head. "Not even her own parents?"

Jack shot her an irritated look.

"You're the first to remind me why people, mostly women, don't report rape."

Chapter Eighty-seven

"Stanley fathered the baby we found in Lisa's coffin," said Tanya. "I doubt that was a consensual relationship."

Jack nodded. "I wish I could get him for that, but it's going to be a lot harder, given our victim's dead."

"What about the cash we confiscated from his car?" said Tanya.

"The lab promised test results by the end of the week. I'm expecting charges for drug smuggling, perhaps money laundering, too."

"But we're still looking for our killer," said Tanya.

"We need to tread carefully so his lawyers can't poke holes, and get a judge to throw everything out. I'm building these cases slowly, one by one."

Jack gestured for her to follow. Tanya picked up her pace, while Max trotted ahead toward the handful of officers gathered on the driveway.

"Stanley's a probable drug dealer and rapist, but is he a serial killer?" said Tanya. "If it isn't him, our pool of suspects has got really—"

"Watch out!" yelled Jack, pulling on her arm.

They jumped back as Dr. Chen's van trundled inches from their feet. Through the driver's side window, Tanya glimpsed the physician's face. She looked her typical stern self, but her face was pale.

"She took it hard, then?" said Jack as they hurried over to the manor.

"I'm just glad she didn't see him hanging from the ceiling."

Dr. Chen parked her van by the front entrance, got out, and slammed the door shut.

"Where's the body?" she snarled.

The officers on the driveway snapped to attention.

"Right this way, Doctor," said one of them, gesturing toward the front door.

Tanya and Jack followed him and the physician inside. As soon as Tanya stepped into the foyer, she felt her throat constrict. It was like a thick smoke hung in the air, strangling the oxygen inside.

The officer led the way, trying not to trip over Max who wanted to get ahead of everyone.

"We found him in his room," said the officer, turning to the doctor. "It's quite the sight, I tell you."

Tanya closed her eyes.

She hadn't shared everything with Dr. Chen after Jack's call. Given what the physician had gone through over the last few hours, she hadn't had the heart to make things worse, but now she wondered if she had done the right thing.

Should have prepared her, thought Tanya, feeling a pang of guilt.

"What are we looking at?" said Dr. Chen, walking briskly up the stairs.

The officer stopped on the second-floor landing and turned to face his small audience. His eyes shone like he had the juiciest gossip to share.

"Have you guys seen that big fat snake he had in the aquarium?"

The doctor nodded.

"No idea how the darned thing got out again, but man did it do major damage."

Chapter Eighty-eight

"Here we are, Doctor."

A second officer was standing by the open doorway of David's room.

Dr. Chen lifted her chin and glared at the two officers, looking more like a bulldog than ever.

"Did you people touch anything?"

"No, ma'am."

With a curt nod, the doctor stepped inside the room. She placed her bag by the threshold and pulled out a pair of plastic booties, gloves, and a face mask.

"What happened to her team?" said Jack in a low voice, as they stepped up to the doorway.

Tanya put a hand on Max's collar so he wouldn't rush in after the physician.

"Carrying out toxicology tests," she whispered.

"On whom?"

"Lisa and Peter. They've confirmed Lisa died from suicide, but want to make sure there were no extenuating circumstances. Peter is still a mystery," said Tanya in a low voice. "The entire team is at the clinic's lab. They looked a little stressed when I left. I think she's working them to the bone."

Jack and Tanya remained at the threshold, knowing the doctor preferred to work undisturbed.

Holding on to her pup, Tanya stared at the grisly scene on the poster bed.

David was in his usual army pants and wife-beater shirt, but looked puffier than normal. His limbs were twisted in unnatural positions, like he had fought to stay alive.

His face was blue and turned to the side so they could see his bulging eyes. They looked like they would pop out of their sockets any second.

Tanya raised her eyes to the aquarium, searching for the culprit. The yellow python was curled around a log, its head turned away from them, like it wasn't proud of its handiwork.

"Bet you've never seen anything like this," whispered the trooper by the door. "It wrapped pretty nicely around his body and choked him to death."

Tanya turned to him.

"How do you know the python did it?"

The officer grabbed his phone and opened the photo app.

"Check this out."

She stared at the picture of David on his bed. His pet snake had wrapped itself around his torso and legs, twisting him into a hideous pretzel.

"Who discovered him?"

"The housekeeper. She said she went to give him his daily vitamins. She's in the kitchen now, shaking like a leaf."

"Was he dead when you saw him?"

"Oh, yeah." The officer nodded. "The dude was a goner—"

"Who put the animal back in the aquarium?"

"That tall guy." He pointed his thumb down the hallway. "The maintenance worker dude. We all helped him because that's one monster snake. Weighs a ton. Never in a million—"

A phone rang inside David's room, startling everyone.

"It's mine," called out the doctor. She stopped her work on David's body, pulled out her glove, and reached into her bag. She plucked her mobile out and barked into it.

"I'm in the middle of an examination. This had better be good."

Tanya and Jack exchanged a glance.

Poor interns, thought Tanya. They had a taskmaster for a boss.

The two troopers, Jack, and Tanya watched as Dr. Chen's eyes widened slightly. She whipped around to them. They leaned in through the doorway.

The doctor hung up and glared at her small audience.

"Everything okay, Dr. Chen?" said Jack.

"Peter Kensington died of a heavy MDMA overdose."

"MDMA..." Tanya stopped as she remembered what that meant. "Ecstasy pills?"

"They induced a heart attack," said the doctor, nodding. "Given his adverse health and heart issues, that would have been expected."

"The question is," said Jack, "did he take them himself or did someone give them to him?"

Dr. Chen shook her head. "My team hasn't finished their report yet, but they tell me the dosage was unusually high. Not an amount a regular addict would take."

"Stanley," said Tanya turning to Jack. "Did the lab only find cocaine traces on the cash? If he was selling cocaine, he could just as easily be selling ecstasy pills."

Jack turned to the troopers. "I need another thorough check in Stanley's room." He pulled his mobile out. "Meanwhile, I'll see what else forensics has found in his car."

The troopers headed off on their job, and Jack stepped away from the room, his phone to his ear.

Tanya felt a tingle on her back, like someone was watching her. She spun around.

"Mariposa?"

The housekeeper was standing right behind her. Tanya hadn't heard her come over.

Mariposa's face was flushed and tear stained, and her hair stood on its ends like she had walked through a wind tunnel.

"I just wanted to tell you," she said, her eyes dark and angry. "We're done."

Chapter Eighty-nine

J ack whirled around.

"That's not a good idea."

Mariposa's face shut down. She looked away, then raised her chin again, this time with a fierce determination in her eyes.

"You can't make us stay."

She turned to Tanya.

"I have something to show you. After that, we're out of here."

Tanya shot the chief a warning glance. She knew Mariposa would be more open to speaking with her alone.

She took the woman by the arm and ushered her toward the staircase. Max trotted in front, like he knew where they were going. Mariposa walked quickly, sniffling and wiping her nose with a tissue every once in a while.

"Seeing David like that must have been a shock," said Tanya as they climbed down to the first floor.

"We're going back," said Mariposa.

"Where?"

"We're going home to Cuba."

Tanya raised an eyebrow. "You know it's not wise to leave until the investigation is over, don't you?"

Mariposa clutched her arm.

"I don't care, but I'm not staying in this madhouse. Every day, I keep wondering. Is it me, next? Is it going to be my husband? I can't live like this anymore."

They entered the kitchen.

Rafael was at the island counter with a bowl full of potatoes and a cutting board in front of him. But he was staring blankly at the wall, his hands on his lap.

Tanya pulled a chair for his wife next to him.

"Doing okay?"

Rafael gave her a glazed look.

Tanya took the high stool across from the couple, but neither Rafael nor Mariposa said a word.

Max strutted over to the bowl of water by the back door, which Rafael had put out ever since they had arrived on the island. The only sound in the kitchen was Max lapping at his water.

"I knew it."

Tanya turned to Mariposa.

"Knew what?"

"I knew this was an awful place when we first came."

She turned to her husband and poked his arm.

"But he wanted to stay because it was good money. More than we ever made. But I felt bad the minute we got on the island."

Mariposa wiped her eyes and blew her nose.

Tanya inhaled deeply.

If I want to get anything out of them, I need to be straight with them.

"Tell me about the Cuban cigars," she said. "How did they get here?"

Mariposa's shoulders dropped and a visible shudder went through Rafael. They stared at her, their faces ashen.

They're guilty.

"We're trying to find a killer," said Tanya. "This is a multiple homicide investigation. Given the circumstances, I think cigar smuggling isn't as significant as you think. But hiding things isn't going to help you."

She leaned in.

"Tell me the truth."

Mariposa turned to Rafael, her face scrunched with worry.

"You tell her," she said to her husband.

"Mr. Charles told me to get them." Rafael swallowed and cleared his throat. "He asked me to call my family back home to find a good source. He said we'd make a lot of money."

"Did you know what he asked you to do was illegal?" said Tanya.

Rafael looked down at the counter, his shoulders slumped. It was Mariposa who answered. She leaned over to Tanya, her eyes blazing.

"Mr. Charles got us."

"Got us?"

Mariposa stabbed the table with a finger.

"Every year we got him his cigars. Just like he asked us. He paid us at first. Two years in, he told us if the authorities ever found out, we'd be in major trouble. He said we'll go to prison. The US

Army will swoop over and kidnap our family and torture them."

"That's when he stopped paying us," said Rafael. "But we had to still find more and bring them over."

Tanya raised a brow.

Rafael sank further into his chair.

"He knew he had us then," he said. "We worked for free for him after that."

"He was a mean man," said Mariposa, stabbing the table again. "He used us. He pushed everyone around. Didn't matter if it was his wife, his daughter, or friends. He always got what he wanted."

Tanya leaned back in her chair. Every nerve in her body said they were telling the truth.

Charles Kensington keeps popping up. Is he still alive? Is he orchestrating the murder of his own family from some secret location?

"Where's Charles now?" she said.

The couple turned to her with surprised expressions on their faces.

"Dead," said Rafael. "He died three years ago."

"Didn't you see his grave by the lake?" said Mariposa.

Tanya nodded.

"Why didn't you leave when he died?"

"Because Mrs. Honoree took over," said Mariposa. "She was as bad as he was."

"Worse," said Rafael.

Mariposa looked at her with frightened eyes.

"Are you going to put us in jail now?"

Tanya sighed heavily.

"The good news is," she said, speaking more to herself than them, "once a judge or jury hears what's going on here, they'll be lenient with you. Your employer coerced you."

"I don't want to go to prison," said Mariposa, dabbing her eyes. "We're not criminals."

Rafael put his arm around her and pulled her in close. Their faces were lined with worry. Tanya's heart sank to see them like this.

"You told me you wanted to show me something," she said.

Rafael glanced over at his wife.

"I can go. You stay here."

Mariposa nodded and pulled the teapot toward her.

"Better hold your nose," she said as she poured herself a cup of tea. "Or you'll lose your lunch."

Chapter Ninety

T anya jumped to her feet.

"Don't tell me you found another body."

Rafael shuffled toward the kitchen door that led to the backyard.

"It depends what you mean by body."

Max trotted over, and whined. Rafael pushed the back door open, and the dog darted out.

Tanya stepped out of the kitchen and into a vegetable garden. Her pup was running back and forth, his nose stuck to the ground.

"Part of my job is to collect food for the snake every month. I catch mice, frogs, birds, and put them in the freezer," said Rafael, gesturing for her to follow him. "The first Thursday of every month, I take a plate of raw meat up, so David can feed his pet."

"I thought *you* fed the snake."

"David would never allow that, and I'm thankful, is all I can say. It took me quite some time to go near that thing, at the beginning."

Max's attention had turned to the row of recycle bins by the garden fence. Rafael shuffled toward them, his head bent low and his shoulders stooped, looking like he had aged years over the past few days.

Tanya observed him.

He's not the scowling man with the ax I first met, that's for sure.

Tanya watched Max sniff the green compost bucket and circle it. Rafael stepped up to the bin and flipped the top cover open. She walked over, bracing herself.

The potent odor of rotting meat came from within. Holding her nose, she peeked inside.

Tanya pulled away, staggered back, and bent over, gagging. The image of Lisa's decomposed body in the coffin slammed to her mind.

"Sorry," said Rafael. "I'm used to it. I didn't think..."

She turned away to take a fresh breath of air, before looking back at the bin.

"I presume that's Xena's monthly feast?"

He nodded.

"How did that get in the bin?"

"I took the meal upstairs last night. I had the meat arranged on a plate, just like how David wanted it, and I left it on his sound system."

"When did you take it upstairs?"

"Around six o'clock. Just as the family sits down for supper. I usually leave it in his room, so David can feed Xena after dinner, like he always did."

"Did you wait in the room or in the hallway?"

"I came down right away to join Mariposa. We eat in the kitchen after we serve the family, and she doesn't like it if I'm late."

Tanya stepped back a bit more, wishing he would close the lid.

"Did you see anyone in the backyard between then and now?"

Rafael shook his head.

"What would happen if the snake didn't eat as planned?" asked Tanya, taking another step back as the odor wafted toward her.

"Xena may be a pet, but she's a python." He shrugged. "Pythons do what pythons do."

"The officers said you got the snake off of him."

"I ran up when Mariposa started screaming. Those young men tried to help, but to tell the truth, they were yelling and sliding all over the place, making things worse."

Rafael shook his head.

"It took a while to get Xena off of David. By then, he wasn't breathing anymore." He paused. "The aquarium door was open, which was unusual."

"Did David forget to lock it?"

He frowned.

"That's what everyone thought when the snake escaped to your room the other day. Veronika and Hazel said it had to be an accident, but I'm no longer sure."

He turned to her.

"David was worried about you, did you know that?"

"Me?" said Tanya.

Rafael gave her a small smile. "He told everyone you came to the island to steal Xena and sell her to a Chinese company for millions. He made up a big story about you being the big bad wolf."

Tanya sighed.

"If someone wanted to kill David, when would be the best time for them to get in his room, open the aquarium door, and take the food away?"

"During supper while the family is occupied and when Mariposa and I are in the kitchen."

Rafael's face turned dark.

"I don't know what's going on in this house. Can you help us get out?"

"If you had nothing to do with this," said Tanya, "you don't have anything to worry about."

"Mariposa booked an early morning flight to Florida. We're heading out tonight. We'll sleep in the car by the airport if we have to."

Chapter Ninety-one

"Leaving will signal guilt," said Tanya.

"We don't care anymore," said Rafael.

Tanya sucked in a deep breath.

"Would you stay in the kitchen for another hour? Make yourselves a cup of tea and wait for me. Don't talk to anyone. Don't go anywhere."

"What do you plan to do?"

"I think I know who is behind this, but I need a bit more time."

A loud buzz made Rafael jump. Tanya reached into her cargo pocket and pulled her public phone out.

Stacey.

"Hang on a minute," she said to Rafael, before walking to the end of the vegetable garden where she would have more privacy.

"Tanya?" came Stacey's voice through the phone.

She sounds distraught, thought Tanya. *No, unsettled.*

"How's George doing?" said Tanya. "Is he—"

"They'll discharge him in two weeks." Stacey paused. "I didn't think he'd make it, but I'm ready to wait two weeks or two months if they ask me to."

Tanya breathed a sigh of relief.

"You have a good medical team on your side, hun. George is strong. He'll pull through this. You need to give him and yourself time."

"I know."

Another pregnant pause. It was clear Stacey had something on her mind.

Tanya waited.

"Jack said you wanted to know about Charlotte," said Stacey, finally.

"Charlotte?"

"She was a waitress at our pub. A sweet girl and a good worker. I really liked her." Her voice broke. "When Jack told me what happened, I didn't know what to think...I was devastated."

Stacey gulped on the other end. Tanya recalled her conversation with Jack only moments ago.

"Charlotte was dating Justin," Stacey was saying.

"Justin?" Tanya frowned. "I thought it was Stanley who asked her on a date."

"She had been seeing Justin for six months, but they were on a break. Justin's work kept him away most nights which didn't make her too happy, so they took a pause to think about things."

"And Stanley?" said Tanya.

"He swooped in like a hawk."

Tanya grimaced. "Because he knew she was in a vulnerable state."

"He pestered her for days until she said yes," said Stacey. "I know because he came to the pub and watched her. It creeped me out. I told her to stay away from him, but she didn't listen. I could have stopped her from getting hurt."

"You can't blame yourself for what happened," said Tanya. "Neither should Charlotte. He took advantage of her."

"I'm kicking myself for not seeing it coming. They were very unpleasant customers. No one liked to serve them when they came over."

Tanya straightened up. "Who came over?"

"Charles was a regular at the pub until he died. When his grandkids were old enough, he brought them for drinks every Tuesday. Then, Peter's family moved to New York, so we stopped seeing him. After Charles died, only Stanley and David came for their weekly pints."

Tanya raised a brow. "So Stanley was a regular?"

"Him and David, but David didn't talk to anyone. His cousins or his grandfather always ordered for him. He brought his comic book collection and spent his time reading."

Tanya frowned. "When was the last time Stanley was at the pub?"

"Two days ago, at their usual time. Him and David."

Was Stanley behind the pub's explosion?

Tanya knew how easy it was to download online instructions to make a homemade explosive device with a timer, and plant it in a public venue. She made a mental note to share that with the fire chief.

When Stacey spoke again, it was in a low whisper. "It was never about Charlotte, you know that?"

"What do you mean?"

"It was all about Justin," said Stacey. "Stanley wanted to one-up on his estranged brother.

She was Justin's girlfriend. That's why he… he attacked that poor girl."

All roads lead to Stanley, thought Tanya.

Stacey began to cry.

"I should have kept her away from that sick man. He hurt her…."

Tanya waited quietly, her phone to her ear, listening to Stacey sob.

Stacey had gone through a lot, but learning what had happened to her young employee had finally broken her. Tanya blinked a tear away and turned around to see where her dog had gone to.

Rafael was sitting on a block of bricks at the center of the garden now, with Max by his side. As she watched, Rafael reached out with a tentative hand and scratched the dog's head. Max licked his hand and wagged his tail.

Max trusts him.

"Stacey?" said Tanya. "Stanley isn't going to get away with this. We'll put the man away in the only place where he belongs—"

A warning bark came from Max. Tanya whirled around. Her pup was on his feet now, darting toward the fence.

All of a sudden, a loud screech echoed through the grounds.

Tanya froze. It had sounded like the howl of a werewolf gone mad.

Rafael jumped to his feet, his eyes bulging.

"I gotta go," said Tanya, hanging up on Stacey. She turned to Rafael. "What on earth was that?"

Rafael shook his head, his face pale, like the scream had swallowed his words.

Max jumped up and down by the fence and let out a ferocious volley of barks. Tanya pulled her Glock out and dashed over.

Keeping her head low, she peeked over the fence.

Chapter Ninety-two

The garden fence opened to the woods in the back.

The furious howl reverberated through the grounds again, sounding more human this time. It had come from the front of the house.

Tanya whirled around to Rafael. "Don't touch the bin. The crew will take prints."

Without waiting for him to reply, she turned around and dashed toward the gate in the middle of the fence. Max crouched low, his muzzle up, and his tail stiff.

He's going to jump the fence.

"Hang on, bud!"

As soon as she pushed the gate open, he bolted out. Tanya raced after him as he bounded toward the front driveway, barking at the top of his lungs.

She swung around the side wall just as Jack slammed Stanley to the ground. They grappled, rolling down the driveway.

"Police brutality!" screamed Stanley, fighting like a maniac. "I'll sue you!"

The chief was trying to control the Kensington, but Stanley flailed with all his might.

"Get off me! You assholes! You won't get away with this!"

He let out another hair-raising screech. Jack flinched but kept his grip on Stanley's hands.

Tanya rushed in. She slammed her knee on Stanley's back. She grabbed his head with her hands and thrust his face to the ground.

"You bitch!" snarled Stanley.

From the corner of her eye, Tanya saw Jack reach for a pair of cuffs on his belt. Sweat was rolling down the chief's forehead.

"Where are Asha and Katy?" said Tanya, digging her nails into Stanley's head.

"They stole my money," croaked Stanley, his mouth flattened by her weight. "Thieves."

Tanya gritted her teeth. "You know where they are. Tell me."

"If I knew, they'd be six feet underground." He tried to wiggle out of her grasp. "When you see those bitches, tell them I'll destroy them."

Tanya wished she could smash his head and make him feel genuine pain.

"You're a psycho criminal, Stanley Kensington. You raped Charlotte and Lisa, didn't you? Lisa was your first cousin. She was pregnant with your baby. Isn't that why she killed herself?"

Stanley fell silent. His back and shoulders slackened. That alone was an admission of his guilt, Tanya was sure.

"Lisa committed suicide because of what you did to her, you disgusting sicko."

Her fingers dug into his flesh. She struggled to suppress the urge to squeeze his throat until he stopped breathing.

Predators like you don't deserve to live.

"Stone?" came Jack's voice. "Let go."

Tanya held on, hot blood swirling through her veins. There were times she wished she was in combat again. Things were easier in the field, where you could make psychopaths pay for their sick sins.

"Let go, Stone."

She released Stanley's shoulders and got up, panting hard. Two troopers pulled the handcuffed man to his feet, while the chief read him his rights.

"As I was saying before you hit a state trooper and ran off," said Jack, "you're being charged with assault of a law enforcement officer and aggravated sexual assault of a minor. You have the right to remain silent. You have the right to an attorney...."

Tanya stood next to the chief, her blood pounding in her ears, wondering how perpetrators were always granted their rights while victims had theirs snatched away so cruelly.

So violently.

The officers pushed their arrest toward the nearest squad car. That was where Stanley would wait until the ferry came over, to take him to the Black Rock precinct.

A prickle on the back of Tanya's neck made her turn.

She glanced instinctively at the second floor of the manor. A curtain on a top bedroom window fell into place, like someone had been watching them.

A chill went down her back.

The more she hung around this island, the more it felt like the ghost of Charles Kensington was haunting them, killing his family off, one by one.

This place is driving me nuts.

She glanced down at her dog for reassurance, but Max was no longer at her heels. He had been born and bred for work. He ran toward fires and never left an active scene unless she pulled him away.

Where did he go off to?

Tanya spun around, her eyes scanning the grounds, her heart beating fast. She spotted a brown and furry tail on the route toward the cove.

Max?

As if he knew she was looking his way, he stopped, glanced back, and barked. Tanya stared at him for a moment before she realized he was following a scent.

She scrambled after him.

"What is it, bud?"

Max put his muzzle back on the path and trotted forward.

"Stone?"

That was Jack.

"He found something!" shouted Tanya as she scurried after her pup.

Jack's footsteps came from behind her, but she didn't bother to wait. Her eyes were on her dog, who was now racing around the cemetery, heading toward the other end of the lake.

Tanya picked up her pace, calling Max to slow down, but he didn't stop until he got on the same boulder where he had spotted Monica's floating body.

Please, no. No!

With her heart in her mouth, Tanya scrambled onto the boulder and glanced down. The human-made rock cairn she had seen earlier was still in its place, secured from the waves by the larger rocks. The tide was high, but she could see the long seaweed strands dancing under the surface.

Her heart thumped hard.

Please don't let it be—

Max leaped into the water with a loud splash.

"What's he doing in the water?"

Tanya spun around to see Jack had caught up to her. He jumped onto the boulder to join her.

Max was now doggy paddling in the lake. They watched him, their brows furrowed.

He loved the water, but he wasn't playing. His snout was raised high, and his eyes were pointed in one direction.

"He's found something," said Tanya. "Or someone...."

Chapter Ninety-three

Max was heading toward the waterfall at the far end of the lake.

Tanya felt sick to her stomach. She whirled around and grabbed Jack by his jacket lapels.

"You told me you checked the cove."

"Whoa, there." Jack put his hands up. "We did, twice."

"Did you look by the waterfall?"

"We inspected the entire lake," said Jack, his voice somber. "Bodies normally sink to the bottom and surface a few days later once they've become bloated. That's what we focused on...."

Tanya let go of him.

She turned back to see where her pup was, then took off her jacket and threw it down.

Jack stared at her. "What are you doing?"

"Your crew missed something. Whatever it is, Max wants me to see it."

With one eye on her pup, Tanya stripped down to her tank top and underwear.

"If you're going in, I'm coming too," grumbled Jack as he unbuttoned his shirt.

Without waiting for him, she dove in, head first.

She sank into the green water, feeling seaweed strands slash against her thighs. She kicked her legs, propelled herself to the surface, and whirled around. Max was paddling next to the chute, his ears drawn back, trying not to get drenched by the flood of water that flowed over the cliff.

A loud splash came near her.

Jack had jumped in. He sprinted past her, spraying water all over her. She turned back to her pup to see him doggy paddle in circles, a confused expression on his face.

What's he up to?

She plunged back in to swim toward him when something soft wrapped around her legs.

She kicked her feet, but whatever it was, it fastened around her foot tighter. She blinked through the murky water to see a tangle of seaweed around her left ankle, threatening to pull her into the deep.

With a curse, she bent down and ripped the twine off, inch by inch, trying not to swallow the brackish water.

I can't breathe.

As soon as she freed herself, she thrust her shoulders above the surface and swallowed a big gulp of air. She treaded water to catch her breath and reorient herself.

That was when she realized she was the only person in the lake.

Around her, the cove was quiet. The yellow police tape that cordoned off the cemetery waved in the wind. The boats tied to the wharf bobbed up and down with the waves, but there was no sign of anyone nearby.

Her blood went cold.

What happened to them?

"Max!" she called out.

Her heart thudded.

"Jack?" Panic crept into her voice. "Max? Where are you?"

"Here!"

Tanya spun around. It was Jack's voice, but muffled, like it was coming from afar.

"Stone!" came his voice again, bubbling like he was speaking through water.

Tanya's heart hammered as she swam toward the fall. Soon, a mist enveloped her. It turned into a light rain, then grew heavier and heavier until the cascade from above drenched her like a monsoon torrent.

I can't see.

She ducked under the surface, but it was even harder to see.

Where's Max?

Hey, bud, where are you?

A hurricane of fear swirled through her mind. She spun around, kicking at the kelp, so it wouldn't grab on to her again. She pushed through the forest of seaweed and swam in circles.

Her throat turned dry and her limbs felt like jelly.

Is there a Bermuda Triangle in this lake?

Her chest tightened and, soon, she felt like her lungs were about to explode.

Air, I need air.

Tanya thrust forward and almost hit her head against the raggedy rock face of the cliff wall. She stopped and scolded herself for panicking.

She put a hand on the rough surface and glanced up, wishing she had eye goggles. She kicked her legs gently, propelling herself vertically along the cliff wall.

Suddenly, her head popped out of the water.

Air.

She took a big gulp of oxygen.

Behind her, the waterfall flowed down like an undulating curtain, thundering like a tropical tempest.

Where am I?

She blinked, panting hard, as her eyes tried to adjust to the darkness. A swirl of terror crept through her as she realized she was looking into an opening in the cliff. She stared into the void, wondering if this was some strange dream.

"Stone!"

Jack!

A bark made her heart skip a beat.

"Max!" she called out.

Someone gripped her arm. She looked up to see Jack trying to pull her out of the water. She dragged herself onto the ledge and collapsed on the cave floor.

"Where are we?" she whispered, glancing around her, disoriented.

"There's a tunnel behind the fall," said Jack, raising his voice so she could hear. "I didn't know this existed. My crew didn't see it. They focused their search under the water."

A furry body bumped into Tanya from behind, and something warm and wet licked her face.

Tanya spun around on her haunches and grabbed Max. She buried her head in his fur and held on tight, her heart thudding.

I thought I lost you, bud.

Chapter Ninety-four

"Hey, Stone?" called out Jack, urgency in his voice.

Tanya released Max and struggled to her feet.

Her pup trotted around her, his tongue lolling and his wet tail slapping against her legs, like he hadn't seen her in ages. She patted his head, trying to take in their new environment.

"How did you find this place?" she said.

"Wasn't me," came Jack's voice in the semi-darkness. "Max did all the work. I followed him into the fall."

Tanya whirled around and squinted to locate him.

Jack was by what looked like an entrance to an underground passageway. He was in his wet boxer shorts, water still dripping down his body, and at his feet was a discarded plastic bag. In his hands were his service weapon and a flashlight.

He came prepared.

Jack turned on his light. Tanya blinked as the cave's craggy stone wall and the dark passageway came into view.

She recalled how Katy had discovered the secret door inside the closet of their guest room. Then, Jack's crew had found more secret doorways.

Are all these connected?

"This place must be riddled with tunnels," she said in a low voice.

Jack opened his mouth to answer, when a sudden holler echoed through the space.

"Help!"

The hair on Tanya's nape stood up.

Max barked.

"Anybody there? Help!"

"*Asha,*" gasped Tanya, her heart pounding. "They're here."

Chapter Ninety-five

Max darted into the tunnel.

"Wait up!" called Tanya.

"Help!" echoed Asha's voice again.

Jack spun around to run after the dog but stopped abruptly. Leaning against the cave wall, he pulled up his foot to examine it.

"What is it?" said Tanya.

"Should have kept my boots on." Jack shone the flashlight along the floor. "Watch these edges. They can cut you."

Tanya squinted to see blood on his fingers where he'd touched his foot.

"Let me take that," she said, reaching over and plucking the flashlight from his hand. "You have your Glock."

Using the flashlight, they stumbled around the jagged rocks. They kept one sharp eye on the floor and another in the direction of where Max had disappeared.

A rustle came from the other end of the tunnel.

"Police!" hollered Jack into the void. "Stop right there!"

Tanya shone the light into the passageway and caught two small moving red dots, at the level of her thighs.

"It's Max," said Tanya.

He was sniffing something on the ground, farther down the tunnel. Jack lowered his weapon.

"Did he find them?" said Tanya, her heart beating a tick faster.

Max scampered over to them and circled around their legs before trotting back down the passageway.

"Slow down," said Tanya, as she stepped around a pointy rock formation.

"I don't like it," muttered Jack. "She's gone quiet."

Tanya was about to call out to her friends when a sickening odor hit her nostrils.

"Did a raccoon die in here?"

Jack grimaced. "I've smelled dead raccoons before. This must be a bigger ani—"

He stopped as Tanya swiveled the flashlight to their left.

It was where Max had stopped to sniff the ground before running off into the dark. Tanya opened her mouth to say something, but nothing came out.

"Oh, man," said Jack, putting a hand over his nose. "How long has he been in here?"

Tanya shone the flashlight from one end of the partly decomposed corpse to the other. Discolored skeleton bits jutted through remnants of his leathery skin. He was lying at an angle, like he had crawled in here and laid down to never get up again.

"I think I know who that is," said Tanya, trying not to breathe in the putrid air that was threatening to envelop them. "Charles Kensington."

"Our missing body," said Jack, staring at their grizzly find. "How in goodness' name did he end up here?"

"I would bet you anything he was murdered three years ago." Tanya's mind buzzed. "The killer didn't want anyone to find out how he died, so they hid him in here. That's my theory."

"They could have thrown him in the sea," said Jack, grimacing. "Much easier that way."

"And have his bloated body float up to be spotted by the fishing boats? No one would think to come here to look for him."

Jack turned to her, a puzzled expression on his face. "Senior Dr. Chen signed his death certificate. It said Charles died of lung cancer."

Tanya stared at the rotting body, unable to avert her eyes. The suicide note she had discovered under the doctor's swinging body flashed to her mind.

I have done terrible things. Please forgive me.

"I think he had more than one reason to hang himself," she whispered. "He probably forged the certificate."

"If Charles was murdered," said Jack thoughtfully, "the killer could have forced him to sign the death certificate. That means, we're looking for someone who had sway over him, or had something they could blackmail him with."

"Honoree Kensington," said Tanya. "I keep coming back to her."

"Let's hope there's some evidence of how he died," said Jack, shaking his head at the corpse. "I need answers. Not more questions."

"Tanya! Is that you?"

Tanya and Jack jerked their heads up.

"Asha?" called out Tanya. She whirled her flashlight around the tunnel.

"They're in here somewhere," said Jack, twisting his neck around.

"Hey, Tanya!"

Asha's disembodied voice sounded far away. Tanya's heart pounded as she squinted in all directions.

Where is she?

Chapter Ninety-six

All Tanya could see was the stone wall, and a tunnel that disappeared into pitch blackness.

"Tanya!" cried Katy.

"We're here!" called out Asha.

Relief rushed through Tanya as she heard both of their voices.

From somewhere farther up the tunnel, Max barked.

"Hang on," Tanya called out as she and Jack stumbled over to him. "We're coming."

Max whirled around in his spot, like he was chasing his tail. He stopped when they got close and let out a howl.

"Max!" said Asha. "So nice to hear your voice."

"Thank goodness you came," said Katy. "We thought we'd be stuck down here forever."

"They're here," said Jack, turning around. "They're right here."

Tanya shone her flashlight around the passageway, her brow furrowed. The tunnel ran deep into the cove, but there were no doors, cross tunnels, or openings nearby. Her eyes flittered to the ceiling and back down again.

What am I not seeing?

Jack turned to Max. "Where are they, big boy?"

Max barked in reply and wagged his tail, but didn't budge from his spot. Tanya noticed he was facing the wall to their right. Seeing her look, he barked again.

Tanya put a hand on the wall in front of him and felt it. It was solid stone.

"Asha? Katy?" she called out. "Where are you?"

"We're locked in here," came Asha's voice from beyond the wall.

Tanya leaned in and felt the stone for hidden latches, pulleys, or knobs.

"Are you ladies okay?" called out Jack.

"Katy twisted her ankle," said Asha. "Other than that, we're fine. Just tired."

"Hey, what are these?" said Jack, tapping the wall.

Tanya shone her light where his hands were. He was pointing at a series of small craggy holes that someone had chiseled in the stone.

"Air vents?" he said, bending to scrutinize them.

Tanya stepped to the nearest hole and put her eye to it. It was dark on the other side, and the gap was too small to make out anything.

She pulled her face away and shone her flashlight through it instead.

"Yay!" cried Katy from the other side. "Light!"

Tanya shone her light across the wall to see if she could find a bigger hole, when her foot scrunched on a hard object.

"Ouch."

She pulled her foot away and swiveled her light down. The object glinted at her in the dark.

"What on earth is this?" said Jack, bending down.

He held it up. Even in the dim light, the enormous diamond in the middle of the earring sparkled.

"The missing earring," said Tanya, recalling its lost pair she'd discovered inside the safe in Honoree's bedroom.

"We found the stolen treasure." Katy's voice came through the wall. "It's all here in an old wooden chest."

"I slipped the earring through that hole in case someone walked by and noticed," said Asha. "We thought that would stop them, and we'd hear them."

Max was sniffing at something on the floor where the earring had lay.

"What is it, bud?" said Tanya.

"A sock?" said Jack, frowning at the small garment that lay crumpled on the ground.

"That's mine," said Asha from the other side. "I stuffed it through the hole about twenty minutes ago. We thought if Max was anywhere around, he'd find us."

"It was my idea," came Katy's voice. "We looked for the smelliest piece of clothing we could find."

Asha mumbled something.

Tanya's head cleared. That was why Max hadn't been able to find them until now. They had been walled-in, underground, hard to detect, even for his sensitive nose.

"Where are you, exactly?" said Jack, tapping the wall again. "Is it a cave?"

"A basement corridor or tunnel. We've been walking around for ages, so we can't say for sure," said Asha. "Can't see much. My phone died."

"I left mine charging in the bathroom," said Katy, sounding wistful. "Asha's already reamed me out, so don't you two start."

Tanya shook her head.

"There's a massive basement under the manor," said Asha. "Several floors deep. It's a real maze down here."

Tanya and Jack exchanged a curious glance.

"You're nowhere near the house, ladies," said Jack.

"*What?*" said Katy.

"You're by the lake."

Silence fell on the other end.

"At least we got what we came here for," said Asha finally.

Tanya frowned. "What are you talking about?"

"We found Honoree's last will," said Asha, a smug tinge in her voice.

Chapter Ninety-seven

"The document was at the bottom of the wooden chest," said Katy. "Under Honoree's stolen jewelry."

Jack put his hand up, though they couldn't see him. "First, tell me, how did you end up here?"

"We followed a call for help, but it was a ruse," said Asha.

"I found the note in your room," said Tanya.

"We got two," said Asha. "The first was anonymous and said they were being framed, and the second was a map."

A map?

"Asha was on her laptop, and I went to the bathroom for a sec," said Katy, "so we never saw Hazel slip them under our door."

Tanya and Jack exchanged a glance.

Tanya frowned.

Hazel had come across as someone who acted impulsively on her emotions, not someone confident or skilled enough to methodically plan and carry out multiple murders.

"The second note was a simple drawing of the basement, saying to meet down here," continued Katy, oblivious to the confusion they were creating in the other tunnel. "I was so sure we were going to—"

"Wait," said Tanya. "Are you sure it was from Hazel?"

"She signed her name under the map, but I'm sure it will have to be authenticated," said Asha. "She wrote 'life & death situation' at the bottom, so we dropped everything and ran to her room."

The first note must have fallen in their hurry.

Tanya shook her head to clear it.

Did the diminutive, bookish woman actually murder Justin, her own son, then go on a killing spree to eliminate the remaining family members? What was her motive? Did her other criminal-minded son put her up to this?

"I don't believe she's working alone," muttered Jack, as if he knew what was going through her mind. "It had to have been Stanley."

"Any idea where Hazel is now?" said Tanya, turning back to the wall.

"We never saw her," said Katy.

Jack shook his head. "They were lured in," he whispered.

Tanya didn't answer. She knew her friends. When they had a stubborn goal in mind, nothing could stop them.

"We went looking for her," said Asha. "Her room was empty, but the closet was open, and there was a small door in the back like ours."

"It wasn't a connecting door," said Katy. "This one led to a stone stairway going down."

"We were halfway down the steps," said Asha, "when the door slammed from above us. We've been stuck in this maze, searching for an exit for hours."

Tanya clenched her jaws.

And you didn't think of warning me before taking off on us?

"You should have called," said Jack, sounding annoyed. "I had a search party out for you."

"We lost cell service as soon as that door shut."

Jack sighed.

"The point is," said Asha, "we found the most recent testament in the chest. No idea who put it here, but it's dated the day of Honoree's death. That's when I lost battery power."

"Mariposa and Rafael signed as witnesses," said Katy. "Just like they said."

"May I say *bingo*, Chief?" came Asha's smug voice.

"Darn that will," muttered Jack. "When I find who's behind all this, they had better have written a will, because I swear to everything they'll regret—"

"Let's get them out first," said Tanya.

"There must be a way from this side to yours," said Asha. "We'll come over, and together, we can figure out who did this."

"Remain where you are," called out Jack.

He turned to Tanya.

"Stay here with your friends and make sure they don't move. I'll look for a way in and bring them over."

He turned to the wall and tapped it.

"Getting you out safe is our priority. Don't go off exploring again. Understood?"

"Yes, Chief," came Asha's voice, quieter.

Jack turned to Tanya and offered his sidearm to her.

"Can we switch?"

Tanya handed him the flashlight. "Keep the gun. You might need it."

"No, you take the gun." Jack thrust the weapon into her hand. "I'll feel better that way."

He walked off with the flashlight, leaving Tanya and Max in the dark, with the Glock for protection.

Tanya glanced around the tunnel. Her eyes were adjusting well enough to see the outline of the passageway that led back to the waterfall.

She thought she saw a movement for a second.

Tanya blinked and stared, but all she could see was the curtain of water streaming down in the far end.

She gripped the gun.

Chapter Ninety-eight

Max whined at Tanya's feet.

She bent down to stroke his ears, when she realized he was shivering. She crouched low and rubbed his back, trying to brush the water off his fur.

"You did a real good job, bud. You found your aunts. Great work."

She was shivering too. She was cold and wet, and barely dressed.

"Hey, do you have any water on you?" came Katy's voice from the other side of the wall. "A small plastic bottle could squeeze through this hole right here."

"I didn't bring...." Tanya stopped.

The waterfall.

The stream cut through the woods before it dropped into the lake. But was it fresh water?

She turned toward the direction from which they had come. At the end of the tunnel, she could hear the chute splash into the cove.

"Back in a sec," she said. "I think I've an idea."

She reached down and felt Max's head.

"Hey, bud. Stay with—"

Max stiffened.

He got on all fours and turned his snout toward the end of the tunnel where the waterfall was. A low growl rumbled in his belly.

Tanya's heart quickened.

Gripping her gun, she squinted at the far end, trying to see what he was seeing.

Max let out a soft bark.

"Shh," said Tanya.

She rubbed his back to calm him, and noticed his ears were pricked and his back was hunched, like he was preparing for an attack.

Tanya turned toward the wall and whispered, "Hey, you guys? Stay quiet."

At her feet, Max growled again.

On the other side of the wall, Asha and Katy fell silent.

With her weapon aimed forward, Tanya stepped along the tunnel and headed toward the cave. She stopped halfway and strained her ears, but all she could hear was the waterfall splashing into the lake.

She took a few more steps through the passageway. Max walked close to her heels, his tail stiff, and his muzzle pointed forward.

Tanya threaded through quietly, her ears and eyes on full alert. She paused at the end where the tunnel gave way to the cave, and listened.

Nothing.

Max growled again, louder this time.

What is it, bud?

Aiming her weapon in front, Tanya slipped into the cave.

Max let out a volley of barks.

Tanya gaped at the apparition standing by the waterfall.

Chapter Ninety-nine

Tanya gawked at the silver pistol in Veronika's hands.

She had seen that weapon before.

It had been hanging in the antique armoire inside Honoree's bedroom. It was the twin of the gun she had killed herself with. That sidearm was now in police custody, while this one was staring her in the face.

Even through the semi-darkness, Tanya felt Veronika's pulsating anger.

Her hair was askew and her face was flushed. Unlike Tanya, who was still wet, Veronika was dry, like she had walked here.

The underground passageways.

Tanya gritted her teeth.

You lured my friends. You were going to leave them to die.

The missing pieces of the puzzle were gradually coming into focus, but she had to be careful how she tackled this woman.

"Heel, Max," said Tanya, not wavering her Glock's aim.

"Veronika, please lower your weapon."

"Do you expect me to just roll over and die?" Veronika's voice was hard and flinty. "You think I'm a simple old woman, don't you? You think I have no agency."

"That's not at all true." Tanya kept her voice steady. "I think you're very powerful."

"I was the naïve little sister," said Veronika, her voice breaking now. "I was the childless whore, then the old maid on the side. I was the extra, always the extra. The quiet shadow in the back. That's what everybody thought of me."

Tanya took a deep breath in and let it out. She could wager that Charles used and abused Veronika for longer than he'd said in the letter to senior Dr. Chen.

"Can we put our guns away and talk, please? I imagine you're in a lot of pain. I'm here to listen."

Tanya took a discreet step closer. Max stepped in with her, his hackles up like he was stalking prey.

"Stop!" Veronika's scream echoed through the cave. "I'll shoot both of you. Don't think I won't do it!"

"I don't doubt you." Tanya stayed in her spot, but maintained her aim. "Isn't it time to be done with all this horror and violence? Don't you think they've learned their lessons now?"

Veronika didn't reply.

Tanya kept her finger on the trigger, knowing the other woman could pull hers at any second.

"You learned that you never had a stillbirth, and that your son was alive, didn't you?"

Veronika remained silent.

"You discovered your sister and Charles had adopted him and brought him up, right under your own nose, without your consent or knowledge. What a horrible thing to learn."

Veronika didn't say a word, but she didn't lower her pistol either.

Tanya's mind whirled like a cyclone, as she tried to figure out how to subdue this woman.

"I can't imagine what you must have gone through," she said, softening her voice. "If it were me, I don't think I could have lived with it."

"I couldn't," said Veronika, speaking again.

"Charles promised to marry me. He even proposed when he found out I was pregnant with his child. But it was all a lie. He sent me away to a hotel in Paris for six months, so no one would know. He was ashamed of me!"

Tanya listened quietly, taking stock of her posture and expression, waiting for the best time to grab the gun.

"I know I shouldn't have believed him."
Veronika's voice cracked. "He pitted me against
my sister, but I was young and dumb. I really
thought he would leave Honoree and marry me.
David was his blood son, right?"

Tanya nodded. The puzzle was slowly coming
into shape.

"Your son was the true heir to the Kensington
wealth."

A tear rolled down Veronika's cheek.

"Why can't anyone understand that!" she
shrieked.

Chapter One hundred

"Charles played with me," cried Veronika. "They all did."

"I'm so sorry for what you've gone through," said Tanya.

"I only found out David was my baby boy when I saw the test results three years ago. It was for an experimental medicine for psychosis."

Veronika swallowed hard, like she was trying to stop herself from crying.

"If I had been allowed to keep him since he was born, I don't think he would've got this sick. I would have taken proper care of him."

"What a terrible thing to happen," murmured Tanya. "Did they do a DNA test? Is that how you found out?"

"Honoree was sick that week, so I went to get the test results myself. She didn't know. That's when I saw the adoption papers and David's birth certificate on his desk."

"His desk?" As soon as she spoke the words, Tanya realized who it was. "You mean, senior Dr. Chen?"

"He was trying to make David better. He got upset when he saw me in his study. He begged me to forgive him for taking my baby away from me."

Tanya kept her gaze on Veronika and softened her voice further. "Have you been planning revenge, since then?"

Veronika's shoulders dropped. The hand holding the pistol was shaking.

Tanya took a step forward.

Then, another.

"Don't come an inch closer," cried Veronika.

Tanya wanted to find out what Jack was up to, and if Katy and Asha were okay, but she knew she couldn't waver her attention now.

She re-calibrated her strategy.

Distract first, then seize.

"Do you come down here often?" she asked, keeping her voice even.

Veronika nodded. Tears were rolling down her cheeks now.

"Is there a passageway from the house to the cove?"

"This house is custom-built," said Veronika. "Charles built it forty years ago. The cove was where he hid his cigars and other things he brought into the country."

Tanya raised a brow.

Charles Kensington had been a contraband smuggler, all along.

"I guess having your own private island with a quiet cove made it easy," said Tanya. "Plus, the proximity to an international shipping route helped. What else did he store in here? Illicit drugs?"

Veronika's eyes widened.

"Drugs? He didn't touch that stuff."

He left that to Stanley.

"What about unauthorized weapons?"

Veronika swallowed.

"He never did these things when the tobacco business was booming," she said. "He did so well, for decades. It's only when things turned bad, he looked for ways to... to diversify his income."

Tanya suppressed a smirk.

Sure, that's what all businesses do. When things get rough, break the law.

Despite herself, Tanya couldn't help but admire the man's ingenuity. But Charles Kensington was dead. It was the living family members she was worried about right now.

"Who helped you dig Charles's grave up, and bring his body here?"

Veronika didn't reply.

"Was it senior Dr. Chen?"

Veronika swallowed a sob.

"David did anything I told him...he... he...."

Tears glistened on her cheeks.

"David got sick because of Charles. He made Dr. Chen steal my baby. This was all his fault!"

Veronika's outburst startled Max. He barked but stayed by Tanya's side.

Tanya nodded to keep her talking.

So it was you who killed the patriarch.

"He was the devil!" screamed Veronika. "He deserved to die. They all did. All of them!"

Veronika's eyes blazed with such fury, Tanya wondered for a crazy second if she'd spontaneously combust.

"You're working for him!" screeched Veronika. "You came here to hunt me down!"

Tanya put her free hand in the air. "I have no connection to Charles or your family. I came here to help you."

Veronika cocked her pistol.

"Stop lying to me!"

Chapter One hundred and one

Veronika swayed on her feet, and her hands trembled.

But she held her weapon close to her chest, its shaky barrel pointed at Tanya.

Tanya observed her, knowing an unpredictable person was the worst kind to face off against. She had to distract her enough to grab the gun, without getting herself or her dog shot.

An old army sergeant's maxim flashed through her mind.

Never underestimate the enemy. That's how you get killed.

At her heels, Max growled.

"Shush, bud."

Large tear drops were rolling down Veronika's reddened cheeks. With her free hand, she pushed a stray blonde hair back, and reached to her neck to touch her sunflower pendant.

It was an instinctive gesture by Veronika, but a pang of agony slashed through Tanya's heart.

The middle-aged woman standing in front of her reminded her too much of her own mother. But her mother had fought for justice in her country, unlike the twisted form of revenge and mayhem Veronika had inflicted on her family.

Tanya pushed the memories of her tormented childhood to the back of her head.

Talking about Veronika's son seemed to relax her.

"Did David ever find out you were his mother?"

"I couldn't get myself to tell him." Veronika spoke in a trembling voice. "He was fighting his own demons. Demons of the mind. The last thing I wanted was to burden him with this....horror Charles put us through."

"Did you tell Honoree?"

Veronika's face cleared and her eyes turned hard. Tanya watched in shock as the weeping woman transformed into a stone-cold statue almost instantly.

"Why do you think she shot herself?" spat Veronika.

Tanya stared at her.

"I slipped a copy of David's birth certificate under her door the day before her birthday. I wanted to see her face at the dinner, knowing she knew what I knew. Finally."

Tanya raised a brow, but something niggled in the back of her mind.

Something is off with her story.

"Did the doctors ever find a cure for David?" asked Tanya.

"They diagnosed him with schizophrenia," said Veronika. "They gave him anti-psychotic pills to calm him down, but it only made him sicker. My heart broke so hard, but I couldn't comfort him like a mother would."

Comfort him like a mother would?

"What Charles did was wrong," sobbed Veronika. "So wrong!"

Tanya nodded, that niggling feeling growing stronger.

"No one should ever separate a mother and her child."

Max growled.

"Settle down, bud," whispered Tanya, not taking her eyes off the woman in front of her.

Max growled again, louder this time.

"I said, settle down."

He stopped, but Tanya could feel his unease.

What's wrong with him?

"I did to Honoree what she would have done to me," Veronika was saying.

"It was antifreeze from the garage, wasn't it?" said Tanya. "Did you mix it into her evening milk?"

"I only wanted to drive her mad, mad like they said my David was."

Max growled again.

Stop it, Max.

"I was sure I'd find her dead in her room one day," said Veronika, "after months of torture from losing her mind. I never expected that birthday dinner spectacle."

"I presume you poisoned Charles the same way," said Tanya. "Did you bring his evening glass of milk to him as well?"

Veronika nodded like it was the most natural thing anyone would have done in her position.

"I read about it in the paper. A woman in Tacoma....how she killed her husband who beat her. She added it to his dinner. " She stopped and swallowed. "It was slow, but I could see Charles lose his mind day by day. It took weeks for him to die, but no one knew."

Veronika paused and her face turned hard.

"I could never forgive him for taking David away from me. Do you understand that?"

Tanya merely stared at her, trying to come to terms with the twisted story she was telling.

"I knew Dr. Chen suspected something," continued Veronika, as if in a trance. "So, I told him how Charles died and asked him to help me hide the body. He knew what he did was wrong the day David was born, so he said yes."

Tanya's eyes widened.

No wonder the senior physician was racked with guilt, guilt that would ultimately drive him to suicide.

"Charles was never in the coffin, and Honoree was too sick to get out of bed," said Veronika.

"Were you feeding her antifreeze, too?"

Veronika nodded.

"Just enough to keep her bedridden until the funeral was over, but then...." She stared at Tanya, her eyes so dark, Tanya felt a shiver go through her. "Then, I realized she didn't deserve to live, either. She kept my son from me."

Tanya remained silent, but her mind reeled.

But your sister didn't know what Charles had imposed on her.

"I couldn't bear to see Honoree lording around, acting like the queen of the manor, after what she did to me. I was her own *sister*. How could she? She didn't even bear a proper heir!"

"And so, the adopted children had to go, too," said Tanya in a quiet voice. "Because David was—"

"David was the only inheritor!"

Max barked.

Veronika's eyes blazed. "Those impostors didn't deserve the inheritance. Thieves. That's what they all are!"

"And Stanley?" said Tanya, wracking her brain to figure out the missing puzzle piece. "What were you planning for him?"

"How I hate that man," spat Veronika. "Every time I tried something, he weaseled a way out. I needed more time, and he'd be gone too. Then David... David...."

Veronika broke into sobs.

Tanya suddenly realized what was wrong with the puzzle she was trying to build. There was one piece that refused to fit anywhere. The way Veronika talked about David meant she hadn't killed him.

Had that been an unfortunate accident, after all?

She spotted a movement behind Veronika.

Max, who had started growling again, got on all fours and barked.

Tanya had been so engrossed in fitting the picture together, she had failed to see the intruder who had crept into the dark cave with them.

Max hadn't been growling at Veronika.

He had been warning her about the shadow standing behind the woman.

Chapter One hundred and two

Tanya whipped around and aimed her Glock at the shadow.

"It was *you* who killed David," she said, her finger on the trigger.

Hazel was clutching one of Charles's old hunting rifles, and it was pointed at Tanya.

Veronika spun around with a startled cry.

"You!" she shrieked as she realized who it was.

Unlike hysterical Veronika, Hazel was calm.

Tanya stared at the shy, soft-spoken woman whom she had thought was fiercely loyal to her family. Her feet were planted squarely on the ground, her back was straight, and her chin was up. Her eyes were cool like she knew exactly what she was doing.

If Hazel killed them now, it would be in cold blood.

Tanya knew why the rifle was pointed at her. To Hazel's mind, her old aunt was a basket case, but the armed cop posed the most immediate threat. She would take Tanya first, then she would take the woman she came for.

Oh, Max. I'll never doubt you again.

At her heels, Max was barking, but neither woman was paying him any attention.

"Was it you?" Veronika cried, flailing her arms, brandishing her weapon at everything and nothing. "Did you kill my baby?"

Hazel didn't blink.

"What did you do to my son?" screamed Veronika.

"I knew what you were up to," said Hazel, her eyes flitting over to Veronika for a split second before coming back to Tanya. "You were killing us all, one by one."

"How could you hurt David? He loved you!"

Tanya's eyes darted from one woman to the other, assessing the risk. They were in a tinderbox. One wrong move, bullets would fly, and they would perish together.

Honoree's last words flashed to her mind. Peter had said his grandmother had wished them all *"a bloodied fight till the end."*

Honoree Kensington's wishes have come true.

"Is this really how you want to go?" said Tanya to the two women. "In a hail of gunfire in this underground tomb?"

Veronika twirled back around, her gun aimed shakily at Tanya.

"I'm not scared to die. I'll join David in heaven."

She swung around to Hazel again. "You took my son from me!"

Hazel scowled, but her rifle was still pointed at Tanya.

"An eye for an eye," she said. "Your son for mine."

Hazel's voice was so cold, Tanya felt a chill go down her back.

"You shot Justin," said Hazel, her fury-laden eyes still on Tanya.

"You took the ferry back with the gun in a shopping bag, like nothing happened. I know because I saw you clean it in your room and put it back in Honoree's cabinet."

"Justin didn't deserve my son's inheritance!" shouted Veronika. "You people were never family!"

Hazel's eyes were still on Tanya, and this time she addressed her.

"I knew her secret crime all along. She killed our father."

"Do you think this will get Justin back?" said Tanya, hoping she still had her senses about her, senses to appeal to. "Please put down your weapon, Hazel."

Hazel's eyes blazed.

"She was killing us one by one, so she could keep all the inheritance for her precious son. She started with our father. She's a cold-blooded witch!"

"So, it was you who tried to dig up Charles's grave," said Tanya, softening her voice. "You wanted to find out what happened to him?"

"I tried last year, but I couldn't. The soil was too hard. I tried again last night, but I had to give up."

That explains the desecrated grave.

"I knew she was up to something with his body," said Hazel. "She took over the funeral arrangements from our mother as she wasn't well, but she told us it was a closed casket event. She forbade us from seeing his remains. That was when I realized something fishy was going on."

Tanya shifted to Veronika.

"You poisoned Charles like you poisoned the others, didn't you?"

Veronika swayed on her feet. She didn't speak, but her chin trembled and her eyes shifted. The guilt on her face was crystal clear.

Hazel turned her blazing eyes on Veronika.

"You cheating tramp! You murderer! You broke our family apart."

"You're not even blood!" shrieked Veronika.

"Veronika!" hollered Tanya. "Hazel!"

Veronika turned to her, her weapon limp in her hand. Hazel remained silent, but Tanya could see she was burning in anger, and could fire at any moment.

"I'm asking you both to stop this right now. Hasn't your family gone through enough tragedy? I know what it's like to lose someone to a violent death—"

"You're not a mother!" screamed Veronika with so much venom, Tanya felt it like a slap to her face.

Veronika turned back to her niece.

"Neither are you! When Honoree kicked Justin out, you didn't even fight back. You spineless idiot. You're a useless excuse for a mother. Your children didn't deserve you."

Hazel's face flushed and her eyes narrowed.

"Everyone knew Charles strung you around like a dumb puppet. Even David. He may have been retarded, but even he knew you were a cheater and a liar."

"Don't you dare talk about my son." Veronika's entire body convulsed. "You killed him! And now you insult him!"

Her finger went to the trigger. The gunshot echoed through the cave.

Hazel doubled over and her rifle clattered to the ground. Her knees buckled as she slipped to the floor, her face contorting in shock. She held on to her bleeding shoulder, just like her son had done in the ambulance three days ago.

Tanya spun around to Veronika.

"Put your weapon down *now*!"

But Veronika's eyes were trained on her niece, gasping in pain on the floor.

Tanya saw her finger go to the trigger again.

Tanya pulled hers first.

Veronika crashed to the ground with a blood-curdling scream, clutching her thigh. Her pistol flew from her hand, toward the waterfall, and Max raced after it.

That was when Tanya caught a movement from the corner of her eye.

Hazel had picked up her rifle.

She aimed it at Veronika and fired. Veronika's head crashed into the wall with a sickening thud, splattering blood and brains across the cave wall.

Tanya jumped on Hazel and kicked the rifle out of her hands.

"What the hell did you do?" she hollered at the woman.

Hazel turned her face up to Tanya and whispered.

"I just wanted to make sure the witch was dead."

Chapter One hundred and three

"What they did to her was terrible," said Stacey, looking up from the side of George's hospital bed. "But she was a monster."

The dark circles around her eyes had deepened since Tanya last saw her.

"Hazel and Monica were adopted, so they and their kids were strangers to Veronika," said Tanya. "As far as she was concerned, David was the only deserving Kensington."

Tanya was standing at the foot of George's bed with Max by her feet. A few hours ago, she and

Jack had taken Hazel into custody at the manor. Jack had handed her over to his crew to tend to her gunshot and take her to the Black Rock precinct.

Tanya hadn't had time to recover from the ordeal in the underground cave, but she knew Stacey and George deserved answers. This was why they were all crowded in his small room.

George had been discharged from intensive care and transferred to a regular ward, but he was still bandaged like a mummy and hooked up to a series of monitors. He was sitting up in bed now, one hand clasping Stacey's, listening with tears in his eyes.

They were in mourning.

"Who wrote those notes?" said Stacey. "Like the one Max found by the ambulance when Justin was shot?"

Hearing his name, Max turned to her and wagged his tail.

"Veronika," said Tanya. "She wanted to unsettle anyone who might claim the inheritance. She's also the one who stole the final will from Honoree's room the night her sister shot herself. But she had the nerve to stand by the door, crying, while I was investigating the mess. She fooled me."

"She fooled us all," said Jack. "Plus, she had help. But it wasn't Stanley, as I suspected."

The chief was leaning against the door, next to Asha and Katy who had squeezed inside the room.

"She had influence over David," said Jack. "Whenever she needed to dig up a grave, move a body, stab and drown someone, she used him. He followed her instructions, like a puppy."

"That's what Veronika said to me too," said Tanya, nodding, "just before Hazel showed up and shot her."

"There was a lot Mariposa and Rafael weren't telling us," said Jack. "They only opened up once they heard Veronika was dead. They were scared. I can't blame them."

Jack raised his eyes to the group.

"For the past two years, Veronika and David spent an hour every evening, bonding over their glasses of milk, in his room. Only Mariposa knew. She said she overheard Veronika tell him stories like he was a little boy. I'm willing to bet these stories graduated to instructions in helping her out with the killings."

"Maybe David knew in his heart Veronika was his mother," said Katy.

Jack shrugged. "What I do know is David was in good physical form, but had the mental capacity of a ten-year-old. It's easy to manipulate someone like that."

"Veronika planned everything well," said Tanya. "The jewelry heist was to distract us from what was really going on. We won't know for sure, but I'd say it was to implicate the staff."

"From the handwriting on the notes slipped under our door," said Asha, "she was the one who lured us underground, too."

"The state forensics team will have a field day in those tunnels," said Jack. "No one suspected Charles Kensington of starting a smuggling venture after his tobacco empire slumped."

"He was a narcissistic sicko," said Katy, making a face. "He exploited his family and his doctor. I'd bet you Honoree suspected his affair with her sister, but she kept quiet. Women those days endured a lot more than we do now."

"What I don't get is why Honoree kicked Justin out of the family," said Asha. "Did Stanley lie about that, too?"

"Justin tried to steal from his grandfather," said Jack.

Stacey and George turned to him in shock.

"He stole money?" said Stacey.

"He was just a kid," said Jack. "I dug up the archived file from our storage."

Tanya looked at him with interest. This was news to her.

"What did you find?"

"Lisa was trying to get away from Stanley," said Jack. "She wanted to leave the island, but she was just a teen. She had no funds or friends, so, Justin did what he thought was best to help his cousin escape."

"Oh, Justin." Stacey wiped her eyes. "He always took in sick animals and was ready to help anyone in trouble. I miss him so much."

George turned to his wife and clutched her hand. Stacey leaned her head against his pillow, more tears staining her cheeks.

"Justin stole a checkbook from his grandfather's office," said Jack. "He wrote a large check for Lisa, so she could start a new life somewhere else. The two teens got caught at the bank for trying to cash in the fraudulent check. Honoree hauled them back home and kicked Justin out, soon after."

"So, that's why Stanley called him a criminal," said Asha with a grimace. "He's one to talk given what he was doing."

"He's in a holding cell, meditating on his deeds, as we speak," said Jack, pursing his lips. "I'll work with the prosecution to make sure his high-paid lawyers won't get him off easily."

"Your work's cut out for you," said Tanya.

Jack gave her a weary look, like he was carrying all their troubles on his shoulders.

"Yours too, Stone. I'm glad you stayed on the team, because things are going to get busier."

Tanya averted her eyes.

You can thank my FBI bosses. I'm here at their command.

Katy turned to the chief. "Did Honoree know Stanley was abusing Lisa? Did she care to find out?"

"That, we'll never know," said Jack.

"My guess is she was more concerned with family reputation, than stopping the rapes," said Tanya. "She probably thought Justin was a troublemaker, especially when the bank and the cops started probing."

"This family held so many secrets," said Asha, shaking her head. "All stemming from shame."

Katy nodded. "Shame of an affair, shame of an illegitimate child, shame of being a discarded mistress, shame of being deceived, shame of being abused, shame of an addiction. Shame ate them alive."

"Shame is like a tumor," said Tanya. "It grows and grows, until it eats you from the inside out."

"That family didn't deserve Justin," said Stacey. "All the money in the world didn't help their dysfunctions. I wish we could have saved both Justin and Lisa, but it's too late for—"

"A visitor!" called out an unfamiliar voice from the corridor outside.

Everyone turned to see who it was.

Chapter One hundred and four

A nurse was standing behind Jack, waving at them.

"You have another visitor, George, but I'll have to remind you folks to leave soon." She flashed a smile at the small crowd. "Visiting hours end in ten minutes, and George needs his rest."

With another cheery wave, she twirled around and disappeared. That was when everyone noticed someone short and petite had been standing behind her, hidden from view.

"Dr. Chen," said Tanya, straightening up, glad to see the physician again. Though the doctor may never admit it, she felt they had a closer connection after what had happened to her father.

Dr. Chen nodded at Tanya as if to acknowledge her, but didn't smile.

She stepped up to the doorway, a serious expression on her face. The room fell silent, as they realized she had something to say, and given it was Dr. Chen, it wouldn't be fun.

"The visitor isn't me," said the diminutive woman.

She gestured at someone in the corridor to approach them.

The sound of a walking stick tapping on the cold hospital floor came from outside. Max scrambled to his feet and rushed to the door, his tail swooshing a million miles a second.

Jack stepped back from the threshold, startled. "What in heaven's name?"

Asha and Katy spun around and gasped out loud.

Soon, Justin appeared at the doorway, a wonky grin on his face. He swayed uncertainly on his feet, next to the doctor, holding on to his crutches.

For the first time since Tanya had met Dr. Chen, she smiled. It was a triumphant smile.

"Justin!"

Stacey's scream could have been heard throughout the hospital.

She dashed out of the room, pushing everyone away, trampling on their feet. With an elated cry, she pulled Justin in for a hug. Barking happily,

Max whirled around their legs, almost bowling Justin's crutches to the ground.

Tanya spun around to Dr. Chen, who was grinning from ear to ear.

"You... you did this?" said Tanya.

"I kept him in the back of the clinic," said Dr. Chen. "Only my team knew."

"What on earth...?" spluttered Jack. "You lied to me."

"Do you think I would have let him go, knowing a killer was rampaging around, eliminating his family, one by one?"

Neither Tanya nor Jack replied, too stunned to speak.

"My father would have wanted me to protect Justin. He did his best to help the Kensington family the only way he knew. I forgive him. But it was my turn to do my bit, my way."

Dr. Chen glared at the chief, her bulldog persona back in full force.

"Go ahead and arrest me for misleading law enforcement," she snarled, "but I'd do it again in a heartbeat."

Jack let his hands drop and shook his head silently, like words failed him.

Tanya smiled at the physician.

A ripple of laughter went through her belly. Suddenly, all the tension of the past three days rolled off her shoulders. Tanya half cried and half laughed, while next to her, Jack chuckled to himself, like he couldn't believe it.

From his bed, George watched his wife and adopted son embrace each other, a gentle smile on his face. He turned his head to Dr. Chen and mouthed silently, *Thank you.*

Tanya watched their silent exchange, so overcome by emotion, she almost didn't hear both her phones buzz in her pockets. She stepped out of the room and pulled the FBI burner cell out to see who had messaged her.

Ray Jackson.

"On my way to Grimwood Estate now," she typed quickly. "Tell the big boss I'm on the job."

She put her mobile away and turned to Asha and Katy who were standing by the doorway, watching Justin and Stacey hug and cry.

Tanya wrapped her arms around her friends, tears welling in her eyes.

"Do you know why I'm mad at you?" She shook them by the shoulders. "Mad enough to kill you for your reckless actions?"

Asha and Katy turned to her with wry smiles.

"You're the only family I have," whispered Tanya, pulling them into a hug, tears rolling down her cheeks. "I lost everyone when I left Ukraine. I can't lose you, too."

She squeezed them tight.

"You're the most capable and smart women I know, but don't ever walk into my crime scenes again, got it?"

"You worry too much," said Asha, squeezing her back. "We're not little girls anymore, running from crime bosses. Sometimes you forget that we're all grown up."

"We know you mean well, hun," said Katy, hugging Tanya tighter. "We love you to bits. Don't ever forget that."

With a resigned sigh, Tanya pulled away from them, and wiped her eyes.

Just like them to not answer directly.

"Go home," she said, giving them a pointed look. "Asha, David is probably waiting for you. Katy, Chantal and Peace are missing you by now." She paused. "I'd drive you to the airport myself to make sure you're on the next plane back, but I have a job to go to."

Tanya was about to call Max to head over to Grimwood Estate, when she remembered her public mobile had also vibrated. She plucked it out and clicked on the message app.

Her eyes scanned the new text she had just received.

"Your brother wants to see you. He's not dead."

The sender: ANON.

To be continued...

———

I hope you enjoyed this story.

Our detective team has done their job and the villain(s) have got their just desserts.

But I have written an epilogue story that occurs five months later. Would you like to know what eventually happens to Kensington Island and its residents?

Five months later, Tanya and Jack are invited to an inaugural function on the island that changes everything.

Asha, Katy, and Katy's young daughter, Chantal fly from New York for the special event. Max is excited to have most of his family around him again, especially little Chantal.

But there's one man in the crowd who has a secret to share. He invites the small group to the cove to reveal what he had been hiding for decades.

Read the final twist to this story that no one, not even Tanya, expected....

....And learn what happens to Justin, who is now the sole heir to the Kensington fortune.

Download the twisty epilogue story for free, here.

Kensington Island Twist

https://tikiriherath.com/fbi-kensington-island-twist

———

Dive into the next spine-tingling, pulse-pounding thriller in this series.

HER PERFECT MURDER

Don't miss out on another fast-paced and spine-tingling murder mystery thriller with Special Agent Tanya Stone, K9 Max, Chief Bold, and the eccentric characters of this small seaside town, each of whom holds a secret they'd rather you not find out.

Will Tanya find out who ANON is and if her brother is truly alive?

Start reading HER PERFECT MURDER next!

https://tikiriherath.com/fbi-book5

Continue the adventure with *Her Perfect Murder!*

HER PERFECT MURDER: A gripping Tanya Stone FBI K9 crime thriller with a jaw-dropping twist.

If I can hear him, he can hear me.

Tanya took a slow, deep breath in. By her heels, Max remained stiff, ready to pounce, but as silent as a clam.

On the other side of the tree, the man had stopped wheezing. He swallowed loudly, choking on his spit, then continued panting, but didn't move from his position.

That was when Tanya realized that in his exhaustion, he hadn't heard them get close. Otherwise, he would attacked.

She quietly stepped forward. A few more inches and she would be able to peek around the tree.

On the other side, the man coughed a rough cough. He cleared his throat and spat.

She took another step and craned her neck to get a glimpse of his silhouette.

The man with the scar was leaning against the next tree over, drenched in sweat. He had one hand on his chest like he was having a hard time breathing.

Tanya's eyes traveled down to his other hand.

An ax.

To be continued...

⟵——⟶

Dive into HER PERFECT MURDER right away!

https://tikiriherath.com/thrillers/

When the killer strikes, there's no warning. Just the sound of the victim's dying breath.

FBI Special Agent Tanya Stone doesn't know she has stepped into a gilded trap.

The tranquil halls of Black Rock's luxurious senior residence hide dark secrets and a deadly killer. In the night, whispers echo louder than screams, and the killer's touch leaves no trace.

Only the chill of death.

Tanya has forty-eight hours to unmask the killer before another precious life is taken. But deadly whispers echo through this small-town resort.

You can't outrun the past.

The affluent retirees harbor more than memories. They hide skeletons in their closets.

As Tanya fights to unravel the threads of betrayal and long-buried vendettas, the violent murder of her own mother haunts her troubled mind.

With help from Max, her loyal K9, she is determined to uncover the twisted truth before the next victim takes their final breath.

Will Tanya survive the storm of lies? Or will the killer claim her too?

Get your thriller fix. And find out how to get early access to all the books in the Tanya Stone FBI K9 series.

———

Dive into HER PERFECT MURDER right away!

https://tikiriherath.com/thrillers/

———

There is no graphic violence, heavy cursing, or explicit sex in these books. No dog is harmed in this story, but the villains are.

———

Available in e-book, paperback, and hardback editions on all good bookstores. Also available for free in libraries everywhere. Just ask your friendly local librarian to order a copy via Ingram Spark.

A Note from Tikiri

Dear friend,

Thank you for reading this book. Did you enjoy the story?

Would you like to help other readers meet Tanya and her K9, Max, and follow their adventures on the West Coast? If you do, tell your reader friends about this book and share on social media. Leave an honest review on Goodreads, Bookbub, or your favorite online bookstore.

Just one sentence would do. Thank you so much.

Hey, have you heard of the Rebel Reader Club?

This is my exclusive reader community where you can get early access to my new mystery thrillers before anyone else in the world.

You can also receive bonus true crime and real life K9 stories, and snag fun bookish swag—from postcards, reader stickers, bookmarks, to personalized paperbacks and more.

You can join the club as a Detective, a Special Agent, or an FBI Director.

The choice is yours.

Or you can just follow the club for free and see if it's something you'd like to become part of. Hit the follow button and you're on.

https://tikiriherath.com/thrillers

(You might have to do a bit of sleuthing to find the door to the exclusive club from my site, but it's there...)

Join the club and AMA.

See you on the inside.

My very best wishes,

Tikiri

Vancouver, Canada

———

PS/ Don't forget! Download the twisty epilogue story here.

Would you like to know ...?

Five months later, Tanya and Jack are invited to an inaugural event on the island that changes everything.

Asha, Katy, and Katy's young daughter, Chantal fly from New York for the special party. Max is excited to have most of his family around him again, especially little Chantal.

But there is one man in the crowd who has a secret to share. He invites the small group to the cove to reveal what he had been hiding for decades.

Read the final twist to this story that no one, not even Tanya, expected....

....And learn what happens to Justin, who is now the sole heir to the Kensington fortune.

Download the twisty epilogue story for free, here.

Kensington Island Twist

https://tikiriherath.com/fbi-kensington-island-twist

PPS/ If you didn't enjoy the story or spotted typos, would you drop a line and let me know? Or just write to say hello.

I love to hear from you and personally reply to every email I receive. My email address is: Tikiri@TikiriHerath.com

PPPS/ Last one, I promise.

I have a secret to share with you.

In this series, Black Rock is set in the state of Washington, USA. But did you know it's based on my seaside hometown in British Columbia, Canada?

Yes, the town exists.

The long pier, the Dog House Brewery & Pub, Lulu's coffee shop, Marine Drive with its gourmet ice cream shops, and even the Pink Palace resort are based on real places.

This town is located ten minutes from the US border, so from my bedroom patio, I can see the San Juan islands, the Olympic Mountain range, and the beautiful blue bay that separates Canada from the USA.

This is an idyllic region where sailing, paddle boarding, and beach picnics are far more common than serial killing—unlike in my novels....

Join the Rebel Reader club to learn more. AMA!

The Reading List

The Red Heeled Rebels universe of mystery thrillers, featuring your favorite kick-ass female characters:

◦—•—◦

Tanya Stone FBI K9 Mystery Thrillers

NEW FBI thriller series starring Tetyana from the Red Heeled Rebels as Special Agent Tanya Stone, and Max, her loyal German Shepherd. These are serial killer thrillers set in Black Rock, a small upscale resort town on the coast of Washington state.

Her Deadly End

Her Cold Blood

Her Last Lie

Her Secret Crime

Her Perfect Murder

Her Grisly Grave

www.TikiriHerath.com/Thrillers

———

Asha Kade Private Detective Murder Mysteries

Each book is a standalone murder mystery thriller, featuring the Red Heeled Rebels, Asha Kade and Katy McCafferty. Asha and Katy receive one million dollars for their favorite children's charity from a secret benefactor's estate every time they solve a cold case.

Merciless Legacy

Merciless Games

Merciless Crimes

Merciless Lies

Merciless Past

Merciless Deaths

www.TikiriHerath.com/Mysteries

Red Heeled Rebels International Mystery & Crime - The Origin Story

The award-winning origin story of the Red Heeled Rebels characters. Learn how a rag-tag group of trafficked orphans from different places united to fight for their freedom and their lives and became a found family.

The Girl Who Crossed the Line

The Girl Who Ran Away

The Girl Who Made Them Pay

The Girl Who Fought to Kill

The Girl Who Broke Free

The Girl Who Knew Their Names

The Girl Who Never Forgot

www.TikiriHerath.com/RedHeeledRebels

This series is now complete.

◄———►

The Accidental Traveler

An anthology of personal short stories based on the author's sojourns around the world.

◄———►

The Rebel Diva Nonfiction Series

Your Rebel Dreams: 6 simple steps to take back control of your life in uncertain times.

Your Rebel Plans: 4 simple steps to getting unstuck and making progress today.

Your Rebel Life: Easy habit hacks to enhance happiness in the 10 key areas of your life.

Bust Your Fears: 3 simple tools to crush your anxieties and squash your stress.

———

Collaborations

The Boss Chick's Bodacious Destiny Nonfiction Bundle

Dark Shadows 2: Voodoo and Black Magic of New Orleans

———

Tikiri's novels and nonfiction books are available in e-book, paperback, and hardback editions, on all good bookstores around the world.

These books are also available in libraries everywhere. Just ask your friendly local librarian or your local bookstore to order a copy via Ingram Spark.

www.TikiriHerath.com

Happy reading.

Debate This Dozen

Twelve (plus one) Book Club Questions

1. Who was your favorite character?

2. Which characters did you dislike?

3. Which scene has stuck with you the most? Why?

4. What scenes surprised you?

5. Did you catch the sentence that had the book's title?

6. What was your favorite part of the book?

7. What was your least favorite part?

8. Did any part of this book strike a particular emotion in you? Which part and what emotion did the book make you feel?

9. Did you know the author has written an underlying message in this story? What theme or life lesson do you think this story tells?

10. What did you think of the author's writing?

11. How would you adapt this book into a movie? Who would you cast in the leading roles?

12. On a scale of one to ten, how would you rate this story?

13. Would you read another book by this author?

Tanya Stone FBI K9 Mystery Thrillers

*S*ome small-town secrets will haunt your nightmares. Escape if you can...

The Books:

Her Deadly End

Her Cold Blood

Her Last Lie

Her Secret Crime

Her Perfect Murder

Her Grisly Grave

←——→

A brand-new FBI K9 serial killer thriller series for a pulse-pounding, bone-chilling adventure from the comfort and warmth of your favorite reading chair at home.

Can you find the killer before Agent Tanya Stone?

www.TikiriHerath.com/thrillers

———

FBI Special Agent Tanya Stone has a new assignment. Hunt down the serial killers prowling the idyllic West Coast resort towns.

An unspeakable and bone-chilling darkness seethes underneath these picturesque seaside suburbs. A string of violent abductions and gruesome murders wreak hysteria among the perfect lives of the towns' families.

But nothing is what it seems. The monsters wear masks and mingle with the townsfolk, spreading vicious lies.

With her K9 German Shepherd, Agent Stone goes on the warpath. She will fight her own demons as a trafficked survivor to make the perverted psychopaths pay.

But now, they're after her.

Small towns have dark deceptions and sealed lips. If they know you know the truth, they'll never let you leave...

⟵———⟶

Each book is a standalone murder mystery thriller, featuring Tetyana from the Red Heeled Rebels as Agent Tanya Stone, and Max, her loyal German Shepherd. Red Heeled Rebels Asha Kade and Katy McCafferty and their found family make guest appearances when Tanya needs help.

There is no graphic violence, heavy cursing, or explicit sex in these books.

The dogs featured in this series are never harmed, but the villains are.

——•——

To learn more about this exciting new series and find out how to get early access to all the books in the Tanya Stone FBI K9 series, go to www.TikiriHerath.com/thrillers

Sign up to Tikiri's Rebel Reader Club to get the chance to win personalized paperback books, chat with the author and more.

——•——

Available in e-book, paperback, and hardback editions on all good bookstores around the world. Print books are available for free in libraries everywhere. Just ask your friendly local librarian or your local bookstore to order a copy via Ingram Spark.

Asha Kade Private Detective Murder Mysteries

*H*ow far would you go for a million-dollar payout?

The Books:

Merciless Legacy

Merciless Games

Merciless Crimes

Merciless Lies

Merciless Past

Merciless Deaths

◄———►

Each book is a standalone murder mystery thriller featuring the Red Heeled Rebel, Asha Kade, and her best friend Katy McCafferty, as private detectives on the hunt for serial killers in small towns USA.

There is no graphic violence, heavy cursing, or explicit sex in these books. What you will find are a series of suspicious deaths, a closed circle of suspects, twists and turns, fast-paced action, and nail-biting suspense.

www.TikiriHerath.com/mysteries

◄———►

A newly minted private investigator, Asha Kade, gets a million dollars from an eccentric client's estate every time she solves a cold case. Asha

Kade accepts this bizarre challenge, but what she doesn't bargain for is to be drawn into the dark underworld of her past again.

The only thing that propels her forward now is a burning desire for justice.

What readers are saying on Amazon and Goodreads:

"My new favorite series!"

"Thrilling twists, unputdownable!"

"I was hooked right from the start!"

"A twisted whodunnit! Edge of your seat thriller that kept me up late, to finish it, unputdownable!! More, please!"

"Buckle up for a roller coaster of a ride. This one will keep you on the edge of your seat."

"A must read! A macabre start to an excellent book. It had me totally gripped from the start and just got better!""

———

A brand-new murder mystery series for a pulse-pounding, bone-chilling adventure from the comfort and warmth of your favorite reading chair at home.

Can you find the killer before Asha Kade does?

———

To learn more about this exciting series, go to www.TikiriHerath.com/mysteries.

Sign up to Tikiri's Rebel Reader Club to get the chance to win personalized paperback books, chat with the author and more.

←—→

Available in e-book, paperback, and hardback editions on all good bookstores around the world. Print books are available for free in libraries everywhere. Just ask your friendly local librarian or your local bookstore to order a copy via Ingram Spark.

The Red Heeled Rebels International Mystery & Crime

The Origin Story

Would you like to know the origin story of your favorite characters in the Tanya Stone FBI K9 mystery thrillers and the Asha Kade Merciless murder mysteries?

In the award-winning Red Heeled Rebels international mystery & crime series—the origin story—you'll find out how Asha, Katy, and

Tetyana (Tanya) banded together in their troubled youths to fight for freedom against all odds.

⊷

The complete Red Heeled Rebels international crime collection:

Prequel Novella: The Girl Who Crossed the Line

Book One: The Girl Who Ran Away

Book Two: The Girl Who Made Them Pay

Book Three: The Girl Who Fought to Kill

Book Four: The Girl Who Broke Free

Book Five: The Girl Who Knew Their Names

Book Six: The Girl Who Never Forgot

The series is now complete!

An epic, pulse-pounding, international crime thriller series that spans four continents featuring a group of spunky, sassy young misfits who have only each other for family.

A multiple-award-winning series which would be best read in order. There is no graphic violence, heavy cursing, or explicit sex in these books.

www.TikiriHerath.com/RedHeeledRebels

In a world where justice no longer prevails, six iron-willed young women rally to seek vengeance on those who stole their humanity.

If you like gripping thrillers with flawed but strong female leads, vigilante action in exotic locales and twists that leave you at the edge of your seat, you'll love these books by multiple award-winning Canadian novelist, Tikiri Herath.

Go on a heart-pounding international adventure without having to get a passport or even buy an airline ticket!

◂——▸

What readers are saying on Amazon and Goodreads:

"Fast-paced and exciting!"

"An exciting and thought-provoking book."

"A wonderful story! I didn't want to leave the characters."

"I couldn't put down this exciting road trip adventure with a powerful message."

"Another award-worthy adventure novel that keeps you on the edge of your seat."

"A heart-stopping adventure. I just couldn't put the book down till I finished reading it."

━━━

Literary Awards & Praise for The Red Heeled Rebels books:

- Grand Prize Award Finalist - 2019 Eric Hoffer Award, USA

- First Horizon Award Finalist - 2019 Eric Hoffer Award, USA

- Honorable Mention General Fiction - 2019 Eric Hoffer Award, USA

- Winner First-In-Category - 2019 Chanticleer Somerset Award, USA

- Semi-Finalist - 2020 Chanticleer Somerset Award, USA

- Winner in 2019 Readers' Favorite Book Awards, USA

- Winner of 2019 Silver Medal - Excellence E-Lit Award, USA

- Winner in Suspense Category - 2018 New York Big Book Award, USA

- Finalist in Suspense Category - 2018 & 2019 Silver Falchion Awards, USA

- Honorable Mention - 2018-19 Reader Views Literary Classics Award, USA

- Publisher's Weekly Booklife Prize - 2018, USA

To learn more about this addictive series, go to

www.TikiriHerath.com/RedHeeledRebels

and receive the prequel novella - **The Girl Who Crossed The Line** - as a gift.

Sign up to Tikiri's Rebel Reader club and get bonus stories, exotic recipes, the chance to win paperbacks, chat with the author and more.

◄———►

Available in e-book, paperback, and hardback editions on all good bookstores around the world. Print books are available for free in libraries everywhere. Just ask your friendly local librarian or your local bookstore to order a copy via Ingram Spark.

Acknowledgments

To my amazing, talented, superstar editor, Stephanie Parent (USA), thank you, as always, for coming on this literary journey with me and for helping make these books the best they can be.

—————

To my international club of beta readers who gave me their frank feedback, thank you. I truly value your thoughts.

- Michele Kapugi, United States of

America

- Laura Edwards, United States of America

- Kim Schup, United States of America. And her dear husband, Stanley, who suffered much teasing for being the namesake of an unseemly character in this book.

———•———

To all the kind and generous readers who take the time to review my novels and share their frank feedback, thank you so much. Your support is invaluable.

———•———

I'm immensely grateful to you all for your kind and generous support, and would love to invite you for a glass of British Columbian wine or a cup of Ceylon tea with chocolates when you come to Vancouver next!

About the Author

T ikiri Herath is the multiple-award-winning author of international thriller and mystery novels and the Rebel Diva books.

———

Tikiri has a bachelor's degree from the University of Victoria, Canada, and a master's degree from the Solvay Business School in Brussels, Belgium. For almost two decades, she worked in risk management in the intelligence and defense sectors, including in the Canadian Federal

Government and at NATO in Europe and North America.

Tikiri's an adrenaline junkie who has rock climbed, bungee jumped, rode on the back of a motorcycle across Quebec, flown in an acrobatic airplane upside down, and parachuted solo.

When she's not plotting another thriller scene or planning an adrenaline-filled trip, you'll find her baking in her kitchen with a glass of red Shiraz and vintage jazz playing in the background.

An international nomad and fifth-culture kid, she now calls Canada home.

To say hello and get travel stories from around the world, go to **www.TikiriHerath.com**

Milton Keynes UK
Ingram Content Group UK Ltd.
UKHW051602270524
443319UK00007B/466